For

Lorcan.

A YEAR IN LISBON

A Novel

LORCAN McNAMEE

First Published - 2016
This edition published 2016
www.ayearinlisbon.com
ISBN 978-0-9954832-0-0
Copyright © Lorcan McNamee 2016
Published by Lorcan McNamee

A catalogue copy of this book is available from the British Library.
Typeset and cover designed by Martin Corr - **www.studioffset.com**
Visit **www.ayearinlisbon.com** for any further information

Lisbon

PARQUE MONSANTO

AMOREIRAS

AVENIDAS NOVAS

CAMPO DE OURIQUE

RATO

GRAÇA

BAIRRO ALTO

ROSSIO

ALFAMA

LAPA

BAIXA

CHIADO

SANTOS

ALCÃNTARA

DOCAS

BELEM

TAGUS RIVER

April 25 Bridge

A YEAR IN LISBON

A Novel

LORCAN McNAMEE

BEFORE

I ended up in Lisbon.

It turned out to be my bolt-hole, the place that I fled to after life in Dublin had become sour and spoiled. There was nothing intentional in my journey to Portugal, nothing meant, nothing willed. It was simply a place to go that wasn't Dublin, a location where someone was foolish enough to give me a job and a temporary place to live. I knew nothing about the city - though in truth I knew little about anything much then - but that was in fact part of the attraction. It was a distant blank slate, an anonymous conglomeration of people and buildings, one thousand miles away, that offered that most precious of options for a person whose every waking second had become shrouded and sore - escape.

I only discovered later that during the Second World War Lisbon had been exactly that, a refuge for thousands of strays, spies, refugees, double-agents, people on the run. Portugal was officially neutral and admitted nationals from both the Axis powers and the Allies, so it was a natural destination for those who were fleeing whatever or whomever. I clearly wasn't the first wanderer to end up in the city, many had come before me.

In fact, years after the War, in 1974, when Portugal's African empire was crumbling, Mozambique declared itself independent from its puny European master. Hundreds of thousands of colonials, white Portuguese settlers and descendants of settlers, got on boats and planes and made their way back to the motherland to escape from the black masses who were now in power. They ended up in Lisbon too, throngs of them, with no more great plan than I would have, thirty-three years later. In leaving, the retornados, as they were called, feared - rightly or wrongly - for their lives, they had heard stories from other colonial outposts that had collapsed earlier, and let their imaginations get the better of them. Nothing as dramatic was behind my escape but it felt, in its own way, equally as urgent. Mozambique wasn't on my radar back in 2007 - I couldn't even have spelled it - but I knew that I needed to leave Dublin, and Lisbon seemed to offer a way out.

The events that led to my flight began in the damp Dublin winter of 2006, when I moved into a house in Rathfarnham, in the south of the city. One of my housemates there was a girl called Maura, and we soon became involved. It went well, then it went badly. Finally, it collapsed. We were both at fault, though me more than her, I suppose. I will tell that story in time, when I can. All I can say is that we were both blind, self-deceiving, clueless, luckless.

Whatever, it ended, and left a hole in me that I hadn't believed was possible, while still allowing me to go on. Maura wouldn't see me, wouldn't answer my calls, then when she finally showed up on my doorstep - I was back in the city at this stage, in Kilmainham - she told me, in so many words, that she wanted all traces of me out of her life. That wasn't all that she told me, but that was enough.

Around the same time as the disintegration of me and Maura, Avatar, the web design company I had been working for for the past three years, went belly up. In anticipation of the crash that was about to come the owner of the firm, Sean McSharry, was living beyond his and his company's means. He had been writing cheques he couldn't cash and had been doing what a whole community of bankers and developers was doing at the same time, though on a slightly smaller scale. Seanie disappeared, and Avatar went into receivership, or examinership, or administration, one of those mysterious nebulous states from which it could in theory have continued trading. Yet that wasn't going to happen, all of the office equipment had just been reclaimed by the office supply firm that had yet to be paid for even a single block of post-its. Avatar was as done as me and Maura. I had to find a job.

I could have looked for another web design position, but that, for some reason, would have reminded me too much of Maura. That was what I had been doing when we met, while we were together, when we split. When all the mess at the end happened. All through our four months of on and off, through what I thought was light and what ended up being the heaviest thing, through my growing desire and adhesion to this woman and the ultimate splitting of what we had, I had been going in every week-day to our office and sitting in front of a coloured screen, writing code, negotiating tricky pieces of Javascript, setting hyperlinks and designing web pages. I couldn't do it right then, I needed my whole life to be as different as possible from how it was when I was with Maura. In an attempt to cleanse the loss, I had to change things utterly.

I ended up teaching English for a summer. I fell into that too, like I have fallen into so much. For two months I stumbled my amateurish way through courses with the children of Europe's middle-class, feeling the relief of doing something different, the relief of change. It wasn't enough, though. Maura still haunted me. I had some brief one-nighters with girls who weren't her, and then stopped meeting women altogether. She had spoiled that for me too. Dublin then was the problem. We had both moved from Rathfarnham at this stage, though this was the city we had inhabited together, a city where she still lived, somewhere. She walked the same streets, breathed the same air, the place reeked of her for me. I had to get rid of Dublin too.

Yet this was a bigger step. The end of the English course approached and the talk in the staffroom was of where everyone was going for the coming year. Some of the others had jobs secured in Turkey, Brazil, Saudi Arabia, Japan, and pointed me in the direction of the best websites that offered EFL job vacancies. If I had thought of getting out of Dublin before it was to go to Limerick City or perhaps Cork, where I had some old university friends, but the idea of leaving the country suddenly became a real possibility. I cobbled together a CV, included a few choice quotes culled from the student feedback forms I had glimpsed when collecting them at the end of the last class – "Cian is good, fun teecher, make us laff," and "Cian friendly, play games, I learn much," – and applied for a few random jobs that didn't require too much experience. I got three replies within a week, had two interviews over Skype and got offered one job. The job offer came by email, two hours after my rejection by the school in Modena, Italy, who had given me the other interview. "Dear Mr O'Dwyer," the email read, "we are pleased to offer you a position as English Language Teacher in the London School, Lisbon, Portugal."

Actually leaving the country was not what I had in mind in escaping the ghost of Maura. It seemed drastic. There was also the fact that leaving would have been a kind of failure, and I don't like failure. I don't like giving in, and - despite seemingly being good at it - I don't like failure. So I had a clear choice. Stay, in a city that spoke to me every day of this woman whose memory I just couldn't shake, or go, admit defeat, but also find some release. The London School needed an answer and I couldn't give them one, so I drank on it.

Some people pray on dilemmas, hoping for divine inspiration to help them make the right choice. Back then I took a different approach, believing in the old Roman view of things, In Vino Veritas. Plastered, I found that decisions became simplified, the extraneous considerations dissolved away in a wave of alcohol until only the essential remained. Simon, my recently acquired flatmate, came with me on a Thursday night, we met some of the other teachers from the English Institute, all of them well able to hold their liquor, and put in place the kind of pub crawl that Dublin is ideal for. We starting in The George, before moving to the Central Hotel, Brogan's and then to assorted bars up and down Temple Bar. I bored my companions with the choice I had to make, the pros and cons, fors and againsts, until Madison, the hard-nosed Boston-Irish girl who had taught with us all summer turned to me in The Turk's Head and said, in her blunt American way, "Cian, why don't you just shut the fuck up and make up your mind already, you're giving us a pain in the balls."

Finally, at half past one, while I was winding my way home with Simon in tow, something happened to tip the balance. I saw Maura. She was taking the alley towards the looming shadow of the Central Bank, tottering over the cobbles on high heels in the company of a bottle blonde woman, also in heels. I hadn't seen her in two months at this stage. I told Simon to go ahead to our gaff in Kilmainham and followed the two women, slipping around the corner to the sound of my housemate asking me, "what the fuck?" I ignored him, lit a cigarette and officially commenced stalking my ex-girlfriend.

Maura's bob of dark hair was ruffled by the wind funnelled down Dame Street, the wind that was only now increasing in intensity. The two women were laughing, holding on to each other as I realised that I felt actual nausea, constriction in the chest. Bile was rising, I felt a strong desire to run away. I had no plan, only a kind of compulsion to see where she was going. I was incapable of looking away, as if she were some kind of massively famous person I had accidentally stumbled upon. My heart pushing blood was like a horse galloping in my chest, one I couldn't slow down.

I didn't recognise Maura's companion, though this wasn't too strange. I hadn't met many of her friends during our three or four months of domestic contentment. Our thing had been more about an escape from the rest of humanity rather than an attempt to meld our lives together. I could hear the blonde girl though, her voice was loud and sharp and sour, uncomfortable on the ears. She was what Maura used to call 'a real Howiya', her term for an authentic working-class Dub. Blondy was in white heels and matching white mini-dress, her legs patchily covered with a form of fake tan that made her look more alien than human. Maura herself was more demure, in a pin-striped trouser suit and dark shoes, though they both trailed a heavily-scented wave of perfume behind them, like the exhaust fumes from a Dublin bus.

They were slow walkers, so it was an effort to stay behind. I kept having to stop and tie my shoe-lace. Maura's friend glanced around at me a number of times, whispering to Maura as she did so. I tried to look at the ground more as I followed them so as not to appear suspicious. It didn't work. Bottle Blonde rummaged in her handbag for a second, finally locating what it was she was looking for, then turned around and faced me. We were about five metres apart now, on a stretch of Westmoreland Street that was between street lights, so I couldn't see the women very clearly. The girl looked right at me and spoke.

"Look fookhead," she began, trying obviously to sound tougher than she felt, "I've go' pepper spray and I'n gonna spray it in yer fookin' oyis if ya coom anny clowser."

She was a real Howiya alright. I put my hands up in a gesture of submission. Just then, Maura ran out in front of a taxi that was going down towards the river, and waved her hands until the car – a 04 Merc – pulled in to the curb. She leaned in the window, speaking to the driver and pointing in my direction. The guy, a large slice of humanity with a shaven head and a look about him that suggested that he would enjoy breaking my fingers one by one, stepped out of the car very rapidly for someone his size, and went for me.

Two things happened in quick succession. I turned to run away from the fast approaching taxi driver, slipped and ended up on my back. The large man, ready to do me damage, had built up enough speed at this stage that he couldn't adjust his trajectory and ended up tripping over my prone figure and hitting his head against the wall of the twenty-four hour Spar. Someone screamed, and then Maura rushed up to the chunky blob of a man, whose head quickly began leaking blood on to the pavement. She bent down to him and spoke, panicked.

"Philo, Philo, are y'all ree'?"

I glanced up at the dark-haired woman. Somehow Maura had exchanged her soft County Limerick accent for the whiny drawl of working-class Dublin. I stood up, knee grazed but unbloodied, and realised that I had just spent the last five minutes trailing a woman who only vaguely looked like my ex-housemate, my ex-bedmate. She had the same dark bobbed hair, was of more or less similar height but had none of Maura's subtle beauty, none of her flickering mischievousness. This woman had a nose that was long and bony and prominent, not Maura's symmetrical little nub.

"Fuck" I said, as I exhaled. "Fuck!" this time more exasperated. As the two women tended to the ailing hunk on the ground, I ran back up Westmoreland Street, past Trinity, around the corner into Dame Street, kept going up the hill, past the Olympia on my right and didn't stop until I reached the threatening shadow of Christchurch at the top of the hill.

"Fuck," I said again, bent over now, chest heaving, hands on knees as cars passed, the occupants watching me as I gulped air. I lit another cigarette and sloped off back to Kilmainham, too spooked by the idea that I might somehow fall into the giant Philo's clutches again to even imagine hailing a taxi.

Back in my house my laptop was sitting open on the kitchen table where I had left it earlier, my Gmail account with its list of emails received there staring at me. I clicked on one, about ten messages down, went to REPLY TO SENDER, and began typing. Thank you for the offer of a position in your school in Lisbon, I wrote, I am now very pleased to accept this post.

Very pleased, I thought, very, very pleased. Get me the fuck out of this city. Now.

Fifteen days later, my plane landed in Lisbon International Airport. I emerged into the arrivals area, blinking from having slept on the flight. Now I've done it, I thought, this is really happening. I've emigrated. My next thought was how much I needed a cigarette.

SEPTEMBER

My decision to accept the job in Lisbon was made in an alcoholic fog, and was spurred by the realisation that I had almost gotten beaten to a pulp for following a woman on the street who only barely resembled Maura. It was made with a still racing heart, a hoarse chest, a cloudy mind, it was made out of fear and regret and self-disappointment, and a desire to flee. Nothing good had gone into the decision, and yet the next day, the following weekend, the next week, I didn't regret it. Getting on that seven a.m. flight to Lisbon that Sunday in mid-September 2007, had now become a necessity. It was the next step in a process that had started nine months before, when I had first met Maura.

My boss, my new boss, was a greying, dapper Canadian who had seemed happy to overlook my lack of experience during our Skype interview, claiming that the London School put more value on personality and an outgoing nature than on teaching technique. That should have alerted me to something right there, but of course I missed the clue in my haste to be accepted by the school. He had emailed me the day before my flight, saying that the school would send a driver to pick me up at the airport. I was impressed by this – no doubt the intention of the gesture – and looked forward to a Limo with darkened windows and a dude in a peaked cap.

I looked out for my name on a card as I wheeled my two and a half suitcases through the winding tunnels of the airport and into the airy, high-ceilinged Arrivals area. It took me a while to locate it. Finally, I spotted a chubby, moustachioed man amid the crowd holding a card, now turned more on its side so that I had to tilt my head to read the words CIAN O'DYER, the W missing from the surname making me wonder if this was in fact my driver or whether there was someone with this actual name being collected. I halted in front of the man, who was now twirling his keys impatiently around his finger, and asked, my voice going up at the end to make a question, as I had been taught in my Portuguese For Beginners book and CD, "London School?"

The man nodded, using the minimum amount of effort needed to carry out this gesture, and turned quickly and headed for the exit. He made no attempt to help me with my bags. I had to half-run to keep up, and saw that he was going in the direction of a blue Ford Focus that was parked, illegally, on the edge of the set-down area, off to the left. The driver, without looking in my direction, slipped in through the front, left-hand side door, shut it with a clunk and popped the boot open. Wheezing now, I hauled the nine months worth of luggage on to my thighs, then into the open mouth of the boot.

Moustachio pulled out just as I slid in to the back seat, and immediately began driving the car as if he were angry with every other road user for their very existence. I asked him questions in my simplified English, but either he didn't grasp what I was saying or my questions were simply too banal to merit a response. He just grunted, pointed and then shut up again.

Instead of making pointless conversation with someone who obviously had no interest in doing so, I examined the city that was to be my new home for the foreseeable future. It was dusty, parched even in September, any grass or vegetation visible was a vague brown colour, something you don't see in Ireland, ever. The road into the centre from the airport was anonymous, block-shaped houses and other buildings lined the road. There were palm trees, though, actual palm trees, in the tiny front yards of some of these buildings. The trees were tall, dominating, authentic, not like the dwarf versions you might see in some pretentious Irish gardens, the Lisbon palms were a reminder that North Africa was only a couple of hundred miles away to the south. More than anything else those first few hours, more than the surly driver, the whiny, babbling sound of spoken Portuguese, the unusual September heat, it was the tropical palm trees that brought home the idea, *I'm not in Ireland anymore.* Their broad, looping leaves even waved to me as we passed. I waved back, hoping the gorilla in front was watching.

Still no reaction came from Fernando, or Franco, or whatever the guy in the driver's seat's name was. Five minutes into the journey he took out a crumpled pack of cigarettes from his top shirt pocket, closed his window and lit a fag. Smoke streamed from his nose and from between his thin, clenched lips, circled around and drifted as far as my prone figure in the back. I thought I caught him glancing at me in the rear-view mirror. Was this an attempted act of hostility? Another one? He had closed his window very deliberately so that the smoke he and his cigarette emitted wouldn't escape out into the Lisbon morning. For someone like Maura, I imagined – Maura hated being forced to passive smoke – the situation would have been intolerable. I was a thousand miles away, but still couldn't stop her intruding on my thoughts.

I sat there for two minutes, the car foggy now with cigarette smoke. My window was open but the driver seemed to be smoking at double normal speed so as to create the maximum sized cloud in the vehicle. I coughed a few times, made a face, allowed him to believe – if that was in fact his intention – that I was massively bothered by his actions, then reached across the seat and extracted my own packet of Marlboro from the pocket of my hoody. I lit up, happily breathing smoke back in his direction. This time he definitely did look at me in the rear-view mirror, his little brown eyes showing – I believed – a profound disappointment at the fact that I was immune to the discomfort he was trying to impose. I took a puff, aimed a smile towards the mirror and blew a great pall of Marlboro fumes into the front seat, his smoke and mine now mixing until they were undistinguishable.

I had never been hated by anyone so profoundly before, and I found it fascinating. Moustachio hated me without knowing anything about me, as if it were the very idea of me that he hated, foreign, probably educated, someone he was being paid to collect at the airport, as if I were important. I softened toward him a little at this realisation. It wasn't me he despised – how could he, we had never even spoken – it was my type. Fair enough, I thought, I didn't like my type either, very much.

We crawled towards the centre of the city. The buildings were now anonymous, the shops with fronts that were mostly opaque, making it difficult to discern their purpose. It all looked run down, a little messy, shabby – which Dublin is too, though Lisbon's particular type of shabbiness was new to me. It felt foreign, the most foreign place I had ever been, right from all of those short people walking along the pavements in jackets and ties in thirty degree heat, to the heat itself, to the sense, looking at the faded dignity of the buildings, that this had once been an almost important place that had sunk back into a kind of quiet middle-age, a complacent antiquity. I couldn't really say how I felt as we moved towards the city centre, other than a kind of bafflement that this was to be my home for the next nine months. *What the fuck am I doing here?* I thought, not for the last time, *am I really going to live here?*

We arrived, eventually, at our destination. It was a busy opening in the city's crampedness, somewhere I would come to know as Martin Moniz. There were four lanes of traffic split in two by an open, flat, paved space which contained the entrance to an underground car-park. On both sides the pavements were wider than before and filled with pedestrians, newspaper kiosks, shoe-shiners, and what looked suspiciously like ladies of the night, though it was not yet lunchtime. My grumpy chauffeur pulled up on the pavement outside another non-descript building that had the words PENSÃO IMPERIAL running vertically up along its four stories and horizontally above the front door. The driver pulled the lever to open the boot, pointed to the doorway and spoke to me directly, for what I realised was the first time.

"It's here."

Then he sat there. At this stage I would have been stunned if he had actually helped in any way, though his lack of movement now seemed like an action in itself, a pointed refusal to make my life in any way easier. I got out, relieved to be away from the oppressive atmosphere of the car's interior. I hauled my overstuffed luggage from the pit of the boot and dumped the bags on to the pavement. I went, as a reflex, to close the boot and then stopped, halted by the realisation that the only reason to do so would be out of social convention, basic politeness, concepts that my driver didn't seem too familiar with. I stepped away, leaving the boot gaping open there like the mouth of a hungry metal animal, and dragged my bags to the door of the pensão. I turned and watched Mr. Moustache as it dawned on him that he had to actually get out after all and close the lid.

"Bye, bye," I said to him from the door of the building as he waddled back to the rear of the vehicle, muttering. "It's been a real pleasure, you're a quality guy."

He cursed at me – I guessed – and seemed briefly to be attempting to squeeze, Cyclops-like, laser beams from his eyes to cut me down where I stood. He closed the boot with great care though, despite his obvious anger. I stood there waving as he pulled out, and cheerfully gave him the finger as he rejoined the Lisbon traffic.

Robert Prior, the head honcho of the school, had explained to me – in the email he had sent after I had accepted the job – what would happen for my first couple of weeks in Lisbon. He went into great detail in his communication, about where I was to stay, about the timetables of the classes each day, the structure of the school, though I only really skim-read it. I didn't care about the nuts and bolts of what I was getting myself into, I just wanted to get away. Only three details stayed with me, there was to be an induction course, seventeen other teachers were starting at the same time as me, and we were all to stay at the Pensão Imperial for a period of time before finding ourselves somewhere more permanent to live.

Yet I met almost no-one that first day. Somehow I felt abandoned, though of course I couldn't be abandoned by people I had never met. I dumped my baggage in my empty shared room, then wandered around the pedestrianised area of the city centre that seemed to be rigidly organised, almost Northern European-like, in a strict grid system. People's voices, the music from the inevitable street performers, echoed off the sheer fronts of the semi-tall buildings and down again to street level. Off in the distance was a giant arch, grand and imposing and somehow out of place at the end of a street devoted almost exclusively to the frivolous act of buying stuff. I suddenly felt a sensation of pure freedom, aimlessness yes, but liberty too. I had no expectations here from anyone, no-one to live up to, no-one to behave for. My impression of the city hadn't changed, the place was shabby-grand, it looked like it needed a polish, a make-over, a good sweep. But it wasn't Dublin, it wasn't alienating, uncomfortable Dublin. It was a blank slate for me and that was enough.

Mike, my Scottish roommate, finally showed up at ten that first Sunday night, smoking and smelling of booze. I was on my bed, flicking through the Lonely Planet Guide to Lisbon I had just bought. I had discovered from the book that the gridded area I had spent my afternoon wandering around was called the Baixa, meaning the low part of the city, as opposed to the high part, which seemed, on first glance, to be everywhere else.

"Hey," Mike said, as he stumbled through the room's door, "Ky-an, right?"

"Kee-an, yeah," I corrected him.

"Ay, right, good to meet you man," he said, shaking my hand.

Mike's head was shaven, he had obviously done it himself, you could see one or two little scabs on his skull where he had been cut. He had a bony face, prominent cheekbones and stubble on his chin to make up for the lack of hair on his head. He looked nothing like an English teacher, or what I though one should look like, though in fairness, I didn't either.

He was happy to discover that I was a smoker. We opened the window, lit up and talked there as the sound of the Sunday traffic reached us from below.

"I thought there were eighteen of us," I said, "I'm not the first to arrive, am I?"

"You? Nah, you're the last. We've been waiting for you."

Mike laughed when he saw how surprised I looked.

"They're all out in Cascais watching the footy. Liverpool and Man U. Well, it's been over for hours but there's an English pub out there and they don't want to leave."

I found out from my now roommate that most people had been there since Friday. The school had told them that they could come two days early if they paid the extra night's accommodation themselves.

"Didn't you get that email?" Mike asked.

I took out my laptop and checked. I had indeed received that message, ten days before, though I hadn't paid it any attention. I was getting out of Dublin, that was all I had needed to know.

"So everyone already knows each other?" I asked, feeling like the new kid in the class.

"Pretty much. Don't worry though, they'll love having someone new to impress with how smart and well-travelled and bohemian they all are. You'll be alright."

"Are you actually a teacher? I mean, in the London School, one of the eighteen? Because you don't sound like you are."

"Aye," he said, "I slipped through the cracks. They must have filled their wanker quota before they got to me." Mike smiled over at me, showing me that he was at least half-joking. He saw me staring at him.

"Let's just say, I'm not a great fan of the Sassanach," he explained.

"I reckon you've picked the wrong business to be in if that's true," I told him, propping myself up on my elbow, "you're a fucking English teacher!"

We laughed at the same time, two Celts bonding, at least temporarily. By eleven that night no-one else had returned and I found a wave of exhaustion assaulting me, the avalanche of newness of the previous sixteen hours finally catching up. I shed my clothes on to the floor of the now smoky room and crawled into bed without brushing teeth, peeing or showering, and slept my first sleep as a Lisbon resident. I dreamed of arches and hills and grids, and angry men with moustaches.

✳ ✳ ✳ ✳ ✳ ✳ ✳

Mike was right, I was a curiosity, at least at first. It was obvious, quite soon, that I was the only Irish person among the eighteen. There was a New Zealand girl, someone small and dark-haired and bird-like called Joanne, and my roommate, Scottish Mike, but apart from that the rest were all various shades of Englishness. There was posh, trendy, hip, earthy, hippie, ethnic and intellectual, but they were all English. Coming late and being from the small island to the left, I was a novelty, like a mascot or pet. "Oh, you're the Irish guy," was said to me more than once those first few days, before we all knew each other so superficially well that our origins were irrelevant. For a while those first few days, I was the token Paddy.

In the flurry of multiple first meetings I played my part well, exaggerating my accent, telling tales of drunken exploits, Sure and Begorrah and Jaysus, Mary and Joseph. It was a part I was playing, doing what I thought was expected of me. I had never been 'the Irish guy' before, and didn't know how else to fulfil the role. This wore off eventually, like all of our initial pretences, until we picked up new ones, and new ones after that.

Our induction course began that Monday morning, my first, and continued for two weeks, until the end of September. Induction soon became known as Basic Training. Who exactly started calling it that wasn't clear, it was one of those communal inventions that may have had four or five different authors. The title was ironic, Basic Training, there was nothing military about our course, we weren't the marines, it was simply a series of half-hearted lectures, seminars and teaching workshops, designed to ready us for life in the London School. There was no hazing, assault courses or weapons training. It might have livened things up if there had been.

It was during Basic Training I found out how little I knew about where I was going to work. The school was not one school but six, with centres in the Algarve, in Porto and four in Lisbon itself. It didn't just teach the Queen's English but also gave courses in French, German, and Portuguese for foreigners. In the flaky world of English language teaching big clumps of teachers left every year to go off and do something more fulfilling, somewhere more fulfilling, and they had to be replaced. Every year the school interviewed and hired those replacements from Britain and Ireland, flying them over and putting them up in the Pensão Imperial, giving them two weeks preparation until they were ready to become obedient cogs in the English teaching machine.

Our class of 2007 was the largest for some time, Robert Prior told us. He gave us the introductory speech that first Monday morning as we sat in a semi-circle, like some great language class, in our plastic chairs with the mini-desks attached to the right hand side. We had all walked over in a mass that morning, it had only taken five minutes from what had already begun to feel like home to the school's headquarters on Rossio, the central square that lay at the top of street-grid beyond. I counted ten women among the eighteen new teachers – most of them attractive in one way or other, I couldn't avoid noticing – and eight men, including myself and my new roommate, Mike. We were shown into a bare but modern meeting room and giggled and chattered like school-kids before Robert strode in in his three piece suit, his hair even greyer now, if possible, than when I had spoken to him on Skype, a month before.

All of the four Lisbon schools needed staff, he explained, in his North American accent softened by years abroad, and at the end of the induction course we would be split up and sent off to the various centres around the city. Actual teaching, at that precise time, seemed too remote even to imagine, I felt like I was on a kind of activity holiday, an 18-to-30 break that was never designed to lead to actual work. Classrooms and students were very far off in the distance, theoretical only.

Basic Training soon brought them back into focus. All eighteen of us were people who had been in English language classrooms before, we all had degrees of one sort or another, as well as the requisite TEFL qualifications. In short we all believed that we already were teachers. The school insisted, however, that we had to learn the London School Method of language teaching before we were to be trusted with actual students. In truth though, once we got into it, few of us could spot the unique features of this method, beyond a certain preoccupation with stationery.

"This is a pen," we were instructed to intone, as we each took our turn practicing The Method in our mock class, made up of the seventeen other new teachers pretending to be clueless Portuguese students. "This is a pen." Everything had to be repeated.

Julio, one of the teachers of Portuguese in the school, was our instructor for this part of the course, he had silver hair and had glasses that hung on a string around his neck when he wasn't wearing them. He had a big mouth and large teeth, and smiled falsely at us when we did something right.

"Is this a ruler?" was the next stage, as whoever was playing the part of the teacher still held the Bic biro in the air in front of the pretend class.

"Yes, is ruler," one of the smart-arses would inevitably reply, to an accompaniment of titters and giggles, "is ruler."

"No", Julio instructed us to say, clearly and unequivocally, "no it's not, this is a pen." And so on, until someone got it right. Once the students had grasped the name for the ink-producing writing instrument, the process would continue with pencils, erasers, books, notebooks and, bizarrely, a hole-punch. A miniature guy that was sitting next to me, who I soon came to know as Jamie, leaned over to me in the midst of this exercise and whispered, in his potent Brummie accent, "Is this a language school", he asked, "or fuckin' WH Smiths?"

Whether it was intended or not, the inanity of Basic Training provided us all with an instant bonding mechanism. That night, in a bar we called Record – though it wasn't the bar's real name, only the title of the newspaper that had its offices on the floor above – the "Is it a Tequila?" game was instigated, and repeated at some stage on every night that first week. It worked as follows. One of our number would be blindfolded, handed an unfeasibly cheap measure of spirits and told to answer the question, without tasting the drink, "Is it a Tequila?" The two possible answers were, or course, "Yes it is," or "No it isn't". An incorrect response would result in the contestant having to down the drink, in one. Though in truth, if you got it right you still had to down it.

Basic Training wasn't taken very seriously. How could it be, when at least fifty percent of us spent the first few hours of every day dealing with hangovers or lack of sleep? There was one of our number, Carly, who had freckles, hippie-straight hair and an air of distinct fragility. She was an assiduous note-taker on everything that happened in our inductions sessions, but she was the only one. We had a talk on the health services in Portugal, on how to get our social services card so we could see a doctor, and on how to get our residency permission, and she took everything down. During our sessions on the London School Method, she took everything down, even the "Yes it is," "No it isn't" responses. The same happened with our talk on finding accommodation in Lisbon, with our presentation on relationships and public displays of affection in the workplace and with the lecture on sexual harassment. She was a nervous young woman, earnest, slightly clueless socially, and seemed to think that by recording everything she could control all of this newness that was being thrown at her. Get it all down in note form and somehow it would make sense.

Yet even Carly was affected by the general level of dissoluteness that set in only a few days into Basic Training. She came out with the rest of the horde on our first Thursday night, got quietly drunk on peppermint schnapps and ended up silently dancing, cheered on by the remainder of the group, standing on a table in the Frágil club at three in the morning. By the second week she had put away her now well-worn note-taking pencil and, like the rest of us, saw the induction course simply as something to be got through each day before we could hit the ridiculously cheap bars and clubs of the city again.

I have used the words 'we' and 'us' a lot to talk about myself and the seventeen other new teachers, as if we were only individual parts of a greater mass. This, in essence, is what we were. The London School crocodile soon became a nightly occurrence, snaking its way around the Bairro Alto, slithering from restaurant to tasca to poky bar, as if we were one thirsty monster with multiple mouths. It was inevitable really, eighteen English-speakers, dropped into the cheapest capital city in Western Europe, with booze prices a third to a half of those in

Dublin or London, what else are they going to do every night except attempt to drink themselves into a coma? Eighteen young people with ten words of Portuguese between them, all placed living in the same hotel, with not one other person in Lisbon who knew or cared anything about them. It couldn't have happened any other way. We formed an instant, fractious, incestuous family, siblings, lovers, cousins, friends, support systems, all at once. Each one of us only really liked about five of the others, though exactly who those five were changed from day to day, and it didn't really matter anyway as we were stuck with each other, at least for now.

We discovered the Bairro Alto early. It soon became familiar territory, the natural habitat of the London School new recruit. The Bairro, as we soon came to call it – as the Portuguese themselves called it – was a slice of the city up high on the hill to the right as you faced the river. There were all sorts of fun ways to get there from our residence down at sea-level. Feeling energetic we would make the trek up Rua Garrett on foot and circle around to the beginning of the cobbled, semi-pedestrian streets where there were more bars per square metre than anywhere else in the city. Otherwise there was an elevator, an old metal box that creaked and groaned its way from the Baixa, the lower area of the city, up to a platform on the hill above. It was a kind of outdoor lift with no building surrounding it that deposited its passengers five minutes walk from the heart of the Bairro. There was also a yellow funicular, a type of mini tram which shuddered and snaked up the hill to the rarefied air above, taking you from sedate Restauradores up to the buzzing Bairro Alto on high. The elevator and the funicular were both part of the public transport system of the city, and so accepted the passes we bought that allowed access to Lisbon's buses, metros and trams. So there was literally no reason whatsoever to avoid going drinking each night, not even the fact that our main drinking destination was a good two hundred feet above our heads to the west.

My Rough Guide to Lisbon told me that the Bairro Alto – the 'Alto' part meaning high, naturally – had evolved during the twentieth century into the cultural and social centre of the city. Indeed it had all the one room tavernas, cramped restaurants, and toilet-sized bars that we could wish for, and so the London School crocodile could be seen there in some shape or form every night of our first fourteen days together. We fit right in to the Bairro, it was a warren of a place with no street wider than a car's width, the cobbles worn smooth by the footfalls of a million pedestrians and a bar or club every second doorway. It suited the expectations of a decadent bunch of English teachers wanting to experience the raw difference of a foreign city without having to make too much effort.

Our first Friday in Lisbon there was a burst pipe on the sixth floor of the Pensão Imperial. This flooded all the rooms on the fifth floor too, uprooting all eight of the London School new recruits staying there and leaving them with nowhere dry to sleep. Amazingly, the rest of the dingy place was full. Myself and Mike, as we lived on the fourth floor, were asked to double up and let two of the fifth floor residents stay in our room. My roommate and I had reached a kind of understanding, neither of us were very tidy but we both had approximately the same limit for our tolerance of mess, and when this limit was reached one of us invariably gave in and straightened out our detritus of full ashtrays, dirty underwear and half-full coffee cups. The arrival of two new guests threatened to upset the delicate balance we had achieved.

Jamie and Rahul were the two new arrivals. Jamie was short, with fair hair that was always mussed, even hours after he had got up. From somewhere in the English midlands, he seemed almost impossible to stir up, it was months before I saw him annoyed or exercised by anything. I suppose his persistent sleepiness was contributed to by the fact that he spent almost fifty percent of his life drunk, at least for those first fourteen days. While nearly all of us took nights off to recuperate, to allow our systems to become temporarily free of alcohol, there was always some London School newbies in the bars of Lisbon come 11pm, and Jamie was always among them. Every night. He had the tendency to reach, after three or four hours of concerted drinking, a kind of waking coma state, where he would smile at people beatifically but where actual communication was beyond him. Jamie was a loveable guy, a harmless blob in the corner after two o'clock each night, though no-one had a clear idea of the motivation behind his nightly bouts of drinking until brainless. Someone should have sent him to AA, but in truth we valued too much the fact of always having someone to go drinking with, if the mood took us.

Rahul was Anglo-Indian, or Indian-English, son of a paediatrician and a surgeon who had expected him to follow them into something respectable and high-earning, like medicine or law. He had rebelled against this – in as much as becoming a language teacher could be said to be rebelling – and had come to Lisbon because he had a Portuguese surname, Mascarenhas. Rahul said that he wanted to connect with this distant Portuguese ancestor who, he believed, must have set sail from Lisbon, before landing in Goa and intermixing with the locals, some four-hundred years before. Rahul had a distinctive style, everything he wore was black or grey, which made it easier when it came to him moving into our room. We at least knew which discarded item of clothing was his, when it came to half-heartedly tidying.

Being at such close quarters with these two only solidified my idea of Lisbon as somewhere to escape to, a bolt-hole for those taking flight. I was there because I couldn't stand being in the same city as Maura – or my own memories of her – anymore. Rahul was there, ostensibly because he had a Portuguese ancestor but really because he was escaping his demanding parents who were imposing their own vision for his life on to their unwilling son. And Jamie had fled in order to leave behind whatever trauma or sadness in his life that caused him to want to drink his brains out every night. Our room had turned into a dormitory but I, at least, liked the extra company. It meant that there was now almost no chance that I would inadvertently find myself alone at any time, with too much time to think.

Jamie and Rahul slept on mattresses on the floor. Their moving in didn't prove to be too invasive, they were both short and neither took up much room. Also, Jamie was out every night trying to fill his alcohol quota and Rahul spent a lot of time with Joanne, the dark-haired New Zealand girl who looked like she should be presenting kids' television. Jamie was a valuable source of information, he would come back from each night out that Mike or I had missed, with all the stories and gossip about the latest scandal from the Bairro Alto. We would all inevitably wake around three, when Jamie stumbled his way in and fell down on to his mattress, and he would give us the slurred headlines of the night's goings on.

"Carly....very pissed," he would say, then giggle, "Adam fell down.... blood, Sylvia and Matt, snogged," then a cough, a sigh, "I got a B.J." At this Jamie would slump down on to his lumpy mattress and be asleep and snoring within seconds.

Remarkably, most of this information checked out the next morning. Jamie would expand on the headlines when he woke again at half past eight, miraculously sober again. He fleshed out detail, added descriptions, talked in full sentences, and what he told us was more or less corroborated by those involved when it was discussed at lunch. Semi-comatose or not, Jamie clearly knew what was going on. We were never able to check his frequent claims of having received oral sex, though we were willing to give him the benefit of the doubt.

Sex, in one form or another, was a constant among the eighteen of us, right from the get-go. How could it not be? How much actual, all-the-way, full-blown sex happened is hard to say – after the fifth day and the pipes burst and there were four or five to a room it was hard to get any real privacy – but stuff went on. Mike, my original roommate, claimed, by the beginning of the second week, to have been with six of the ten women, but one evening the other three of us in the room began guessing who they were, and he didn't seem very clear on exactly which six.

"Laura?" Rahul suggested, as we passed an expertly rolled spliff around. He and Jamie were on their mattresses on the floor, Mike and I were laid out on our beds, Jamie's Coldplay CD droned away in the background.

"Yeah," Mike replied, "had a quick fumble with her last Saturday night".

"You told me that that was with Anna Cameron," I said, inhaling and exhaling slowly.

"Did I? Maybe it was," Mike said. "Which one is Laura again?"

Rahul had quickly formed a sort of friendship/couple with petite, dark-haired Joanne, and after the first Monday they were rarely seen apart. They seemed to have found each other like a pair of separated identical twins. It was sweet, and sickening at the same time. Rahul could usually be found in the room that Joanne shared with Carly and two others on the floor below, until Joanne's roommates objected to Rahul's constant presence and he came back upstairs to us. Joanne rarely showed her face in our room, there was too much concentrated maleness there for her, and in fairness it probably didn't smell too good either.

Keeping in mind what I had just fled from in Dublin, I tried to keep out of the pairing off, especially when it would inevitably involve someone I shared a living space with. I didn't want to go there again. Yet biology, alcohol and the libido are stronger than good intentions and I got drawn in to the general debauchery. Our first Wednesday there I ended up on the streets of the Bairro Alto, with Melissa Simpson from Manchester squashed between me and the side wall of the Record Bar, my hands inside her shirt and her tongue in my mouth, being cheered on by at least six of the others, as well as assorted passers-by. By the weekend Melissa had moved on to Adam, the most athletic of us, a guy who seemed to sleep in sweat pants and runners, while I had a fumbled snog with Carly, our conscientious note-taker, in the back of the Jamaica Club. It was like kissing a nun.

Then night twelve, our second Thursday there, Melissa's friend Sylvia slipped into bed with me as the others slept around us and Jamie's snoring annihilated the silence. Sylvia's full name was Sylvia Saint James, she was attractive enough as she was but had become a kind of prize among the male teachers for having the name of a porn star, and I was surprised by her attention. In our cramped room, in my narrow bed, Sylvia gave me hand relief while I tried to find her clitoris in my drunken clumsiness. I think we both passed out before it could go any further, though I couldn't be entirely sure about that.

The next morning, a Friday, was a day off, the third last day that the school was willing to pay for our accommodation. We were due to start work on the Monday, and had the option of staying on in the Pensão Imperial, though the cost of the stay would have to come out of our first month's wages. The last week of Basic Training the school provided some help for us to find somewhere to live – phoning landlords, arranging viewings, negotiating rents – but we had to do the legwork ourselves, travelling from flat to prospective flat, checking out travel and local amenities, forming little flat-share groups. By that final Friday I had done nothing, it all resembled too closely the nightmare that was accommodation search in Dublin. I only realised how screwed I was when Sylvia squeezed past me at eight o'clock that next morning and made for the door.

"Where are you going?" I asked her, hoping that we could maybe have another go at what had stuttered to a halt the night before.

"I'm moving this morning," she said, "I've got a place with Melissa and Anna."

Sylvia, Melissa, Anna. They were already becoming known as 'The Three As', just because of the last letters of each of their names. 'A' also stood for 'Ambitious', 'Assiduous', 'Applied', it should have come as no surprise that they were one of the first groups to get organised enough to find a home. The Three As were the most worldly, head-screwed-on women in our varied bunch. Still, it was a jolt for me, I hadn't even got myself involved in a flat-sharing group yet, never mind actually having found a place.

I had had an offer, back on the Tuesday before. Rahul and Jamie, recently parachuted into our room after the deluge of the previous week, proposed that I go with them to look at a flat in Benfica. Mike had gone off to look for someone to sell him some grass, and the two others had taken advantage of this fact to try to co-opt me into making their duo a trio, without having to include our Scottish roommate.

"You don't want to live with Mike?" I asked, feeling some kind of loyalty to the bloke who I had shared the room alone with for the first five days in the city.

"Mike's a good guy", Jamie began, "......but we don't want to live with him," Rahul finished his thought. "He's a pig".

They didn't want to share with Mike, although I was apparently acceptable. The thing was, I was easily as messy as he. I just hid it better, I suppose. I was flattered, and then that strange loyalty kicked in again, and I found myself turning them down. I had decided - I told them, making it up on the spot - to live with people who weren't London School teachers. We already spent so much time together, I explained, that I thought it was unhealthy, I wanted to branch out, maybe even live with some Portuguese. Rahul and Jamie looked at me as if I had just told them that I was leaving to become a Buddhist monk, then shrugged and went to see their flat. They ended up taking the place in Benfica, inviting sporty Adam as next choice flatmate, moving on without much fuss. After all, we had only known each other for nine days.

It was certainly this last idea that I had – or pretended to have – that of living with locals, that they found most surprising. During Basic Training the Lisbon Portuguese hardly existed for us as real people, we had formed such an airtight group that it was surprising to realize that others actually lived in the city in any authentic way. In truth it was the same for me, I had no intention of living with real-life Portuguese people, though the idea of avoiding forming another little pod of London School-ness in one of the flats around the city did appeal to me. I wasn't the only one feeling smothered at that time, though it had taken until that moment for it to dawn on me how claustrophobic our little community had become.

Still, typically, I didn't do anything about escaping it. It was almost Dublin all over again. I had good intentions but my inertia and ability to procrastinate meant that I was somehow paralysed. In truth I didn't know where to start, even if I had been as dynamic and organised as the Three As. I figured that something would turn up, that the universe wouldn't just leave me stranded in the Pensão Imperial for the year. Bizarrely, that's exactly how it turned out.

Saturday night came, and I was still potentially homeless. The pensão was emptying out, Rahul and Jamie had just that afternoon flown the coop, only after I had seriously considered asking them if I could belatedly accept their offer of a place in their Benfica flat. What had held me back wasn't pride, it was the knowledge that it would be futile, I had just that morning seen sporty Adam hauling his luggage down to reception, his bags no doubt filled with barbells and tracksuits and tubs of Creatine.

Pride didn't hold me back from breaking down and suggesting that Mike and I move in together. We were two of the last new teachers left, the hallways now seemed to echo as we walked through them, though of course this was my imagination, the hallways had never been full of people anyway. Myself and Mike were back in our room, smoking the last of my roommate's weed. The place had reverted to its previous semi-hovel status, in only a few hours. It was clear that Mike and I would have made terrible housemates, we both needed the balancing force of someone tidy to live with. I don't know if he suspected this too. Whatever, he turned me down.

"Nah, man," he replied, to my suggestion that we find a flat, "I like it here, it has everything I need. I'm gonna stay."

I looked around at the brown colour scheme, the bareness, the lack of lamps, pictures, adornment of any kind. He saw me looking.

"What can I say? I'm a man of simple tastes. I'm surprised you're still here though," Mike went on, "I thought you'd be living with Rahul and Jamie. I can't believe that they wanted to live with that prig Adam instead of you."

"Yeah," I said, "hard to believe".

Despite my predicament, it was still Saturday night, and not going out drinking wouldn't help me find a place to live any sooner. For some reason most of our number had arranged to meet in The Irish Rover, a bar just on the edge of the Bairro Alto. The place was faux-Irish, a plastic paddy set-up that displayed all the usual clichés on its walls, Guinness advertisements, a bodhrán, an Irish flag, even a leprechaun or two, built from some pub-design catalogue that included other formulas like 'Salsa Bar', 'Strip-club', 'Wine Bar'. There was only one Irish person there, a girl from Monaghan who had come to Lisbon to study for a year and had ended up waitressing in The Irish Rover. That's how inauthentic it was, it had waitresses.

Still, it also had booze. The Guinness there was undrinkable, though surprisingly the Murphys wasn't too bad, so Mike and I had a few pints while waiting for our fellow London Schoolers to arrive. We, of course, were still only ten minutes away from the Bairro Alto, while most of the others had now dispersed out to apartments in Lumiar, Lapa, Benfica and Odivelas, and needed to take buses and metros to get back into the centre. I was standing at the bar, ordering my round in English, figuring that if there was one place in the city I could avoid having to use my terrible Portuguese, it was in an Irish bar. A guy standing beside me seemed to notice my accent and turned to face me.

"You Irish?" There was something Southern Hemisphere about his accent, a hint of wallaby, a smidgen of kiwi.

"I am. You?" My question was ironic, but he took it seriously.

"In a way, born in Durban, second name Callaghan."

"Durban", I repeated, trying to run through my knowledge of

Antipodean geography without appearing ignorant of what country he was talking about. The guy could see that I was struggling.

"South Africa," he said, "though my Irish passport allows me to work here. Useful thing, an Irish grandfather."

There was nothing Irish about the way he spoke, unsurprisingly. I recognised the accent now, all clipped, squeezed vowels, sharp, precise consonants.

"Charles."

The guy stuck out his hand and I shook it. He was taller than me with fair, sun-bleached hair and – I supposed from his Celtic side – freckles pocking his face. He wore baggy clothes, loose-fitting chinos, a large, linen shirt. Again, apart from the freckles there was no Callaghan in Ireland that looked like him.

As happens smoothly with English speakers in a non-English speaking city, we formed a quick, easy intimacy. Charles was with his girlfriend and they both joined Mike and I in our semi-snug down the back. The girl was tallish too, and slim, flat-chested and lithe, with the same air of sunburnt health that Charles displayed. Instead of shaking hands she went in for the Portuguese style of greeting, the kiss on either cheek for both myself and Mike. From her accent she was clearly English.

"I'm Charlotte," she said, after the awkward kisses were over.

"Really?" Mike said, still a little off balance after her greeting, "that must get confusing, Charles and Charlotte."

They laughed, as if they hadn't heard this before.

"Yeah" Charlotte said, "people are always mixing us up."

We drank and talked, barriers down, the usual suspicion and restraint between new acquaintances now absent. We were, after all, a little English speaking island in a sea of foreigners. Charles and

Charlotte had been there a year already, they worked in a school with the grand title of The Communicate Institute. They had come from Manchester in 2006 to try something new, to get some sun, to see some of the world, the usual bland clichés of the EFL teacher. I had heard a variation of this story seventeen different times in the previous two weeks. It was all I could do to smile, look interested and try not to make my own back-story as tedious. *What are you running from?* I couldn't help thinking, now stuck on this idea that all these foreigners that I kept meeting were doing the same as me - fleeing.

Charles and Charlotte revelled in their position as one year veterans of Lisbon, happily recommending to us bars and restaurants we had already been to about five times each, giving their slant on the Portuguese, how enthusiastic they were as students, how much more introverted they were than the Spanish. Mike and I exchanged quick glances, I imagined we both felt that we could do without the lecture.

To stem the flow, I asked them if they knew of a good way to find somewhere to live. It was our new friends' turn to exchange glances.

"Are you both looking?" Charlotte asked, in a way that suggested that she was trying to be casual, but really wanted to know.

"Nah," Mike answered, "I'm fine for the minute, in a pensão. It's just Cian here, he didn't get off his ass in time to get sorted."

Charlotte and Charles looked at each other again.

"What? What is it?" I asked.

Charlotte gave her boyfriend the nod.

"We have a room free in our flat. It's small," he said," but the flat's nice. Why don't you come and have a look."

"Really?" Here it was again, somebody offering me somewhere to live. I had never thought of myself before as a person who made a good impression, as somebody instantly trustable, but for the second time in a week here was a group of people I hardly knew willing to let me live with them. Was it the Irishness, the soft, disarming accent we were supposed to have? Or was I just a better actor than I had thought I was, capable of the pretence of trustworthiness without even trying?

They gave me the address – the flat was in a part of the city called Graça – and left, saying that they were having an early night. *A very early night*, I thought. It was eleven o'clock.

Mike tapped me on the arm with the back of his hand once they had left.

"Charles and Charlotte, eh?" he said, "your knights in shining armour."

Then he smiled broadly, as if he had just thought of something, showing thick, square teeth.

"You could be living with a right pair of Charlies".

I went to inspect the room in their flat the next afternoon, still woozy and vague from the hangover brought on by getting smashed, as smashed as Jamie usually got, the previous night. Our fellow teachers had finally shown up in The Irish Rover, and we had hit the town knowing that this was the final night before we actually had to enter a classroom and do some work. It was an end-of-holiday kind of blowout and gave me, the next morning, the familiar desire never to drink again.

At the door of the pensão, on my way to Charles and Charlotte's place, I met Carly, and helped her with some of her bags. She had got a place with Laura and Caroline, and was just back to collect the rest of her stuff. She had brought more than anyone else, she had paid one hundred pounds sterling, she told me, almost proudly, for excess baggage on the flight over. Carly had six large suitcases. The ones I lifted were heavy too, no doubt filled with pencils and notebooks. She seemed nervous, a little frazzled, though this was entirely normal for Carly.

I waved down one beige taxi for Carly, and then one for myself, and gave the driver the address, written for me by Charles. The driver grunted, and we set off. I wasn't at all clear on where exactly Graça was, but we headed towards the river and then turned left up towards the Castle, in the opposite direction to the Bairro.

The taxi snaked up the narrow cobbled streets of this part of the city, climbing all the time, on occasion getting stuck behind one of those squat little yellow trams with a number 28 on its back, the cab driver cursing each time the tram stopped to pick up passengers. There was no way to pass, space was just too limited, the buildings on either side felt like they were leaning in over the road at various stages, ready to come together and crush anything in their way.

We stopped at a spot at the top of a hill where the road widened into a kind of triangular space with shops and businesses lining the street on either side.

"Largo da Graça," the driver announced, as if he were a grumpy tour guide. I paid him, looked for a number twenty-four and found it, just a door basically, set into the space between a barber's and a restaurant. I pushed the button on the intercom and was buzzed in.

The apartment itself was on the first floor, and was reached after a walk up a dark, bare corridor and some plain steps. A door with light emerging from it was half-open to my left. Charles and Charlotte were standing there in the hall, waiting for me. Charles shook my hand, his freckles especially prominent today for some reason, and Charlotte did the cheek-kissing thing again. It was almost an organised welcome committee, I thought, the couple not for the first time creeping me out. I got an image of the Two Charlies beckoning a series of flatmates into their spare room, murdering each one and then dismembering the body, before advertising again for their next victim. Even if this were true, I knew I would still consider taking the room, just to get out of the pensão.

The flat was compact, Charles and Charlotte's bedroom was at one end, next to the kitchen, both looking out on to a bare little internal yard. At the other end of the long, wood-floored corridor was the free room, which faced out on to the street outside, the Largo da Graça where the taxi had let me out. In the middle were the windowless bathroom and living room. It all looked new, with freshly painted white walls, varnished wooden floors, basic but functional furniture. I thought of the brown-tinged gloom, the still flooded sixth floor of the Pensão Imperial and almost accepted the room there and then.

For form's sake, I had to view it first. Charles had described it as a box-room and that's what it was, a cube-shaped space that wasn't much bigger than your average cardboard box. There was a small, built-in wardrobe in one wall opposite the window, a single bed slotted into the corner under this window, only leaving a foot and half of space before the opening of the wardrobe, and a tiny desk and chair – as if for a child – on the other side of the room. Apart from a plain, wooden-framed mirror on the wall behind the door and a blue painted shelf above the desk, that was it, they were the total contents of my little cell. It was a place I imagined Mike could be happy in, he could smoke a lot of dope there, meditate and enjoy the frugality. I wasn't quite sure I would adapt so well.

Still, I burned no bridges, and made appreciative noises.

"I know it's small," Charlotte said, sounding like an estate agent, "but it's cosy, and you get the view."

She pulled a cord to the side of the window and the metal shutter came up, revealing Graça outside in all its sedate Sunday glory. Two old people walked by, arm in arm. Nothing else moved.

I told them that I would think about it, went back down the dark steps and out into the September sun. There was a tram passing just as I reached the Largo so I hopped on and draped my arm half out of the open window as it screeched and wound its way down through the now tourist-filled streets of the Castle quarter of the city. The breeze felt good on my hungover face, though the sharp turns and sudden dips of the tram jolted and jostled my already disturbed digestion. I got out in the Baixa, one hundred yards from the river, now at sea-level again after my visit to Graça on the hill, and strolled back to the pensão.

The place was really empty now. I took the elevator and then walked slowly up to our room. The door was slightly ajar, I pushed at it, and walked in silently. Mike was under the duvet, jerkily making what could only be masturbatory movements. I turned and left as quickly as I had entered. Fifteen minutes later I had rung Charles to accept the room in their flat. Four hours after that, I had moved in.

OCTOBER

I didn't have time to regret my decision to move in to what was basically a shoe box. Nine hours after I had hauled my hastily packed suitcases into no. 24, Largo da Graça, I was at work.

The school I had been assigned to was near the campus of Lisbon University. There was a metro stop there – Cidade Universitária – sixty seconds walk away from the London School, and the school itself was unmissable when I meandered up there at ten o'clock the next morning. ESCOLA LONDON the sign on the first floor boomed, in distinctive blue, red and white lettering, pasted to the front of another one of those anonymous, flat-fronted buildings that could have been a block of flats, offices of an insurance company, a high class brothel. Apart from the sign, nothing on the outside told of the activity that went on inside those ten or so rooms.

The eighteen of us new teachers had been split up between the various London School centres in the city. Five, including Mike and Jamie, had been assigned to the headquarters school in Rossio – the consensus opinion was that these two had been sent there so that the top brass could keep an eye on them. Four others had been sent to the school out on the coast at Cascais, the once seaside village that was now basically an extension of the city. Five, among them Carly, Sylvia Saint John and Rahul, went up to the London School centre near the big roundabout at Marquês de Pombal, which left myself, Adam, Joanne and Laura, who were given a map of the city and told to report to the university school at ten o'clock on October first.

I was relatively relaxed that first day, bearing in mind that I had had eight weeks teaching experience in my life. The other three that started with me were among the people I had had least contact with in our extended group of eighteen. Joanne was Rahul's other half, the Kiwi girl with the dark hair and shy smile, who said she was twenty-three but looked fifteen. She and her boyfriend had almost melded at this stage, they didn't live in the same flat but had begun to spend every waking and sleeping hour together. To see her there that day in the staffroom, on her own, was an indication that this was really happening. Joanne was there without Rahul. It hit me then, we're in work now, playtime has ended.

Joanne wasn't exactly innocent, that would be the wrong thing to say. A better word for her would be 'uncorrupted'. I got to spend more time with her that first week and found that she was a person seemingly determined to avoid cynicism of any kind, to think the best of people, even in the face of all the evidence. I found this refreshing and infuriating all at once. There were times when she made me feel better, more hopeful, just by her being around, and others when I just wanted to shake her, to tell her to wake the fuck up and to stop deluding herself. I wanted to say that the world was a hard place, with hard people in it.

Laura, on the other hand, needed no such reminder. She was a semi-detached member of The Three As group of Sylvia, Anna and Melissa. Significantly though, they never became The Four As. Laura was a little younger than the others, a little shorter, a little more rotund, slightly less organised and sophisticated, that bit more hard-drinking. She was like their wilder younger sister. She was different enough from the other three for it to matter, not different enough for them not to be friends, of a sort.

Adam was the fourth rookie that began work in our London School that autumn. It was actually a shock to see him that first day in formal trousers and a pair of shiny black leather shoes, I had only ever seen him through the days of Basic Training in sportswear, only in garments with Nike, Adidas, Le Coq Sportif, on them. Someone had called him Sport Billy early on, and this had stuck. Just looking at him made me feel lazy and sedentary. Adam was the guy that Melissa Simpson had moved on to, after her brief assignation with me, and was also who Rahul and Jamie had gone to after I had earlier turned down their offer of a room in their flat.

For these reasons he seemed to me to be the anti-me. Three times that first week, and every subsequent week, he came into work with wet hair, looking flushed, having just worked out in the University gym. I had never, at that stage of my life, even been in a gym, and found that lighting twenty-five cigarettes a day was all the exercise I needed. Adam looked a lot better than me in swimwear, but I didn't envy him his cult of the body. It just seemed like a lot of hard work.

We four – Laura, Joanne, Adam and I – were all seated on a bench outside the busy office at half past ten that morning in the London School building at Cidade Universitária. We whispered among ourselves to hide our apprehension, all of us had made it in at the appointed time of ten o'clock, and had been told to sit where we were now sitting by a particularly stern looking secretary. It was like being in primary school, waiting to talk to the principal. For thirty-five minutes, nothing happened.

"Ok, who's Ky-an?"

A woman had appeared before us from one of the doors to our left. She was tall, solidly built, with a lot of hair, a mountain of hair that looked like a small mammal of some kind had decided to live on her head.

"I think that's me," I said, trying not to sound too put out, "though it's pronounced Kee-an."

"Ok, whatever, follow me."

I did as I was told. The woman had an English accent, vaguely Estuary, was in her mid to late thirties and could have been attractive if Gok Wan had got a hold of her and restyled her. She took me to a functional office with a desk, chairs, shelves, a bulky three-year old desktop computer, few items that betrayed the personality of the occupant.

"Sit down".

The woman motioned to a hard wooden seat that faced her more padded office chair on the other side of the desk. Again, I obeyed. I kept waiting for her to introduce herself, and then gave up waiting.

"I'm sorry, are you the school director? Are you Elizabeth?"

We had been given her name the previous Thursday, along with a map indicating the location of the school, and instructions to be there promptly at ten.

She stared at me, wide-eyed, as if I had just asked her if she were the same woman I had just seen turning tricks down on Martim Moniz.

"Well who else would I be?"

It wasn't aggressive, what she said, just impatient, verging on the contemptuous. She was right, I even began thinking, how could I have been so stupid? Our encounter was a formality, simply to fill in some paperwork and to go over basic rules and regulations.

"And these are your classes," she said, handing me a slip of printed paper, "Your first one starts in about an hour".

This was unexpected. I had to actually teach? Two weeks of

pretending to be on an eighteen-to-thirty holiday had totally failed to prepare me for genuine work. I returned to my companions, who obviously noticed my expression.

"What's she like?" Joanne asked, "is she nice?"

Her voice was low as Elizabeth's door was open, and she was just now coming back towards us. Laura took one look at my face and snorted.

"Oh yeah," she said, much louder than Joanne had spoken, "I'd say she's a real princess."

Our school director had now reached our little group and turned to the last person who had spoken.

"So you're Joanne?"

Laura looked incredulous.

"Far from it. I'm Laura."

She stood up and stuck out her hand. Elizabeth took it, unconvinced, and let it go quickly.

"Follow me," she said.

We all had our turns in the principal's office. Joanne was last, and when the door finally opened we all saw her protesting to Elizabeth, in as much as Joanne was capable of protesting about something, about the fact that we had to teach that day.

"But I haven't had time to prepare," she was saying, "if I had been told last night I could have had lesson plans and....."

"Look Joanne," said Elizabeth, cutting her off, "get over it. You have a class in half an hour."

This – not having time to prepare – was literally traumatic for Joanne. Her lesson plans soon became legendary, they were printed out from her laptop on a mini-printer she had brought with her from New Zealand. The various sections of the class were then <u>underlined</u>, <u>with a</u>

<u>ruler</u>, in different coloured inks, five or six plans a day, five days a week. Some of us, me included, were lucky to scrawl together a few ideas on the back of an envelope before a class, while Joanne constructed these intricate plans that seemed to want to make teaching into a kind of science.

For me it was much more art than science. Being told, with an hour's notice, that I had five hours teaching that first day didn't bother me too much in the end. It meant that I had to wing it, and that's all I really knew how to do anyway. I was pleasantly surprised by the students that first day. They were a mixture of adults and teenagers. Some were in their forties and fifties, there for work reasons, with an eye on the future, some were thirteen or fourteen, sent there by their parents to improve their grades. I also had one group of ten year olds who came after school and seemed gratifyingly intimidated by a lumbering Irishman at the top of the class who only had a vague idea of what to do with kids so young. Almost to a person they were enthusiastic, eager to learn more, interested in me for some reason. English, for them, was a secret code that allowed access to another world, one where the real business of humanity was done, and I held the key to this code, simply by the language that I had spoken since birth. It was a new experience for me. I found that I was being prized for a part of myself I had never previously given any thought to, the language I spoke everyday with about as much reflection as I gave to breathing.

So I breezed through the first day, managed to exchange a few words with the other various members of staff wandering around, the four other teachers, the secretaries, even the security guard, Senhor Eugenio, who directed me to the balcony at the back of the staffroom when I asked him where I could smoke. I had to use gestures for the old geezer. He seemed, strangely for the head of security in an English language school, to understand no actual English, though he did twig the international sign of me holding an imaginary cigarette to my lips and blowing imaginary smoke out into the still unpolluted atmosphere. The balcony, which doubled as the smoking area, looked out on to an anonymous concrete area that was itself surrounded by four, five and six storey buildings, just like the one we now worked in. They were all bland, blank constructions with windows like dead eyes, staring down blindly on to the empty patio, on to me inhaling my Marlboro.

In Dublin, the summer before I left for Lisbon, Avatar had closed and I had to decide what to do. There were other web-design jobs out there, positions still being advertised in the appointments sections of the newspapers and on the recruitment sites, yet I couldn't bring myself to apply for any of them. Getting another job would imply permanency, an active decision to stay there in Dublin, faith in the future. I didn't have a lot of that. I wanted something temporary, uncomplicated, commitment-free. I wanted time to think. Simon, my new flatmate, gave me the out I needed.

He was teaching English in a language school in Dame Street, acting basically as part Entertainments Officer, part-babysitter for the teenage sons and daughters of the European middle-classes. I had done a full semester of a TEFL course seven years earlier, a Humanities option that they were offering in order to broaden the education of the bunch of focused nerds in my Computer Science degree, so I applied to Simon's school on the off-chance. Amazingly, after a rapid interview where I believe I successfully displayed the fact that I had retained almost nothing from that English Teaching element of my course in

DCU, The English Institute gave me a job. I soon found out that their summer course started in two days, and they desperately needed warm bodies to act as teachers.

For July and August of that summer of 2007 I spent four or five hours of every day in a classroom, basically winging it. The job was so different to what I had been doing previous to that – sitting at a rectangular desk, staring at a coloured computer screen every day – that it took me two or three weeks just to really consider what I was doing work. It felt for all the world like being involved in some volunteer programme at a summer camp for needy children who wanted to pick up a bit of English.

Whether I got lucky with the kids I had, or whether I was actually a better bullshitter than I had suspected, my charges didn't seem to see through to my fundamental incompetence. The classes were fairly chaotic but far from disastrous. We played lots of games, drinking games like Fizz-Buzz that I adapted to the classroom, as well as others like Alibi, which were taught to me by some of the other teachers who took pity on me when I admitted in the staff-room that I barely had a clue what I was doing. This last game, Alibi, became a favourite of mine, and of my classes. It involved two students, who were to play the part of suspects of a crime, disappearing into a corner for five minutes to agree on their common alibi for a particular time in question. They had to decide where they were, what they did, what they were wearing for a defined period of four hours, before being questioned individually by the rest of the class, who played the roles of the detectives investigating the case. The idea was that the two suspects' stories would have to be identical – which they almost never were – or else they would be found guilty by their peers who, now morphed into judge/ jury, would decide on a punishment. It usually resulted in bedlam and hilarity, which soon became the yardstick by which I measured a successful class. Bedlam and hilarity, that's what I was going for.

We had debates too, and discussions. I showed excerpts from my DVD collection, from Godfather and Pulp Fiction for the boys, from The Sound of Music for the girls. We played Pictionary, Charades, Hangman. The only time the classes went wrong was when I tried to use a textbook to actually teach them something, when my ineptitude and lack of grammatical knowledge came out. I was a performing monkey, a Butlins redcoat, a children's party organiser, only very vaguely could it be said that I was a teacher.

That said, I got bizarrely good feedback in the end of course questionnaires that the students filled out. And I do think that they managed, probably accidentally, to learn some English along the way through my scatter-gun approach. I seemed to have wandered into something I had an unformed aptitude for, and which I found was a relief from the dead stare of a computer screen. Going to work and interacting with some actual human beings was a whole new experience for me, even if they were adolescent, loud and barely able to string a coherent sentence together. By the end of the summer, I thought that I kind of knew what I was doing.

This delusion was dispelled quite quickly in The London School. Things got tougher, after day one. Joanne, frazzled into a near nervous breakdown by the first day's sudden workload, settled into the job easily that first week, her conscientious, hyper-organised approach eventually showing up my lack of basic professionalism. Soon it was me who felt overwhelmed. This was serious business now, it dawned on me, it was no summer school, we had classes who would have exams at the end of the year, and people who were paying good money to have their English turbo-charged by the London School. Hangman, Pulp

Fiction and debates about who was better, men or women, weren't going to get me through the year. I realised that I was going to actually have to figure out how to teach people things.

On top of that, in my life in general I was assaulted by newness of all kinds. In those first few weeks of October every waking second of my day was filled with novelty. Even in sleep I felt it, my dreams were more intense and vivid than ever, jammed with collisions of old and new, Dublin and Lisbon, Ireland and Portugal. My job was something I really hadn't done before and only had a vague idea how to approach, my colleagues were people I had just met, my friends were friends of twenty days duration. The language I heard every day, on the trams and on the streets, was this strange nasal conglomeration, with all those Ows and Shs, like nothing I had heard before. In restaurants I ate fish whose name I didn't recognize, even in English when I looked them up in the dictionary later. The cars and buses came from surprising directions, and I barely avoided being hit on two separate occasions those first weeks. And of course I was now inhabiting the smallest bedroom I had ever lived in, in the same flat as a couple who genuinely seemed, as their names appeared to indicate, to be two versions of the same person.

More even than Joanne and Rahul, I soon noticed that Charles and Charlotte were almost never apart. Literally never. About ten days into my stay in the flat in Graça I walked into the kitchen and found Charlotte on her own, stirring something in the frying pan. I looked around the room for her partner and realized that, for the first time ever, she was unaccompanied. I was just about to ask her where Charles was when I heard the toilet flush and he walked through the door, drying his hands. In fact, I was surprised that they even took a dump separately, such was their union. They slept together, shopped together, cooked

together, they even had the same teaching timetables so that, although
they couldn't actually be together in each others' classes, they were
always in the vicinity. Apart from the four or five hours teaching a day,
Charles and Charlotte shared the same physical space at all times.

They also hardly ever left the flat. They were in a foreign country,
with beautiful October weather and a city full of cheap activities to do,
and yet number 24, Largo da Graça, first floor, was seemingly the only
place they wanted to be. They worked at more or less the same times
as me, and on Saturday nights they did go out, but always after I had
begun my night, and they consistently returned hours before I did.
They were always there, always at home, always together.

So it was no surprise that the Two Charlies' presence soon became
oppressive. There were only two communal areas in the apartment,
the kitchen/ dining area that looked on to our bare back yard, and the
interior, windowless living room. The rooms were next to each other,
and both had doors that opened on to the long corridor that ran the
length of the flat. Charles and Charlotte had perfected the technique
of inhabiting both rooms simultaneously. While cooking dinner they
would wander over and back between the rooms, one watching a
programme on television while the other chopped or stirred or fried,
then they would meet up and discuss the progress of the dinner, or the
soap opera, or both, before swapping places and shouting in and out
instructions, updates, pieces of news, as if nothing was really worth
experiencing if it wasn't experienced by both of them simultaneously.
There was no escape from them.

And then there was the PDA problem. Of course it's hard to call
them *Public* Displays of Affection, when technically they were in their
own home, but I was a member of the public and I didn't need to be a
witness to the daily kissing, stroking, squeezing and rubbing that went

on. Especially as neither Charlie wore anything more than a light t-shirt and shorts around the house. My digestion – usually so unflappable – became slowly knocked off balance by having to watch Charlotte rubbing her mate high up on the thigh, or him massaging her feet while I tried to eat my evening meal. They seemed to make absolutely no concession to the fact that I was now living in the house. There remained the possibility, though, that the way they acted with me in the house actually *was* a modification of their previous behaviour, that this was them toning things down for my benefit. The mind boggled.

So whether they meant to or not, they drove me out, out into the streets of Graça and Alfama. The apartment had become so claustrophobic, so filled by the overwhelming presence of my amorous flatmates, that there was only one escape, and that was the front door. If I spent more than a half an hour in my own room I began to get the impression that the walls were closing in, making my box-shaped space even smaller. I had to get out of there.

I found a cheap restaurant, right next door. It was called A Lua, which my pocket Portuguese dictionary informed me meant The Moon, though there was nothing remotely lunar about the place. I soon recognized it as the standard design of Lisbon eateries. It had a narrow, deceptive façade that gave way to a long interior that stretched back about seventy feet, with tables – each a standard square and covered with a crisp white paper tablecloth – lined up in threes either side of a central aisle. The floor was, as always in Portuguese restaurants, hard, porcelain tiles. There was a counter on the left as you walked in, where people stood to have a quick coffee, a gooey pastry or simply to chat with the corpulent owner, Sergio, over a Super Bock beer. Just at the entrance was the fish tank, made of clear plastic or glass, that allowed the customers to see the shellfish – usually fat, grasping crabs – that may or may not have been on the menu that night. I imagined Sergio just putting his hand into the tank when someone ordered one of the crimson crustaceans, and grabbing one of them, throwing it straight into the pot as its little legs clawed uselessly in the air.

I took to eating in A Lua, three or four times a week. I tried some of the other restaurants in the area first, but found them more expensive, with worse food and a more suspicious atmosphere. It wasn't as if A Lua was particularly welcoming – Sergio was gruff and no-nonsense and seemed not to care if his customers were put off by his manner – but it wasn't as actively distrustful as one or two of the places I had been in down the main street in Graça. In A Lua there was a sense of benign neglect, Sergio and the regulars simply didn't care very much about this stray foreigner who came in every second night to order in bad Portuguese or incomprehensible English. *So you're not from around here*, was their initial attitude, *whatever, we're not impressed*. That was an attitude I could deal with. I had briefly entertained the idea of becoming an intrinsic, respected member of the local community, a kind of foreign mascot for the people of Graça, but I ended up gladly settling for the indifference of our next door restaurant.

Evenings, after my solid meal in A Lua, I would wander over to an outdoor coffee shop near Graça church. This consisted of a wood and concrete shed with a hatch in it that allowed coffee and other beverages to be served to the mixture of tourist and local clientele that went there to digest their dinner outside. I began drinking *bicas*, which were those short, thick espressos that left a bitter, bracing aftertaste once downed. They were like shots for coffee drinkers, small, powerful, drinkable in one. A bica was ten cents more expensive there, outdoors, than in A Lua, partly because of the bonus of being able to sit and breathe fresh air while you got your injection of pure caffeine, but also because of the view over the city that you got while doing it.

Lisbon is all hills, and Graça is right at the top of one of them, just along from St. George's Castle, which dominates this eastern side of the city. The other main hill in the city centre contains the Bairro Alto, where we London School teachers usually ended up each weekend night. Between the two hills is squashed the low-lying Baixa area, where the streets are all set out in a grid pattern, like an electric circuit-board, and where most of the shopping is concentrated. The two hills stare stonily across at one another, the traditional Graça/Castle side suspicious of the bohemian debauchery of the Bairro Alto. They both look down with disdain on all the vulgar commercial fuss in the Baixa below.

From the viewing area next to the Graça outdoor café you can see nearly all of this and more. The river is just visible off in the distance to the left, as a glimpse of grey water in the daytime and a dark absence at night, and the regular sized buildings that the grid creates are laid out like morsels, little cookies you almost want to reach out and nibble on. The castle juts out too, on the same level as Graça, stony and stern. Yet from Graça there is also a view of deeper into the city, away from the open presence of the river, a view of Socorro and Intendente and Avenida da Roma, where the streets lose their grid shape and become as chaotic and random as they should be in a city like Lisbon. The view from the castle makes the city seem organised and tidy, but from Graça you see more of what it really is, you can look down like God at all the mess and traffic and frantic movement of people.

Mario, the guy who worked at the coffee hut, became my first Portuguese friend, after a fashion. My Portuguese was only just above non-existent, and his English was scatter-gun and rudimentary, yet he always seemed pleased to see me. Mario learned my name a week after I started going there and soon began greeting me with a "Hey Cian, what's up?" which he had learned from some American teen series or other. Foreign programmes on Portuguese television are subtitled, not dubbed, and so the natives pick up strange bits and pieces, little undigested nuggets of language that they don't always know how to use properly. "I'm so pissed!" was another one of Super-Mario's favourite one-liners that he would come out with at random times around me. I tried to explain the expression's different American and British usages to him but I was wasting my time. Words didn't necessarily have to mean things for Mario, he liked the poetry of them, the sound, the emotional association. He enjoyed the fact that they were exotic samples of a culture far from his, that made him feel more international just by saying them.

So if nothing else, the Two Charlies and their obnoxiousness got me out into the world. I soon became a regular in A Lua, if I didn't eat there I would descend from our first floor flat after dinner and take a swift coffee at the counter with the rest of the Graça residents. I liked listening to them as they joked with each other affectionately and gossiped for the ten or fifteen minutes it would take them to complete the ceremony of the *bica*. The *bica* was that tiny little mini-cup of coffee that the Portuguese drank constantly throughout the day. The sugar was a key element in the ceremony, the sachet had to be tapped multiple times to move all the contents to one corner before the paper was torn and the white granules poured into the already viscous liquid. The coffee would be sipped and savoured, often accompanied by a glass of water or an almond pastry. I felt like an anthropologist, observing the behaviour of a remote tribe and trying to fit in. I must have been more successful than I realised. Mario noticed my attempts at integration.

"Cian," he said, one evening in my third week in Graça, "you drink coffee now like *Português*." He smiled, obviously proud of me. "Before," he went on, "foreign!" And mimed me rushing my *bica*, treating it like a measure of tequila, "now, *relax*. Is good."

The days soon slipped like this into a rhythm. They began with me enjoying the hour I usually got to myself between when The Happy Couple set off for work and I had to leave, and more often than not ended with some combination of A Lua and Mario's. Charlotte and Charles started teaching around the same time as me but liked to go in an hour early to prepare their classes, for which fact I gave great thanks. It was my favourite hour of the day, between eleven and twelve, when I would often just sit in the kitchen in silence, with a cup of tea and two slices of toast smeared with raspberry jam, before opening the window and having a leisurely cigarette while the smoke drifted out into the Lisbon air. I could briefly luxuriate in the solitude and the absence of pawing hands and The Two Charlies' overwhelming presence.

The journey to work also became habitual, though the tram trip from Graça that snaked down towards the Baixa and the Metro stop there, was never really routine. It was too much of an event. Those toiling, block-shaped trams soon became a constant part of my days, they were the only form of public transport that reached us up there on the hill. The window of my room gave on to the Largo da Graça, where there was a tram stop. So the first sound that I heard each morning, whether I was aware of it or not, was the rumbling of the number twenty-eight as it approached, then the screeching and the squealing of the brakes that sounded like metal animals being tortured. Out on the street later, at the stop, at the beginning of my daily journey to work, the ground carried the message of the tram's imminent arrival before it even swung into view, the vibrations travelling thirty, forty, sixty metres ahead of the slow-moving yellow vehicle. The trams also had a staccato, insistent bell that would sound impatiently if any puny car dared to get in their lumbering way. They were relics of the early twentieth century, cutting edge when introduced but faintly comical in the year 2007, yet were still a vital part of the city's transport system, and were the only way – bar walking – that I could get from the hill in Graça down to the centre of things, the Metro stations in the Baixa.

As I have said, it was never mundane to me, riding one of those creaking yellow boxes. It was always novel, there was always someone to watch, some old Senhora dressed in all black, Spanish tourists talking loudly as if they were in their own country, adolescents hanging near the back and trying to decide if they were going to rob anyone that day. At a number of points along the way the road was so narrow, squashed between two old, tall buildings on either side, that it seemed impossible that two trams could pass each other going in opposite directions without doing some kind of damage. They were on rails, and had done it thousands of times before, of course, but every time it happened, every time two of the rickety yellow trams met – one going up to Graça, one going down – I would wait for the sound of the scraping of metal on metal, wood on wood. The sound never came. They always managed it unscathed, the windows of each tram close enough that the passengers could reach out and touch hands in passing though the vehicles themselves never so much as kissed.

So my trip to work began with the gentle rollercoaster of the twenty-eight and finished with the Metro. I usually caught the train at the Baixa/Chiado station, two minutes walk from where the tram left me off. The contrast with the tram couldn't have been greater, we moved underground into an environment that was closed in, modern, pristine and slick – everything in fact that the awkward yellow trams weren't. I normally just shut down until the tiled interior of the Cidade Universitária station came into view. People were busier on the metro, less leisurely, more business like. It wasn't conducive to staring at the other passengers.

In school, after my relaxed first day, shit got real very quickly. I had a First Certificate class for two weeks before I even found out what the First Certificate was. It turned out that it was a Cambridge exam for students at an almost advanced level and not, as the name suggested, a token qualification for beginners. I was corrected by students in my lower-intermediate class when I told them, with the certainty that I knew was necessary even if I wasn't sure, that the past tense of the verb 'to lay down' was 'lied down'. And even the ten year olds in my junior class made me feel inadequate. Their teacher from the year before, who was from deepest Sussex, had taught them the words for various fruits, including 'ba-nah-nah', and they found my pronunciation, with the flat Limerick 'a' in the middle, hilarious. *Shit*, I thought, after one more long stumbling day trying to pretend that I knew what I was doing, *I can't fucking do this.*

The truth was, I realised, that I was a Computer Science graduate who had fallen into web design, and who had become fairly good at it, before the catastrophe of Maura, and Avatar going belly up. I had a straight, up-and-down mind, a mind that organised things into boxes and expected them to stay there, with a dash of creativity that I had had to develop while designing sites. The mixture of patience, good humour, subtlety, organisation and linguistic sensitivity needed to teach a language well was, at that time, foreign to me. I was a fish out of water, a pig on a bicycle, a monkey in a dinner jacket. I was out of my depth and needed help.

Amazingly, the school attempted to provide it. At the end of our second week of work we four newcomers were informed that we were to arrive in a half an hour early that Friday for a meeting. Laura, Adam, Joanne and I reluctantly showed up at twenty-five to midday, five minutes late, and were shown in to one of the classrooms, where we stayed, silent and expectant, as if we ourselves were students, waiting for a class to start.

A round man walked in and stood smiling at us. He was sweating, had receding hair and walked in a way that suggested flat feet. He was all circles, he had a rounded belly and a spherical head, though he wasn't fat as much as pudgy. He had flesh you wanted to just push your finger into and watch it sink in.

"Ladies and gentlemen," he said, apparently delighted to see us, "I'm Perry Owens."

He was, he went on to explain, both the school director over at the Avenida school and the school support officer for first year teachers.

"Why are we only meeting you now then?" Laura asked, direct as normal.

"I've been on holiday, darling," Perry said, utterly unapologetic. "But now I'm here and I'm here to help."

Laura put her hand up, as if she were in school. Perry looked at her and raised his eyebrows.

"I don't need any help," she said, "can I go?"

Perry thought that this was hilarious.

"I like you already," he said, not answering her question. "So what we're going to do, you are all going to talk to me about your classes, and I'm going to tell you where you are going wrong."

Perry looked at each of us in turn and, seeing how unimpressed we were he added,

"It's a joke, I'm joking. I'll be supportive and encouraging and all that good stuff. So madam," he said, now looking back at Laura, "you go first."

We all lied, of course, me more than anyone. I admitted to some teething problems, but didn't come close to letting my colleagues, and this camp man I had only just met, know how badly I was struggling. Joanne, if anything, lied in the other direction. I knew that she was so super-prepared for every eventuality in a class that nothing serious ever went wrong for her, yet I could see that she felt obliged to make up difficulties, exaggerate problem students, hype up her cluelessness, just to be part of the gang. I don't think she had any idea how patronising this was, or was aware that everyone else knew exactly how in control she was of everything.

Perry, to his credit, knew what was happening and called me aside just as our session ended and the others disappeared back to the staffroom.

"Cian", he said, "that's a nice name." He had his hand resting lightly on my shoulder. It passed through my mind that he was going to kiss me. "When is your first class?" he asked.

"Two o'clock," I replied.

"Let me come and observe you. You don't mind, do you?"

"Well actually...," I began.

"Great," Perry exclaimed, as if I hadn't even spoken, "I'll see you then."

My two o'clock was with a bunch of mostly older people, retired or near to retirement, who were doing English classes in the same vein as others learned to knit, or went hill-walking or did Tai-chi. It was a social atmosphere, and the students – six women of advanced years and two men who flirted with them all in turn – seemed to like me, despite my obvious lack of training.

Perry sat in the back, a little separated from the students. He said something to them in Portuguese and they all laughed. I gave him a look that I hoped communicated hostility. He just smiled back and clenched his fist briefly, as if I were about to compete in the Teaching Olympics.

At the end of the class the students all filed out, all smiles and encouraging nods. Antonio, the older of the two men, even shook my hand. The eight of them had laughed at my jokes and had made an almost super-human effort to seem interested, educated, entertained. Their efforts to paint me in a good light probably made me look even worse, however, they were so obvious. The class hadn't been the worst, we had done some listening from a CD – difficult to fuck up, even for me – and I had asked the students to work in groups and to recreate the story they had just listened to. If Perry had been hoping to see me at my worst he was to be disappointed.

"Cian", Perry said to me, once we were alone in the classroom, "take a pew."

He motioned to one of the chairs that had just been vacated, as if he were in his own home. The wooden chair still retained the heat from Antonio's backside.

"First of all," he said, still standing, "I like the look of you in the classroom. You're tall, solid, good-looking in your own way. You should use that, flirt with the ladies a little, they like that, even with the men, if you like. You can be more commanding, you have the physique for it. Don't be so apologetic about being at the top of the classroom. You're the teacher, you're the authority here. You're the sheriff, wear the badge with pride."

Perry stuck out his chest and mimed a badge over his heart with his right hand.

I looked up at him, wondering if he expected me to respond. He paused for breath and kept going. There were now two tiny damp stains under his arms, turning the sky blue cotton there dark.

"The second thing you should know," Perry continued, tilting his head a little to the left, "is that the fact that my position exists – the one supporting first year teachers – is no accident. The school hires you guys, kids with hardly any experience, totally by design."

He leaned in towards me and lowered his voice.

"I'm not supposed to be telling you this, and if it gets back to me that I said this, I'll deny it," – Perry looked like he was enjoying himself, playing Spies and Informant – "but the London School likes having teachers it can control. If they hire experienced staff, with a bit of knowledge, who are more sure of themselves, then they can't order them around so easily. Teachers in their fourth or fifth year won't take their shit. So they go for greenhorns, like you and your friends."

Perry had sat down at this stage, and was perching on the edge of his seat.

"If you're feeling lost," he went on, "then you're not alone. You're all clueless. That's why they gave you the job in the first place."

Perry picked up his briefcase, smiled once more at me and handed me his card.

"If you have any questions, these are my contact details. I must fly. Remember one thing - You're the sheriff. Cheerio."

I looked at the card. It was a lime-green colour and had Perry's home phone, mobile number and email address on it, and a little round caricature of him on the left-hand side. I put it in my wallet, along with old receipts and scraps of paper with phone numbers on, and went back to the staffroom.

In the next days I found, surprisingly, that Perry's little pep-talk made a difference. I looked at the other first year teachers in a new way, as fellow strugglers who simply covered up better. And much as I tried to forget Perry's sheriff metaphor, I did find myself sticking the chest out more, attempting to be more authoritative. I hitched up my imaginary holsters, spun my invisible spurs.

It also helped that Carol started feeding me ready-made lesson plans. Carol was one of the four teachers that had returned from the previous year, in fact she had been there eight whole years by then. I imagine I brought out her maternal side and she took pity on me, taking me aside at the lunch hour and giving me detailed plans for lessons. What she gave me were failsafe schemes that a monkey could follow, not too tedious while managing to result in the students at least learning *something*, the height of my ambition at that stage.

Carol was in her fifties, heavy now and tired looking, though you could still see the traces of the looker that she must once have been. She had a wide open face, green eyes that sometimes looked grey, and fair hair that seemed to change shade each day. She was scatty and a little chaotic, always forgetting her glasses or umbrellas, always losing wallets, keys and money, but equally she seemed to find the business of teaching the most natural thing in the world. We developed a rhythm, if I was lost and clueless about a particular class that I had to teach, which was most of the time, I would retire to the far end of our shabby staffroom, find a chair and a desk and put my head in my hands while staring at a page. Carol would inevitably find me, pull up a chair and ask me if I needed some help. I would pretend that I was fine for a few moments, before Carol would insist on seeing what I was working on and give me some simple, foolproof ideas that even I couldn't mess up.

"I know you know what you're doing," Carol lied, "but if you find these useful, use them."

We both kept this pretence up. I stayed with the myth that I was a capable teacher and Carol continued pretending that she was simply offering some extra ideas that were totally optional, and not in fact planning a whole day of classes for me. As the weeks passed in that first month of October, I began to realize that, more than simply handing me ready-made classes, Carol was – deliberately or not – showing me how to teach.

I saw the way that concepts were introduced in simple form, with real examples, at the beginning of her lessons, then students were given controlled practice with whatever tense or topic that was being taught, where they had little opportunity of making a mistake. Finally, things would move on to free practice, where the teaching point was used in a more or less real situation. Here, students would talk together in twos and threes using the present perfect, or the third conditional, or vocab and expressions for the doctors, or booking a hotel room, or arguing about politics. It was all systematic, gradual, carefully paced, bit-by-bit and totally, blindingly, rational. It appealed to the computer programming part of my brain, where everything had to be precise, clear, organised and unambiguous. *Shit*, I thought, in the last week in October, by which time Carol had been helping me for the best part of twenty days, *so this is how you do it.*

I began retreating to my desk and putting my head in my hands less and less. There were some days when I could even answer honestly to Carol that I didn't need any help, when she asked. I could see that she was doubtful, even a little disappointed that I was no longer dependent on her. For me it was like taking the training wheels off, and realizing I could stay up on my own.

Consequently – and it took me until the end of October to do this – I decided that it was time to speak to Patricia Coelho. Patricia was a student, the best one, in my teenage Level Six class of Tuesdays and Thursdays, and in many ways the leader of the gang. She was a strange case, pretty enough with a wide open face and still childish chubby cheeks, but also hopelessly square, style-less for a fifteen year old. She wore red or green cotton shirts, buttoned to the top, or pinafores that her little sister would have rejected, and still used pencils and pencil-cases with cartoon characters on them. Her hair was a mound of unstyled curls, forming a frame around her face. She was easily the uncoolest kid in the class, and yet got no abuse for this from the converse-wearing boys with one earring, or the girls in mini-skirts and carefully applied makeup. If anything the others listened to her, and mostly did what she said, as if there had been an election I hadn't been aware of and Patricia had been installed as president. Simply through good humour and the force of her personality she had gained a kind of respect.

And she took an instant liking to me. Her musical tastes were skewed and middle-aged, obviously inherited from some aunt or uncle. She liked The Eagles and Neil Young and Journey, before they became cool again and, Irish bands from the nineties like The Corrs and The Cranberries. Her attachment to me was sealed when I told her, one day after class when she brought in the sleeve of a Cranberries CD to ask me about some of their stodgy, juvenile lyrics, that I vaguely knew the brother of the band's drummer. It was as if I had told her that Britney Spears was my sister, Cher my aunt, Patricia's petty little crush bloomed right there into fully-formed devotion.

In class Patricia saw herself as my enforcer. She usually sat in the middle of the language class semi-circle, beside her insipid friend Sofia, and gently, or not so gently, encouraged those who were slacking off to pay attention. She made sure the three or four kids to her left kept on topic, and the ones on her right didn't act the idiot when they got bored. Yet she did it all with such charm, she cajoled rather than ordered, that no-one told her to fuck off, no-one told her to mind her own business, as would certainly have happened in a class of Irish teenagers. I was helped by the fact that, fundamentally, these kids wanted English, they saw it as the key that they needed to access the outside world. Patricia reminded them of this, kept them in line, allowed no messing. She, in truth, saved me those first few drowning weeks, in a class that could easily have gotten out of control.

This had to stop though. If I was weak, she was making me look weaker. It got to the stage where if I said anything João or Filipa or Catarina didn't understand, they would turn to Patricia for an explanation. To use Perry's terminology, she was the sheriff in my Level 6 class, not me.

"Patricia," I said one Thursday evening when the class was dribbling out in twos and threes, the boys punching each other, the girls linked arm in arm, some of them already singing, "can I talk to you for a second?"

Her smile was disarming, broad, toothy, dark eyes wide and looking at me as if I were the only person on the planet. I had a real craving for a cigarette and had another class in fifteen minutes.

"I want to thank you Patricia," I began, once we were alone, not really knowing where I was going with this, "for your help in class. The other students see you as an example, and they follow your lead. It makes everything work well."

"I really enjoy your classes, Cian," Patricia said, "I really learn a lot".

This was sheer flattery. Patricia only really picked up bits and pieces from my aimless approach. Her English was already much better than anyone else's there.

"Good," I replied, "but I need to ask you to let me be the teacher".

I stopped, waiting for a reaction, indignation, tears, a trembling lip. Her smile did indeed falter for a fraction of a second, then she regained control.

"I see," she said.

"If someone needs an explanation, for example," I went on, wanting to be crystal clear, "it's important that they know that they have to ask me, not you."

I looked at my watch. I now only had ten minutes before the next class.

"Do you understand, Patricia?" I asked.

The smile was still there, but was now empty.

"I think so."

I felt that some kind of gesture was necessary before I fled and lit up. I reached out my left hand to give her a reassuring touch on the right upper arm, the intention was to make a brief, split second contact to show that we hadn't fallen out. At the same moment she turned to leave, the tears now coming, no doubt she wanted to hide her watering eyes from me. As she turned I missed her arm and, before I could pull back my left hand, brushed against her right breast.

I couldn't tell whether she had noticed the contact. She had turned fully at this stage, and all I could see was the black curly bush of her hair.

"Patricia," I said.

She half smiled at me over her shoulder, eyes a little red already.

"I'll see you next week, Cian," was all she said, and then she was gone.

I wasn't sure how much Patricia, her crush, and my inadvertent, inappropriate touching of her breast was on my mind that weekend. Whatever, I got healthily drunk on Saturday night, I was almost Jamie-like in my inebriation. The occasion was a suggestion, from the dissolute bunch at the Rossio school, that the eighteen of us new teachers celebrate having survived four full weeks of work all together. And such a celebration was never going to be restrained or sober.

The atmosphere, when we all met in the Record Bar at eleven on Saturday night, was giddy, edgy, verging on hysterical. It was our first mass meeting since work had begun and the holiday atmosphere had ended. There had been weekend nights out, we had met up in our fours and fives on occasion, but the London School crocodile as it had existed had gone into hibernation for the previous month. So that Saturday night at the end of October had the sense of a reunion about it. Every newbie dutifully showed up: Joanne, Laura, Adam and I from the University School; drunken Jamie, my old roommate Mike, Sylvia St. James, Melissa her flatmate and Karen from the central school in Rossio; Rahul, Matt, Paul, Lizzy and Sheila from the Rotunda School; and then Carly and Anna, along with Flora and Mark from Cascais. No-one missed out, no-one cried off. There were hugs, kisses, friendly punches, immediate downing of shots, as if we hadn't seen each other for years.

Only Mike and I didn't live with other London School teachers. He had stayed on in the Pensão Imperial for two weeks, by then it had gotten too much even for him so he had moved in to what sounded like a squat somewhere in Alfama with a couple of Aussies. I only lived ten minutes walk away, but he hadn't as yet invited me to see his place. I figured that it was some kind of hovel. Still, he was the same, laid-back, unimpressed by all the fuss yet happier than he would have admitted to be out again and together with all these people. I was glad to see him there. I saw him as something of an ally, someone I would have liked on my side if I ever needed anyone.

The night, however, was unremarkable. We drank, we danced in the Jamaica club down at river-level, we ate *feijoada* in the ad-hoc restaurant that was set up every Saturday night in someone's apartment down the road from the Bairro, and then drank some more in an all-night club in Alcântara. These places, these place names, were now as familiar to us, after six weeks in the city, as the streets where we had grown up.

There was, though, a sense that we were going through the motions. It was as if we were following a script written for the people that we had been five weeks previously, before work had started, when we were all under the same roof like an extended, incestuous family. No matter how drunk we got, no matter how insistent the leaders of the revelry – Jamie and Sylvia – were that we all stick together, it was now clear that we were no longer one conglomerated mass of humanity, no longer one animal with eighteen heads. It was daylight when I emerged from the club in Alcântara, the city slowly becoming visible again in the weak morning sun, a bakery somewhere emitting that unmistakeable odour of slowly hardening dough. I was drunk, glad to get away from the London School gang, perversely happy to be alive as I weaved down the uneven cobbles, tripping a few times, scanning the road for a taxi.

By one o'clock the following afternoon the joy of living had faded. Charlotte was knocking on the door of my cell, though it took me about five minutes to grasp the fact that I wasn't dreaming her. My mouth was sealed shut, my skull felt like it was full of hardened concrete, the very act of opening my eyes hurt.

"Cian," Charlotte said again, as I groaned in response, "there's a guy at the door here, a Portuguese guy, says you're playing football today."

I shifted on the bed, rolling on to my back. Football? How could anyone imagine that I was playing football that day? I would be lucky to make it to the bathroom before evening. Then, a vague memory of my conversation with Mario on Friday night seeped into my consciousness. He had served me my *bica* as usual, and had slid my euro coin back to me when I went to pay.

"It's from the house," he said.

"The house? What house? Oh, ok," I realized what the expression was that he had mangled. "You mean it's *on* the house. Where did you learn that?"

"*Televisão*."

This, television, was where Mario picked up all his shiny bits of language, like a magpie.

"So Cian," he went on, as I began the sugar ceremony, tapping the paper sachet while holding it at one corner, "I make favour for you, you favour for me."

I should have seen this coming, Mario never gave me free coffee. He explained, as best he could, that two of his regular football team were injured – he said something in Portuguese and pointed to his leg – and so they needed an extra player for a game on Sunday. I agreed, quickly, thinking that I could do with the exercise and half-hoping that I could get some more free coffee from Mario. Now that the end of the month was approaching my account balance was shrinking rapidly. Charles and Charlotte were charging me a pittance for my cupboard-sized room but were costing me much more by forcing me to flee at meal times. A Lua was cheap, but it wasn't free.

By lunchtime on Sunday, of course, I was barely conscious and Mario was standing in our hallway, waiting. Charlotte eventually pushed the door ajar, I could hear Mario talking to her in the corridor in mostly Portuguese, she either understood or pretended to do so. I fell out of bed, picked myself up and couldn't decide which to regret more, ever agreeing to the football game or letting Mario know where I lived.

"Cian," Mario said when he saw me, "you sick?"

I suddenly saw a way out.

"Yes, very sick."

"He's not sick, Mario," Charlotte said, making the Portuguese gesture for 'drunk' or 'drinking', her hand a fake bottle, her pointing thumb the neck as she tipped the imaginary liquid down her throat, "he has the *ressaca*."

Charlotte had now started talking like Mario, mixing English and Portuguese, using articles in the wrong places. Mario was amused by my hungover state.

"It's ok, football only for fun. Don't worry".

My flatmates rallied round. Charlotte made me some coffee, Charles offered to lend me shorts and trainers. They were more enthused even than Mario that I was playing football that afternoon, and were certainly more excited than I was.Mario insisted that we walk to the pitch, despite my suggestion that we get a taxi. We took a short cut, over by the viewing area where his cabin was and down a steep cobbled hill where the road was lined with cars, even though it was barely wide enough for one vehicle to travel along. The sun felt hostile in its brightness, even with my sunglasses on. I lit a cigarette, my hands shaking a little as I held the lighter.

"Very bad", Mario said, pointing at my Marlboro, "*cigarros* no good for football."

"Fuck off, Mario," I said to him, but without venom. He looked mock-shocked, though I was sure it was the first time he had heard the expression outside of films. We wound our way past the old houses of the city, down cobbled lanes whose surfaces reminded me only of deformed, pimpled skin, through minute squares that had one bench, one tree, two old men. Mario laughed to himself as he walked, and practiced his new favourite expression. "Fuck off," he said, to no-one in particular, then with a little more force, "Fuck off!"

We emerged into what I recognized as Portas do Sol, one of the stops on the 28 tram route. It was still on a height, and had a viewing platform that looked out at the expanse of river in the distance and down to the terracotta rooftops of Alfama below.

"We go here," Mario said as he crossed the road, went over the tram-tracks and pushed at the creaky gate that led down a flight of concrete steps.

"This is the pitch, Mario?" I asked, "this is it? Jesus."

I had imagined something more salubrious. We were descending towards a paved area that I had seen quite a few times, even in my six short weeks in the city. The pitch was directly below the viewing area, where tourists gathered at all times of the day to stare off into the distance as if they were doing something profound. The pitch seemed cut into the side of the hill, like a ledge on a cliff, and was placed just before the houses and buildings of Alfama started. The houses themselves were packed tightly together, as if huddling up for mutual support, and were built all the way down the hillside as far as the river bank. The football pitch was the only blot on this view, a rectangular patch of black that emphasized even more the earth-coloured roofs that continued in their chaotic way down towards the Tagus.

It was a five-a-side pitch, though by the look of it ten players would be a crowd squashed into the small space. There was a low wall surrounding the playing area to keep the ball in and fences behind each goal with the same function, though the nets in those goals were eaten through by age and damp. Just next to the uneven concrete surface was a makeshift bar from where some kind of Portuguese dance music thrummed out through one large speaker. There was a set of white plastic garden chairs and a table placed directly in front of the bar's open hatch. The whole place had the feel of the Third World, like an improvised football pitch in some Rio favela where the next Pele or Ronaldinho would play until sunset, maybe in his bare feet.

Mario introduced me to the other players on our team, an assortment of fat and thin men, hairy and bald, Mario's age – early twenties – and more decrepit. They were already out on the dark tarmacadam warming up, firing shots into an empty net with more violence than I felt capable of at that moment. My new teammates all came to shake my hand, Nuno and Jorge, Artur and Pedro. They seemed impressed to learn I was Irish. They indicated - by gestures and a few words that I managed to pick up - that, by dint of my nationality, they expected me to get stuck in, to be the midfield enforcer on the team. Maybe break a few bones. We obviously didn't have a reputation for skilful, subtle football.

I warmed up, tentatively, already regretting the half slice of toast that Charlotte had convinced me to have a half hour before. Mario came up to me before kick-off.

"You," he said, his arm around my shoulder as if he were a manager, "*substituto*. You understand? Artur is old and......," here he puffed out his cheeks, moving his arms out from his sides indicating great girth, as if he were the Michelin Man. I looked over at Artur. He was heavy looking alright.

"After ten minutes, he finish," Mario clarified.

The fact that I didn't have to play right away was the only good news I had heard since waking, forty minutes previously. I lit another cigarette, sat on one of the wobbly plastic chairs and watched the kick off. The other team, who had shown up just two minutes before the starting time, were smaller than ours, but also quicker and more skilful, and were soon two-one up. Mario wasn't a bad player, and had taken on a leadership role, even though he was the second youngest. Artur, the heavy man in his forties, started like a train, scored our goal but soon ran out of steam. Just on schedule, after around ten minutes, he was soon puffing and holding his side. Eventually he gave in, wandered over to where I sat while the ball was out of play and beckoned me with a jerk of his head.

"Ô irlandês," he said, between wheezes, "*tu jogas.*"

He had told me that I was playing, I understood that much.

I wandered on to the pitch, still fragile, looked up and noticed that we now had an audience of tourists who were standing at the viewing point above. For the first five minutes I had to watch as the game went on around me. I would run towards where the ball was only for it to be swept away quickly by our nippy opposition or even by someone on my own team. Growing up in Limerick I had played mainly rugby, as a butterfingers full back, or as a clumsy centre-half forward in hurling. Like any kid though, I had kicked a ball around on the street and had played some five-a-side football in school, so the game wasn't completely alien to me. Yet it felt that way for the first ten minutes until I stopped trying so hard and took to hanging out in midfield where Artur before me had typically loitered.

The ball started coming in my direction regularly then, though my lack of close control was soon shown up. There was one player on the opposition team, a small wiry guy with very dark stubble, who looked to be waiting for me to be in possession. Every time the ball came to me he would nip in and steal it from me, once scoring himself, twice more laying it off to others who forced diving saves from Paulo, our stout goalkeeper. I looked at the others in bafflement each time, they looked back at me as if they couldn't believe that Roy Keane and I came from the same country.

To my relief half-time came. Mario bought me a bottle of sweet, fizzy drink, as if in commiseration for being so bad at football. I took a few long gulps – all of a sudden my dehydration had kicked in – and then something about the action of the carbonated liquid hitting my oesophagus made me certain that I was about to vomit. I made it to the back wall of the enclave before emptying the liquid contents of my stomach against the uneven bricks there. Everyone else – the six members of the opposition, the guy running the makeshift bar, as well as Artur, Pedro, Nuno, Jorge and Mario from my own team – cheered and laughed and clapped, as if I had just scored a goal.

Old fat Artur resurrected himself and started the second half while I sat on the sidelines, trying to keep my insides inside. Artur stabilised things, our team got more possession and we pulled back to four-all by about ten minutes from the end. Still, the exertion had worn the old guy out and he shuffled to the side, wheezing and coughing, and plonked himself down beside me on one of the other rickety plastic chairs. The others called out, Mario louder than anyone, for him to rejoin the game, to give it one last push, but Artur just sat there hacking up phlegm and waving away his team-mates' pleas. I stood up, not really knowing what I was doing, put my hand on Artur's shoulder and said, pointlessly, as I was sure he didn't understand me, "I'll go on".

Nobody on our team looked very delighted to see me trotting back on to the pitch, though our opposition slapped hands and made jokes as if they had just won the game. Mario sent me up front to hang out near our opponents' goal, presumably where I could do less harm. The game had reached a stalemate, players were getting tired, and I now found that it was a little easier to keep up. Perhaps my purging of a quarter hour before had done the trick. Whatever the reason, suddenly I wasn't as inept as I had been in the first half.

Hugo, the bearded man who was running the bar for us, was also the designated time-keeper. After I had been on the pitch long enough to start feeling like shit again, he bellowed out, "*Dois minutos!*" Two minutes left. Mario came forward with the ball after having robbed stubble-face, the thin, wiry guy who had made my life a misery earlier in the game. I was free out to the right, and put my hand up to demand the ball, but Mario ignored me and, though there was an opponent directly in front of him, tried a shot at goal.

The ball swerved off the side of the leg of the defender and flew in my direction on the right wing. Without thinking, maybe drawing on some hidden childhood instinct or other, I stuck out my right leg. The ball glanced off it, changed direction again and ricocheted into the bottom corner of the ripped, straggly net.

I was mobbed by my team. Even Pedro the goalkeeper came out of his goal to pat me on the back and, bizarrely, pinch my cheek. We managed to hold out for the final ninety seconds, I was pulled back into defence where I basically got in the way of both teams. Hugo, from his place behind the wooden partition that formed the bar, finally blew the whistle that ended the game.

Mario came up to me afterwards and put his arm around my neck, though he was four inches shorter than me and had to reach up to do so. I had suddenly become a hero of the team. Mario wanted, I reckoned, to enjoy some reflected glory and to remind the others that he was the one to have invited me along.

"Cian," he said, the smile of a winner on his tanned face, "is very important to win. We first now in *liga*. Your goal.....*uma coisa bonita*, a beautiful thing."

"You told me that it was just for fun, Mario," I said to him, smiling now myself, "just for fun you said."

He detached his arm and put his hand on my shoulder. Charles's Manchester United shirt was sticking to me there now, sodden with sweat.

"I no want to give you pressure," he said, "but you have fun, yes?"

"Yes, Mario," I assured him, realizing as I said it that I wasn't lying, "yes I did."

Pedro, our heavy-set goalkeeper, ran a café down in the bowels of Alfama, so we went there for a victory beer. I tried, half-heartedly, to leave, but my new-found best friends insisted that I stay. Just getting there was a journey I couldn't have done without the others as guides. There are practically no roads, or proper streets, in Alfama, it is built on the side of a hill and consists of a jumble of houses of various heights, cafes that can seat six people at a time, churches, tiny restaurants and minute, semi-enclosed squares, all linked together by a network of paths and alleys that meander up and down and across, seemingly randomly.

It is a section of the city where cars, bicycles or any form of transport that has wheels or – like the trams, rails – is absolutely useless. The Baixa is the area of the city at sea-level, the one Germanically arranged in a rigid grid pattern. Alfama is, if anything, the anti-Baixa, built on a slope, proletarian, labyrinthine, organised chaos. Disorienting if you don't know where you're going.

After ten minutes of meandering along through the maze, down steps, over cobbles, through mini arches, we reached Pedro's café. It was a dark place on a corner with a bar inside, where coffees and pastries, beers and sandwiches were served, while the two sets of tables and chairs outside were where our team sat. Pedro brought us all out a Super-Bock, cold from the fridge, and made a comment while delivering my bottle, which the others laughed at. I supposed that it had to do with my vomiting, or with hangovers or with being drunk, they were the obvious jokes to be made. I didn't mind, I laughed along just to show what a good sport I was. Mario tried to explain what Pedro had said, and made even less sense. It didn't matter, we were all men together, drinking the same beer, soaking in the same October sun, having played on the same team and won. They laughed at me and my throwing up, and then moved on to Artur and his extreme lack of stamina. All was as it should be.

The café looked on to one of those tiny squares in Alfama that was bordered on one side by a row of terraced houses and on the other by the side wall of a minuscule chapel whose entrance was around the corner. There were two scrawny benches set back to back in the centre of the square, with a thin, sickly looking tree between them.

The beer, nasty at first, now seemed to be reviving me, negating the hangover which was, after all, a reaction to the withdrawal of alcohol. The sun had now fully reached our little corner, and it felt good on my face as the conversation went on around me, good-humoured and mostly incomprehensible. Mario tried to involve me but I was happy just sitting there, feeling the smoke from my cigarette soak the chemicals into my bloodstream through the walls of my lungs, temporarily part of something just by being there.

A figure crossed the square in front of us and sat on one of the benches. He had a shaven head and wore sunglasses with the arms connected to a string that went around his neck. The string looked homemade. He had on baggy Hawaiian shorts and flip flops, and wore nothing on top, as if he were on the beach. Only half of the bench was now in sun so the figure shuffled over and moved from the darkness into the light. He tipped his head back so as to expose more of his skin to the incoming rays, and took off his glasses. His skin was pale, Celtic-looking, like mine.

My teammates had spotted him too. Mario began speaking first, indicating, with a tip of his head, the pale-skinned man on the bench and saying something that ended with "........*na praia,*" – "....on the beach." Artur, Pedro and Nuno all found whatever he had said hilarious and added their own takes on the idiocy of the clearly foreign man who dressed, in the middle of the city, in October, as if he were in the Algarve. The guy on the bench was oblivious to their laughter, maybe he heard it, maybe he even knew it was directed at him, but he didn't care. He had the warm touch of the sun on his skin and that was all that counted.

I had suspected that it was Mike – fellow London School teacher, Glaswegian ex-roommate – from the first, but once he took off his sunglasses I recognised his small eyes, pale features, the very blonde eyelashes that made them look almost invisible. It was him alright. Some of the blokes at our table began speaking louder now, almost calling over to my Scottish workmate, though it was all in Portuguese so Mike wouldn't have understood, even if he had been listening. He didn't move, his pale, shapeless body was tipped back and absorbing all the ultra-violet that he could, like a flower turned towards the sun.

He did look ridiculous there, even to me. Still, I stood up and walked towards the bench. Mike didn't move, even when I lowered myself gently down beside him. I could hear Mario's voice coming from behind me.

"Ô Cian," he was saying, "what you do?"

I ignored him. At the sound of my name, Mike opened his eyes and turned towards me.

"Hey man," he said, his eyes bloodshot, I could now see, "what you doing down here? You look better now than you did last night. Fuck, you were wasted."

If Mike, of all people, was impressed by how drunk I had been, I must have been bad.

"Playing footy," I said, "having a drink after."

I indicated our outdoor table across the square. Mike only glanced over. Then he leaned forward abruptly and smelled my breath.

"Hair of the dog, eh?" he said, "Cian, you bastard". He smiled, as if in admiration at my stamina.

"So you're sunbathing?" I asked him.

"Yeah, too hung-over to go to the beach, I live just here." He pointed to one of the houses that were squashed together, just in front, a kind of tie-dyed sheet or wrap draped over the balcony on the first floor indicating which was his.

"That's the commune, then?" I said, "The People's Republic of Alfama."

"That's it mate," he said, "you should call in some time and meet the guys. They're careful about who they let in though, got some plants growing there at the back they want to keep quiet. Better text me first."

I agreed to do that, and went back to my table. We shook hands on parting, as the Portuguese do. While I had been talking to Mike my team-mates had quietened a little, curious to see what I was up to. Mario looked up at me as I approached.

"Your friend?" he asked, half piss-taking, half actually wanting to know.

I shrugged. Was Mike my friend? I wasn't entirely sure.

"I suppose so," I said, finally.

Pedro, the café's owner, said something to me, with his hands raised, palms outward, as if apologising for their previous taunting of Mike.

"Don't worry about it," I said, not knowing how to begin to explain that Mike had been oblivious to it all anyway. I sat down again, went back to my beer, lit another cigarette and offered my pack around. No-one took one.

I realised that there had been no need for me to approach Mike. I could have just sat still, drunk my beer and waited until my companions had got bored of shouting at him and had started to talk about something else. Yet I had stood up, I had displayed my connection to this eccentric stranger sunbathing in an Alfama *largo*. The conversation at the white plastic chairs went on around me and I was back to being a foreigner again, someone distant and incomprehensible, not from the known world of these men. No matter how many goals I had scored, of course, I had never been anything else.

NOVEMBER

At the end of October all of the teachers in our school received invitations, printed on card and slid into envelopes of the same colour, to a party on November third. The party was being thrown by Fabian, our occasional French teacher, who spent Tuesday and Thursday at our school. The other week days he was in other London School centres. The London School advertised itself as a language school, as if it offered all languages equally, but the truth was that there were twenty-nine English teachers, one part time German teacher, a teacher of Portuguese to foreigners. And our French Fabian.

For this reason we, the English teachers, had never really seen Fabian as part of the staff. He was in and out, often we would forget that he was there, it was nearly always a surprise to see his big Gallic face twice a week in the staffroom. His English was mediocre, and in the rapid-fire exchanges of the English teachers in the staffroom he was frequently lost. Only Adam had any kind of relationship with him. Our sporty workmate had done A-level French and so was surprisingly fluent in the language for someone so normally gormless. For most of us though, Fabian was pleasant but unknowable.

For that reason it was a surprise to get the invitation to his party. In fact, the very existence of a printed invitation was a surprise in itself. There had been lots of parties in the flats of London School teachers around the city, but usually they had been planned and decided upon three or four days in advance, and publicised through a few text messages and entries on the London School Facebook page. The school grapevine then did the rest. No-one had ever gone so far as to print formal invitations, or indeed formally invite anyone. It was usually a free-for-all, invitations assumed rather than presented.

Yet Fabian's invitations were on pale green card, in pale green envelopes, inviting the bearer – in French, bad English and, according to Carol, worse Portuguese – to a soirée on November third, to celebrate his moving into a new flat in Lumiar. We all had little personalised cubby-holes in the staffroom, for memos and messages from the boss, and it was a Wednesday morning when we came in to find the pale green rectangles sitting in our slots, promising more than just another drunken Saturday night.

It took a while for the excitement to build, but when it did it went viral. The Facebook page was alight with discussions about what people were going to wear, if it would be acceptable to turn up already plastered, if there were to be cocktails served. It turned out that every teacher at each of the centres Fabian worked at around the London School empire had received a little pale green present in their mail box that week. Those who hadn't got one began wondering if it really was a party that they couldn't crash, if there was going to be actual *security* on the door, as if Fabian's bash was the Oscars. He had caused a real stir – a *frisson*, in fact – with his little pastel-coloured rectangles, whether he had intended to or not.

In the days leading up to the party Laura and Sebastian, our Senior Teacher, had a private joke going. There were secret looks between them, they would burst out laughing for no apparent reason, Seb kept calling her "a hag", Laura countered with "fag!" Most of the rest of us just ignored them, they were clearly looking for attention. Carol, though, wanted to know what was going on.

"Come to the party," Laura told her, with something close to a leer, "and you'll find out."

It was quickly becoming the social event of the year. For once I put on a shirt with an actual collar that Saturday night, and was glad that I had done so when I met Rahul and Joanne on the way to Fabian's flat from the metro stop at Campo Grande. Rahul was stylish as always, in a black jacket and trousers, with a shirt of the same colour and a purple tie. Joanne had gone for a little black dress that came to just above the knee, with high heels and her hair done up in ringlets. I was taken aback. Joanne, usually so demure and girlish and controlled, was *sexy*. Her perfume had spice in it, her heels were high and stretched out her figure into a vision of femininity I hadn't suspected she was capable of. On our five minute walk to Fabian's apartment I had to concentrate so as not to stare at her, and purposely stood in front of the two of them as we rode the lift up to the third floor where the party was taking place, so I wouldn't be caught glancing down the low-cut front of her dress.

It turned out that everyone had made an effort, not least Fabian himself, who circled his three newly furbished rooms in a tailored suit and a green silk tie a shade or two darker than the colour of his invitations. He was a tall man, with tightly curled dark hair – some of which fell over his left eye – and pale grey eyes that were as absent of all real colour as I had ever seen. His skin was pale too, paler even than mine was then, much paler than skin should have been for someone who had grown up in Marseille. This skin, his height and a certain haughtiness all combined to give the impression of a well-dressed, good-natured vampire.

That said, he was a civilised, attentive host. When we arrived we were handed empty wine glasses and were shown to a table in the kitchen filled with bottles of French and Portuguese red, white, rosé and vinho verde. The table beside that held piles and plates of food, nothing heavy but everything elegantly displayed, crudités, canapés, salad with feta and olives, smoked salmon, cow and goat cheese, saucisson, paté, crackers, garlic mushrooms, roast peppers and other dishes that were as good as unrecognisable to us uncouth Anglophones.

This was obviously a party the like of which we teachers hadn't seen before. Most of the eighteen first years were there as well as a good sprinkling of those who had been in the school longer. The main topic of conversation initially became how all of our get-togethers in future should be like this, how much more civilised and European it was to eat food on a Saturday night instead of trying to break some kind of alcohol drinking record. The grub also acted as soakage and slowed down the usual rapid onset of drunkenness. Even by one o'clock, by which time most of us had moved on to beer and spirits, things were still reasonably restrained, no-one had yet started doing shots or dancing on tables, two things that were almost compulsory at a London School party.

Another reason for our collective restraint was that, though a good half of the crowd there were from our school, our normally boorish presence was diluted by clumps of unknown randomers. I recognised some faces from trawling around the Bairro Alto at two in the morning, faces that hung out in the same bars, walked the same streets as we did, though I had no idea what their story was or who they were. And then, slowly, we London Schoolers began to do something unfamiliar, something we had forgotten was possible. We began to mix with those who didn't belong to our incestuous little group.

There were other English teachers there, from other, less self-important language schools, but the majority of the unknowns were creatures we had almost come to forget existed – people who didn't make their living teaching English to the Portuguese. There were French people, naturally, some arrogant and disdainful of our very existence, others only too delighted to practice the language of Shakespeare and Fifty Cent. There were two Swedes in the corner – a couple looking stereotypically tall and blonde – a sprinkling of Germans, and one Icelandic boy who seemed to be intent on playing the role of drunken oaf normally occupied by one of us. Also, three Spanish girls arrived around midnight, all somewhere between ugly and exotic, all dressed in black, like witches, and whose English was, amusingly, even worse than Fabian's. I hadn't felt so cosmopolitan since arriving in the country in mid-September.

There were even some Portuguese there, students of Fabian's. They seemed as bewildered and entertained as we were to be surrounded by so many foreigners. They, at least, were in their own country, we actually were the outsiders. One of them, João, a nervy-looking guy with quick, darting eyes, began talking to me. He had this habit of smoking in jerky, abrupt movements that began to put me off my own cigarette. He explained that Fabian had invited his whole class, but that only he had shown up. It seemed that he was looking for someone to latch on to, and I was it. I started looking around for a way out. I was glad to see that Sebastian had arrived.

Our Senior Teacher immediately began playing a prominent part in the festivities. Seb had arrived with this guy, Fernando, who may or may not have been his boyfriend, and quickly slipped into the role of social butterfly, flitting from group to group. He was charming and affectionate without going overboard, briefly being the entertaining centre of attention in each little knot of people, before moving on. He seemed to know just the right thing to say, and when to say it, and to whom. Fernando just stood in the corner and looked bored.

"Hello Cian," Seb said, just as my new BFF, João, disappeared to talk to one of his classmates who had just come in. He had made me promise to email him at joaowow@gmail.com.

"Seb," I replied, "the life and soul as always."

Sebastian was very slightly shorter than me, but always seemed taller. He was lanky, had long thin limbs and hands and a large forehead, all of which gave him the impression of height. His hair was wispy, as if one good gust of air would blow it all away, and he had a boyish face that made him look five or six years younger than the thirty he claimed to be.

"Cian," he said, arching his eyebrows, "lurking in the corner as always."

"So this thing you have got going on with Laura," I said, ignoring his taunt and trying to pretend that I knew more than I did, "can anyone join in?"

He and Laura had kept up whatever fake conflict that they had begun almost immediately after receiving their invitations. I was now a little curious to find out what they had cooking.

"In theory," he said, smiling, "but this is one contest I really don't think you want in on. You're too much of a straight boy."

Sebastian put in his requisite six minutes with me before moving on to the next victim of his charms. I was still none the wiser as to what intrigue was going on between him and Laura. Things became clearer after I talked to Mike later in the evening. We were in the living room, the place was slowly beginning to resemble a more traditional London School party, with empty bottles on the floor now, people kissing in corners, music loud and insistent. Fabian had been playing the host all night, refilling glasses, introducing people to each other, forcibly mixing English and non-English speaking tribes. Now though he had taken a break, and was standing beside a lamp that cast a greenish light on to his features, making him appear even less human. Mike jerked his head in Fabian's direction.

"Look," he said.

Laura was standing near Fabian, looking at him almost lovingly, while Sylvia St. James placed herself by the lamp. Both tiny, they had to look up at him as he was speaking. Sylvia took his hand, as if examining it for a life-line, caressing it a little as she did so. Laura too was tactile, she kept touching the French teacher on the arm, the face, the stomach of his white shirt as they conversed.

"Is Sylvia involved in this too?" I asked Mike. He always somehow seemed to know what was going on, despite appearing clueless.

"Her and the other Two As," Mike said, "it's a game they've got going on."

Myself and Mike stayed in our corner and watched the show. The Three As were now a tag team, Sylvia drifted away but Anna Cameron, taller, blonder, more flat-chested than her friend, moved in in her place and carried on the affectionate touching, the attentive looks in Fabian's direction. Sebastian then glided towards the little group, whispered in Laura's ear and, with some protest on her part, took her place to Fabian's right. Fernando, Seb's friend, then arrived. Sebastian stayed long enough to introduce him to Fabian before hovering away, almost soundlessly, to the next group he was to favour with his presence.

The pantomime continued like this. Fernando wasn't bored any longer, and had stopped smoking for the first time all night. He whispered something into Fabian's ear, standing on tip-toe a little as he was only slightly taller than Laura. Fernando then began showing our host all of his tattoos, giving a commentary on each one, beginning with his forearm, moving to his neck and chest and ending with the top of his left ass-cheek. Fabian showed polite interest in each one. As this was going on Melissa, the third member of The Three As, took Anna's place and gave Fabian a single, slow, lingering kiss on the cheek as a greeting.

Laura stood off to the side a little, pretending to listen to Jamie's drunken slurring but keeping an eye on goings on over by the green lamp. I sidled up to her and whispered in her ear, bending down as I did so to reach.

"I know what you're doing," I said.

Laura was chubby but looked pretty that night, with her big blue eyes, her full lips, the round cheeks of a child.

"Really?" she said, hardly glancing at me.

"Yeah, you're competing for him. Fabian is the contest, and the prize."

"No shit?" she said. "You needn't be too proud of yourself, Cian, it doesn't take a genius to work that out. Just look at Fernando, he's so fucking obvious."

Indeed, Seb's friend had Fabian's tie between his fingers and then rubbed it on his own cheek, as if testing how soft the fabric was. He then fixed the knot at Fabian's neck, tightening it and smoothing it, and held on to the end as he spoke to his target.

"Anyway," Laura continued, "you haven't got the whole story right. The question is, Is Fabian gay or straight? Sebastian thinks that he's gay – though he thinks that practically everyone is gay – and we don't. The only way to win the bet for sure is to bed him."

"So how's it looking?" I asked.

"I'm quietly confident," she said, with a half-smile.

By three o'clock chaos had properly set in. It was reassuring, in a way, most of the remaining food was now trampled into crumbs and mush on the floor around the kitchen table, Jamie was asleep in the corner by the flatscreen TV and a bundle on the sofa moved and shifted, and looked like it was made of two bodies. This was more the aftermath we had come to expect from a London School party, as if our overwhelming presence had poisoned Fabian's careful Gallic civilisation.

Before passing out Jamie had christened the three black-clad Spanish girls Hubble, Bubble and Toil-and-Trouble. Looking at them, they were indeed witch-like. I met one of them – I believe it was Toil-and-Trouble – in the queue for the one toilet in the apartment. Once we had exhausted the limited extent of her English and my Spanish we began kissing, sloppily, drunkenly, with tongues and saliva and bumped teeth, even as people nudged us out of the way to take our place in the queue. She had big teeth and a prominent nose and thick, unplucked eyebrows, and tasted strongly of cigarettes, but there was something about the disproportion of her features that made her fascinating to look at, like some form of sexy alien.

"Toil-and-Trouble," I said, once we had taken a break from trying to devour each other, "come home with me."

The girl showed no sign of having understood what I had said. The bathroom door opened, and she made a dive for it, saying something like "un momento" and slipping in before Anna Cameron, who was next in the queue, could stop her.

"Hey Cian," she said, loudly, as if it were my fault, "your girlfriend just took my spot, and I'm fucking bursting."

I shrugged, as Anna banged on the door and told Toil-and-Trouble to hurry up. I went back into the main room to get my jacket, which was buried under a pile of similar ones at one end of the sofa. I looked around me, there were still some people there, scattered around the space, but Fabian had disappeared, as had Sebastian, Fernando, Laura, Melissa and Sylvia. Had they all seduced him? I wondered. Was there an orgy going on at that moment in Fabian's apartment? Jamie had woken now and called me over to his nesting place under the TV.

"Who won?" he asked.

I couldn't tell if he was talking about the contest for Fabian or about the Benfica-Porto game of that evening, or whether he was still dreaming.

"Dunno, Jamie mate," I said, "go back to sleep".

Back in the corridor, I couldn't tell how much time had passed. There was no longer anyone in the queue for the bathroom, though the door opened just as I got there. It was Anna Cameron, looking thin and pale, her eyes bloodshot.

"Where's Toil-and-Trouble?" I asked her, pointlessly.

"Who the fuck is Toil-and-Trouble?" she asked, tired now, not really interested.

"The Spanish girl."

"Oh, she left," Anna replied, "vamoosed. You can certainly pick them, Cian, she was no Penelope Cruz."

Anna went back to the party, laughing at her own dismissal of my taste in women. I opened the front door, peered into the stairwell, put my hand on the closed doors of the lift, as if I could detect if it had been recently in use, just by touching. There was no-one, anywhere, and no sound in the sleeping, still building. I took the stairs down to ground level, almost tripping on the last flight but clutching on to the handrail, just in time. It only took me two minutes to flag down a taxi and we were back in Graça in eight more minutes. Four minutes after that, in my narrow bed in my narrow room, I was dead to the world.

Perhaps something changed for me after that party. All of that flirting, the overt, unapologetic desire of Laura and The Three As, the game that made guessing Fabian's sexuality into a contest. And then Toil and Trouble, even though she ran out on me just as things were getting interesting. It reminded me of who I used to be before Maura happened, it reminded me that I was just a guy, and just a guy who liked women, despite the shambles I had made of things in Dublin. Maybe it made me more open to the possibility of being with someone, of shaking off my months of chastity. Or maybe it was just luck.

Whatever, I met Dina soon after. Inevitably it was in A Lua, our restaurant next door. I say 'inevitably' because I was there most nights. If I didn't have dinner there then I clomped down the stairs from our flat at no.24 Largo da Graça and popped into no.26 for a coffee instead of going to Mario's, or else I would call in after work for a quick beer to help me face The Two Charlies with a little less resentment. If I was going to meet a Portuguese mother of one, five or six years older than me, then it was going to be in A Lua.

The place was the kind of one-stop-shop that didn't exist where I came from. It was somewhere you could have a solid, reasonably priced meal at lunchtime or in the evening, or where you could pop in to for ten minutes for a coffee or a pastry, a beer or a measure of spirits. All your comestible and beverage needs in one spot. It was a restaurant, a café and a local pub all in one – like hundreds like it in the city – and at least there you could, despite the attempts of a new anti-smoking law, have a cigarette along with your *bica*, your Super Bock, your *feijoada*.

The regulars didn't pay me much attention at first. I came, ate, drank and left, they gave me a "*Bom dia*," or a "*Boa tarde*," without great hostility or much interest. That suited me fine. Sergio, the large, sweaty man who owned the place, nodded at me and served me promptly each time, tried out a few words of English on me on occasion, but mostly just treated me like everyone else. This was Graça, just up the road from Alfama, they were used to foreigners of all kinds, tourists, eccentric German artists, English teachers, backpackers, blow-ins of every variety. I was no big deal.

And then, slowly, I became one of the regulars. I learned the names of people from the area, Mario was in once or twice when I was there and proudly introduced me as "*o meu grande amigo*", and expounded on the story of my winning goal of the month before with what I was sure was enormous hyperbole. And I soon achieved the treasured status of being able to simply nod to Sergio after I finished my meal to indicate that I was ready for a short, thick coffee. It got to the stage where, if I had to prepare some classes or do some admin work for school, I would haul my papers down to A Lua and spread them out on some empty tables there rather than have to brave the kitchen area in our cramped, Charlie-filled flat.

After a while, I was semi-adopted by The Two Manuels. These were a pair of guys who spent so much time in A Lua that they had to be given nicknames to distinguish them – Manuel da Moto, and Manuel da Barba. Manuel da Moto – literally, Manuel of the motorbike – was thirtyish, prematurely balding, and spent most of his time in bike leathers, his Yamaha parked directly outside the restaurant. Manuel da Barba – bearded Manuel – was so named simply because he had scrabbly, thick-in-patches facial hair, and his motorcycle-mad mate didn't. They weren't very imaginative, their nicknames, but they served their purpose.

The Two Manuels quickly appointed themselves my instructors in the subtleties of the Portuguese language. The Portuguese I learned from them, of course, wasn't the type of language I could use with

Senhor Eugenio, the security guard in the school, or with Fatima, the cleaning lady Charles and Charlotte had hired to come to our house twice a week.

They taught me *Foda-se* and *Filho da puta*, *Caralho*, *Merda* and *Vai-te foder*, some of the Portuguese contribution to the world's rich store of swear words. It was great entertainment for the Two Manuels to hear me bungling the pronunciations, and then eventually getting them right, and they usually took turns giving me sentences to say with the words in, as if I were some kind of performing parrot. They were ok, I usually didn't mind them, if I wasn't in the mood for them I would retire to the end of the restaurant with some files and papers I never looked at, the furthest point from their hangout up near the counter.

It was the Tuesday evening after Fabian's party. I came back to Graça late from work, near ten o'clock, and decided to see if I could get through a whole day without seeing my flatmates. Charles and Charlotte had already left by the time I got up that morning, and luckily they normally went to bed early, about eleven, so I figured that I had an hour to kill. Naturally I went to A Lua. I ordered a black beer, stood at the counter and chatted to Manuel da Barba about nothing much while Sergio looked on.

Manuel da Moto then arrived, his bike leathers creaking as he walked. As always happened when the Two Manuels got together, the bearded one immediately became more mischievous, more playful. Separately they were fairly pleasant people – at least Manuel da Barba was – but together they pretty much always wanted to take the piss. It started almost immediately.

"Cian," Manuel da Moto began, giving the two syllables of my name their full weight – Key-Ann, "I have a new word for you."

"Really?" I said, faking interest.

"Yes really," Manuel da Moto said, taking a sip of the beer that Sergio had just served him. "Your word today is *Cona*."

I was standing between the Two Manuels and facing Motorbike Manuel as he spoke. I heard a snort of laughter from behind me as he told me the word.

"You know it?" Manuel asked.

"No, I don't know it."

Over my shoulder his mate with the beard was struggling to control himself.

"It's a very beautiful...Portuguese flower, very....," here he looked over at Manuel da Barba and said something to him in Portuguese, looking for a translation.

"Pink," Manuel da Barba took up the baton, "is very pink, very beautiful when it open." He had managed to control his hilarity by now, was getting into the swing of it.

"And good to eat," Manuel da Moto added.

Manuel da Barba had gone to stand beside his friend, had his left hand on his shoulder now. They both had to suppress a giggle.

"Yes, taste good."

Manuel da Barba licked his lips suggestively, his tongue even reaching the outer edge of his beard. I looked over at Sergio behind the counter, he was smiling his disconnected smile, like a parent watching his kids at some harmless play.

"Can you say it, Cian?" Manuel da Moto asked me, "*Cona. Cona.*"

"*Cona*," I repeated, obediently.

I knew they were fucking with me, of course, they did this every time when they taught me a new word. It was like Monty Python and the English/Hungarian dictionary, the Two Manuels would teach me a word or expression and give me a totally erroneous meaning for it.

Vai-te foder was one of the first gems that they had presented me with, telling me it could be used to tell a woman she was very beautiful. *Vai-te foder* is, of course, the Portuguese expression for "go fuck yourself".

"Can you say this, Cian?" Manuel da Moto said, warming to his task now, "if you give this flower to a woman, you can say, *Gosto da tua cona.*"

"*Gosto....,*" I began.

"*Gosto da tua cona,*" Manuel repeated.

"*Gosto da tua cona.*"

"*Posso ver a tua cona?*"

"*Posso ver tua cona?*"

"Good, almost."

By now Manuel da Barba was in stitches, he literally had to bend over to catch his breath, his face was red, eyes filled with tears. The other Manuel himself was just about holding it together. Sergio just shook his head.

While I was semi-unwittingly entertaining the locals, a woman, standing behind us in the aisle, began speaking to the Two Manuels. To my ears her tone was strident, it sounded to me like Portuguese always did when spoken at any kind of volume, the intonation going sharply down at the end of sentences as normally happened when someone was displeased, or insistent, or anxious to get a point across. It gave her speech a kind of whining, nagging quality. I did recognise one word she used while speaking to the Manuels – "*vergonha*". This meant 'shame'. The Two Manuels had taught me this word only the week before.

Manuel da Barba replied to the woman, a little sheepish now but attempting to be defiant still, and this time I heard the word '*brincar*', another word they had taught me. '*Estamos a brincar,*' was what the Two Manuels always said after revealing, for example, that the word they had just taught me meant a type of vehicle was in fact slang for a penis. "*Estamos a brincar, Cian,*" they would say – "we're only joking." And this is what they were replying to the angry woman facing us. *We're only messing*, I imagined they were saying, *chill out woman*.

I was ignored in all this, irrelevant to the discussion. This gave me a chance to examine her more closely. The woman seemed to be caught between two urgent appointments, her hair was a little mussed, she had her phone in her hand, jacket on, handbag over her shoulder. I couldn't tell whether she was on her way in or out. She had highlighted hair that framed her face, and the first pair of green eyes I had seen in the country. She was in her early, maybe mid-thirties, a half-decade older than me. A real adult.

She said something else, a parting shot, still indignant. She looked at me once, then turned and went on her way into the back of the restaurant, the heels of her boots click-clacking on the tiled floor. The Two Manuels looked at each other and laughed, slightly abashed, but keeping up their front.

"That's Dina," Manuel da Moto said, "she's very serious." Here he put on what was supposed to be a serious expression, in imitation of the woman called Dina. Manuel da Barba joined in, and this entertained them for another five minutes.

As it was still a quarter to eleven I ordered another black beer, still hoping to achieve my goal of a Charlie-free day. When the Two Manuels left to go home to their wives – I found it hard to picture them both married, but apparently they were – I sat down at one of the tables with a copy of a newspaper. The paper was called O Público, from the day before, and I felt proud when I recognised a few words. I even worked out the meaning of a sentence or two. The beer was a black liquid, nothing like Irish stout but tasty all the same, tart but richer than the usually chemically tinged Sagres that they normally served in A Lua. I enjoyed savouring it, letting time pass at its own pace until it was safe to go home.

A shadow fell across the mostly incomprehensible words I was trying to read.

"You know," the woman called Dina said, in English now, when I looked up at her, "those guys are idiots. I went to school with them and they were idiots then too."

I didn't know how she had snuck up on me, how I hadn't heard her approach. Her heels made such a definitive, assertive sound.

"They're ok," I said, "they're harmless".

I defended them out of instinct, out of some kind of masculine solidarity, though I wasn't sure I was required to. I wasn't sure if we were friends or not, me and the Two Manuels.

"They're children," she said.

Her hair was straightened now, tamed, she was altogether more composed than before. Dina's English was much better than my two possible-friends, the Two Manuels, it had a slight American tinge to it.

"Do you mind?" she asked, pointing at the seat opposite me.

"Of course," I answered, with a wave, indicating that she should sit.

Dina did so, and made a gesture to Sergio, like a regular in a Dublin pub might signal for a pint. Sergio turned around to the coffee machine.

"I'm Dina," she said.

"Cian." I put out my hand and she took it, firmly, squeezed and let go. I found her eyes distracting, cat-eyes, green like Monet's water-lilies.

"You know that that was a bad word they were teaching you to say," Dina said.

"I know," I said, "it's not the first time. That's what they do. It amuses them, and I don't mind. What did it mean exactly?" I asked her.

I had a good idea what it meant, of course, but I somehow wanted her to tell me. She looked me straight in the eye.

"'Cunt'," she said, "*cona* means 'cunt'."

"Wow," I said, actually not knowing what else to say.

"You're not American," she said, then. It was a statement, not a question.

"No," I agreed, "not American."

"I know because you don't have the accent. I lived there for seven years, in Rhode Island. There's a Portuguese community there, like little Lisbon."

"And you came back?"

"Yes, separation."

She said this – "separation" – as if it explained everything. I nodded.

"And you're not English, I don't think," Dina went on.

"No I'm not." We were obviously playing a guessing game here, or at least she was.

"Scottish?"

I shook my head. I felt that she was enjoying herself, and that she liked that I didn't just tell her the answer.

"You're not Australian, not New Zealand, not Canada. Maybe Wales, maybe Ireland." Dina was watching me with her green eyes, waiting for a reaction.

"I'm going to say Ireland," she said, her eyes narrowed now.

"Correct."

She seemed genuinely pleased to have gotten it right, after having gone through the whole English-speaking world.

"Liam Neeson," she said, "I like him. And Sean Connery."

I didn't bother correcting her about Connery. Dina sat there still, showing no sign of wanting to leave. She began telling me about her son, who was nine, and her husband, who was Portuguese but who had stayed on in the States after their split. I told her, after she asked me, about the London School – which she had studied in as a teenager – about the classes I had, about where I lived, leaving out the bit about my irritating flatmates who were the reason I was in A Lua at that moment.

"So," she said, after a brief lull in the conversation, "I have a proposal for you." She suddenly sounded very American.

"Shoot," I said.

"My son, Rui, grew up in the States, bilingual, Portuguese at home, English at school and with his friends. Now he's here he's losing his English, and I don't want that. I need someone to spend some time with him, play with him, remind him of his English. I thought that that could be you. In return," here she looked at Sergio, "for every hour you spend with Rui you get a free meal here. I know you're in here a lot, so that must be worth something, I think."

Two things occurred to me then. The first was that she knew that I was a regular, she had obviously been discussing me with someone. The second thing, I asked her about.

"I don't follow," I said, "how can you be so sure that I'll get a free meal here?"

She was his mistress, I imagined, immediately, she was fat Sergio's bit on the side. The thought annoyed me a little. How the fuck did Sergio get a woman like that?

"Sergio's my cousin," Dina said, "he's happy to help me and Rui."

I looked at her. I knew that this was something I was going to say yes to, but didn't want to appear too eager.

"It would have to be at the weekends," I said. She nodded.

"Let me think about it." I added.

We exchanged numbers, Dina and I. Within twenty-four hours I had rung her and we had arranged that I would call to her house in Graça on the Saturday morning to meet the boy.

Saturday came and I found myself reluctant to call over in my usual weekend get-up of Manic Street Preachers t-shirt and jeans and smelling of cigarettes. When Dina and I had first met I was in my smart-casual work clothes, wearing a shirt with a collar and trousers not made of denim. For my visit to Dina's I compromised, put on a dark shirt with short sleeves that my mother had insisted I take with me, and a pair of Levi's cords that helped to dilute the foreign slacker look that I suddenly wanted to avoid. And then I began wondering if I looked like I was trying too hard. I felt like I was going on a date.

Dina lived on one of the narrow back streets that myself and Mario had passed through on our way to the football pitch a month before. Her street was cobbled, her road slightly more than the width of a car, with narrow, concrete pavements for pedestrians on either side. Despite the lack of space there were still cars parked outside every second house, mostly compact vehicles like Puntos, Yarises and Clios, though there was one Merc halfway down that almost blocked the road. Hers was number fifteen, an old building in an ancient slice of the city, though secreted away from all the buzz and clamour of Lisbon in its secluded little street. With the silence, the lack of people, the sedateness, it could have been a street in a village in the Alentejo, the Algarve, in the central plains.

The door was opened by a short, elegant lady in her sixties. She was in full makeup and wore dark trousers and a white blouse, with tiny pearls on a chain around her neck, as if she had just dressed for a reception or a business meeting.

"Hello Cian," she said, shaking my hand, "I'm Maria, Dina's mother."

There was something of her daughter in her, alright, the compactness was Dina's, the prominent cheekbones, though her mother had standard issue Portuguese nut-brown eyes, nothing like Dina's emerald disks.

"Come in," she said.

The interior of the house was a contrast to the outside, it was pristine, modern, with wooden floors and the whitest of walls. In the uncluttered living-room was a flat-screen television, tidy, proportional bookshelves filled to just the right extent by hardbacks, novels and journals in Portuguese, English and French. The kitchen was like something from a catalogue, the surfaces, hob and draining board all looked as if they had never been used for actual cooking. The décor was the definition of taste, minimal and poised, with muted colours. There was no ostentation. A twenty-first century space in eighteenth century Graça.

"You drink coffee?" Maria asked, as she motioned for me to sit on one of her sturdy wooden chairs.

"Absolutely," I replied.

I looked around for Maria's daughter, but couldn't see any evidence that Dina even lived there. Maria made us coffee and sat down with me, as if it were her I had come to see. Her hair was greying, but she still retained a certain solid attractiveness, and obviously still took care with her appearance. There were thousands of women of her age in the city, some of them illiterate, many of them keeping with the country tradition of wearing the mourning black for their whole lives after the death of their husbands. Few of them, especially in the old neighbourhoods of Alfama and Graça, were so well preserved.

"I was in Dublin last month," she said, "for an architectural conference. Beautiful city."

"Really?" I replied, "you're an...."

"I'm an architect, yes. I was one of the first female architects in Portugal in the seventies." She made no attempt to hide how proud she was of this fact.

"You're an architect, and you though Dublin was beautiful?" I asked her, "I think you're being polite."

Maria smiled, and touched my arm, almost flirting.

"The city was charming, I thought," she said, "so much character."

She told me some more about her work, mentioned some of the buildings in Lisbon that she had designed. I pretended to know which ones she meant. As she talked I felt like there was something I wasn't being told, a plan in place that I had no knowledge of but which I was intimately involved in. I nodded and played the part of the cooperative visitor, and waited for my chance to ask where her daughter was.

A dark-haired child put his head around the white kitchen door. He and his grandmother exchanged some words in Portuguese, he approached her and she grabbed him, kissing and hugging him, stroking his hair. An Irish boy of Rui's age would have squirmed and struggled at such over-affection, especially in front of a stranger, but the little guy seemed perfectly content for his granny to paw and slobber over him while I watched.

"This is Rui," Maria said to me, "say hello Rui."

Rui did as he was told. I had almost forgotten that I had come to spend time with the kid, in all my preparation for seeing his mother again. Rui was slight and had the dark fringe and nut-brown eyes of – I assumed – his father. His colouring was different to Dina's but there was a strong resemblance between mother and son, though I found it hard to pinpoint exactly what that was. Perhaps it was that they were both very controlled and careful in their movements. Nothing was rushed. Unusually for a kid every action was deliberate and precise. He patted his hair down after his grandmother had mussed it, and placed his narrow backside into the chair at right angles to mine.

Grandmother and grandson exchanged another few words. Rui then turned to me and asked,

"You wanna play Madden?"

He had turned into a mini American person in just one sentence, his accent pure New England.

"Maybe," I answered, "you'll have to explain to me what it is first."

"Madden" turned out to be an American football game on X-box. Rui showed me how it worked, once we had moved into the living room and switched on the flat-screen. In the game you had to choose which team you had, which players would play for you and then you got to control what they did on the pitch. Rui handled the joystick like an expert, his little fingers a blur of dexterity and finesse. Mine felt and looked clumsy beside him as we sat on the floor and stared at the screen.

He trounced me in the first match, of course. I had never played the game before and had only a vague idea of the rules, so it was hardly surprising. Rui had chosen the New England Patriots, their blue and silver CGI figures swarming all over my poor immobile guys in green and white. I had picked the New York Jets, for no other reason than that they were a team I had heard of, yet they were anything but jet-like under my control. The Patriots won 48-3.

"You're not very good," Rui said.

I had to explain to him that I didn't even know the rules of the real sport of American football, besides the fact that a touchdown was six points and a penalty goal – "it's called a field goal, silly" – was three. I got him to explain to me how to play and despite myself this actually turned out to be useful practice for the kid's English. He had to trawl up half-forgotten terms and pieces of vocabulary that had all but disappeared in his ten months back in Portugal. He did well, in general, describing what all the different buttons on the controls did, and how the various movements of the joystick allowed you to make your players complete different motions, but then he got stuck on relatively simple words like 'helmet' and 'tackle', and I had to help him out. I felt, at least, like I was earning my free meals, if they were ever to materialise. I had my doubts about that at that very moment, given that Dina had yet to show her face.

Rui only beat me forty to ten in the second game. I felt secretly pleased to have improved on my first, miserable showing.

"Give me a few more weeks," I told him, "and I'll beat you."

Strictly speaking I shouldn't have mentioned anything about us meeting again. This first Saturday was supposed to be a trial run, to see if we got on, if I could stand him and if he trusted me. Still, he seemed to be not too big of a pain in the ass, and playing video games in exchange for a free meal appeared to me to be a good deal.

I was about to leave when Dina finally showed up. She looked different to the first time we had met, preoccupied, less assertive. I was standing in the living room, putting my jacket on, Dina ignored me and spoke to her mother briefly. Then she grabbed Rui, as his grandmother had done earlier, kissed him on the cheek and released him, and finally turned to me.

"Cian, I'm sorry I wasn't here, something came up."

"Don't worry," I said, trying to make it look like I was genuinely not bothered. As if I was only in it for the free food.

"I talked to Sergio," she said, "the meals are all arranged. You've been here, what, two hours?"

I looked at my watch. It was true, it was now past one, I had arrived around eleven. I hadn't felt the time passing.

"Yeah, two hours."

"So you have two free meals this week."

"I'll enjoy that," I said, "I'll order lobster, or something. Maybe champagne." I was still trying to keep things light.

"Thanks again, Cian, I can see that Rui liked you."

I was sure that she couldn't see that at all, she had just come in.

"Will we see you next week?" Dina asked, as I was walking out the door.

"I'll give you a ring," I said.

I used my first freebie that very night. I thought that I would test Sergio's conception of what a meal entailed, so I ordered a starter of soft goat's cheese and a warm bread roll, and a main course of *bacalhão com natas*, Sergio's rich cod in cream, that came with a side salad and chips. With that I drank a glass of Dão red, and then finished with one of those sickly-sweet gooey desserts that the Portuguese love so much, along with a milky *galão*. Manuel da Barba came and sat with me for a few minutes while I smoked my after dinner cigarette, his beard obviously recently trimmed but dampened a little by his own milky coffee. I told him about my deal with Dina and he wanted to know if he could put a bottle of beer on my tab. That, I told him, would be pushing it, on my first night.

At the end of the meal I stood up, sauntered over to the glass counter and waited for Sergio to present me with a bill for at least part of my feast. Instead he reached up to a box on a shelf above the bottles of spirits and took down a tightly rolled brown cigar.

"É para ti," he said.

He had just given me a cigar instead of the bill. I put it under my nose, sniffing the odour of rich, dried vegetation as I knew you were supposed to do, and wished everyone a good night, before Sergio had time to change his mind. I found that I enjoyed it, swanning out of A Lua without paying, as if I were some celebrity and Sergio was my personal chef. Back in the flat I lit the cigar and smoked it at the kitchen window, knowing that the smell would reach Charles and Charlotte in the living-room where they were watching 24. It would probably annoy them. I didn't care, it tasted good, my rich, free cigar.

✳ ✳ ✳ ✳ ✳ ✳ ✳

In school that next week there was tension in the staffroom. The light-heartedness of the week prior to Fabian's party had been replaced by a sense of uncertainty and friction. Most of it came from Laura and Sebastian. They had begun sniping at each other right from the Monday after the party. It had started off harmlessly enough.

"What did you get up to on Saturday night?" Sebastian asked Laura, as she shared a cigarette with me on the back balcony, overlooking the concrete desolation of the central yard. "You witch," he went on, "you put a spell on my Fabian, Nando and I were wearing him down and you spirited him away. I think you and the Three A-holes dragged him off to some girl-dungeon and ravished him, gave him no say in the matter."

The London School Facebook page had been active in the forty-eight hours after the party, with claim and counter-claim as to what had happened with the night's competition. Still no-one knew who had won, or whether Fabian was gay or straight. Laura stayed uncharacteristically quiet about it all, and strangely seemed to be doing something else, somewhere else, whenever Fabian was in the staffroom that week following the party. Seb noticed this, as he noticed everything, and commented on it.

"Jealousy is not a good look on you," was all that Laura had to say, back to him. I had never seen her so reticent.

I went back to Dina's again on Saturday. I had used up all my free meals already by Monday night, and so almost resented having to pay when I ate in A Lua on Tuesday and Wednesday. Within three days I had become hooked on free food. Only Maria and Rui were in when I called to their house, this time ten minutes late and in my old Nirvana t-shirt and Levis. Rui and I played Madden again, he very obviously let me score fourteen points before half time – only three points behind him – before crushing me in the second half. Then we played some computer games that were more typical of a little kid, including one where a host of cartoon characters were engaged in a race, using a variety of eccentric vehicles, diving over abysses, landing on toadstools, flying on clouds. There was another with shiny, angular aliens and yet another involving an array of animals who fought in an animated boxing ring. Again Rui took pity on me, allowing my kangaroo to pummel his gorilla, his congratulations afterwards exaggerated and false. I was being patronised by a ten year old.

Maria put her head in the door as we battled.

"I have to go out for a few hours, but my daughter is coming now. She will be here in fifteen minutes. Is it ok?"

I told her to go, not to worry. The truth was that I was having fun. I should have been flattered that she had decided to leave her grandson with a guy that her daughter had only known for three weeks, that she herself had only recently met. Having lived through the previous decade in Ireland, with all the relentless, horrific details of what had been revealed, in her position I wouldn't have left Rui alone with an unknown, twenty-eight year old foreigner, even for five minutes. Still, the kid was quite content, unconcerned by having almost a complete stranger as his guardian. He continued kicking my ass on screen and on the scoreboard, he had run out of pity for my incompetence.

The promised fifteen minutes became a half hour, then an hour, and still Dina hadn't shown. I called her, it went to voicemail. Rui was getting hungry so I made him a sandwich and mixed some of the chocolate Cola Cao powder into milk for him, at first not putting enough in for his taste and having to add more. Rui drank his chocolate milk, ate his ham, mayo and cheese sandwich and chatted away to me in his pure American English about the other video games he wanted, the milk forming a subtle brown moustache along his top lip. After a while I stopped listening, the kid was getting plenty of speaking practice at least. I sat and tried to tot up how many free meals this extended morning's babysitting would net me.

The front door rattled and swung open at ten past two, but it was Maria, not Dina.

"You still here, Cian? Where's my daughter?"

I stood up, ready to make a break for it. I needed a cigarette. I had had enough of the company of this ten year old and his grandmother, charming and all as they were. I shrugged in answer to her question.

"She not here yet?" Maria said something in Portuguese, Rui looked at her, mock-shocked, as if she had just cursed.

"I'm sorry, I don't know what she's doing." Maria went to Rui and kissed him.

I said my goodbyes and bolted, enjoying the fresh air, the open space, as if escaping from a period of detention. I lit a cigarette and walked up the hill to Mario's for some semi-adult conversation.

That evening our intercom buzzed, angrily, it seemed, and Charlotte answered. People almost never called to our door, my flatmates didn't seem to have friends other than each other and I almost never invited anyone I knew to our Charlie-infested apartment. Charlotte was excited to beat me to the little phone device that connected to the caller at the front door.

"*Sim?*" she said, exaggerating her Portuguese accent, putting a sing-song into just one word. She listened to the reply and then turned to me – I had come halfway down the corridor by the time she had picked up the handset – and said, plainly disappointed, "it's for you Cian."

It was Dina.

"Cian," she said, her voice distant though she was only twenty feet away, "can you come out here?"

I considered telling her to fuck off, then realised that that would make me look even weaker. I opened our apartment door, slowly descended the steps and took my time getting to the street door, as if that would teach her a lesson. She wasn't there. I looked around and heard a call from just up the street. Dina was in the driver's seat of a pale blue Renault Clio with the engine running.

"Get in," she said, "I want to apologise."

I didn't do as she said immediately, the passenger side window was open so I put my hands on the roof and leaned in.

"Dina," I said, "I agreed to help your son with his English, but I'm not a babysitter."

My indignation was forced. The situation – and my self-respect – demanded that I be pissed off, as if I had been kept from an urgent appointment that morning. Dina played along.

"I know," she said, "that's why I'm here, I'm trying to apologise". This last word was full-on Rhode Island, the vowels elongated and nasal. "Get in the car. Please."

She had turned seductive and soft now. I did as I was asked. She put on the indicator, pulled out into the road and did a U-turn in the middle of Largo da Graça, finally steering her Renault down the hill towards the city centre. The sun was setting right in front of us, the sky a mixture of reds, oranges and dirty yellows. I looked over at Dina as she drove, her eyes were hyper-green in the light now being squeezed from the sunset. She had recently sprayed herself with perfume, something spicy and rich that went straight from my nose to my bloodstream, and from there to my nervous system.

"Where are we going?" I asked.

Instead of answering she bellowed something that sounded like "Sighdafrent carasash," at a Volkswagen that had pulled out in front of her. She drove with little caution, braking just before the moment when not doing so would have been disastrous, not slowing down for corners, running red lights. Still, we wound more or less intact down the twisty cobbled streets until we arrived to the Baixa, and saw the dark flowing shape of the river to our left. The bridge – a slightly smaller version of the Golden Gate – loomed in the distance, its large metal bulk in the semi darkness looked like a giant creature straddling the water. Dina took a turn and we wound up towards the great structure, the car wheels humming as they moved on to the ridged surface of the road that coated the bridge, making a noise like a swarm of metal wasps.

"Where we're going is a secret," she announced, finally, once we were up high, traversing the Tagus, the river below looking grey and green and brown in the fading light.

In truth I didn't care where we were going, secret or not. The smooth movement of the vehicle, the tang of Dina's perfume, the sunset burning the sky in the distance, were enough for that moment.

"You know what the bridge is called?" Dina asked.

"It's the April twenty-fifth bridge," I replied, feeling like I was being tested.

"*O Vinte-cinco de Abril*," she said. "You know what happened on that date?"

I had a vague idea, but I could see that she wanted to tell me.

"Not a clue," I said.

"It was the revolution, 1974. A peaceful one. We put carnations in the guns of the soldiers."

She spoke as if she had been there. At most, in 1974, she could have been a foetus. Dina went on to give me a history lesson about the brutality of Salazar's pre-'74 dictatorship, the torture, the secret police, the way many women of her mother's age and older had been left illiterate as a deliberate policy.

I could see that she liked having an audience. She was passionate, vehement, contemptuous of the old rulers. We had now crossed the mile-long bridge and left the river behind, we were travelling in the direction of Setúbal and the South. She talked and drove effortlessly, continuing the lecture while negotiating the twisty, tree-lined road we had now driven on to after turning off the motorway. She knew where she was going, that was obvious, the sharp turns and steep gradients didn't bother her, even as she continued my education on the history of her country. Like the Two Manuels, I realised, in her own way Dina was making sure that I wasn't just some ignorant foreigner. I was obviously someone who looked like he needed instruction.

We pulled in, finally, to a car park in front of a building, after twenty minutes along almost empty country roads. The place was all built of wood, set back into the forest with a substantial gravel parking area out front. The words "O Covil" were on a wooden sign. I didn't ask Dina what it meant, but looked it up later when I got home. "Covil, n. masc: den, lair," the dictionary told me. Now that did make me smile, she had taken me to her lair.

The place was a restaurant. Dina obviously knew the staff, she greeted two of the waiters and the receptionist and, once we were seated, a balding guy in a double-breasted suit came to our table. Dina introduced me in Portuguese to the bloke she called Bruno, and then they chatted animatedly for a while. I just sat and looked like I knew what they were saying.

"I used to work here," Dina explained, when Bruno had left, "it's the best restaurant I know. I wanted to take you here to say sorry."

I nodded. I had to remind myself what she was apologising for.

"It's just that, Rui's father is here, and I had to see him. I didn't want to tell my mother, and I thought I could get back in time before you had to leave. But Paulo – that's my husband – kept talking and talking."

She put her hand to her hair, gripped it briefly and let it go.

"He's very....persistent."

"Is he Portuguese?" I asked.

"He's from Lisbon, like me. Alfama."

"Why did you separate?" I felt I could ask this question, seeing as she was supposed to be apologising.

"The usual reasons," Dina said.

I nodded, happy to let her leave it at that. I didn't care that much. But then she went on.

"He lost interest in me and Rui. I think he was having an affair, though he never admitted it. He wants me to go back with him, but I don't want that. In the States things were bad between us. He lied all the time. You know the story, it's the same with a thousand couples, a million marriages. It's boring to listen to, I know, so boring, such a cliché. You think, when it's happening to you that you're unique, but really it's happened a million times before."

As she talked she held a slim knife, a butter knife, and used it to repeatedly stab the pale round goat's cheese that Bruno had left for us. When she had stopped the cheese was annihilated, its soft insides exposed, bits of it lying all over the plate. Dina looked down at what she had done, then pushed the plate to one side, lifted a chunk of white cheese flesh to her mouth and popped it in. She forced out a smile, and then the smile looked real, and suddenly this Paulo, her wayward husband, was forgotten.

"So how about you?" Dina asked, bright again, "did you leave some girlfriend – or wife – back in Ireland? Or is that why you're here, you're escaping from someone? A broken heart, perhaps."

She was half-joking, half-wanting to know. Again I got this urge to tell her to fuck off, to mind her own business. As if she were trying to walk into my house without being invited. I took a piece of the dismembered cheese and chewed slowly.

"Hey," Dina said, "you don't have to tell me. I was just, you know, making conversation."

I looked at her as she observed me, and suddenly found that I was tired of not talking about this.

"She was called Maura," I told her, "it was a bit of a disaster."

Dina now stopped her chewing, her toying with the cheese, and looked at me steadily.

"What happened?"

"Do you really want to know, or are you just being polite?" I asked her. I was being defensive, I knew, but I just couldn't help it. I didn't feel like telling this story to someone who had no real desire to know it.

"I really want to know."

So I told her. Up until then Dina had done most of the talking. I was happy with that and she enjoyed my undiluted attention. But now I had something to say.

I began at the beginning, the damp Dublin winter of 2006. I was living in Clanbrassil Street, just off one of the main link roads between the south of the city and the centre. I liked it there, I shared the place with a big GAA head from Athlone who was almost never in the flat. He was always back home for the weekend playing matches or off in his girlfriend's place in Harold's Cross. I believed, rightly or wrongly, that I was near the living, breathing centre of things there, the steady heartbeat of the city. It was a ten minute walk from Dame Street or from Whelan's, fifteen from Temple Bar, close to the city's grassy hub at Stephen's Green. In my naive way I often imagined living there forever.

Then, Billy, my landlord's marriage collapsed and he turfed us out. His wife had caught him boinking one of his tenants from one of his stable of flats around the city. He was very open about the reason why we had to leave, even a little proud, I thought. Athlone lad and I were given until the end of November to get out. To make it up to us he promised to overlook the damage we had done to the place and return our security deposit. *You're too kind Billy*, I mouthed as he told me of his magnificent generosity over the phone, *you're too fucking kind.*

Flat hunting in Dublin is a penance, at the best of times, and I put it off until I had only a few days to find somewhere to live. My mother came to the rescue, or so she believed. Through the south County Limerick grapevine she heard of a room coming free in a house way to the south of where I was living, in Rathfarnham. The daughter of one of her cronies from the neighbouring village to ours, Meelin, was taking a six month sabbatical from the Civil Service and flitting off to

Australia, and was looking for someone to hold her room for her until she got back. The girl's name was Justine. A viewing had been arranged for me, through my mother and her little coven back in Ballyhayes. She texted me the address and the buses I needed to get there.

The whole arrangement stank, to me. Rathfarnham was too remote, hardly even still in the city, it was practically County Dublin. It felt like banishment. And only a six month stay would mean that I would have to venture out into the humiliating, squalid world of Dublin flat-hunting again, less than half a year later. Looking for a place to live was a little too much like a series of interviews for jobs you didn't even want.

Yet the greatest drawback, as I saw it, was that the other two tenants were also Limerick girls, people from 'home'. They had their roots in the village of Meelin too, like Justine, just four and a half whispering miles down the road from Ballyhayes and the listening ears of my people. I knew well how the flow of information worked between city and country, between metropolis and village, and if there were just one informant in the capital relaying information back then every person who cared within a ten mile radius of Ballyhayes inevitably ended up knowing your business.

That said, I went to see the house. I visited some apartments with free rooms around where I had been living – Thomas Street, near St. Patrick's Cathedral, down as far as the canal – and they were, without exception, vastly overpriced, cramped, musty and full of people who were potential sociopaths. It was out of desperation that I went to see the house.

The place in Rathfarnham was a pleasant surprise. The bus, direct from Clanbrassil Street, stopped just four minutes walk from the front door. The place was a semi-D, the free room was en-suite with a shower that could have power washed cars and trucks, and there were tidy gardens front and back and satellite TV. It had a neat, civilised, *feminine* air about it that I had almost forgotten could exist in a place of residence. The rent too, was fifty euro less than I had been paying in the centre, and the kitchen itself was about half the size of my whole flat back in Clanbrassil Street. It was so suburban, so tranquil, I momentarily forgot that I lived in our smelly, misshapen capital city.

The girl who showed me around was called Sheila, a year or two younger than me, small and dark and pretty, with little bird arms and legs that looked like they would snap with a wrong turn. Justine, their Civil Servant housemate, had already left on her six month holiday. Sheila was gossipy and talkative, happy to know we were more or less from the same place, reassured, in that very rural way, that if she didn't know me then at least her people knew my people. Her cousin, the other resident, Maura, was asleep at that time, she was a nurse on night shift, but Sheila assured me that she would be delighted to have a Limerick man in the house. I smiled, on my best behaviour, and made appreciative noises. I made no commitment, but said I would get back to her.

It only took another day of the purgatory that is Dublin house-hunting for the place in Rathfarnham to begin looking better and better. I only had another four days before Billy the landlord would kick me out. So, not thirty hours after I had viewed the house I found myself – cursing myself all the while – calling Sheila and telling her that I would gladly accept the room in their fragrant, distant house. When she heard the news she sounded like I had told her that she had won the lotto. *Boy*, I thought, *are your illusions ever about to be shattered.*

Two days later I, and all my stuff, had moved into number 22 Templewoods, Rathfarnham, Dublin 14. It took me a week to get over the pleasure of falling out of bed in the morning, still half asleep, and stumbling the three and a half steps to the shower, without having to open or close any doors. At first I couldn't sleep at night, it was too quiet, the silence, when I woke at three a.m. made me think I had gone deaf. And the neat, controlled orderliness of the kitchen left me scared to dirty a saucepan or leave toast crumbs on the counter. It felt like staying in one of my friend's parents' pristine place, an abode of real grown-up adults.

I hardly saw Maura for the first month I was there, she was like the ghost flatmate, at work when I was asleep, asleep when I was at home. One sign of her presence was the tang of her shampoo emanating from the shower most days when I came home from work. There were half-opened pots of yogurt in the fridge and runners and slippers in the living-room of an intermediate size somewhere between my tens and Sheila's child-sized shoes. Echoes of her existence, nothing more. We only glimpsed each other once or twice in the mornings – when she was coming home and I was stumbling late out the door – and in the evenings before she left for work.

Our first real conversation came two weeks before Christmas, in Shelia's room. The two cousins were sitting on Sheila's bed, with the door to the landing open, as I passed on my way downstairs. It was Sheila who spoke when she saw me.

"Cian!" she called out, "can you come in? We need a guy's perspective on things."

The topic was Maura's love-life. I sat down on a delicately made white wicker chair that didn't look like it could support my weight, as Sheila talked about Jeremy, apparently the latest in a long line of non-committal, uncommunicative men that Maura had been out with. Maura herself hardly said anything as Sheila described how the dude would disappear for two or three weeks and then show up out of the blue. He would then bombard Maura with calls and texts and presents, take her out and tell her how much he liked her, before vanishing again for another month.

They both sat on the edge of the bed, looking over at me with the same nut-brown eyes, as if I were the oracle of everything to do with male unreliability. The cousins were quite different, Maura was more solid, rounder, less fragile-looking, still short but taller than Sheila. But whatever genetic element that they shared could be seen in their faces, almost as a hint, a whisper, their dark hair the same shade, though of differing lengths, both with thick eyebrows and long lashes, their skin sallow, their eyes quick and all-seeing and no-nonsense.

Instead of providing an answer, I asked Maura a question.

"What do you want?"

I was buying time, only now aware that I wanted to say something intelligent to this girl. I suddenly cared what she thought of me. She paused for a second and then replied.

"I want someone I can trust, someone I can believe, someone who's not going to fuck me around."

The swear-word registered with me, as a sign of some slight intimacy. Sheila never swore, that I noticed, but Maura didn't seem to be so careful. I stood, still not wanting to prolong the conversation

"Then tell this Jeremy guy that, and if he can't give you what you want, dump him."

The advice was obvious, far from rocket-science, but it pleased me that Maura seemed to find it insightful and profound. All of a sudden, with no warning whatsoever, I really wanted to be thought insightful and profound by this girl.

I gave Dina an edited version of this, the beginning of my story, right up until the evening when I had to give Maura advice about the feckless Jeremy.

"That's a trick we women use," Dina said, "we ask the guy we like to tell us what to do about the guy we're with."

As she spoke a waiter appeared from her left, my right. He was carrying a tray, on the tray was a pig.

"What the fuck?" I said, as a reflex.

In truth it was more of a piglet, roasted on a tray and placed on the middle of our wooden table. There was no apple in its mouth, but its expression was one of surprise, something I could identify with. Dina was watching for my reaction.

"It's called *leitão*," she said, "it's roast pig."

"No shit?" I replied.

The whole pig was, in fact, only for show, to shock and impress the foreigner. The waiters took it away, smiling as they did so and chatting among themselves. They then brought us back a platter of its meat. Dina served me some, along with salad leaves and chunky beef tomato slices. The ubiquitous chips were there too, I took a few for variety though I wasn't really hungry anymore.

"Keep going with your story," Dina said, "it was just getting interesting."

I had become dinner entertainment for her, me and my failure. Still, I couldn't stop now, I was too committed to letting it all out. The meat was cold, chewy, strangely tasteless, talking at least gave me an excuse not to have to pretend to like what was on my plate.

I went back to ten months before, to January 2007, two weeks after I had advised Maura to dump her boyfriend, Jeremy, if he couldn't give her what she wanted. It was a Wednesday evening, I had just come home from work and was coming out of my shower, a too-small towel tied around my waist. Maura knocked, walked in without waiting for an answer and didn't bat an eyelid to see that I was almost naked. She looked me up and down.

"I've made some lasagne, it's downstairs. Just to say thanks."

"Ok," I replied, "thanks for what?"

"For your advice. I cut Jeremy loose, though I don't even know if he noticed. He disappeared again so I had to leave a voice message."

I only vaguely remembered who Jeremy was, and couldn't even really recall what my advice had been. Still, once I had got dressed I accepted her lasagne, it was delicious, with spices of some kind – cinnamon, or ginger perhaps – in the sauce, giving it a kick. There was only the two of us there, in our warm, neat kitchen, with Lyric FM on in the background and a bottle of red Portuguese wine to go with the pasta.

We made small talk at first, awkward at being alone together for the first time ever. Slowly though, after a couple of glasses of the ink-red Dão, we got on to our romantic histories. I was non-committal, revealing the bare minimum, but Maura revelled in discussing the parade of useless, feckless, cheating guys she had tended to fall in with. She laughed hard about each one, strong, full laughter with her mouth open and her dark hair shaking as she guffawed.

"I knew right then," I told Dina, "that there was something between us." Dina just nodded, and kept chewing the insipid pig-meat.

During that first meal that Maura and I ate together, I couldn't take my eyes off her when she spoke. She was animated, her eyes enlivened, her mouth fuller, more sensual than I had previously noticed. Her hair was hedge-thick, I just wanted to reach out and stick my fingers into it, to burrow down in, take a grip and hold on. It was cut in a dark bob, which accentuated the roundness of her face, her felineness. Sitting there and laughing with her, listening to her speak, I imagined stroking her, like a cat.

We danced around each other for a month. I cooked for her the following week – a student style chilli con carne – though I made it look as if I had simply made too much and she would be helping me out by eating it. This became a habit, once one of us was cooking we would make extra so the other could share in the meal. Sheila had a new boyfriend at this time and was out a lot with him, so this threw myself and Maura together more, now that she was single again and she was working the day shift.

We led largely separate lives outside the house. Yet within the walls of 22 Templewoods, Rathfarnham, Maura and I spent more and more time together. We rented crappy DVDs and watched them in the evenings, laughing at them and slagging them off with a pleasure we didn't get from watching good movies. We took turns cooking for each other and on Maura's insistence we had one night a week – usually a Wednesday – when we would play loud music and clean and hoover the house, upstairs and down, while drinking a bottle of wine. It was the first and last time that I took pleasure in housework. We had tournaments on my X-box, which she eventually began winning without me even having to let her. In a matter of weeks we had formed a temporary but solid bond where the possibility of sex was there constantly but always unspoken, a step neither of us wanted to take just yet. Yet on nights when I knew Maura was going to be at home I couldn't stop myself from checking the time constantly in work, often leaving early so as to make sure I caught the 4.50pm bus back to Rathfarnham, back to this woman who was, at that time, still nothing more than my housemate.

Perhaps it was Sheila who tipped us over the edge. A Thursday evening in late February she arrived in the door, before 10pm for once, and found her cousin and me splayed out on the couch, both of us in sweatpants, each of us with a glass of red wine on the floor in front of us. We were making fun of the latest crop on I'm a Celebrity, Get Me Out Of Here. Sheila just stood there at the open living room door, staring down at us, her cheeks still red from the cold outside.

"You two look like an old married couple," she said, only half-joking, "when are you going to get it together?"

This was the first overt mention of what would have been obvious for weeks to anyone watching, if there had been anyone around but Maura and I. Maura was unfazed, she simply ignored what Sheila had said and began teasing her about her new boyfriend, Philip, and asking her why she was home so early. I joined in. This, though, was a blatant attempt at deflection. The idea was out there now, the idea about Maura and I getting together. Sheila was the first person to articulate it out loud, and it couldn't be unsaid.

"It happened two nights later," I told Dina.

I had basically stopped eating now, Dina was only grazing, nibbling on salad, cold chips, bland pig meat. She had let me speak, without interruption, for ten minutes at this stage. The waiters had lit candles, on our table and on the walls, and Dina's eyes were eerily green in the stuttering light as she observed me.

As I recounted the events of the night to Dina I could picture them in my mind as if they were happening right in front of me. It was the first time I had ever spoken about any of this out loud, the act of verbalising it seemed to bring it into being again, an exact virtual replay being called up as I talked. It was a Saturday night, Maura and I were out drinking separately, she with her nurse buddies, me on a more or less monthly excursion with my work colleagues, a kind of combined team bonding exercise and excuse to get drunk.

We went in our twenty-strong pack to the Long Acre, then to the Oliver St John Gogarty, before winding up in the Turk's Head, a place with multiple levels and violently loud music. I found that I had had enough quite early and escaped before two, walked out into a chilly Dame Street without saying goodnight to anyone, and hopped into a taxi that was passing. Fifteen minutes later I put the key in my front door in Rathfarnham, cursing the twenty euro I now had to pay to get home after having been able to walk home for free to my flat in Clanbrassil Street, just four months before.

Maura was in the kitchen when I entered, heating up baked beans. She was in that half at home state, still perfumed, in a dark skirt and blouse but in slippers, makeup still on but her hair pulled back with an old, white scrunchy.

"Good night?" I asked her.

"Good, yeah," she said, "out with the girls."

This was something we laughed about, her and her mature band of fellow nurses calling themselves "the girls."

"You?" she asked, in return.

"Oh, you know," I said, "the same. Out with my two great aunts, Dora and Flora. The girls."

Maura took a bean from the pot and flicked it at me with her spoon. I caught it and ate it.

"Any action?" she asked, looking at me closely.

"Was chatting to this Australian girl," I said, "but she was not my type."

"Oh yeah," Maura asked, "and what type would that be?"

We both felt it then. Really there had been a change between us since the night, a couple of days before, when Sheila had made her comment about us finally getting it together. Maura stopped eating, and pushed her plate to the other side of the table. We both stood, I leaned across the table, plunged my right hand into her thick hair and drew her towards me. Our first kiss was awkward, a kitchen table between us, both of us off balance. She tasted of tomato sauce, wine, Chanel, her lips careful and tentative, the kiss probing, precise, and then more passionate, with biting, tongues, breath becoming heavier. The table edge was digging into my thighs and I was falling over, though I didn't want to stop, I didn't want to break the spell. It was Maura, ever practical, who halted things, took my hand, led me out into the middle of the floor where we sprang back together again, like iron to a magnet, no obstacle now between us.

"You know the way," I said to Dina, there in the main dining area of O Covil restaurant, another, entirely different table now between me and her, "when you're with someone for the first time, when you sleep together, things can be awkward, uncomfortable. Maybe you are unsure what to do, how fast to move, where to put things?"

I waited for her to answer. She looked surprised that she was now expected to speak. She hadn't had to say anything for a quarter hour.

"I was married to Paulo for ten years, and I didn't cheat on him. So I don't really remember a first time with anyone."

This was matter-of-fact, almost wistful.

"But sure," Dina confirmed, "I suppose I can see how it can be awkward at first."

"Well it wasn't with me and Maura. It was like we had been doing it forever. I suppose it was because we had lived together for two months, we saw each other every day, slept twenty feet apart. I had seen her in her night clothes, with hangovers, I had seen her painting her toenails, putting on makeup, moisturising, she had seen me in my underwear, watched me shaving. She had cooked for me, bandaged my finger when

I cut it chopping carrots. We had already reached a level of intimacy a lot of couples never do, so the next step felt natural. It was like we had had two months of foreplay, and it was all leading to that night."

Sitting there, talking to Dina, who was within touching distance, about my first time with Maura, it was like that whole night was happening again, somewhere at the back of my skull. I could still feel Maura's skin from that night, the tightness, the heat of it, if I wanted I could summon the taste of her mouth, the salty flavour of the perspiration from her breasts, her inner thighs, could feel what it was like to have her hand on my ass, pulling me closer, deeper. I could hear her still, whispering in my ear as we fucked. I was drunk that Saturday night with Maura, but the alcohol hadn't clouded my memory, practically every detail was still clear as I sat opposite Dina in the restaurant. I had a semi-erection as I spoke about it. I shifted a little in my seat to rearrange things.

"What happened next?" Dina asked.

Bruno, while I was recounting, had brought dessert, and then coffee. I hardly ate anything, the sight of the very lifelike pig had put me off, but the coffee tasted sharp and inviting.

"You mean, after the first night?"

"Yes, the next few weeks. You still had to see each other every day."

There was now a cloud of smoke about us, drifting and circling. The restaurant was emptying. I had no idea what time it was. Bruno kept bringing us coffee, I had a couple of cognacs. Dina took another cigarette.

"It happened again three nights later," I said, in answer to Dina's question, "and again the next weekend. We didn't talk much about what we were doing, things went on more or less normally. Maura and I still cooked for each other, still went out separately at night, still watched trashy television in the evenings. Now though we usually ended up in bed together once or twice during the week, and once at the weekend. We almost developed a routine, like a married couple, just like Sheila had said."

Dina took a drag of the cigarette and nodded.

"Maura hadn't told Sheila at this stage, she said it made it more exciting that it was a secret. Some nights she would come in, late from work or from the pub, and I might be in bed, maybe asleep, and I'd hear her pushing open my door and closing it quietly, and then soon feel her little hot body beside me under the duvet. I pretended to be annoyed, the first few times, when she woke me up, but I wasn't, not really, and soon, if I knew that she was out late and I was at home, there was no way that I would sleep, even if I was in bed I was listening out for her footsteps on the stairs, waiting for my door to creak open, waiting to smell her gin-breath on my cheek. She was always more daring those nights when she came to me, I think she liked it, she liked the control, liked the idea that it was her and not me who had started things. It excited her more."

"So you never saw each other outside the house?" Dina asked.

"Almost never."

"And you never went out, like on a date?"

"Once, about three weeks in. I suggested it, it felt like something we should do. But it was a mistake. We went out to dinner but our conversation was awkward, all the intimacy we had at home disappeared. We were on a date and that's what it felt like, something artificial, something for relationships different to ours. We went for a drink after, travelled home together in a taxi. We didn't know what to say to each other. When we got back to the house we went to our separate beds, like two people who were just housemates, not lovers. It was like taking an experiment out of the laboratory and seeing that it doesn't work."

"So that's what it was, an experiment?"

"I suppose so."

"And that's when it ended?"

"No, not then, later. It ended later on. This time, after our date things went cold for two weeks or so. We didn't know how to talk about the night of the date, or about what we had together, in case there was really nothing there, in case it was all a fantasy. Like some old artefact that disintegrates when you expose it to the air outside. She started to go to bed early – to avoid me, I thought – then so did I. I thought that it was all on the verge of finishing. And then Sheila told me that Maura was planning to move out."

"Sheila, the cousin? So what did you do?" Dina asked.

As the waiters cleaned around us, I told her the next part of the story. I told her how the thought of not seeing Maura again made me actually nauseous. Dina took my hand briefly as I continued, then took her hand away to light another cigarette, her fourth or fifth. She listened as I recounted the Saturday morning after Sheila had spoken to me. Maura and I met in the kitchen, she gave me a half-smile and then tidied her dishes away quickly and made to leave.

"Maura," I said, "I don't want you to move out."

"Did Sheila speak to you?" she asked, "I fucking told her not to. But I think it would be best for both of us."

"I don't agree," I told her.

We sat down at the kitchen table that had been a barrier between us, a month before.

"You know," she said, "I liked what we had before. We had no demands on each other. It was something we never talked about because we didn't have to, it was all understood, there was no pressure. I had my life, you had yours, and we had our thing here, it was the perfect set-up."

"So let's go back to it," I said.

And that's what we did. It was that simple. We slotted back into our routine, fell back into our old rhythm like smokers going back on the fags. It was so easy, as if we had been doing it for years. What she had said was true, we had the perfect set-up. We had our own lives, work, friends, social life, and then we could always come back to our semi-spouse at home, back to undemanding, captive affection, back to support, desire, passion. We didn't try to make it something it wasn't, we stopped forcing ourselves to be more conventional, to put a name on what we were doing. Two or three times a week we ended up in her warm bed or in mine, and enjoyed every second that we spent together. Maura and I each had our lives, and then we had our time together, the holiday from our lives.

"For two months there," I said to Dina, as the restaurant staff swept up around us, "we were happy."

Bruno, the balding manager, came up to Dina and whispered in her ear. She nodded, then looked around her. We were the last people in the place, the wooden tables were being cleared and stacked, even the staff were putting on jackets, ready to leave.

"I guess it's time to go," Dina said.

There were only a few cars in the gravel car-park when we went outside. The wind had gotten up now, the trees brushed against each other, swaying and clashing, making a sound like a hundred thousand aspirins dissolving in water. I went to get in to what I thought was the passenger side of Dina's Peugeot, until I saw the steering wheel there. Of course, it was on the right. I was distracted now, not really concentrating on what I was doing.

I found the passenger seat, finally. Dina put on a CD, some female singer – maybe Alanis Morissette, maybe Edie Brickell, perhaps Feist – began singing wordy, clever songs as we wound back through the narrow roads in the dark. The trees on either side looked threatening as they were briefly lit up by the headlights.

"So you lived happily ever after, for two months," Dina said, after we had both been silent for some minutes, "something must have happened."

"I've talked enough," I said, as Alanis, or Edie, or Feist sang about rejection, heartbreak, moons and sea-lions, "you tell me about you, I'm bored of the sound of my own voice."

"But I want to know how it ends," Dina said, like a kid told to go to bed before her show finished.

"It's not a soap opera, Dina," I said, "it's not a rom-com, it's my life. Maura and I made mistakes. We did everything backwards, first we lived together, then we slept together, then we....well, whatever it was, we lived as a couple. It was never going to last, and it didn't. Can we leave it at that?"

Dina looked over at me. At this stage I was slumped in the passenger seat, hands in the pocket of my hoodie. I was suddenly drained, the desire to speak had left me. Dina didn't say anything. I couldn't tell what she was thinking. I just stared out of the window while she drove. We didn't speak again until we had rejoined the motorway and reached the bridge, its giant shape alien in the semi-darkness after the tight green spaces we had come from.

"Rui likes you," Dina said, after what seemed to be hours of silence, "I hope you can keep coming, it's good he had some male influence. With Paulo mostly in the States, he hardly ever sees him."

Now I was to be the surrogate father-figure, after having already played the role of babysitter. We were on the bridge now, the lights of the city spreading out before us.

"He's a nice kid, smart," I said.

"Yes, he is smart. Paulo is smart too, but in a way that you can't trust."

Dina drove slower now than earlier. We went uphill, past the Cathedral on our right, up Rua de Limoeiro – Lemontree Road, Dina had translated it for me – through Portas de Sol, beneath which lay the football pitch where I had scored my last minute goal, and then around the twisty ancient streets, back to Graça. Dina stopped in front of A Lua, now closed and dark. There were few people around Largo da Graça. I couldn't tell what was going to happen now. Dina turned off the engine and leaned towards me. She kissed me on the cheek, once, rather than the more usual twice.

"So am I forgiven?" she asked, slightly flirty.

"Sure," I said, "but just this once. Next time the price will be higher."

I opened the passenger door and stepped out on to the pavement. There wasn't as much wind there in the city as there had been at the restaurant, even up on the hill on Graça. Dina pulled out, did a rapid U-turn and turned the corner on the way home, flashing her lights once as she departed.

DECEMBER

I came out of my class with Patricia Coelho and her teen colleagues one Tuesday in early December, and found that I had a text from Dina.

"*Cn we meet tonite?*" it went, "*buy u a drink in a lua?*"

Since our visit to O Covil, the lair, I had seen her twice more, but always in the company of her son, in her mother's house in Graça. Dina called these meetings "playdates". This was how she saw me, I thought, a big kid for Rui to play with.

We had coffee each time, and talked in a civilised, polite manner, Dina happy to relay the latest annoyance her husband had contributed to her existence, obviously avoiding asking me about the story I had told her in the restaurant. I was on my best behaviour, skirting the issue of Maura, trying to work out if there was something developing between me and Dina or not. I still couldn't be sure. I had never been with anyone non-Irish before, or anyone with a kid, and never anyone in their thirties. And I had definitely never been with anyone who was paying me for a service I was providing, even if it was only payment in food. It was all new territory. Dina was in A Lua when I arrived at ten o'clock. I sat down, she signalled to Sergio for another beer to be brought to our table.

"So what's the occasion?" I asked, as I held the glass at an angle and poured the bubbling liquid into it.

Dina looked straight at me, in that way she had, unblinking, her eyes like two green searchlights.

"I just felt I needed some time talking to an actual adult who isn't my mother".

"I get it," I said, "can't be easy. I know I couldn't spend more than a week in a house with my mother."

"Don't know which is worse," Dina said, "living with Paulo or living with Maria."

I didn't say so, but Maria – Dina's mother – had stuck me as the most laid-back of women. Still, I had had some familiarity with mother-daughter conflicts, Maura had had a fraught relationship with her Limerick mammy.

"And then I had a call from Paulo," Dina said, "he's back in the States. It wasn't a fun call."

Dina told me some of the things they had called each other, many of the words I recognized from my swearing lessons with the two Manuels.

"How did you two ever get together?" I asked her.

"We fell in love, Cian," she said, "you must remember what that's like."

"Vaguely," I said.

"And how about you?" Dina asked, "you won't tell me about the split up, but you must have been with other girls since. And before."

We don't say 'split up', I almost said, *it's 'break-up' or 'split'*. I resisted the impulse just in time.

"Sure, I've been with people, with girls. I've been with a few." Suddenly I was babbling, having trouble making a simple sentence. "Maura wasn't the last, if that's what you mean."

Should I tell her about Sylvia Saint John, I wondered, or about snogging Carly? Or about the Spanish girl we had christened Toil-and-Trouble?

"But you still think about her?" Dina asked me.

"I try not to."

Dina nodded, as if I had said something significant. Manuel da Barba came in and stood at the counter, ordered a coffee and performed the whole sugar ceremony, stirring two full sachets into his tiny *bica*. He glanced down and saw Dina and me sitting opposite each other, just ten feet from where he was. Dina saw him too.

"You know," she said, "I'd be curious to see where you live. Maybe meet the two Charlies, they sound interesting. I've only seen the outside of your place."

I had told her about Charles and Charlotte during one of Rui's playdates, I was pretty sure that I hadn't made them sound interesting enough for Dina to be dying to meet them.

"I don't know," I said, trying to keep things light, "it's a long way. You got your walking shoes on?"

Dina didn't smile, she just stood up. Her beer glass was still half-full, mine had a good three mouthfuls left in it. I was about to protest, but she was already half-way out the door. Dina and Manuel da Barba nodded to each other as she passed. I managed a quick "*boa noite*" to him as I followed Dina outside.

She was already standing at our street door when I left A Lua.

"What have you got against Manuel?" I asked, trying to be mild.

"I told you before," she said, "I was in school with him and his friend with the motorcycle. They're idiots. And I don't like everyone knowing my business."

What business was that, exactly, I wondered. We walked up the steps in silence. The flat was unusually quiet when I opened our front door.

"That's right," I told her, as she stepped carefully over the threshold, "my flatmates have gone out. They're working on their relationship."

Charlotte had confided to me earlier that she and Charles had come to believe that their relationship had gotten stale and predictable. That they needed to get out more together, to do different things. *No shit!* I had almost said to her.

"You mean that we are alone?" Dina said. I smiled. It was like the dialogue from a bad porn film.

"All alone."

I did what I imagined she expected me to do, and stepped up to her as she stood on the parquet floor of our silent corridor. Her green eyes watched me, inexpressive. I moved slowly, I could almost watch myself from the outside, transferring my hand to her hair, circling the back of her neck, pulling her closer, bending down, touching my lips to hers. Even in heels, Dina was five or six inches shorter than me. Her lips were a little dry to begin with, but she licked them, mid-kiss, and continued. The taste of her mouth had layers, first there was lip gloss, cherry flavour, then beer, a hint of garlic behind that, then a flavour that was all her, moist and rich and human.

Dina didn't comment on the tininess of my bedroom, when I led her there, or on the lowness of my bed. We undressed in stages, kissing, removing an item, touching, removing another one, until we were down to just underwear. All her clothes – loose linen trousers, light blouse already half unbuttoned, white cotton t-shirt, boots opened with just a zip – had been easy to take off, as if she had dressed with precisely this idea in mind. It was a degree or two below a comfortable temperature to be naked, so we got under my duvet.

The sheer pleasure of her skin was the first thing that struck me, smooth, taut, hot, a little sweaty, a surface that was designed to be touched. It was good that she was small, there wasn't much room in the bed, on one side was the wall, on the other the edge of the bed, every manoeuvre had to be done with great care. One wrong move and we both could have ended up toppling off and lying naked on the multi-coloured rug that covered the wooden floor of my bedroom. The tight space forced us together, made things slower and more intense. It joined us up. Afterwards, we stayed entangled there, limbs intercrossed, our heads on the narrow pillow. Her green eyes stayed open, emitting their own light. I wanted her to close them for a second, to give me a break from their gaze, but she kept looking, watching.

"You're the first guy I've been with since Paulo," she said, "it's strange, after being with the same man for ten years."

"Yeah?"

"Yeah. You two are so different."

The word "so" was elongated, emphasized. I didn't know how to take this.

"Different good or different bad." I had to ask.

Dina blinked once before answering.

"Just different." And then she smiled.

We lay there lazily for a time, then Dina threw back the duvet, rolled over and hopped on to the floor. In about thirty seconds she was dressed again, faster even than she had gotten undressed.

"Are you going?" I asked, sitting up, my hands behind my head. Her rapid movements reminded me of Sylvia Saint John, more than two months before, who had left my bed equally quickly.

"I have a son, Cian," she said, as if I could have forgotten, "I need to get back home."

Dina zipped up her boots, leaned over and kissed me, briefly, on the lips, before making for the door.

"So I'll see you Saturday, yeah?" she said, "for the playdate?" She was all business, back to being my sort-of employer.

"Playdate?" I said, in a mock American accent, "gee, sure, I'll be there."

She didn't react to my attempt to make her smile, just opened the door and left. Her heels rat-a-tatted on the wooden floor of our corridor, and the front door closed with a definitive thump, which seemed to reverberate around the flat for about five minutes afterwards. I had no idea if the Two Charlies had come in while I was with Dina, or if they had heard anything. And then I realized, quite quickly, that I didn't actually care if they had.

Christmas started as early in Portugal as it did in Ireland, by mid-November there were the beginnings of window displays featuring the red suit and white beard of Pai Natal, and by early December everything was Natal-this and Natal-that. There were also elves and stars, cribs and tinsel and – bizarrely, as they are never seen in Lisbon in real life – snowmen. Just like everywhere else it was all in the service of shifting as much product as possible, supporting the glorious enterprise of commerce.

In the particular enterprise of The London School, each individual branch had its own Christmas party. Ours was scheduled for the fifteenth, a good four days before the school closed for the holidays. Elizabeth, our director, took charge of the party planning herself, something Sebastian grumbled about, as she used this excuse to palm off on her Senior Teacher mid-year reports that she herself was supposed to do. In the end it turned out that the extent of Elizabeth's party planning was a phone call to a restaurant down in Campo

Pequeno, one metro stop away, where we were all going to go to have dinner. Because of his extra work, Sebastian missed one whole valuable weekend of drinking, socialising and being charming. He was not pleased.

All the academic staff, plus Mafalda and Paula, our two secretaries, attended the party. The restaurant was called O Mar, and provided us with dish after dish of succulent seafood. I had thought that A Lua's food was good, but this was of a different order altogether. Naturally, as the tab was being picked up by our employers we ordered bottle after bottle of red and white, as well as aperatifs, brandy and port. No-one was sober when the dinner finally ended. After the meal it was Carol who suggested that we go to the Brazilian bar. The eleven of us piled into two taxis, I was in the back seat of the final one next to Fabian and Laura as they seemed to be attempting to eat each other, starting from the mouth area. Fabian had somehow found out about the contest he had been unwittingly involved in back in October during his party, and hadn't spoken to Laura since, but our boozy Christmas dinner seemed to have solved that. I had to tap Laura on the shoulder when we finally got to our destination, she had Fabian backed up against the door and was almost lying on top of him. I paid the grinning driver and the other two stumbled out onto the cobbles and into Bar Brasilia.

The place was around the corner from Portas do Sol, where I had had my triumphant game of five-a-side, and only ten minutes walk from my place in Graça. It was on the cobbled path to the castle. There was no sign outside, it seemed like just another building, except for the strong, rhymic bass sounds coming from within. We clomped up the stairs and found our workmates dancing and drinking in what looked basically like someone's apartment.

Most of the furniture had been taken out, and the floorboards were largely bare, except for a few cheap, multi-coloured rugs. It had the layout of many of these old-fashioned Lisbon flats, a larger living-room at the front, a long corridor with rooms, all of them windowless, coming off it, leading to a kitchen/dining area at the back. There were armchairs dotted here and there, and an improvised bar in one of the rooms, but that was it as far as furnishings was concerned, except for a few beanbags in various corners, on which people of all the colours of humanity were sprawled.

A band played in the front room, rhythmic, driving Afro-Brazilian music that was almost impossible to sit still to. They had a bass, hand-drums, bongos, a guitar, the sound emerged from some portable speakers that were simply plugged into a socket in the wall. The singer, who also played guiter, was a small man, very black, with dreadlocks that looked like thin snakes, and a loud voice that needed no amplification. Eight or nine people danced there on the bare floorboards, among them Sebastian, Joanne, Mafalda and – letting it all hang out – our overdressed boss Elizabeth.

Laura dragged me off to find the bar. For someone so small she had an amazing capacity for alcohol. A grinning white guy in a Brazil football top was standing at a long table in the second room down from the corridor, mixing, serving and taking the money for one basic type of drink, a green, cloudy liquid poured into plastic glasses.

"Caipirinha!" the barman said, when Fabian asked him what it was. He explained, a little like Mario, half in English, half in Portuguese, that the drink contained sugar, lime juice and cachaça, a Brazilian spirit. We got two each, downed the first and took the second with us back to the dancing area.

And that was pretty much the last thing that I remember. I have had hazy nights before, usually connected to consumption of spirits, but never a complete blackout where I was conscious but totally unable to recall anything that happened. Cachaça seemed to have some magic memory stealing property that not even Poteen had inflicted on me in the past.

I woke the next morning about ten, felt as if I were paralysed, slept again, dreamed, woke, slept and finally came back to consciousness sometime around lunchtime. I peeled myself from bed and staggered to the kitchen, made some coffee and had a slice of toast with banana, letting the mushy fruit dissolve slowly in my mouth.

Charles and Charlotte were out again, they had gone from one extreme to the other, now they left the house at every opportunity after months of almost monk-like behaviour. I almost missed them at that moment, or at least I missed having someone to talk to to help me recall the events of the night before, after we had reached Bar Brasilia.

As I sat in our silent echoing kitchen, images and scrambled impressions of the previous night returned to me gradually, but it was all so fleeting, so tenuous and surreal that I couldn't be sure whether I had dreamt them or whether what I remembered had actually happened.

I rang Laura.

"Hello Cian," she said, a smile in her voice, "how are you this morning?"

"How do you think? You?"

"Oh fine, bit of a dodgy stomach, but OK." I should have known this, Laura drank large quantities but didn't really get hangovers.

"I have a few questions about last night."

"Oh yeah?"

"Yes, it's a bit of a blur. I have a memory of Sally and Joanne, did they, like, kiss? I can picture them snogging while the band played Girl from Ipanema."

There was a snort of laughter from the other end.

"This is just one of your sick fantasies, Cian. I'm really learning a lot about you from this. That did not happen, though I imagine that Joanne could have some Sapphic tendencies."

"Though maybe I can help jog your memory," Laura went on, "why don't you tell me more about Dina. And maybe about this girl Maura too."

The Irish name sounded strange in Laura's estuary accent, more like 'Mora'.

"Oh shit," I said, "was that you? We were sitting outside, on someone's doorstep, you bummed a cigarette from me and we could hear the music coming from upstairs in the bar."

"Yeah, it was an interesting conversation, very revealing."

"What did I say, exactly?"

I hadn't told anyone else except Dina the story of me and Maura.

"You didn't say much about this Dina woman, other than that you thought she might be too old for you," Laura said, "most of it was about Maura, though I couldn't follow a lot of what you were saying. You kind of rambled."

"Jesus, I must have been wasted."

"No shit."

I didn't know what else to say. The image of me sitting on a doorstep, hunched into the small space beside Laura as we shared a cigarette, had now returned vividly. Though I still couldn't remember what I had said.

"Cian? You still there?" Laura asked, on the other end of the phone.

"Yeah, just thinking. One other thing, do you remember Patricia Coelho being there?"

"Who the fuck is Patricia.... whatever her name is?"

"She's a student in my First Cert class, Tuesdays and Thursdays. Small, pretty, big mop of curly hair. I seem to remember chatting to her outside the bar, though I may have dreamt that too."

"I have enough trouble remembering my own students," Laura said, "how do you expect me to know yours?"

"But you didn't see me talking to any teenage girls outside on the street?" I asked her.

"Oh man, really? Teenage girls? I really hope that that was a dream."

"Yeah, it probably was."

"Which is almost as bad. It means that you're dreaming about one of your female teenage students."

"Where are you now?" I asked her, happy to change the subject. I heard a voice in the background, male, possibly French.

"Oh, you know. In Fabian's."

"I thought you sounded smug. All is forgiven then?"

"Of course. I can be very convincing."

"I bet."

Laura hung up, I got dressed and took a tram down to Portas do Sol. The 28 was almost empty, unusually. I took the cobbled street that led to the castle and stopped outside the building that, the night before, had housed the Brazilian club. There was still no sign, it was up there on the first floor, windows shuttered, looking for all the world like any other apartment. I wondered briefly if I hadn't dreamt the club into existence too. I strolled around the little square in front, there was a bench there with two drooping trees on either side, and an occasional out-of-season tourist in hiking boots and windcheater taking the steep path up to the castle. The scene was incredibly sedate, there was a weak December sun squeezing out some rays over the tops of the buildings, some stray leaves blowing around, no people there. I sat on the bench, the almost bare branches of the trees moving slightly to and fro above me.

My memory, whether it was dreamt or not, was of sitting on this same bench the previous night, with Patricia Coelho on my left. I had given her a cigarette, she had never tried one before and she coughed and gagged as she tried to inhale. She said that she lived near there and pointed up the road towards the castle to indicate where her house was. She had a green, chunky padded jacket on, suitable for the winter but not very stylish for a fifteen year old, though typical of what Patricia would wear. At one point I tried to get her to drink some caipirinha, which she took one sip of and spat it out on to the cobbles. Then her friends came to drag her away, she gave me two kisses, one on each cheek, and disappeared.

It was a simple scene, there was nothing surreal or dreamlike about it, yet I couldn't be sure if it had really happened. I still felt somewhere between drunk and hungover, the flashing images of the night before - whether remembered or dreamt - still hadn't realigned themselves. I took a taxi the two minute drive back to Graça, paid the driver the one euro fifty and went back to bed for the afternoon. I dreamt about dreaming, about dreadlocks and benches, doorsteps, sea-monsters and whole roast pigs that were delivered on silver salvers and who suddenly came back to life, oinking loudly.

✳ ✳ ✳ ✳ ✳ ✳ ✳

Three days later I was on a plane to Dublin. It was seven a.m. flight and I hadn't had much sleep. Dina had stayed the night before and had gotten up with me at ten past four to help me finish packing, and then returned to her own house to be there when Rui woke up.

She had texted me that evening, wondering if she could come over. It was the third booty call - or booty text - that I had received since our first night together. The pattern was the same with each, usually around eight or nine my phone would shudder and beep, as if in anticipation, as if it knew who the message was from, and I would read Dina's few words - "Rui in bed, u free?". Normally I left at least fifteen minutes before replying that I was, though I wanted to text back straight away. Within an hour I would be touching her taut skin and licking her smooth neck in my narrow, narrow bed.

The night before my departure for home she had caught me mid-packing, which I abandoned when she arrived. We slept a cramped, intimate, fitful four hours before the alarm went off and dug me out of my semi-slumber. Dina was already awake.

I tried, but I couldn't really sleep on the flight. I was in a middle seat, with two dozing passengers on either side. There wasn't much room and I was preoccupied with the fact that Ireland was waiting on the other end of the journey. I had managed my escape, and now I was going back.

Dublin airport was in the first stages of bedlam when I arrived. At the baggage reclaim alone there were hoards of travellers, some already drunk, others with tinsel in the hair, offering kisses under the mistletoe. Baggage trolleys were full with presents, gaudily wrapped, piled high. The Arrivals area, basically an unadorned cavern, was a carnival of signs and balloons, screams and crying and embracing, with a Santa Claus or two wandering around. The diaspora had come back, with kids with London, Sydney, New York accents, dollars, pounds in their pockets. And then I realised, as I watched grandparents meeting grandchildren for the first time, that I was officially one of them now, an emigrant, one who had left.

The city was frosty, with white edging roads, buildings and bridges. Pedestrians breathed out mist. It seemed like darkness was closing in, though it was still mid-morning when I caught the coach to Heuston Station. It really felt like Christmas, there was a giddiness in the air, an atmosphere that is only experienced at one other time of the year in Ireland, namely on those out-of-the-blue sunny days in April and May when the place is transformed and people forget the claustrophobic, stubborn country that they really live in. There is a licence about Christmas time, a sense, maybe not that *anything* could happen, but that if it did it wouldn't be too surprising.

I was hoping for a seat on my own on the train, but on December twenty-first there was no chance of that. I had to settle for sitting beside an elderly man from Ennis who smelled a little of damp and porridge and old age. He wore a worn suit and flat cap, and insisted on asking me about my 'people' and telling me about his - he had been up in Dublin for a few days staying with his nephew and the nephew's wife, who had been "awful nice" to him. Eventually I faked exhaustion so I could close my eyes, and then realised that I didn't have to fake, and fell into a staccato sleep.

I was awoken by loud voices, screeching. I thought someone was being harmed in some way, but it was just a bunch of teenagers in the seats ahead, tickling each other. By the time we had passed Limerick Junction, fifteen minutes from the city itself, the full force of the country I had returned to had hit me hard. It may sound idiotic, but I had forgotten just how *Irish* Ireland was. After sixteen weeks away from all I had known, the various aspects of Irishness, all at once, was a lot to take. The accents, the bad skin, the quick courtesy, the determined superficiality, the horror of being considered impolite, the softness of the facial features, the apparent lack of guile. *Is this what we are?* I thought. *Were we always like this and I hadn't noticed?* I hadn't been confronted by my nationality before in this way, and suddenly being surrounded by the kind of mass of Paddies I had been separated from since September was eye-opening.

My mother was at the station when I walked down the platform. The place was simultaneously warmed by the heat from the idling engines of the trains and chilled by the winter wind funnelled straight down the tracks. We hugged, and she held on a long time, longer than I would have. I glanced at her as we walked to the car, she looked to have aged in the three months that I had been missing. Her red hair was thinner, the lines at her eyes deeper. She was frailer. The car was the same, though, her 1999 Toyota Starlet, a little battered on the outside, pristine and clean-smelling on the inside.

"You look tired, Cian," she said, predictably, "have you been sleeping well?"

I assured her that I had been sleeping, that I was fine. I could already feel the old irritation growing, the itching to be away, though I had just arrived.

"Your father is looking forward to seeing you."

I doubted that this was true, though it could just as easily have been. You could never tell, my father lived in his own benign little semi-detached world, a kind, bland word for everyone, though nothing of any import. We pulled out and headed for the roundabout that led to the Dublin road.

"You look good though," my mother said, almost despite herself, "some colour in your face."

I nodded, though she couldn't have seen my reaction as her eyes were now glued to the road. She rarely even liked to talk while driving, she found it so stressful.

It was dark when we turned off the Dublin road and on to the poorly lit way to the village of Ballyhayes, the place where I had grown up, where my parents had grown up. It is usually described as "picturesque", and I suppose it is, though it is difficult to recognise beauty in somewhere that is so familiar. Ballyhayes hadn't changed, as I somehow had expected it to, even though I had only been gone three and a half months. The same stone bridge brought us into the village proper, the same Centra store stood on the main street, the church still loomed there at the end of this street, the dark grey stone the colour of purgatory. We passed many people I recognised, and buildings that were as familiar to me as my own face. We moved around to the part of Ballyhayes that is usually called 'the back', and pulled into my parents' driveway, a driveway just like the one next to it, and the one next to that, in a row of ten identically shaped houses.

My father too looked as if the passing of time was lessening him somewhat, his features were a little more pinched, as if age were slowly sucking at him from the inside. At dinner he asked me about Portugal, stuff you'd get asked in Geography class, its people, population, the big cities, the main industries, the state of its democracy. I had known that this gentle but insistent interrogation was coming, of course, this was the way my father approached the world, with facts, quantifiable measurements, information that could be put in boxes and confirmed. This was how he communicated with me, with everyone. "That Ray O'Dwyer knows what's what," people said about him, "nothing gets past him." He was a retired primary school teacher, had taught half the village at one time or another. He was liked and respected in Ballyhayes the way anyone who has lived there long enough was liked and respected, provided they weren't a total bollocks.

For answers to his questions, Dina's lectures came in handy. I told my father about the peaceful revolution in 1974, the carnations in the rifles, the secret police before that who had arrested people at will. Most of the rest I made up or guessed at, it would have been inconceivable to him that someone could live in a country for three months and not know - like I didn't know - the exact population, the makeup of the political opposition or the main agricultural crop. It reassured him to see that my time in Portugal wasn't a total waste, and I knew that he didn't have the internet at home, so it would take him a while to check my answers.

My old room had been tidied and there were new sheets on the bed. It felt cavernous compared to my cell in Graça, though it was only about twice the size. My mother had kept my old schoolbooks on the shelf there, and medals I had won for hurling when I was fifteen, as well as my X-men comics she had resurrected from somewhere and laid out, as if to welcome me back. I flicked through a few, and got lost in the story quickly. The narratives all seemed new to me, as if I had never read the comics before, though I knew that I had pored over their inky, coloured pages between the ages of thirteen and sixteen, following Wolverine and Rogue, Storm and Cyclops, imagining myself with powers, saving the various girls of the village I had crushes on from the clutches of some über-villain from Limerick City.

The next few days I borrowed my mother's car and drove the eight miles into the city. Ballyhayes, in its understated way, was prepared for Christmas. The bunting was up, the crib was in the entryway of the church, the main street lit with green and red and yellow fairy lights. Limerick City was of a whole different scale, the window displays in shops lavish with reds and whites and fake snow, the lights draped across the top of O'Connell Street arranged into complex shapes, reindeers and sleds, snowmen and stars. The level of shopping too was at a higher level, hordes of people - still in the midst of the boom, not yet facing up to the imminent collapse - assaulted the stores, stripping them bare of produce, like vultures at an antelope corpse. I saw people with wodges of cash, two and three and four credit cards, arms full of carrier bags from five or six different retail outlets, as if the coming deadline of Christmas signified the end of shopping as we knew it. It made the Lisbon retail experience look tame in comparison.

I had gone to secondary school there in the city, so bumped into people I knew from time to time.

"Oh really?" was the reaction I got from a girl I used to know when I told her I was in Lisbon, "lucky you, out there in Spain, with the sun."

I didn't bother correcting her, we were never really that friendly anyway. And her protestations of jealousy were false, too, I knew, just as the expressions of approval and admiration were from everyone I met. "Portugal!" they invariably said, "lucky you!" Yet they were all making too much money, or at least pretending to, at that time before the crash. Everyone I met was too engaged with the busy push to get rich to be really envious of some loser who had had to emigrate to get a job, as if it were the nineteen-eighties. "Lucky you!" they said, when what they really meant was "You poor sap, couldn't cut it here, had to leave."

I knew the subtext and didn't care. In O'Mahony's bookshop on O'Connell Street I bought my father a history of Fianna Fail and my mother a Darina Allen cookbook. It felt strange, they were the first presents I had ever bought for them independently of my sister Catriona, who was eleven years older than me. Usually Catriona did the shopping and I gave her some money towards the gifts, if I remembered, if I got around to it. It gave me some strange pleasure to do the legwork myself this year, like something an adult would do.

While in O'Mahony's I spotted a guidebook to Lisbon I hadn't seen before. It had just started to sleet outside so I stood there, flicking through the glossy pages, waiting for the weather to improve. The monuments, buildings and bairros of Lisbon looked sanitised in the shiny photos, much newer and more exotic than I remembered. Still, I carried it to the cash register along with the books for my parents, and when the woman there asked if I wanted them wrapped, I said that I did, even the guidebook. I liked the idea of having something else to open on Christmas day, even if I knew what it was, even if it was only from me, to me.

It was the twenty-sixth before I entered a licensed premises of any kind. The twenty-fifth had passed off peacefully enough, in the typical stupor of a country Christmas. We went to mass - which I did to please my mother, though I sneaked a listen to my iPod during the sermon - visited neighbours and called my sister Catriona in Cork where she was spending the holidays with her in-laws. I tried, in vain, to squeeze some conversation out of my two year old nephew, Sean, as my mother mumbled baby-talk down the line, getting more of a reaction than I did. The three of us had turkey and ham, Brussels sprouts and mince pies, my father fell asleep in front of the television and my mother got semi-drunk on two glasses of sherry and dropped plates and glasses while insisting on helping me clean up the kitchen. It was a pattern that was followed, with subtle variations, in thousands of households across the country, year after year after year. By nine o'clock I felt claustrophobic, trapped, and so took a bottle of wine to my bedroom, briefly considered ringing Dina, decided against it and then drank and smoked myself to sleep after counting the days - and then calculating the hours - I had left until my flight back to Lisbon.

On Stephen's Day I met some guys from my alma mater, CBS

Limerick, in Cissie Mack's in the city. It was four o'clock when we began drinking and, with comings and goings, we had a constant presence in the pub until closing at half past twelve. Again I found it briefly strange to be surrounded by so much Irishness, and by so many people who hadn't escaped from anything, who had stayed put and tried to work with what they had, in the country of their birth.

The others were now accountants, surveyors, microbiologists, plumbers, Guards. There was even another teacher there, a tall, intense guy called Martin Duffy, though what he did bore no relation to my day to day experience. He was in an inner city Dublin school trying to get kids with names like Decco and Charlene, Spudster and Jayo, interested in Shakespeare and Seamus Heaney. For all my twice-weekly contact with Patricia Coelho and her group of teenagers, after a brief conversation together Martin and I agreed that we did very different jobs.

Still, it might have been the effects of seven pints of Guinness, or the ill-defined Christmas spirit, or perhaps just the passing of time, but I temporarily found this rag-tag collection of my contemporaries much less odious than I had ten years before when we were enclosed in our blue uniforms, trying to survive in the echoing corridors of the CBS. Had we all become more open, less bitter, had we all *grown*? I wasn't sure that I had, necessarily, though I supposed it was possible.

I went into the beer garden for a cigarette, the smoke I exhaled mixing with my breath, now become visible in the two degree weather. Manus Sheehan joined me, in our group we were the only two smokers.

"So, O'Dwyer," he said, maintaining the tradition carried over from school of only using surnames, as if calling someone by their Christian name would display far too much intimacy, "you're from Ballyhayes, aren't you?"

"I am".

"Myself and my wife have just bought a property there," Sheehan said, "it's quiet there, like the nineteen fifties."

No-one bought houses anymore, they all bought 'properties'. It seemed extraordinary to me that this guy - short and ginger and not especially smart, who had only survived secondary school on his wits and his unbreakable good humour - had managed to buy a 'property' at twenty-eight, and also had an actual wife. I think he too found it remarkable that a woman had decided to commit to him for the rest of her life, judging by the number of times he used the words "my wife". It was as if he were trying to reassure himself that she was real.

"Yeah," I said, in response to his comment about Ballyhayes, and resisting the urge to defend my village from the idea that it was stuck in the past, "there was a burglary there last year, the first one this decade. It's all anyone has talked about since."

Manus sniggered. He was a city boy, like most of the others.

"I like it though," he said, "it's good to get away from it all out there."

You'd think that he worked in the City of London, or on Wall Street the way he talked, and not in his father's garage in Dooradoyle.

"It is quiet, alright," I said, agreeably.

"We're having a party on the thirty-first," Sheehan went on, "me and my wife. It's kind of a house-warming stroke New Year's thing, we just moved in last month and haven't had anyone around yet. My wife's friends are coming, loads of single girls, with enough Champagne even you wasters could pull them. I was going to ask the others, you'll come too, I hope. Sure it'll be just around the corner for you."

I could see that Manus was desperate to show off his new pad, and his wife.

"Thanks for the offer," I said, "but I'll probably not be around at New Year."

Sheehan gave me his address anyway. By one o'clock, when the barstaff were trying to evict us from the pub, guys had come and gone, partners, wives and girlfriends had arrived, then left, a core group of six of us had spent the whole day drinking together, and had made the solemn promise to meet there every December twenty-sixth until we all had kids, or until one of us died, whichever came first. I stumbled to the taxi rank at half past one, semi froze while waiting, and finally got back to Ballyhayes at two o'clock, strangely warmed by the bonds of male solidarity.

What I had told Manus Sheehan was true, I had planned to spend New Year in Dublin and fly out on the second. Yet the friends I rang there were all either spending the thirty-first with partners or immediate family or had left to see in 2008 on some Australian beach or other, stealing a march by ten hours on the rest of us. I was left stranded. The week ticked by, only relieved by the arrival of my elder sister Catriona and her son Sean, who quickly took over the house and everyone in it.

"What's wrong," Catriona asked me one morning, when I complained that the kid had eaten the last of the Weetabix, "you can't deal with not being the centre of all attention anymore, little princeling."

This was a common theme of hers, how I was treated as the golden child, spoiled and cosseted, and how she, by coming first, had made things easy for me. Although it was partly true, this routine got a bit old after a while, and I was relieved when she and my nephew left again for Cork city, the day before New Year's Eve.

The thirty-first came. I was going to stay in and go to bed before twelve, there was no danger of being woken by fireworks, out here in the wilds of County Limerick. Yet my mother had decided that we, as a family, were going to ring in the new year together, watching the RTE show that they called, with some optimism, The New Year Extravaganza. Going to bed early on New Year I could take, having to be there with my retired parents as 2007 turned into 2008 I couldn't. At eleven o'clock I faked a phone call, told my father and mother that it was from a school friend that was having a party - as if it had just come up - and left our house at half past, after shaking my father by the hand and kissing my mother on the cheek.

Manus Sheehan's house was in one of those developments that had sprung up like toadstools all over Ireland in the last decade. The estate had been built further behind 'the back' of the village where my parents had their house, forming a new 'back' of Ballyhayes. It was literally four minutes walk away. The sky was clear, a frost was setting in, the few cars parked in the various driveways were already sheathed in a brittle white layer. I slipped at one stage, black ice forming already on the ground, and just managed not to break the bottle of Portuguese Dão that I had originally brought back from Portugal for my mother, who, I soon remembered, didn't really drink. The wine would have still been there, unopened, if I had returned the following Christmas, so I liberated it and took it with me to Sheehan's as an offering.

Manus's property was number eleven, a bland, three-bedroom rectangle identical to all the other houses in the development. A small blond woman answered the door after I had been standing there ringing the bell for five minutes, the tip of my nose now semi-numb. I explained who I was, and she smiled, shook my hand and said her own name. I didn't catch this, the sound of music and voices in the background was loud now, though I assumed that standing before me was the almost mythical Mrs Sheehan. She did exist after all.

More than just existing, she was, in fact, undeniably attractive, shorter even than her husband, small enough that you could imagine picking her up and putting her in your pocket. She had small eyes, a button nose, neat child's teeth, and also, I noticed, prominent ears that stuck out a little from the side of her head, giving her the look of a pixie or elf. She motioned for me to come in. I followed, still clutching the bottle of wine I suspected that no-one would drink.

When Sheehan's blond wife opened the door to the kitchen the sound of party assaulted us, that mixture of too-loud music, raised voices, screeches, the thud and shuffle of feet dancing, intermittent cheers, glasses clinking. The gathering was spread over the living-room and the adjoining kitchen, fifty or sixty people squashed together, jostling, moving in time to Beyoncé on the stereo, downing shots, spilling beer, shouting, flirting. I spied some of our classmates that had been in Cissie Mack's on the twenty-sixth, Philip Casey was there, lanky and awkward, Senan O'Connell and Phantom Hayes were chugging beers in the corner, Billy Reddan was trying his luck with a couple of girls by the cooker.

Manus, the man of the house, spotted me, came over and half-wrapped his arms around my torso, as if not sure he was drunk enough yet to be hugging other men but willing to give it a go.

"O'Dwyer, ya fucker," he said, as he grabbed a bottle of Miller and popped the metal cap off using the edge of his own kitchen table, "I knew you'd come."

Sheehan's ears and neck were red - from drink or heat I wasn't sure. He placed the beer bottle into my hand as if handing off a relay baton.

"Drink," he said, "you have to catch up."

I did as I was told.

"C'mon O'Dwyer," Sheehan said, his arm again half-draped around my shoulder, "I'll introduce you to the gang. We've only got twenty minutes til midnight, you better hurry up and find someone you want to kiss."

For the next five or six minutes I had names and faces thrown at me, none of which really registered. I shook hands, kissed cheeks, nodded, said my name twenty, thirty times until it sounded strange and meaningless in my mouth. Sheehan seemed to either be showing me off, or - more likely - showing off to me how many people he knew, how many people he could attract to his house on New Year's Eve. I was easily the soberest person there, and not at all prepared for the hysteria that had been building for the last three hours, as if midnight on the thirty-first would actually *change* anything, as if something profoundly different would come with the dawning of the new year. *It's just another day*, I felt like saying, *you'll all wake up tomorrow, you'll still be you.*

Sheehan handed me two shot glasses, with a dark red liquid in them. I threw the contents down my throat, without asking what it was. The alcohol burned a little, not unpleasantly, and tasted a bit like cough syrup. At this stage we had reached the far end of the room, the furthest extremity of the party. There was a knot of perfumed femininity there, four or five girls all drinking alcopops, laughing loudly, admiring each other's jewellery, pointing at someone at the other end of the room. I wasn't paying much attention, by now I had been introduced to every other guest at the party and had no more space left in my short term memory.

"Girls, girls," Sheehan said, his arm still on my shoulder, "ye're looking fine tonight, so ye are."

He had a loud, resonating voice for such a short man, and all the women turned to look at him. One of them was the blond girl who had opened the front door for me. She smiled and sidled up to Manus, sliding her arm through his, the only person in the room who had to tilt her head upwards to look him in the eye. In the restricted lighting of the party she looked even more elfen than before, her eyes mischievous and darting, her hair a pure, eery blond, as if she had stopped off in our world only briefly before returning to her own supernatural realm.

"Have you met my other half, O'Dwyer?" Sheehan asked me, "isn't she gorgeous?"

"Absolutely," I said, at that moment meaning it, "but I didn't catch your name on the way in."

"San-dra," she mouthed, as if I were slow, "and these are, let's see, Gráinne, Michelle, Penney and......that's Maura there with her back to us."

Looking back on that moment now, I feel a certain pride that I didn't react. I was poker-face personified. I didn't blush, I didn't go slack-jawed, I didn't cough in surprise or shock, I didn't utter out loud the words I was thinking - which were a mangled mixture of inarticulate curses - and I didn't turn and flee. I think that I eventually managed to smile benignly, as I imagined a visiting ambassador would in a foreign court, and kept my mouth shut.

The girl called Maura turned to look. It was her alright, definitely her, not some other, random Maura who had turned up to the party, but my Maura, the dark-featured, full-haired Maura I had shared a house with for six months, the small-of-stature, full-figured Maura I had slept with two or three times a week for three of those months. It was the same Maura that had told me, six months before, that she didn't want me anywhere near her ever again, she didn't want me to phone her, see her, write to her, email her. It was the same Maura that wanted to forget that I existed, that I had ever been born, who had said that, if she could, she would wipe clean every trace of me off the earth.

She too managed not to react. Nobody in the room knew about our shared history. We both gave an impression of total indifference, as if we really were the complete strangers we were pretending to be. Maura looked almost the same, there was a bit more roundness to her face, she had let her hair grow out, it was now past her shoulders, but it was still so recognisably her I thought I could even make out the Chanel perfume she always used to wear from the tangle of scents in the air there at the far extent of the party. We had woken up together on thirty, forty occasions, seen each other showering, I had watched her as she put on makeup, she had cut my hair at least twice, and now we stood there, frozen, feigning ignorance of one another, as if I was just some guy, as if she were just another dolled-up girl.

"We were talking about New Year resolutions," one of the women - not Sandra - said. Sandra's friends formed a mass of pastel shades, earrings, potent perfume, styled hair. They were - to me in my dazed state - indistinguishable in their common femininity, their vague drunkenness.

"Yeah, my resolution," began Penney, or Gráinne or Michelle, "is that I'm going to turn Mark from Westlife straight. I reckon I'm the woman for the job."

There was a collective cackle, and then the predictable jibes and protestations. The girl to her left - Michelle or Penney or Gráinne - was next.

"I'm going to learn to ice-skate," she said.

"Ice-skate?" her friend to her left said, "I tried to teach you to ride a bike last year, you kept falling off."

I tried to keep my attention on what they were saying, as if the conversation was fascinating to me. It kept descending into hilarity, mockery, faux-bickering. Eventually the girl on the end, the one whose hair was dyed russet, the one that was called Gráinne or Penney or

Michelle, put her hand out and touched Maura on the forearm.

"How about you, Maura?" she asked. I had to look at Maura now, as I had been pretending to follow the conversation.

"Oh," Maura began, glancing briefly at me before looking back to her questioner, "my resolution is to find one man in this country who isn't a complete prick."

Predictably this brought the house down. Sheehan pretended to be offended on behalf of his whole gender, and two of the women clapped, emitting a combined cackle and cheer that could be heard, I figured, in every part of the semi-D.

I watched Maura as carefully as I could while not being too obvious. She was as deadpan and controlled as she had been in my flat in Thomas Street, six months earlier, when she had informed me that I was persona non grata. She had this knack of suppressing upset and pain, discomfort or annoyance, and showing her best face to the world. Though the emotions always came out eventually.

It was now three minutes to midnight. Someone, at the other end of the room, began a countdown, from one hundred and eighty, but got down to one hundred and sixty four and lost count. While Manus was talking to his wife and her friends, and the excitement built around us, I slipped away, weaving through the warm bodies squashed into the small space and finding the door to the hall. The stairs were carpeted, I was able to walk up without noise, the upstairs was dark and deserted and quiet, the complete opposite to the bedlam below. I checked the time on my mobile, eleven fifty-eight and ten seconds, eleven, twelve.... I resolved to stay up there until well after all the hysterical joy at the coming of a new day had subsided.

Someone had pissed on the toilet seat. I wiped it off and sat down, with the door open and the light off. There was moonlight coming in the upstairs window, it showed that all the doors to the rooms on the first floor were open. I had no desire to go nosing around at that stage, I found that I had no curiosity about Manus Sheehan and his wife's lives, they seemed so removed from mine, so settled. It was impossible to imagine that I would find anything revelatory tucked away in a drawer somewhere, anything that would demonstrate deviation from the suburban norm.

As I sat there, trying not to think, the babble from downstairs increased, as if excitement was diffusing through the room like a gas. I checked the time - eleven fifty eight and forty seconds, forty-one, forty-two. A door opened below and closed again. Someone started climbing the stairs, almost noiselessly, though very deliberately, as if concentrating on not tripping. It was a strange time to be leaving the party. I hadn't turned on any lights, so when the figure emerged at the top of the stairs it was silhouetted only in the milky light of the moon coming in through the curtain-less landing window.

"Are you hiding from me, Cian?"

I knew the voice, of course, I had know it was Maura since the minute the door had opened downstairs. I couldn't see her face but the outline was all her, the solid halo of hair, her small stature, her full, squat torso, the way she stood, with her right hand gripping her left forearm, as if in protection.

"Just taking a break from the mayhem," I replied, from my position on the closed toilet seat. I felt at a disadvantage, looking up at her.

"Strange time to take a break," she said.

"I could say the same about you."

"I wanted to talk to you," she said.

"Really?" I was genuinely surprised. "I seem to remember that you never wanted to speak to me again."

"That was before. Things change."

This didn't sound like the Maura I had known. She paused then, as if listening to the growing murmur from downstairs.

"Things change, Cian," she said, again, "you learn to rethink things, to forgive."

I nodded.

"You didn't sound very forgiving downstairs. And don't forget that there was two of us in it," I told her then, unwilling to assume the role of bad guy, "remember what you did too."

"TEN......NINE......EIGHT.....SEVEN.." came the shouts from downstairs.

Maura just looked at me, perched there on the toilet.

" SIX.....FIVE.....FOUR......"

"We should talk," she said, simply.

"THREE......TWO.....ONE......HAPPY NEW YEAR!"

There was an explosion of noise from below, cheers, party horns, someone - inexplicably - yodelling, the sound of a glass being dropped, shattering. I sat, still on the toilet, looking up at Maura. The door to the living-room opened downstairs and released a blast of noise, a wave of sound like something solid that polluted our previous quiet. Bladders that had been stoppered, held in anticipation of the turning of a new year, were now ready to be released. There was a rush for the stairs and the house's one bathroom.

"We better move," Maura said, "they're coming up here."

She held out her hand to me. I took it, and stood up.

JANUARY

In March of 2007 Maura and I were - I think the appropriate word is - happy. Of course I didn't know this at the time, you never do, and the happiness was illusory anyway, or at least temporary. But that was what we were, for a short period.

We had tried to normalise things between us briefly, going out on our one date, but this very quickly showed us that ours was not a 'normal' relationship, whatever that was. Eventually, by March of 2007, we had accepted what we had, which was: independent lives, with our own jobs, friends, interests, frustrations and pleasures, and then a compartment separate to all this that we both inhabited, where we were a kind of couple. It was almost as if, within the walls of 22 Templewoods, Rathfarnham, there existed some kind of force-field that held the world out and allowed Maura and me to create our own little untainted space, where the future, the past and the rest of existence had ceased to be.

We stopped talking about 'us', that is, if we had ever really started. There was no mention of where we were going with all this, if we were now girlfriend and boyfriend, if we could see other people. When Maura and I were together we existed in a kind of eternal present, which lasted until one of us left the confines of our house, when the boundaries would collapse and our space would become part of the rest of the planet. It was our own dirty little secret, except that there wasn't anything really dirty about it. The fact that it was a secret of sorts, though, was part of what made it work.

I don't know if Maura was thinking about the future, I suppose she must have been, despite never mentioning it. I repressed any thoughts of what was to come in favour of living in a sweet, transient present that seemed to offer me the best of both worlds. I had a life out in the messy civilisation of Dublin City, and then a holiday from the chaos, in my and Maura's sweet domestic idyll.

The truth though, was that I had fallen into something I had never experienced before. I can see that now, of course, but back then it never occurred to me to examine what was going on, or how it was effecting me. I squashed any idea I may have had of facing up to the reality that Maura had got under my skin and was now in most of my night-time dreams and waking thoughts. I suppose this, the infusion of Maura into every aspect of my consciousness, must have come from living together, from sharing that space so intimately and so frequently. The house soon came to seem like it was ours. Sheila was still spending most of her days with her beau, and so had left myself and Maura the run of our Rathfarnham residence. Each passing day made us more like the joint owners of that house, we talked together about what home improvements we would make if we didn't have a landlord, and even discussed investing in a set of garden table and chairs, imagined repainting the kitchen in pastel shades, with stronger, more primary colours for the living room. It was like we were playing house, dressing up in our parents' much-too-big clothes and imitating their strange adult ways. We played at being a grown-up couple, both of us forgetting that we were already fully grown adults, too old to be indulging in this kind of make-believe.

This was not a game, much as I fooled myself that it was. When she would go out for a night with her work buddies, I took to desperately ringing around my friends - and then vague acquaintances - for someone to drink with, just so I didn't have to imagine her out in the shark-infested Dublin scene without me. At least semi-drunk I could fool myself into believing that we were both enjoying some independent social activity. I had honed my powers of denial and self-delusion to this extent, and successfully managed not to admit to myself the truth. Which was, of course, that in the space of two months I had become incapable of imagining not having Maura in my life.

May, though, was coming closer. The room I inhabited wasn't mine, - even though it felt like I had been there for years - and Justine, the original inhabitant, was due back May tenth and had already emailed me to tell me she wanted her old room back. I thought about telling her that I was staying put, but I had signed a contract and I knew that Justine was returning from Oz with her boyfriend, Tadhg, the lawyer, in tow. I repressed this fact, though, and managed not to worry about where I was going to live. Five months later in Lisbon I would, inevitably, take the same approach.

In mid-April Maura's mother was diagnosed with breast cancer. Maura took two weeks off so the two of them could have some time together, they went down to Kenmare where they used to spend summer holidays. All Maura's nursing and daughterly skills were employed in taking her mother's mind off the coming treatment. The truth was, though, that mother and daughter had never really got on, Maura had little patience for the guilt complexes of the Irish mammy, and by day four of their stay in Kerry she was reduced to ringing me at midnight when her mother was in bed to let off steam.

"She's been waiting to have cancer all her life," Maura said about her mother, "it gives her an excuse now to be a complete pain in the ass."

This was all very different. A parent with cancer was very real, and couldn't simply be packed away as being part of the world outside, irrelevant to the comfy nest that we had formed inside our Rathfarnham house. I was now cast in the role of support-provider, which hadn't been in the original game-plan for whatever it was that Maura and I were doing. I tried my best to put on a caring, listening front, but it wasn't me. I had been playing a part - we both had - for months now, but this was one change that was too far outside the character I had been inhabiting for comfort. Cancer wasn't something you could just shut out and pretend was irrelevant to our cosy little arrangement.

By the second week that Maura was away she had stopped calling, and I found that denying to myself that I missed her was no longer possible. Sheila hardly spent any time in Rathfarnham at all at this stage, so I found myself alone most evenings. I took to wandering the house, which now seemed enormous and echo-ey, looking through the attic, where Justine's stuff was stored, reading some of her diaries - mostly tedious stuff about her resentment for one of her co-workers and complaints about her boyfriend's obsession with rugby - and cooking long, elaborate meals that only I was going to eat. Two days that first week I slept in Maura's bed, woke to the smell of her and showered using her shampoo and gel. When I finally went back to my own room I sprayed some perfume of hers on to my pillow, so my subconscious was fooled into believing that she was there beside me, even as I dreamed.

And then I found that I couldn't sleep at all in my own bed, and was only able to get some fitful hours of unconsciousness if I slipped into Maura's pastel coloured room. I sent her emails that she didn't respond to and texts that received hurried, badly spelled replies - "up to mi eys, Ma playing the martir" - and resisted calling her lest I reveal too much of the hole she had left by departing. She did ring me twice, and I her once, but our conversations were strained and made awkward by neither of us knowing the changed rules of this new stage of our game. I thought about going down to Kerry to find her, yet rejected the idea quickly, imagining being roped into looking after a bad-tempered middle-aged woman who I had never met. Instead I attempted to find extra work to do in the office in Avatar, and ended up going to see films I didn't want to see and drinking with people I didn't like, just so I didn't have to spend any more time than was necessary in my now Maura-less house.

Sheila showed up the following Wednesday accompanied by Philip. He was an estate-agent, Clongowes-educated, though not such a dick as most of them I had encountered from that school. I was glad to have other living, breathing people in the house. While Sheila showered we had a beer, and Philip mentioned that he had a friend, Simon, who was living in Kilmainham and who had a room free in his house. He was looking for someone to move in immediately, asked me if I knew of anyone. Like four months later in Lisbon, it seemed that the universe was providing me with somewhere to live.

I still had thirteen days left in the Rathfarnham house, but rang Simon anyway. It was true, he had a free room and wanted to fill it that weekend. Simon's French housemate, Rudi, wanted his friend, Monique, to move in, but Simon didn't want to be outnumbered in the house - "I don't want to be stuck with two frogs," was how he put it. His Parisian housemate was away in the West until Sunday, and Simon wanted to stage a coup, have a native installed there before Rudi returned. Present him with an Irish *fait accompli.*

Maura had been gone two weeks at that stage, and her presence had begun to fade from the house. I still itched a little when I was there, and felt uneasy and incomplete wandering around the silent, empty place. It felt like she had abandoned it and, by extension, me. *Two can play at that game,* I thought, as I planned my exit.

The process was very swift. I called to see Simon on Friday after work, the room was adequate, twice the size of the cell I would move into months later in Graça, though smaller than my Rathfarnham room. The house, too, was much more cramped than my residence in the south of the city, and lacked that feminine touch, but it was ten minutes walk from Dame Street, fifteen from Temple Bar, and reasonably close to where I worked. Philip had vouched for me, and so my nationality - as it would be months later, for the house in Graça - proved sufficient for Simon to invite me to stay.

By Saturday morning I had thrown my things together, piled them in a taxi and had left the Rathfarnham house, a good twelve days before the deadline that Justine had set. To pack I had had to sneak back into Maura's room, I had left pyjamas, toiletries, books, two pairs of jeans and my iPod in there, after having practically moved in while she was away. Trying not to spend too long among Maura's strewn possessions, I grabbed everything I could and squashed it into a suitcase and sat on it to make sure it would close. Soon after I was back in the city centre, and had left suburbia behind.

Maura returned to Rathfarnham on the Sunday. I didn't know this at the time, I didn't know she was coming, she hadn't phoned, she hadn't texted. Anyhow, with the urgency of moving and the housewarming drinks of Saturday night, I hadn't had time to work out how to tell her I had left. In fact, I had deliberately avoided thinking about it at all. *What did I have to explain?* I thought. We were only having fun, keeping each other company, giving each other pleasure. Why would she be upset? We could still carry on our little fling that was nothing more than a diversion for us both, what did it matter where I was living?

Maura, though, knew that our thing relied on the special circumstances of our cohabitation, the magic spell that being thrown together in that house had cast. Coming back that weekend she found my room empty, stripped bare, except for the dust under the bed that I hadn't had time to hoover up. Although of course it wasn't my room anymore, it was Justine's, my room was now four miles away, in the heart of Dublin City. To me this appeared to be inconsequential, a simple change of address. Maura realised that it was much more than that. It was a break, a tear of that delicate membrane that kept us both apart from the rest of the world and allowed us to create our own intimate little universe.

I finally rang her on Monday night. I left a message, explaining briefly what had happened, not knowing where exactly she was anyway. I asked her to return the call, which she didn't do. I rang again Tuesday. It took until Wednesday for Maura to finally answer the phone.

"You didn't hang around," was the first thing she said, "I leave Dublin for a couple of weeks and, whoosh, you're gone."

I explained the reason for my rapid exit, the necessity for speed, Simon's desire not to be left with his two frogs. Normally she would have enjoyed the story, but she wasn't in the mood for anecdotes.

"You know," she replied, "you haven't even asked about my mother." Her voice was a wall, blocking out apology, light-heartedness, entreaty.

I paused. This was new territory.

"Ok," I said, in truth without much feeling, "how is she?"

We were both out of our comfort zone here, our twosome had been based on in-jokes, sex and the fact that we inhabited the same building.

"You don't even really want to know," Maura half-shouted, "you leave, without saying anything, and then you...fucking....urrrrrr!"

There was a thud on the other end of the line, as if she had just thrown her phone, then the line went dead.

I did ring back every day, though, but none of my calls were answered. That week something changed. The fantasy that I had been living by for months became harder to sustain. It was soon impossible to continue with the myth that Maura was nothing more than a pleasant pastime. My dreams were filled with her, or a version of her, sometimes hurt and wronged, sometimes sweet and childlike, once or twice ready for vengeance. I was distracted in work, and twice at going home time I found myself standing at the bus-stop for the number 59 that would take me out to my old house in the suburbs, before I remembered, with a twinge of something close to loss, that I didn't live there anymore.

Saturday, I decided to go out to our old house, and talk to her face to face. I took the 59 to Rathfarnham, walked up to Templewoods in the spring warmth, foxgloves and crocuses flowering now, making the place seem like a rural retreat after coming from the city centre. The house, though, looked asleep, the blinds were down, the curtains drawn, there was no sign of life. I had left my key when I moved out, so I simply hung around like an inexpert stalker, sitting on the front step, circling the place and looking for an open window. Nothing happened, there was no way in, no-one came home. I left. I felt stupid for coming at all. I had given up phoning Maura at this stage, I had had my calls ignored for long enough and had got the message.

Without knowing it, and without intending to, I had broken the spell. I had moved out without telling her, without preparation. It was like the bends, diving to great depths and then coming straight up, with no gradations. The magic, whatever it was, that Maura and I had created and maintained over the space of three months had been scattered in the one short day that I spent moving out. She realised this, and resented me all the more because I didn't seem to.

And I went and made it worse. I'm not entirely proud of what I did, but neither do I think that it was the worst thing in the world. The night of the day I had spent hanging around my old Rathfarnham house I went out as usual, got semi-drunk, and arrived in the door of my new gaff in Kilmainham at two in the morning. There was a slight figure on the sofa, sitting in the semi-dark, lit only by the streetlight coming straight in the window. It was Monique, smoking and looking pensive.

Monique had been sleeping on our couch since Monday. She was Rudi's friend, the one he had wanted to move into what was now my room. There was an element of protest about her presence on our sofa, and there was no indication of when she was planning to leave. I came in that Saturday night, sat down beside her without a word, and took one of her cigarettes when she offered. She had been drinking Tia Maria and was a little drunk herself.

"On your own?" I asked her.

Monique looked at me with something close to pity.

"No, I have Gerard Depardieu and Colin Farrell in the kitchen, can't you see?"

I found her disdain amusing. She was slim, lithe, and arched her eyebrows when she spoke. She and I should have by rights been enemies, but her snarky Frenchness entertained me and she seemed to like me. Monique continued drinking from the bottle of Tia Maria, and gave me a glass. I sipped the sweet liquid, felt my drunkenness take on a new quality.

What happened, happened naturally, as if it were the only thing we could have done. We moved closer, left hands on knees, brushed thighs, gave each other those go-ahead looks, and then kissed, and fucked lazily there on top of her sleeping-bag. It was languorous, almost relaxing, there was little of the fire that came with being with Maura, and afterwards we lay in silence, smoked a cigarette each and fell asleep together, tangled up in Monique's green Highlander. I slept well that night for the first time since I had left Rathfarnham, it was a solid sleep, despite the cramped conditions. About seven o'clock I extricated myself from Monique's semi-embrace and made my way back to my room, the one I had snatched from her a week before.

As is the way of these things, news of our liaison spread. Monique told Rudi, who mentioned it in passing to Simon, who then passed it on to his friend Philip, who was of course Sheila's boyfriend. And Sheila, of course, was Maura's cousin. I only pieced this together later, though it wasn't actually difficult to work out if I had thought about it. Still, while engaged in an encounter with my new housemate, I didn't seriously consider the prospect of my old housemate finding out.

That's not to say that I didn't think of her at all. In fact, I had to stop myself saying her name out of habit when I was with Monique. Maura had never left my mind for the whole of the act, as if she was a presence there observing. Maura had been freezing me out for a week by then, and Monique was a kind of payback. *Take that, Maura*, I thought, as Monique slipped off her bra, as she undid my belt, *I can hurt you too.*

Yet the question was there, silent, latent, hovering over my brief few hours with the French girl. Was what I was doing there - in light of whatever it was that Maura and I had together - acceptable, advisable, was it right? A combination of a night of drinking, a pretty, sweet-smelling French girl on our soft, cushioned sofa, and a week of being ignored by the woman that I really wanted to be with had quickly got rid of my doubts though. It was just sex, after all, nothing serious. And I had no inkling that Maura would come to learn of what had happened.

Of course she did. News - and especially news about sex - is like the

Ebola virus, it spreads rapidly, is potentially fatal. By the Wednesday after I had been with Monique I had given up calling Maura. I came out of The Screen cinema after watching a new print of Citizen Kane, to turn on my phone and find that I had a voice message. Going to the cinema on a Wednesday night was part of my routine and Maura knew this, she had rung when she knew that I would have my phone off, obviously only wanting to leave a message. I still remember most of it, word for word.

"Cian," Maura began, saying my name as if it were a word like "tosser", or "wanker" or "bollocks", a word designed to express anger or contempt, "I'm done with you. I'm tired of you, stop calling me. You know that you were just a bit of entertainment for me, until something better came along, just a fucking pastime."

Her voice was hard, like a weapon. There was a pause there, as if she were summoning herself to continue in the same vein, tough, dismissive.

"...and I know about your French slapper, I heard about it, though you probably thought that I wouldn't. You didn't waste any time, did you? You couldn't wait to get out of the house, and now I know why. Well fuck you Cian, fuck you and I hope she gave you the clap, I hope she gave you AIDS!"

"You're not worthy of me, you asshole," and then came a deep breath, as if trying to stop herself crying, "and if I ever see you again, I'll stab you in the fucking heart."

Maura stopped speaking, though didn't hang up immediately, there was a dull hiss there, and a clicking sound, and the vague sense of someone breathing, as if she were thinking of what else she wanted to say. Finally the message ended.

Standing there outside The Screen cinema, beside the statue of the cinema usher, having just listened to Maura's rant, was the first time that I really grasped that she cared. That I had the power to wound her. That was how slow I was. It was clear that what she had begun her message by saying - that I was just a pastime for her - was not even slightly true. Whatever it was that we had been doing, whatever it was that we had had together, it wasn't just to pass the time, for me or for her. And she had managed to hide that fact from me until that moment, or I had managed to hide it from myself. I felt nauseous, and had to sit down on the low concrete surroundings of the statue there outside the Screen cinema. It felt like something was ending that I had only recently realised had started. I felt the beginnings of a kind of grief.

Weeks passed. I phoned Maura, then I phoned Sheila, then, when I still got no response, I went out again to the house one Tuesday evening. Sheila opened the door, I could see her trying to muster up a disapproving look at short notice when she saw me standing there.

"I want to see Maura," I said.

"She's not here."

"I don't believe you," I told Sheila.

I had had enough of being ignored. I pushed past Sheila as she stood blocking the way, it wasn't difficult, she was five foot nothing and weighed about seven stone. She tried to grab my arm, I shrugged her off, and climbed the soft carpeted stairs that I knew well. I pushed open the door to Maura's room, the one next to the door which had been mine but which was now Justine's again, and was met with a room that was empty except for a bed with a bare mattress on it, a large wooden wardrobe in the corner and a dresser to the side whose flat surface had always been covered with perfume bottles, tubes of foundation, hair scrunchies, chocolate wrappers, photos of Maura's nieces. It was now bare. It looked like a completely different space to the one I had slept in a couple of times a week, the one that had spoken of Maura's personality so strongly. Like me she wasn't the tidiest of individuals and so her room always appeared so full of *stuff*. Now it was deserted, stripped clean.

"You see now what you've done?" Sheila said, standing behind me, "she's moved out. She couldn't stand being in this house anymore, you've ruined it for her."

I went in and, futilely, opened the wardrobe, then looked out the window, as if Maura might be hiding somewhere. Sheila still stood there, hands on hips, staring. I walked past her without a word, without even looking at her, descended the stairs for what I knew would be the last time, and walked back out to Rathfarnham, neglecting to close the door on my way out.

I only saw her once more before our accidental reunion in Manus Sheehan's house in Ballyhayes, though it was she who found me. I had searched, but soon discovered that the fact that we had kept our lives outside of our little Rathfarnham nest so separate now made it impossible for me to find her. I had never met her friends, apart from Sheila, and although I knew that she worked in Tallaght hospital I had no idea where exactly. I went there one day, after I had spent a whole night in a disrupted, insomniac state, but the place was enormous, full of long, identical, squeaky-clean corridors painted in pastel colours, with multitudes of people in bland uniforms walking around looking busy. Maura used to talk about 'the ward', but I didn't know which one - or else she had mentioned it and I hadn't been paying attention - and so I wandered, without direction, staring at any diminutive figure in a nurse's uniform that I came across until I could be sure that it wasn't her. I went to the canteen and stared some more, and stopped random nurses in corridors and asked them if they knew Maura, all without success. She had disappeared, and I had no idea how to find her.

The collapse had been so sudden I found I had no real way of dealing with it. One week we were locked in this part-time but intense couple, then Maura left for Limerick to be with her sick mother and two weeks later what we had had disintegrated, as if it had never existed. In fact it was like she had never existed. I rang her phone one day and a girl who sounded like she was a teenager answered and said that a woman had stopped her on Parnell Street one day, had given her the mobile, and walked away.

And then she showed up at my door. I had left my address with Sheila, in case any post had gone to Rathfarnham, so Maura had obviously got my location from her cousin. There was a knock at the front door one Sunday afternoon in July, and I opened it to find the woman I had been searching for for two months just standing there, looking at me defiantly. Neither of us said anything for a few moments. Finally she spoke.

"Invite me in, Cian," she said, as if she were some kind of vampire.

I opened the door wide and stood back, still struck dumb. In truth I had so much to say that anything at that moment would have seemed inadequate.

I went inside and sat on the couch where Monique and I had slept together two months before. Maura stayed standing. She looked a bit heavier in the face, her cheeks that fraction rounder, though most people wouldn't have noticed the difference. I found myself drinking in the sight of her, attempting to retain every detail, her white lacy top that showed off the olive skin on her arms, the azure necklace that she wore, the sky blue eye-shadow that was a new innovation. Her perfume was so familiar, and brought back so many sensations, I was glad I was sitting down. I think I was holding my breath.

"Last month," she began, as if she had rehearsed the speech, "I flew to Manchester to stay with my friend Callie, and then I went to a clinic to have an abortion. It was yours. It was all over in two hours. Then I came home."

This I had not been expecting. Still I couldn't speak. Then I said the first thing that I thought of.

"I don't believe you."

It was true, I wasn't sure I could trust her now.

"I don't care if you believe me or not," Maura said.

"Then why did you tell me in the first place?" I asked, not unreasonably, I thought. "You're trying to get to me, to stick it to me. Is this revenge? Is that what the abortion was? Or this made up story of an abortion? Revenge?"

"You believe what you want, Cian. I've told you about it, I felt that I should. That's all I came to say. We're now done."

She turned to go. I couldn't tell if she was upset or was really just eager to go.

"Where are you living, Maura? I looked everywhere for you, I've been looking in random strangers' faces on the street hoping to see you. Are you even still in Dublin?"

I was walking after her now as she made for the door, trying to get in all of the questions that I had been wanting to ask her for months. Her story about the abortion hadn't really wounded me yet, if it was even true I couldn't process the information, it was too much. I was just, in a perverse way, happy to see her, happy to have it confirmed that our four months together wasn't some kind of mirage.

"Don't go, Maura, you didn't let me explain. We can talk it out."

Talk it out. Some stupid phrase I had heard on some American day-time talkshow. She seemed to hesitate at the door, opened it and turned around.

"Do you want to know why I had the abortion? Apart from the fact that I would be a terrible mother at this time in my life? I did it because I had something of you inside me, and I wanted it out. You betrayed me, you motherfucker, and I didn't want your blood and mine mixed in some poor unfortunate child. I thought that what we had was different to all of those other wasters that I was with, but you're worse, if possible. At least they didn't pretend to be better than they were, you did. You made me think that I had found someone worth my time, after so many dead ends. But you're not worthy of me, you betrayed me without a thought, you never even considered how that would feel for me. I would have cut that child out of me if I hadn't made it to Manchester."

At this she flung herself down the steps and out into the street, walking up towards IMMA and Heuston station, and away from me. She had retained all her anger, even months after my moving out, after my night with Monique. She was still angry enough to come around and tell me about this abortion, whether it had happened or not, to see the look on my face. She obviously hated me that much.

And then we met again in Manus Sheehan's New Year's party when I, and I imagine she, had least expected it. Though if I had thought about it it shouldn't have been such a shock, Maura's folks only lived four miles down the road in Meelin, and we were inevitably going to know some of the same people.

Upstairs in Sheehans', in the first moments of 2008, just as celebrations were dying down and party-goers rushed to be the first in line to relieve their straining bladders, Maura took my hand and led me into one of the empty rooms. We left the light off and closed the door, Maura lay down on the left side of the bed - the same side she would always sleep on back when we had shared beds - and patted the right side, indicating that I join her. I sat down, though didn't feel ready to stretch out.

I lay my head back against the head-rest and looked down at Maura.

"The last time I spoke to you you told me that you had aborted our child because you didn't want any part of me inside you."

Maura looked up at me, unblinking.

"I was angry back then."

"I noticed. And you're not now?"

"It's hard to keep it up," she said, "It kind of runs out, even if you try to keep it going. Though I can't say that I've forgiven you."

The noise from outside the door was getting louder, someone was singing a Westlife song. Flying Without Wings, I think it was.

"Was that abortion real?" I asked her, "or just to hurt me."

"Did it hurt you?" she asked, still expressionless.

"Of course. Was that the intention?"

Maura sighed, as if tired of this whole thing.

"The abortion happened, Cian, do you really think I would lie about that?"

"Honestly, I don't know. We didn't know each other as well as we thought. I have no idea what you're capable of."

"You'd be surprised what I'm capable of. Though I told you already, the abortion was real. I flew to Manchester on June twenty-third of this year, last year, stayed with Callie, went to the clinic the next day. They give you a pill, you know. I thought it would be worse."

Maura was lying on her side now, turned towards me, with her head resting on her folded right arm.

"I didn't tell anyone," she went on, "not even Sheila. I knew she'd be all judgemental, you know how holy she is."

I looked down at her. It was still good to see her, a kind of sick pleasure to be in the same room as her, despite all that had happened.

"What was it like? The abortion."

"It was horrible," she said, "but I don't regret it. I was in no state to be a mother. And we made it by accident, remember."

"You made it very clear why you did it, back in July."

"I was hurt," she replied, "what do you expect? You left our house without telling me, as soon as your little legs could carry you. You obviously wanted to be rid of me, and ran as soon as I was missing for a few weeks. We had a good thing, and you took off, ruined it. And then the French girl. Insult to injury."

I had had this conversation with Maura tens, hundreds of times, all in my own head, in the weeks between my moving out in May and her calling to my Kilmainham house in July, in those months where I couldn't locate her and couldn't shake her presence. I had prepared my arguments carefully, a rebuttal for every accusation that she had for me, and of course in my fantasised scenario Maura always came around to my side, always admitted that she had over-reacted, that my behaviour wasn't ideal but that it was understandable. Yet, I just realised something. Since I had landed in Lisbon back in September those self-justifying, imaginary discussions had dissipated, evaporated in the Portuguese sun. I found that I no longer cared about winning, or scoring points, or making her grasp how wrong she had been.

"You and me only worked in one small space, during one short period of time. Then our window closed," I said, "so it doesn't matter why what happened happened, we were never going to last anyway. Our thing was like some old artefact discovered in a bog somewhere, once you expose it to the air, it disintegrates."

She looked up at me, still expressionless.

"You don't know that," she said, "you never gave it a chance. It makes you feel better to tell yourself that so that you didn't ruin anything worth saving."

I had the sensation that what she said was right, but only partly.

"I think we both ruined it," I replied simply. Six months before I would have had a list of self-justifications and counter-accusations, but I had run out of them by now. Maura didn't reject what I had said, she just stared with those nut-brown eyes of hers, which were just about visible in the half-light coming in through the curtainless window.

"I hear that you're in Portugal," she said, instead.

"Have you been asking people about me?" I said, unable to stop myself teasing.

"It's a small part of the county, Cian, everyone knows everything about everyone."

"I know nothing about you, in the last six months at least," I said to her.

"That's 'cause you've been in Portugal. County Limerick doesn't extend that far."

"Yeah, well, I have a life there, I think," I told her, realising as I said it that it was almost true.

"Good for you," she said, without much congratulation.

"It's good to see you, Maura," I said, looking down at her as she shifted on the bed, as she hauled herself upright. The skirt of her dress had ridden up a bit, I could see parts of her thighs. I realised that I still desired her, despite everything. I wondered what she would do if I tried to touch her.

Maura looked at me and said nothing.

"I think I'll go down to the party again," I said, as she stood up. "Shall we go down together?"

"Just because I'm talking to you now, doesn't mean we're friends, Cian. We were never friends anyway. I'm going home. I just came out 'cause I couldn't stand to be at home with my parents at midnight."

"And your mother? How is she?" I was asking the questions now I should have asked back in April.

"Still a pain in the ass. In remission. She has a good few years yet left to be a thorn in my side."

We were both standing now. The party seemed to have moved upstairs, the noise level on the other side of the door had increased, I could hear some of the other guys from our class out there, Philip Casey and Billy Reddan, maybe one or two others. They were singing rugby songs.

"So how do we do this?" I asked her. "Do we just walk out into the middle of the hordes?"

Maura, instead of answering me, walked up to the door and pulled it open. Nobody seemed to notice for a second or two, though the landing was full of people. She pushed through the queue and, as she started down the stairs, one of the women there, obviously Penney or Michelle or Gráinne from earlier, called out, "Hey, it's Maura. What were you doing in there?" Maura walked on, paying the mob no attention. "No, *who* was she doing in there?" one of the other sirens shouted, as half the crowd broke out in cat-calls and hoots.

I was still inside, in the twilight. I managed to slip out and join the gang as most people's attention was focused on Maura, who was now near the bottom of the stairs. I stood and watched as she had to vault over a couple there who were entwined on the second step. She then grabbed her coat, opened the front door and banged it shut. The sound would have been loud in an empty house, but amid the bedlam it hardly registered. I came half-way down the stairs, thought about following her, then was caught by Manus Sheehan coming up the opposite direction.

"O'Dwyer, ya fucker!" he said, drunker now than before. I envied him this, at least. "I heard you were up here with some babe. You're a dark horse, only been in the door half an hour and you've scored already."

Sheehan gave me a beer, then became distracted by a girl with a large chest who was the inverse of his wife in every way, and I slipped past. I left the beer on the kitchen table, pushed my way to the coat rack that was now on its side on the hall floor, and burrowed through the pile until I came to my black leather jacket. I pulled the front door open. The air outside, when I emerged, was sharp, as if the cold had teeth, blades. It felt good though, clean, uncomplicated. There was no trace of Maura, other than some small marks in the frost on the barren lawn that could have been her footsteps. Still, it was good to be out of there. It felt like a release, being in the open air, being away from the throng. It felt like an escape.

❄ ❄ ❄ ❄ ❄ ❄ ❄

My return flight to Lisbon also had the feeling of escape. It was good to be in Dublin airport, to be on the Aer Lingus plane, to be surrounded by Portuguese speakers again. In Lisbon airport this time there was no sullen driver to pick me up, only an Arrivals area that was bright and airy, high-ceilinged and full of the faces of strangers. Despite this, despite the fact that I wasn't likely to run into a single person that I knew there, for a brief second I thought, *wow, home.*

My little box-room hadn't grown, however, though Charles and Charlotte were still absent when I returned. They had spent New Year in a cottage in the Lake District, and had stayed on to "work on their relationship." Charlotte had emailed me this explanation. I, in truth, couldn't care less why they weren't there, I simply luxuriated in all the space I had and took my time to wallow in the total absence of Charlies. I sprawled on the couch, took up all the room I could and flicked through the channels on the TV in a way that I knew would have thoroughly irritated Charlotte. After ten days with my parents the solitude was a pleasure.

Work started again on the Monday. Everything was the same, yet felt changed. I had been away from Lisbon, and had come back, so that now made it a place that I had returned to. This fact made the city different somehow, you don't return to a place that is alien and hostile. You don't come back to a last resort. I had told Maura that I had a life there, and it somehow appeared that that was true.

Hopping on the tram that first Monday of January was like slipping on an old, comfortable shoe. As usual the 28 snaked down from Graça through the narrow streets bordering Alfama, dipped down and then up towards Portas do Sol before plunging again, past the Cathedral and landing on the flat, civilised streets of the Baixa. It was the same groaning, shivering roller-coaster as before, the same route that it took through old Lisbon, a route that it had been following for one hundred years. I found myself smiling as I sat there beside the left hand window, looking at familiar landmarks that had been, just four months before, foreign to me, apparently unknowable.

My workmates commented on my mood.

"What's happened to you, Cian?" Sebastian asked, "you're uncomfortably tranquil. Did you have lots of nasty Irish sex for yourself over the holidays or something?"

He was right, in hindsight, though I didn't recognise any of this myself at the time. I must have mellowed in the three weeks of the holidays, I even let earnest, Ireland-obsessed Patricia Coelho in my teenage class quiz me about the Christmas traditions in my country. It was after class, she was eating into my break yet I indulged her, made up some shit about Mummers and candles in windows and fairies leaving presents for people. Patricia was fascinated, she asked if we could meet some time to discuss it more, she was doing a project for school on different cultural traditions and wanted to hear my experience. I didn't shoot her down there and then as I would have done a month before. Instead I told her I'd look at my schedule and get back to her.

It was only when she turned to go, her questioning of me done for now, that the memory of seeing Patricia outside Bar Brasilia after our Christmas party back in December returned to me. I should have just let it go, but for my own sanity's sake I felt I had to quiz her, to find out whether I had dreamt the whole thing or not.

"Did I see you, Patricia?" I asked her, trying to tread carefully, "at any time outside class. I mean, over the holidays?"

Patricia played the innocent.

"What do you mean, exactly?" she asked, half-smiling.

"You know, maybe at night somewhere. Around Portas do Sol?"

Patricia looked at me, still a smile in her eyes as she did so.

"You're funny when you're drunk, Cian," she said, not entirely answering my question, "my friends couldn't believe that you were my teacher."

This sent her off happy, and even reassured me. At least I hadn't imagined the whole thing, at least I had one clear memory from that inebriated night in December. If anything, the little encounter with Patricia served to solidify my new found serenity. Laura, my usual partner in cynicism, demanded an explanation.

"I don't like the new you, Cian," she said, as we shared a cigarette on the back balcony overlooking the concrete wasteland below, "have you found religion, or are you on some kind of anti-depressant?"

"What can I say," I said, smiling benignly down on Laura in a way that I knew would annoy her, "you should try a bit of positivity, it would do wonders for you."

I know now that being back in Lisbon was an element in my mood change. I found that I was suddenly back in a place that I knew my way around and that had shed the hostility I had seen in it in those first few weeks. I knew how the transport system worked now, when to catch the trams, where to stand so as to get a seat at some stage on the twenty-eight's journey up the hill to Graça. I could go into A Lua and simply nod at Sergio, who would take thirty seconds to prepare me a revivifying, potent little cup of coffee, which would make everything better. I had forty basic words of Portuguese that served as a survival guide for the necessities of life in the city, and I found that wandering the streets of Graça, that village within the city, down to the Pingo Doce supermarket or across to the newsagent on the other side of the street, I would see scores of faces that I had seen before, many of whom now recognised me in turn as a real, if temporary, presence in the community.

And part of it, of course, was down to having seen Maura again. She had disappeared, back in May, then showed up again briefly in July, and had left a whole process incomplete that I couldn't finish on my own. I lived in the same city as her, through the summer of 2007, knowing she was there somewhere, unable to locate her among the other million people that walked the streets of the capital. I eventually had to leave Dublin to escape this absence, and carried this hole with me, in one form or another. New Year's Eve had, somehow, completed the circle.

Maura was alive, we had talked, the clumsy shambles of our break-up was fading into the past, and could hopefully now be left there.

I was also looking forward to seeing Dina again. After my encounter with Maura I had unavoidably fallen into comparing the two women. I had thought about Dina while in Ireland, romanticising her with the luxury of distance. Her maturity, her stability, those green green eyes, were set against Maura's apparent lack of all these qualities. Even Dina's status as the mother of Rui gave her points for a maternal instinct that Maura obviously lacked, having aborted the child that would have been half mine.

So the thought of Dina, waiting for me back in Lisbon, had made watching Maura walk away from me again a little less dispiriting. Dina and I exchanged texts, and she replied to voice-mails that I left with messages of her own, non-committal, ten second, two-line utterances that expressed nothing other than the fact that she had got my message and that she was returning it. I worked, that first week of January, taught my classes with more enthusiasm than the students themselves showed, and tried to enjoy the last few days of Charlie-less existence before my flatmates arrived back on the tenth.

The next Tuesday evening I walked into A Lua, escaping now the overwhelming presence of Charles and Charlotte, who had only just returned and had set about taking over the flat as they tended to do. I saw Dina and Rui, sitting at a table on the right, under a large, ornate mirror. A dark-haired man sat with them, his back to me as I approached. Dina saw me coming and reacted.

"Cian!" she said, standing up and opening her eyes wide, as if in some kind of signal, "this is Rui's father, Paulo."

I turned to this Paulo character. He was in short sleeves, despite the January drizzle outside. He was short, I could see that even though he was seated, and had powerful, thick forearms, like Popeye, and a look of the military about him. He took my hand to shake, squeezed it briefly, but with force, though didn't smile. Dina said something to him in Portuguese that included my name, their son's name, and the word "inglês".

"You should speak in English," Paulo said to her, in an accent that was less American than hers, "it's rude if he can't understand."

Dina looked at him, using an arrangement of her features I hadn't seen before, but which I took to be a result of being married.

"*Tu não me dizes.....*" she began, and added some other words I didn't catch. "You don't tell me..." was what she started to say. I found that I liked that she looked at him that way, that mixture of suspicion, resentment, defiance.

Paulo just nodded in reply, muttering, "*muito bem, muito bem,*" sarcastically. Rui had obviously seen all of this before, he continued eating his ice-cream, humming to himself and smiling intermittently up at me.

"OK, I'll see you later," I said, and inched off down the aisle. I had seen all I needed to see. Dina gave me a tense, fleeting smile. Popeye didn't even look in my direction as I disappeared.

I sat down close to the back. I could watch the family group up near the door without being obvious. I ordered some grilled *bacalhão*, it arrived with a salad, the tomatoes chunky and solid, the lettuce plant-like and crispy, as if it had just been picked. Paulo stood for a time and chatted to Sergio, no doubt the world's least animated conversation. Dina didn't look towards me, though Rui did turn around once or twice and wave, or stick his tongue out.

Manuel da Moto came in, in his motorcycle leathers, his large frame casting a wide shadow that almost reached my spot down the back. He and Paulo obviously knew each other, the two men shook hands and then Paulo went outside to look at Manuel's Honda. I saw Dina stand then, she said a few words to Sergio while pointing at Rui, and then came quickly down the aisle between two sets of tables, the heels of her boots clomping definitively on the floor tiles as she approached.

I had my head raised but she blew right by, didn't even look at me. I was sitting by the entrance to the Ladies'. Dina pushed at the bathroom door, opening it a little, and then turned rapidly and spoke over her shoulder.

"I'll talk to you when I'm coming out," she half-whispered, "I haven't got much time."

I felt like I was in a spy story. I finished my glass of wine slowly, and forced myself not to look around every time the door behind creaked on its hinges. I lit a cigarette and tried to savour it. Finally the door opened and swung shut, and Dina was standing beside me. I could smell her perfume, faint now and mixed in with the ambient odours of briny fish, cigarette smoke and strong coffee, but enough to stir me, to make me want her again.

"You look good," I told her. It was true, she was her compact, womanly self, the perma-brown skin on her throat and near her neck crying out to be touched.

"Don't," Dina warned. She was all business. "Paulo doesn't know about us, and it's better he doesn't find out. He's a jealous guy."

The voice of Brian Ferry intruded on my thoughts, right at that moment - *I didn't mean to hurt you, I'm just a jealous guy.* I tried to repress it.

"But you're not....," I said.

"We're not living together," Dina interrupted me, "but we are trying to be civil to each other, for Rui's sake."

I risked a more direct look up at her. Paulo was still outside, there was no danger.

"And," she went on, "he is still Rui's father. He thinks that that gives him some rights over me."

"Well I can still come over to see Rui," I ventured, more to see what she would say than really meaning it, "you know, for his English."

Dina looked at me for a few seconds. I couldn't tell what was going through her mind. It occurred to me that she was beginning to find me more trouble than I was worth.

"We'll see," she said, "I'll call you."

With that she turned and strode back to her son, who was now happily drawing on one of the disposable white table covers that Sergio used. Her highlighted hair bounced as she moved away, the men at the other tables finding their eyes drawn to her too.

✳ ✳ ✳ ✳ ✳ ✳ ✳

January ticked by, and Dina didn't call, as I knew she wouldn't. I phoned, left messages, got the treatment Maura had given me seven months before. No reply. I went to her mother's house one evening, after my coffee at Mario's, and knocked politely on the front door. Maria answered. It was raining, that kind of irritating, insistent rain that I thought I had escaped when I left drizzly Dublin. I had no real plan, I simply wanted to have a conversation with Dina that didn't involve us playing Tinker Tailor Soldier Spy.

Maria was pleased to see me. She kissed me on both cheeks, wished me a happy New Year and invited me in.

"I don't see you for a long time, Cian," she said, "are you too busy for us?"

Dina, of course, hadn't told her anything about me and her, and so obviously couldn't explain the real reason for my absence.

"Never too busy for you, Maria," I said, going into charm-the-mother mode.

She made me a coffee, asked me for a cigarette, just as Dina had done after our meal in O Covil. I gave her a Marlboro.

"I don't usually smoke," she said, "Rui doesn't like it but I enjoy a cigarette from time to time."

It was when she smoked that I saw more of a resemblance with her daughter. The way she sucked on the thin white stick, and pursed her lips as she exhaled, was exactly the way Dina did it, both of them sexy, despite themselves. I wondered if Maria was flirting with me.

"Dina and Rui are out with Paulo," Maria explained, "you know, her husband." As she mentioned Paulo she frowned a little. Perversely, it pleased me, that little frown.

"You don't know when they'll be back?" I asked.

"I can't say," she said, taking the last drag out of the cigarette, "it could be late. Dina likes Rui to spend time with his father." Again, a souring of her expression around the mouth.

We talked aimlessly about our respective Christmases, about the London School, Graça and the neighbourhood. I tried to string the conversation out, hoping I would be still there when Dina arrived home, but time dragged on and it got to the stage where I had to either take my leave or make a move on Dina's mother. I stood up, asked Maria to let her daughter know that I had called, and emerged back into the tepid air of Graça, the streets wet but the drizzle now gone. Dina was proving difficult to track down.

I stood at the viewing point up beside Mario's coffee shop on my way home. The city looked sedate from way up there, it still sounded like a living animal but this time it was a dozing one, a light snore of noise made its way to me standing up there on the hill. Mario had closed up, I went down the steps by the church and back to Largo da Graça.

The place was taking on a feeling of night-time. The cafés were shut or shutting, all the older and younger people had disappeared, all that was left was the odd straggler, out walking a dog or moving briskly from one place to another. As I approached my front door I sensed a movement to my left behind a parked blue Seat. I looked again and believed I could make out the dark curly top of someone's head. There was a person hiding behind a car just up the street.

I thought briefly about wandering by casually to see who it was, but quickly realised that I didn't care enough. I had other things on my mind. I finished my cigarette before going inside, sucking the last dregs of tobacco goodness from it, and then pushed our creaky street door open.

Inside, I thought again about the hidden person. Charles kept a pair of binoculars in a cupboard in the kitchen, so I grabbed those and went to my window that looked out on to Largo da Graça. My metal blinds were mostly down but there was space at the bottom to look through. I probably didn't need the binoculars, but using them made it more of a game, and I felt in need of a bit of entertainment.

With the naked eye it was difficult to make anything out very clearly, it was too dark, despite the streetlights. I tried the binoculars. Everything was a blur until I twisted the lens at the front in order to focus. The vague blobs I had seen before formed themselves into the shapes of cars, tram-tracks, the tram stop, the cobbles on the street, the shoe-repair shop across the road. The binoculars were surprisingly heavy. I held them tight to my eyes and pointed them in the direction of the Seat, behind which I thought I had seen someone lurking, five minutes before.

The figure stood up, just as I focused on the area. It was Patricia Coelho. Conscientious, fifteen year old Patricia, student from my teenage class. Her dark curls were especially prominent that day, perhaps the moisture in the atmosphere made them springier. She had been crouching, as far as I could see, but now remained standing, staring at the very window that I was observing her from. It occurred to me then that I had never got back to her about her project, the one she had been doing about world cultures, the one she had wanted to interview me for. I edged back a little, though she showed no signs of being able to see me, I had left the light off and the blinds three-quarters closed. I waited to see what she would do, and then realised that I was holding my breath.

Eventually Patricia edged her way around her hiding place, the blue Seat, and walked out on to the street. There were no cars. She crossed it in a series of short, quick steps, looking back once in my direction before heading down the way I had just come from when I returned from Dina's.

"Hello Patricia," I said, there in my room, aloud, to my student's retreating back, "could it be that I have a little stalker?"

The thought actually cheered me up. I fell asleep, chuckling at the idea.

FEBRUARY

The stalking soon became a little less amusing. After the night that Patricia was in Graça I said nothing to her, didn't even mention that I had seen her. We had a class, then another, then another, and she was her normal over-eager, bossy, likeable self, finding everything fascinating, constantly shocked at the fecklessness of her classmates, determined to learn every last scrap of English that she could, no matter how trivial.

Back in October, when I had had to talk to her about her domineering approach in class, about letting me be the teacher, she had sulked for a few weeks, remaining unusually quiet in class and sometimes refusing to answer questions. Slowly then, she had returned to normal and become a useful member of the class, curious, quick, slightly overbearing, but always pleasant and enthusiastic. The new year brought a change in her, or perhaps it was just that I was only noticing it for the first time. She was more grown up, as if she had gotten some maturity pills for Christmas. Back in October, when I had first met Patricia and her class, she was still a child, she had had a Disney pencil-case with Elmer Fudd and Tweety Bird on it, carried a back-pack that was in the shape of a teddy bear and sometimes held her hair back with a pink headband with a flower on it that I had seen ten year olds wear.

In the space of a few months, however, the pencil-case went, she cut her hair into a more manageable, adult style and stopped dressing so much like a clueless tween. She even started wearing some subtle make-up. I walked into the classroom one evening in early February, a couple of minutes early, and found Patricia and her friend Sofia reading Portuguese Cosmopolitan and giggling over a sex quiz. She was still on the cusp between child- and adulthood, swinging one way and then the other, sometimes in the space of a few minutes, but by 2008 Patricia Coelho was subtly shedding her girlishness - whether by accident or design - and slowly growing up.

Two weeks after my first sighting of her in Graça she turned up on the Metro. It was a Saturday, I went to an exhibition in the Gulbenkian museum. I met Mike there. We strolled from exhibit to exhibit, pretended we were cultured, stared at the arty women who were also milling around, and then went and had a few beers in the café there. After the beers we made plans to meet up later.

The nearest Metro stop was São Sebastião. Mike and I walked there, then he headed north on some mysterious errand that he was very vague about, and I caught the first train heading south, back to the Baixa and the city centre. I put my iPod earphones in my ears, sat down and switched off.

And that's where I saw - through the glass door that separated my carriage from the next one - the top of someone's head, with a mass of black curls perched there. As well as the door there were other passengers, seats, poles in the way, so I couldn't be sure who it was. There was also the fact that I had imagined, about three or four times in the previous two weeks, that I had seen Patricia, once in a pharmacy in the Baixa when I was buying, among other things, condoms, once in the Brasileira café in Chiado and once amongst a crowd that was watching us play football on our tiny pitch in Portas do Sol. Each time I was mistaken, each time the person was, in reality, another young female of small stature and with dark curly hair. Once the imagined

Patricia even turned out to be a guy, a short heavy metal fan with a Metallica t-shirt and hair to match. So I had by now lost faith in my ability to spot my supposed stalker in the act of stalking.

To test my hypothesis that it was Patricia there in the underground train I stood up slowly and peered through the connecting door between our two compartments. The person, whoever he or she was, had pulled their head in and was just about out of sight, though I could see a shadow of black hair to the left. The train stopped at Avenida station, two stops before the Baixa, where I would normally get out. Just as the doors were about to close I stepped out on to the platform and went to a bench along the tiled wall of the station. The train pulled soundlessly out and I clearly saw my fifteen year old student, Patricia Coelho, in her seat in the carriage next to the one I had been in, herself now peering through the connecting door, staring - I imagined - at the seat I had inhabited until ten seconds before.

That first time that I had spotted Patricia in Graça, late on a midweek night, may just have been coincidence. She lived in the Mouraria, a ten minute walk away, and had told me, when I mentioned that I lived in Graça, that she knew it well, that her grandmother lived there. Meeting on the Metro, though, was something else entirely. I tried briefly, sitting there under the ground amid the tiled splendour of Avenida station, to calculate the odds of a teacher and a student occupying, by chance, the same train at the same time, one carriage apart, in a city of two million people, four Metro lines and sixty Metro stations. The maths were too much to do in my head, though I was pretty sure that the chances were miniscule. It was beginning to become something that I needed to confront.

Mike agreed with this. I spoke to my ex-roommate that night. We met up with Jamie, Sylvia Saint James, her flatmate Melissa, and some of the second and third year teachers in our favourite bar - Casa do Miguel - just on the edge of the Bairro Alto. The bar decor was bare, with formica tables and hard, classroom chairs, but suited our view of ourselves as bohemian and earthy. The eponymous Senhor Miguel was a bad-tempered, greying man in his sixties who took orders at the tables and never got one wrong, no matter how complex and lengthy it was.

"You need to talk to her," Mike said, as we sat drinking black beer at the end of three conjoined tables of London School teachers. "You need to talk to her before things go too far and she ends up accusing you of doing the very thing to her that she's doing to you. I should have done that."

I looked at him more closely.

"What the fuck did you get mixed up in, Mike?" I asked him.

"I met this wee doll," he said, lowering his voice, "looked twenty-one, said she was eighteen, turned out she was fifteen. I dumped her when I found out, then had her at my house at three in the morning, knocking on the door. And then her fucking father turned up. I had to move in the end. The other communards weren't too happy with all the commotion. Any publicity is bad publicity for a squat."

"So that's why you moved."

Mike had found a new place to live after the Christmas break, again with people not in the London School. He now shared with a bunch of Brazilians who were all in a capoeira group, in an apartment down past Largo de Camões, near the Bairro. At the time he had been vague about his reasons for moving.

"Aye," he said, "that's why I moved."

"And you were involved with a fifteen year old?"

"Let it be said, it was legal. The age of consent is fourteen here. And she was gorgeous. But it's still dangerous territory, and I did get out of it as soon as I knew."

He seemed insistent that I not think badly of him for it. And I didn't, judging people held no interest for me, especially not judging Mike. He was someone that, as my grandmother would have said, had no badness in him. Someone I would probably have been happy sharing a place with, though undoubtedly he had his own bad habits that would have made me wish for the safety of the Two Charlies.

"Anyway," Mike went on, "you need to have a word with her."

I got my chance sooner than I had expected. The next day, a Sunday, was my mother's birthday. I had neglected to buy her anything and so went to the shopping centre, Amoreiras, over the far side of the city, to pick something up.

As usual I got distracted. Shopping for my mother was impossible. I realized that I didn't even know her very well anymore and had no idea what she liked. I wandered into a men's clothes shop and moved from rack to rack of discounted items. Idly I picked out a salmon-pink shirt, thinking that I should try to expand the range of colours that I wore, and held it up to my chest in front of a mirror to see what it looked like. The mirror, as well as showing me how unsuited to pink I was, reflected the scene behind me in the tiled arcade between shops. There I saw, half-hidden by one of the pillars but definitely looking in my direction, my stalker, Patricia Coelho.

I didn't react immediately, just kept trying different shirts. Finally, I placed the garments I had selected back on to the Sales pile, and moved off further back into the store, and hid behind a rack of trousers. Patricia was still there, I could glimpse her through the gap between the hangers and the rail. The clothes store was on a corner so I was able to slip out an alternate exit on the right-angle to the one Patricia was guarding, and then circle around, covered by a group of dejected kids and frazzled adults, until I was standing right behind her as she peered into the shop I had just left. It struck me that she wasn't very good at this stalking business.

"Hello Patricia," I said to her back, taking care to pronounce it in the Portuguese way - pat-REE-see-a.

For a second she didn't move, as if she hadn't heard me.

"Hello Cian," she said, just as she turned around, "are you shopping?"

She was totally unruffled. She gave me her full-beam, eyes-wide smile. In heels, with a calf-length navy skirt and dark blouse, Patricia was looking grown up. Her make-up was subtle, though she had too much mascara on. Only her mound of hair, still unruly despite the haircut, spoiled the almost womanly image.

"It's a coincidence to meet you here," I said to her.

"Lisbon is a small place," Patricia said, talking about her city of two million people.

"I think I also saw you outside my house last week, and on the same Metro train as me recently."

It came to me that this was not the first time that I had had to confront Patricia. Back in October I had asked her to let me be the teacher in the class, after she had almost taken over my role in my first month in the London School. That was when I had inadvertently brushed her breast with my left hand. She had been upset, and had turned away so I wouldn't see her crying, so I still had no idea if she had noticed the accidental boob-touch or not. Had I precipitated this current bout of stalking back in October, by my clumsy slip of the hand? This thought made me want to go easier on her there as we stood in Amoreiras.

"Outside your house?" Patricia said, looking surprised. "Where do you live?"

"I live in Graça, Patricia, we had a conversation about this, about how we live close to each other."

"Oh, yes, I forgot," she said. She may have been bad at stalking but she was a good little actress.

"You know," I began, not knowing exactly how to put what I wanted to say, "these coincidences make me a little uncomfortable. I think it would be better if they didn't happen any more."

I looked at her to see if she had gotten my meaning. This was, after all, her second language, the subtleties of which may not have been obvious to a fifteen year old.

"You know it's my birthday this month," Patricia said, giving no indication that she had registered what I had said. "I'm sixteen."

"Congratulations."

"Thank you," she said, "I'll see you in class."

She flashed me her smile again, then turned on the high heels of her black boots and walked off down the corridor, looking at her reflection in the shop windows as she passed.

After our conversation in Amoreiras I was concerned that I hadn't been clear enough with Patricia. The stalking, however, did seem to stop. The only place I saw her in the next few weeks was in her usual seat, in the centre of the language class semi-circle, every Tuesday and Thursday afternoon. She was her usual self, keen as mustard, bright, subtly encouraging her classmates. I admired her, she seemed immune to awkwardness or discomfort. I had caught her in the act of following me and yet she was exactly the same as before, avid and light-hearted.

Either she was getting better at concealing herself in my surroundings, or else the talk that I had had with her had worked.

It briefly made me feel good to think how maturely I had handled the situation. Now that things had returned to normal I soon forgot about Patricia, I had something else to preoccupy me, and that was my imminent interview with the mythical Marie-Ange.

Robert Prior was the well-dressed Canadian who directed the day to day running of The London School. He had originally interviewed me, and all the seventeen other new teachers, he had hired us and overseen our induction, but the owner, and official head of the school was a woman named Marie-Ange. I heard her name a number of times in my first few months there, always in connection with some administrative decision or other, some minor change to the external signage, or some diktat from on high regarding syllabus. She was a shadowy, almost mystical figure, the Wizard of Oz, whose name was invoked to explain any kind of vague adjustment to the school's running, no matter how small.

And I only ever heard her referred to as Marie-Ange. She was never Senhora Marie-Ange, or Madame Marie-Ange, and a surname was never mentioned. There were just the two bald, hyphenated Christian names, as if that were sufficient, as if she were Madonna or Beyoncé or Shakira, an icon that needed no elaboration.

Each new teacher had, as a matter of course, a mid-year evaluation with the owner. The veteran teachers had a lot of fun with us first-years, inventing all kinds of bizarre initiation practices that we would have to go through on our visit to the old lady.

"You have to kiss her ring," Sebastian claimed, as we all sat in the staffroom one Wednesday, the day before I had my appointment with Marie-Ange, on the fourteenth.

"Yes, and you have to stand in front of her while she drinks a brandy and stares at you, like a bond villain," Carol added, "you spin around and you're not allowed to speak."

Even our school director, who happened to be present at the time, got in on the act.

"She gives you all a job to do," Elizabeth said, "cleaning her car, mowing the lawn of her villa, vacuuming all her Persian carpets. The task you're given depends on your mid-year evaluation."

"It's like penance," Carol added, "to make up for your sins."

We four new teachers forced ourselves to laugh along with the inventions of our colleagues, but we were all - I suspect - a little apprehensive about our audience with The Great Leader. I was first up, they had even given me a class off to go and visit her lair in the Rossio school, right in the centre of the city. Sebastian was teaching my three o'clock Intermediates so I wouldn't be late for Marie-Ange.

On arrival to the reception on the ground floor of the Rossio building I was pointed towards the elevator and told to go to the seventh floor. The buttons on the inside of the lift only went up to seven, the top one was red, unlike all the others, which were white, as if the floor I was instructed to visit were some sort of Twilight Zone. A floor that didn't exist in our space/time. When the lift reached the top I stepped out and into a short corridor, with a closed, blank door on my left and another one, this time ajar, on my right. There was nothing else there, just the three metre long corridor, the wood panelled wall and the two doors. I was already a little intimidated, but was also enjoying myself, it was like I had reached a secret, hidden part of the building, perhaps where The London School lodged away its old teachers once they had ceased to be useful. It was all very cloak and dagger.

A voice came from my right, through the open door.

"Cian? Mr. O'Dwyer?"

I stuck my head around the corner. Marie-Ange - I assumed it was her - sat behind a heavy, ornate wooden desk, much too large for the few objects she had scattered around it. There were paintings mounted on the walls on both sides and behind her, traditional landscapes with peasants and horses and burgeoning vegetation. A window to my left gave a view out to Praça Dom Pedro and to the scurrying crowds of people below, going about their business, utterly ignorant of this office and of this elderly woman behind the ministerial desk.

"Sit down please."

Her accent was laced with the elongated vowels of French. She was said to be French-Swiss, though that was unconfirmed, like everything else about her. She was a small woman, tiny really, with large glasses and make-up that gave the impression that she had a lot to conceal. The way she peered out at me, amusedly, as if waiting to see what I would do, put me in mind of an old priest in the confessional box, braced for the torrent of sins to come, but unconcerned, having heard everything before.

We began with small talk. Marie-Ange asked me about how I had settled in, how I liked my students, what I thought of Lisbon. I gave her the usual bland answers - "Fine", "they're very enthusiastic", "The city is great, full of life," - hoping that she couldn't see through my insincerity. I felt that there was a script that I needed to follow, that I was playing the part of the obedient useful employee, the efficient cog in the London School wheel.

"Hmmm," she said, in her old lady way, in response to my platitudes. Then she fixed her gaze on me through the thick lenses of her glasses, giving the impression that the real business of the interview was about to start.

"So tell me about your future, Cian," she said.

Her question made it sound like I must have some kind of psychic ability, that I should know what was coming.

"I'm enjoying teaching for now," I said, improvising fast, "but in the future I hope to combine my experience of web-design and multimedia with EFL, and perhaps get into producing interactive learning materials for students."

This had just come to me, in fact it was the very first time that such an idea had crossed my mind. Marie-Ange nodded as if my reply had been satisfactory.

"And do you see yourself as a *leader*, Cian?"

Again she peered at me through those thick lenses. Another of the many rumours about her came back to me then, that she had been a supporter of the dictator Salazar and his regime, before its fall in 1974. I wondered if she had learned any interrogation techniques back then from the PIDE, Salazar's secret police. Were there electric connections in my chair, ready to administer a nerve-buzzing shock at an inadequate answer?

"Eh, yes," I replied, not even convincing myself, "absolutely." I had to repress the sudden urge to giggle. "Absolutely I see myself as a leader. Every teacher has to be a kind of leader," I went on, amazing myself at the bullshit I could come up with without any preparation, "to be able to manage and teach a class."

Another "Hmmmm," from Marie-Ange, another knowing nod. I still couldn't work out the purpose of the interview. It was possible that it had some real, yet hidden significance, yet it was also entirely plausible that Marie-Ange met each new teacher simply as a piece of theatre, as an attempt to create the impression - to herself and to others - that she still had some power in the school. *I am in charge*, I imagine she thought, *look at them cower before me.*

"And tell me Cian," she went on, "who do you admire?"

This question, I realised, was going to tax my powers of invention. Names flashed through my mind, the usual suspects, Muhammed Ali, Jesus Christ, Gandhi, Pele, Che Guevara, Bertie Aherne, Bill Gates.

"My father," I replied, finally, when the silence had gone on too long and I had to say something. This was my biggest lie yet, I didn't really admire him at all, we could have been from different planets.

"He always does what he believes in, he has worked hard all his life and doesn't compromise."

Some of this was actually true, though it was only by accident. I was still improvising, saying what I thought was required in the situation. Again Marie-Ange nodded, as if she were, filing all of this away as information she would need access to later.

The interview concluded with a few more questions from Marie-Ange. I couldn't work out if they were incredibly inane, or very insightful - "What is your greatest achievement?", "What improvements would you suggest for the London School?", "How would you sum yourself up in one word?" In answer to the last question I came up with "versatile". Again, it seemed like the appropriate thing to say, even if it wasn't strictly true. I nearly got a dose of the giggles, however, it was hard work playing the part of this committed, solid employee, and hilarity was getting the better of me. I turned the laugh into a sudden cough, and was relieved to hear Marie-Ange, in her squeaky, Frenchified old-lady voice tell me that the interview was over.

She let me go with a limp shake of the hand. As I stood in the elevator, on its way down from the seventh floor, I realised that, despite the air conditioning in the building, the underarms of my shirt were soaking wet. Marie-Ange was a small nut of a woman, on the face of it granny-like and unthreatening, but the rumours had obviously gotten to me and made me feel like I had just been through a particularly terrifying session with PIDE's top interrogator.

Having been the first of our school in to see the head lady, it at least gave me the opportunity to join in with the generalised exaggeration of the experience. Mike, Rahul, Jamie and I were, as usual, trawling the tepid streets of the Bairro Alto that Saturday night. We came across Laura, Sebastian and Fernando, standing outside the Record Bar, drinking bloody-looking Sangría, pieces of fruit floating in their plastic cups.

"You'll want to sleep well Sunday night," I told Laura, who had her appointment on the Monday morning, "that Marie-Ange character is no joke. She left me standing for a whole hour, asked me these questions about pedagogy and linguistics, it was like a fucking inquisition."

"You're a liar, Cian," she said, "and a bad one. You're full of shit."

She was right, of course. Laura was the best liar I knew, and could see through the weak lies of others.

"I heard that she was a sweet old lady," Laura went on, "who forgets your name and only wants to know that you're eating enough fruit."

"Now whoever told you that," I said to her, "is definitely lying."

Sebastian, Fernando and Laura were on their way to a gay club, Envidia, that was situated at the top of the hill, towards the outer reaches of the Bairro Alto. Rahul and Jamie disappeared when they heard this, they were off to a club in Alcântara where they were meeting Joanne. Mike though, wanted to go.

"Ah man," he said to me, as the other three set off up the cobbled hill towards Envidia, "have you ever been to a gay bar? The women there are extraordinary."

He split this last word into "extra-" and "-ordinary".

"It's a gay bar, Mike," I said, realising as I spoke that I didn't know what I was talking about, "the only women there will be interested in other women. That's why they're there."

I had never actually been to a gay bar before, but didn't want to admit this, for some reason.

"Nah, man," Mike said, "gorgeous straight women love gay bars. They reckon they won't get hassled there, it's the only place they can go to get a bit of peace."

We followed the other three through the now thronging streets. There were lots of underage kids around, sitting on steps, gathered in doorways, drinking naggins of vodka, smoking, kissing in alleys. It was one o'clock, there was an air of barely suppressed hysteria, an excitement that seemed like it couldn't build any more without some kind of riot taking place.

Envidia was sedate by comparison. There was a shaven-headed bouncer on the door. It ran through my mind that he was going to do a gay-test on us, to assess our suitability to enter, but he just nodded as we walked by, unsmiling like every other bouncer at every other club. Inside the place was not large, it had space to hold seventy or eighty people, with enough room for dancing. There were no bare-chested men dancing in cages, no men kissing in corners, and no-one at all in leather trousers, as far as I could see. I was kind of disappointed. At first glance it seemed like the usual cramped, dark, quirky Bairro Alto dive, except with cheesier music than normal and a severe shortage of women.

Mike was right though, the few women that were actually there were stunning. I joined Sebastian at the bar, and commented on the beauty of the few females there. Sebastian ordered quickly, and then turned to look at me, leaning on the bar as he did so.

"Unless you want to change teams for the night," he said, "keep it in your pants, little Cian. The fag-hags are not here to be pawed over, those alpha-bitches like the gays, they know that we have no interest, they come here to relax. So leave it alone."

"Who died and made you King of the Gays?" I asked him.

Sebastian looked at me again, haughtily. He was an inch or so shorter than me, though he managed to make himself appear as if he were looking down on me.

"You know what, Cian, you should go for it. See how far you get with one of these goddesses. Entertain us."

I looked around the room. Along one wall, at the edge of a group of four men of all different heights, was a tall girl with blond streaks in her hair, drinking some form of clear liquid with ice and a straw in it. She had the air of a model about her, poise, controlled boredom, not one hair where it shouldn't be. Most striking was her eye-makeup, green and pink mascara shading into one another, giving her a science-fiction look, like a woman from the future. With the false confidence of a straight guy in a gay club, I walked right over.

"*Como te chamas?*" I said, asking her her name, knowing she would change to English when she heard my accent.

The girl turned her head without moving her body and looked at me, painted eyes narrowing. She was only very slightly shorter than me. I felt that I was being evaluated, weighed up, as if I were a handbag in a boutique, a messy work of art on a wall.

"*Tu não es uma bicha, pois não?*" she said.

I must have looked baffled. She just shook her head and smiled, her colourful eyes crinkling and elongating as she did so. The girl took a careful drink of whatever was in her glass, her gaze not leaving my face for an instant, and then said one more word - "*coitado*" - while shaking her head. She then simply turned and walked away, to join another group of men across the dancefloor where she pointed at me and laughed along with her new companions, as they all looked in my direction.

I walked away with as much dignity as I could muster. I found Seb, Laura, Fernando and Mike over by the bar. I actually knew what "*coitado*" meant. Dina had used it with me on a number of occasions, when I had complained of being tired, or of having a cold or about one of my co-workers. "*Coitado*," she too would say, as insincere as she could be, - "you poor thing."

The round figure of Perry was there too, I found, when I rejoined the group. Perry, the advisor appointed by the school to help first year teachers, the one who had told me to remember that I was the sheriff in the class. He was red-cheeked and smiling, and kissed me on both cheeks when he saw me.

"Cian," he said, "welcome to our world. Anything you want to know about, so you don't stick out too much?"

"Actually," I said, taking a swig from my Miller Lite bottle, holding it by the neck, "there is something you can help me with. What's a *bicha*?"

Perry opened his mouth to indicate his delight. He looked like I had just made his night.

"Sebastian," he said, grabbing our Senior Teacher by the shirt sleeve, "Cian wants to know what a *bicha* is."

Fernando overheard, and joined in, light in his eyes for the first time that night, as if something had finally piqued his interest. It was unclear whether he and Seb were lovers or friends or both, but usually where you found one you found the other.

"He's a *bicha*," he said, pointing at Sebastian. Then, pointing across the room at each member in turn of a couple that was standing there, "and he's a *bicha*, and he too." Then he turned towards Perry, who was standing beside him, and pointed at our corpulent colleague, "and he's *definitely* a *bicha*!"

They all laughed, even Laura, whose Portuguese was almost non-existent.

"And this one here," Perry said, taking over, putting his hand on Laura's shoulder, "well we're not sure about her, she's not a *bicha*, but she'd like to be."

Laura punched him on the chest.

"I'm also a *bicha*," Fernando said, "I've known that I was a *bicha* since I was thirteen. And you honey," here he ran the back of his index finger down along the side of my face, "*tu não es uma bicha*, though maybe we could convince you."

The posse clapped and hooted at this last suggestion. I didn't mind, I was doubly an alien there in Envidia, a straight Irish guy in a gay Portuguese club. I was glad to be able to play a part in any way in the evening's entertainment.

What the girl with the pink and green had said to me was now clear - "you're not gay - you poor thing!" She had pitied me for my heterosexuality, as if being gay were some kind of higher calling, some golden state. As I watched my companions, and the other men in the club, *bichas* all, except for me and Mike, I could see where the model might be coming from. They danced with abandon and confidence and rhythm, flirting effortlessly, being hugged and pawed at and touched by the ten or twelve mostly beautiful women there. It seemed to me that there was little of the obvious angst and conflict and insecurity of a straight bar. I wondered if being gay was something you could pick up, like acquiring Portuguese or learning to cook. In my confused, dazed state after being summarily dismissed by the girl who was clearly out of my league, I imagined a future where I could be gay part-time, gay at the weekends.

Mike had a dance, got chatted up a few times by guys, tried it on with a number of the languorous, celestial women in the club and then, by two o'clock, when he had been shot down every time, announced that he was off. It appeared to me then, that I was the last male hetero there. The theme of the night, among our group up until then, had been a discussion as to who was giving me the eye, but it was only when I went to the bar to get myself and Laura another beer that someone approached me.

The guy wasn't what I imagined would be considered attractive, his nose was a little bent, he had hair sticking up at the back and his stubble was uneven, like an unwatered lawn. Still, I found it flattering, in a twisted kind of way. This must be what it's like to be a woman, I thought, cloudily.

"*Boa noite,*" the guy said. It was an oddly formal greeting - "good night" - in such a setting. "*Boa noite,*" I said back.

The next sentence from his mouth I didn't get, something involving the word "*aqui*" - "here". Was he asking me if I came here often? I quickly admitted my status as foreigner, though not my identity as rogue breeder. The guy looked taken aback.

"You look Portuguese," he said, in English now.

No-one had said that to me before, me with my colour-drained skin, my Northern blue eyes. I had only been chatted up three or four times in my life before, and only by women. I assumed that it was a line he was using.

"So do you," I said. He half-smiled, showing uneven teeth. I really hadn't hooked a looker.

"I just arrived a few minutes ago," the guy said, his English crisp and unhurried, "and noticed you immediately."

Among the beginnings of anxiety and discomfort, I also felt flattered.

"My name's Manus," I said, and stuck out my hand. I wasn't sure if gay Portuguese men enjoyed the handshake as much as their straight counterparts, or if they preferred to go directly to the two cheek kisses.

"Marco," he said.

We talked a while. Marco told me about his job as a journalist with a tabloid there in Lisbon, and about his two years in London where he learned his English. I described the village I lived in back in Limerick, and the semi-D I had just bought there, though I didn't mention Mrs Sheehan, my blond pixie of a wife. I was on holiday, was my story, Manus Sheehan, getting away from it all on a city break.

I found that I liked Marco. I didn't even mind being in the situation where I was being seduced. I began to imagine, in a different universe where I was a different person, going home with him, letting what would happen, happen, having a new experience. Like doing a bungee jump or eating snake, something you would only do when, like Manus, you were on holiday.

"So why don't we go for a walk," Marco suggested, finishing his vodka.

"Now?" I said, playing the innocent, "but it's half past two."

"Well, we don't have to walk far," Marco said, looking directly at me now, "I live down near Santos."

It had just stopped being a game and become real. It was time to 'fess up.

"Marco, you're a nice guy," I said, hearing myself trot out the platitudes a woman would use if she wasn't interested in a guy, "but I actually like women. I'm not gay, I'm only here with friends."

Marco looked at me doubtfully, his nose appearing even more bent as he faced me straight on.

"I've heard that before, Manus," he said, "you should really stop pretending, before you waste anyone else's time. You don't need to be ashamed."

"Oh I'm not ashamed," I reassured him, though I did feel bad now for leading the guy on.

Marco didn't hang around, he disappeared as quickly as he had appeared. I rejoined our group.

"I see you've found someone," Fernando said, as I returned.

"He didn't believe that I wasn't gay," I told him.

"Maybe he's right," Fernando said, "you never thought about it?"

"Have you never thought about being with a woman?" I asked him, trying to deflect the conversation from the uncomfortable turn it had taken.

"Sure," Fernando said, "for about five seconds. Then I see some cute guy and remember who I am."

It was three o'clock when we gathered up to leave. Fernando went to look for Seb, Perry had already gone though no-one knew if he had left accompanied or not, and Laura and I sat on a sofa in a corner, the last two heteros in the place. Laura lay her heavy head on my shoulder and closed her eyes. There were fewer people in the club now but more action, couples were dotted around the space, some kissing, others getting more intimate, one or two only talking, as yet.

I spotted my friend Marco against the wall in the distance, his hair still sticking up at the back. A dark-haired man stood close to him, his back to us as we sat. The two men were talking, then they touched hands, Marco's right and the other man's left. Marco's companion was shorter, his forehead only reached Marco's nose, and Marco wasn't that tall. Laura stirred beside me, having been poked by Sebastian, who Fernando had just found. There was a crease on her cheek where she had been lying against me. I gave her a hand to stand up and put my arm around her shoulder as we moved towards the door, feeling the need to remind myself of the warmth of a woman all of a sudden.

Marco and his mate were by the front door. I was glad for him that he had found someone, my leading him on for ten minutes hadn't slowed him down too much. He saw us coming towards him, caught my eye and then, just as I was passing, leaned forward and kissed the shorter, dark-haired guy full on the mouth.

And then I realised that I knew him, that I knew Marco's companion. Seeing him from the back something had called out to me, a tingle of familiarity, the stockiness, the dark hair on the forearms, the thickness of those very forearms. Like Popeye. *I yam wot I yam.* He had his eyes closed as we passed, totally involved in his kiss with Marco, but it was unmistakably Paulo, Dina's husband, Rui's father, the jealous guy who Dina didn't want to find out about us. Paulo and Marco wrapped arms around one another and looked like they were only beginning. I stood and watched, still with my arm around Laura's shoulders, unsure what was appropriate in the situation.

"Hey Cian," Laura said, now half out the door and dragging me behind her, "it's rude to stare. If you're so interested why don't you join them?"

The two guys didn't see me, and didn't hear Laura. They were oblivious, in another world, lost in each other. For a brief moment I think I was even a little jealous. We emerged back out into the Bairro Alto, which was more sedate now but still with people wandering the streets. I saw Laura to a taxi, took one myself, and within five minutes

I was back in Graça, sitting in my empty kitchen with a lit Marlboro between my first two fingers, wondering what I was going to say to Dina.

✳ ✳ ✳ ✳ ✳ ✳ ✳

Dina had promised to ring me, back in January. She had spoken to me covertly in A Lua, on her way from the toilets so her husband wouldn't notice, saying that she would be in touch. But she didn't ring, as I knew she wouldn't. She didn't text and she didn't buzz on our front door at eleven at night for a quick roll on my child's size bed before going home to her son. She disappeared from my life as quickly as she had come into it.

That is, until late February. The Wednesday after I had seen her husband in a Lisbon gay bar with his tongue down another man's throat, I got a call just as I was descending the steps of the school. Dina knew my timetable, knew when I finished each day.

"Cian," she said, her voice sounding distorted but recognisable, "can we meet?"

No, I wanted to tell her, *no we cannot.*

"Where?" I said, instead.

"In the Brasileira café," she said, "it's in Chiado, you can get the Metro to Baixa/Chiado, then...."

"I know where it is, Dina," I told her.

I thought that it was a strange place to meet if she was trying to be discreet. It wasn't exactly close to Graça, but was located on one of the main routes from the Baixa up to the Bairro Alto, where anyone could go by and see us, or even come in. A Brasileira also wasn't some anonymous locale, it was where a generation of Portuguese writers and intellectuals used to gather, near the beginning of the twentieth century. Lisbon's Doheny and Nesbitt's. The place had history.

Dina was already there when I arrived. A Brasileira was of a similar design to A Lua. The cafe showed a narrow, restricted face to the street while stretching back and back and back, becoming deceptively spacious the further you entered the seating area. There were paintings on the wall to the left as you walked in, just above the head height of the seated patrons there, and a high, ornate ceiling that gave the place an air of the nineteenth century. Waiting staff were dressed that little bit better than in most Lisbon cafés, there were fewer stained, shabby shirts, the men wore ties, all had a sense of occupying an important position, despite their, no doubt, five euro an hour wages.

Dina stood and kissed me on both cheeks as I entered. She signalled for a *bica* for me, and then sat and smiled in my direction.

"You look good," she said.

"Thanks," I said, not returning the compliment, though wanting to. She looked exquisite sitting there, green eyes dimmed by the subdued lighting, but still striking.

"How's Rui?" I asked.

My question wasn't innocent. I wanted to remind her that if I hadn't seen her for two months then I hadn't seen her son either, and he was missing out by this. The waitress brought me my tiny coffee.

"Look Cian," she said, ignoring my question as if she had rehearsed what she was saying and just wanted to get it out, "Paulo and I, we're going to try again. I want Rui to have a father, we're looking for a house here. Paulo's going to sell his business in the States and come back here."

As we sat there I could still picture her husband, from four days before, his mouth on Marco's, his hand at the back of Marco's neck, pulling him closer. I laughed.

"What's funny?" Dina asked me.

I didn't answer, I just continued laughing, put my hand to my forehead and looked down at the table top.

"Cian!" she said.

I looked up, finally, and shook my head.

"Oh, Dina," I said.

"Cian, you're acting very strangely."

I straightened my face, and looked directly at her.

"I'm curious, why did you want to meet here? It's quite public, isn't it?"

"Oh Paulo never comes in here, he hates it," Dina said, looking wary, "he says it's just for the foreigners."

She looked around at the abstract art, the high mirrors behind the bar, like in that Manet painting. The beautiful, elevated ceiling.

"I like it though," she added.

"Me too," I said, looking straight into her green eyes. She stayed silent for a time, ten seconds perhaps.

"So we can't see each other again, Cian," she said, speaking more quietly now, "and I'm sorry, I think Rui's English classes will have to stop too."

This I had assumed, though I still felt regret at not seeing her son again.

"Just do me a favour," I said, "don't lie to Rui and tell him that I decided not to come any more. Make something up, but don't tell him that it was my decision."

Dina took a drink of her milky *galão* and watched me over the top of the glass as she did so.

"Ok," she said. She had a thin moustache of foamy coffee on her top lip and didn't, for the moment, wipe it away.

I lifted my cup and downed my *bica*. It was luke-warm now, bitter. I stood up and put the straps of my black bag over my shoulder. Dina remained seated. She didn't attempt to give me the two kisses goodbye. I looked down at her for a moment, wondering if I should say something, if I should tell her that her husband wasn't who she thought he was. I went to speak, caught myself in time, then turned and left.

On Friday, February twenty-ninth, the leap day, I received an email from Maura. Of course she didn't write out of the blue, she was replying to one that I sent had sent her. I had drunk-mailed her one night, after a standard Saturday night in the city where much alcohol had been consumed and no sense had been spoken. That night Rahul had disappeared as usual with Joanne, Mike had scored with Melissa of the Three As and even Jamie, plastered as he was, was chased around the Bairro by a Spanish girl who had taken a shine to him. I arrived back to Graça feeling lonely and a little horny, and sent off a rambling, at times morose email to maura_tiernan@yahoo.com. This was an old address of hers, I knew, and I wasn't even sure that she used it any more. It was a shot off into the ether, an opportunity to get things off my chest without having to deal with the consequences.

Of course there was a consequence. One short reply from Maura, about two weeks later, on February the twenty-ninth. It was to the point.

"Cian", it began, "I've met someone, and am trying to learn how to be happy again. He's the first guy I've been with since last year, since you. Please leave me alone now. You had your chance, and blew it. Or we both blew it. Whatever, it doesn't matter. Don't contact me again."

She didn't sign it, didn't put her name at the end. "again" was the last word in the message. There wasn't even a solitary letter 'M' at the foot of the mail, like she would put on her notes that she occasionally left for me back in Rathfarnham. It felt unfinished, brutal. I couldn't stop reading it.

I finished work at half past seven that day, and found Charles and Charlotte in the kitchen when I got home. They were in the midst of one of their elaborate creations where they would both strip down to shorts and t-shirts, and chop and stir, sauté and roast, until they had totally colonised every inch of the kitchen. It made it impossible that I could prepare anything for myself, even if I wanted to.

In my room, before I went down to A Lua, I opened my laptop and read Maura's message for what must have been the twentieth time that day. I took my computer with me downstairs to A Lua, ordered a soup and a beer and read the email again, three times. I closed the matte black top of my Dell and tried to enjoy the thin Sopa Alentejana.

Manuel da Barba passed on his way to the bathroom. I was sitting at the back, away from the main knot of locals near the counter.

"Cian," he said, "you here? Come up and talk, I have some new words for you."

"Not tonight, Manuel," I said, lifting the lid of my computer, "working". I indicated the Dell.

Manuel looked down at the screen and scratched his beard.

"Is the weekend. You need to relax, you work too much."

If I had been in less of a funk I would have smiled at the realisation that this was the first time anyone had ever said those four words to me - "you work too much."

"You ok?" Manuel went on, when I didn't reply, "you look....*triste.*"
Here he put on what must have passed for a sad face, though it was
difficult to see through the beard.

"I'm good, Manuel, thanks," I said, putting on my best false smile,
"I might see you later." I turned back to the screen as if I was doing
something important.

Manuel da Barba returned to the counter. As he did so Dina came
in and stood beside him. Manuel da Barba was the one Manuel she
could stand, she had told me. The other Manuel was the instigator
of whatever mischief they got up to, but the guy with the beard, Dina
thought, was alright on his own. They stood and chatted for a minute
or two. I couldn't tell if she had seen me, I presumed that she had. Dina
rarely missed anything that was going on or anyone that was around.

Paulo then came in and joined them. He slid up to stand beside
Dina, made a joke that she laughed at - falsely, I thought - and then
leaned over and kissed her on the lips. They both got coffees and began
the Portuguese sugar ritual together, tapping the sachets as you would
tap a vial before injection, before tearing the paper sugar containers
open and spilling their sweet contents into the dark, thick coffee. Paulo
drank with his left hand, Dina with her right, she draped her left arm
over his right shoulder as they slowly consumed their *bicas. The happy
couple*, I thought, looking at them.

Of course I could have told Dina what I had seen in Envidia the
previous Saturday night. I could have told her, right there in A Brasiliera
café, where we had met two days before, when she had told me that
we couldn't see each other again. I could have told her in ten different
ways, with a voice mail, in a text, by email, even in a written letter on
actual paper. I could have, and had chosen not to. On Wednesday she
had just dumped me for her gay husband, and in a way it felt good - or

at least less bad - how deluded she was and how certain her marriage was to fail. She had dropped me and gone back to Popeye Paulo, and would eventually find out that her not having a penis would prove to be the key obstacle to the success of their union. These things have a way of coming out, I thought, it didn't have to be me to spill the beans.

There was a strong chance that, even had I told her what had happened in Envidia, she wouldn't have believed me. Eventually she would have put two and two together, would have battled denial and discovered the reasons for all Paulo's unexplained absences, for the way he looked at other men, for his disinterest in her sexually. By that time though, she would have painted me as the jilted, jealous lover, capable of inventing any kind of slander to undermine her newly reformed marriage. She was prone to this type of self-delusion, I knew, just to keep her family together.

The last reason that I said nothing was less selfish, less mean-spirited, though still self-interested, I suppose. Dina had said that she wanted Rui to have his father back, well now he had him and I didn't want to be the one to take him away again. I had no doubt that the shit would hit the fan eventually, but as long as it wasn't me to cause it to fly, I was good with that. Let the kid have a bit of time to live within the illusion of happy families, what harm could it do?

I reassessed my decision to keep shtum when I saw Dina and Paulo there at the counter in A Lua, whispering together, all touchy-feely, each of them involved in their own massive pretence. Sergio passed by, I ordered a double brandy, he delivered it thirty seconds later. It made me feel better as I sat there, swirling the liquid in its bulbous glass, there was a taste of sweetness and comfort about it. I put my laptop on the tabletop in front of me, which shielded me somewhat from the accidental gaze of anyone looking in my direction, and muttered a little mantra under my breath as I looked up towards Dina - "You're the wrong gender, you're married to a bender. You're the wrong gender Dina, you're married to a bender." It made me smile, if nothing else, and I kept it up, on and off, until they had both finished their coffees, said goodbye to Sergio and Manuel, and gone back out into the tepid February evening.

It was a relief when they left. I didn't really feel like eating or going home, so I ordered another double brandy. Sergio brought me what looked like a triple. Feeling masochistic I read Maura's email again. Sergio had just got wi-fi into A Lua, - though he pronounced it "wee-fee", which always amused me - so I looked stuff up on YouTube, people reciting bad poetry, cats falling off roofs, monkeys in dinner jackets, video of an old Flaming Lips gig. People passed every five minutes or so on their way to relieve themselves. Manuel da Barba came down once for a chat. He told me about some idiot who had decided, that day, to cycle around Graça, and got his front bicycle tyre stuck in the tram tracks just as the 28 came around the corner. I tried to smile and nod politely, but Manuel left when it finally dawned on him - minutes after it would have occurred to anyone else - that I was not in a very sociable mood. I was glad when he left.

I sat, drank and browsed the Net. After a while I looked up to see the flash of a pale face peering in the front window of the restaurant. A small figure then pushed open the front door, hinges squeaking as it moved, and walked directly towards me. She pulled out the chair opposite me that Manuel da Barba had just vacated, and sat down.

"Hello Patricia," I said. I couldn't even muster up any real surprise to see her.

"Hello Cian, are you well?" It was like we were old friends.

"Not especially, no."

"That's too bad," she said.

I had taught her that expression to use when you wanted to be sympathetic to someone who has just told you bad news about themselves. "I've got cancer," - "That's too bad." "I'm all alone," - "That's too bad". "My ex-girlfriend aborted our baby and has now found another man, and my most recent lady-friend just dumped me in favour of her gay husband," - "That's too bad."

"You know I'm sixteen now," Patricia told me, "it was my birthday last week."

She seemed very insistent that I know this fact about her age, she had mentioned it before too. I remembered something Mike had told me about the age of consent in Portugal, that it was fourteen in some cases but that sixteen had some significance too. He seemed to be an expert on the topic.

"Congratulations," I said, "did you get any nice presents?"

"Driving lessons," she said, "cosmetics, a TV for my room, CDs, a trip to Madrid."

"Wow," I said.

I took what I hoped would be a good slug of my drink, though the narrow topped brandy glass prevented this. I realised that this would be the time to be telling Patricia to go home, or to be going home myself. I didn't do either.

"Can I get you a drink?" I offered her, instead.

It felt good, and harmless, all of a sudden, to be sitting there with this teenage girl, who may have been stalking me for the previous two months but who also smelled good, and who wasn't about to abandon me for a guy who preferred men. She blinked at me, still smiling, and then answered, "I'll have a pineapple juice."

I think I had been expecting her to order something adult, a vodka tonic, or a scotch. I caught Sergio's eye as he was clearing a table about half way up the room, I pointed at my glass for a refill and then mouthed the word "*pineapple*", while indicating my companion. Sergio, I knew, had a daughter Patricia's age. He looked at me as if he wanted to warn me to be careful, then nodded and went to get the drinks.

Patricia began talking. Words came easily to her, one after the other, she moved from subject to subject without pause. I was happy just to listen to her and not feel that I had to correct her mistakes. Sergio deposited our drinks without a word, Patricia stopped her flow of speech for half a second to thank him brightly - "*obrigada*" - before continuing with her monologue. She talked about school, about her brother who was studying in Coimbra, about how she was learning the violin, so she could be just like Caroline, her favourite member of The Corrs, about how her ambition was to live for a year in Dublin and get a job in the music business. She talked on, revelling in her own ability to hold court like this in a foreign language, while I listened, made encouraging sounds, smiled about once a minute.

The brandy now tasted bitter, I regretted having ordered it though I kept drinking. It was clear that Patricia didn't really expect me to contribute, though it got to the stage where I felt that I had to butt in.

"Patricia," I said, my two hands now around my brandy glass, "why are you following me around?"

Again, she didn't bat an eyelid, didn't twitch a muscle.

"Following you?"

"Yes," I said, "I saw you in Amoreiras, in the shopping centre, I saw you on the Metro, outside my house one night last month. Now you're here, in the place where I often have dinner."

"I live close to here," she said, "in the Mouraria. I often come in here to meet friends. I thought I would find some of them in here tonight."

I had never seen her in A Lua before. I knew she was lying, she knew she was lying, but she gave no sense that this was so. *A good little actress*, I thought, again. I admired her right then, so self-possessed in her dissembling, absolutely believing, for the few seconds that mattered, every word that she said.

"But I'm happy to meet you like this," Patricia went on, "it's good to chat sometimes outside class, don't you think?"

She was the only one chatting, really.

"Sure," I agreed, "cheers!"

I held up my glass, now almost empty, Patricia clinked it daintily with her own.

"Cheers!" she said, "that's a funny thing to say." She looked like she was having the time of her life there, with her English teacher, saying words in English she had never uttered before.

"Cian," Patricia went on, after taking a longer drink of her juice, "do you know what day is today?"

"It's Friday."

"No, the day, the....."

"You mean the date?"

"Yes, the date. Do you know what it is?" She couldn't wait for me to answer. "It's the twenty-nine of February."

I didn't bother correcting her lack of an ordinal number.

"So it is," I said.

"It's the leap day. Didn't you teach us that last week?"

"I think so, yeah." Last week was a blur at this stage of the evening.

"It only happens every one thousand, four hundred and sixty days," Patricia continued. "I like the idea that women have more power on this day, that we can declare.....no, what's the word?.....propose, to a man."

"That's true."

"What would you say," she was grinning now, but also taking her time, as if trying to ensure that she got the wording right, "if I asked you to marry me?"

I smiled, too, despite my slight unease. She was using our conversation to practice the contents of the previous week's classes. *"What would you say if I asked you to marry me?"* was pure second conditional, exactly what we had just been studying. A question or statement with 'would' in one clause and 'if' plus the past tense in the other, putting forward an imaginary or hypothetical situation and speculating on what would result. "What would you do if you were rich?" "If you could kiss one celebrity, who would you choose?" "If you were President, what would you do?" - these were some of the second conditional examples we had used in The London School that week.

"I would say," I replied, carefully, in answer to Patricia's question about marriage, "that you were too good for me."

She giggled.

"You know that I'm not really asking you," Patricia said, "it's just hypo..., hy....., hypotekital."

She laughed at her inability to pronounce the word.

"Hypothecital," I said, which made her open her mouth even wider in laughter. I smiled, pretending I had butchered the pronunciation on purpose, though in truth I was tripping over my tongue by now, drunker than I had realised.

Patricia went on with her grammar practice.

"If you could go on a date with any one of the Corrs," she asked, "who would it be?"

"Jim," I replied instantly, thinking, for some reason, of Paulo and Marco.

"If you could change anything about yourself," Patricia went on, "what would you change?"

"I'd have smaller ears."

"If you could do any job in the world, which one would you choose?"

"Camel racer."

I was replying without thinking, trying to make her laugh. I felt infused with alcohol now, I hadn't really eaten any dinner, except for that soup two hours earlier, and had that intense concentration on one subject that drunkenness can bring, that complete shutting out of the rest of the world that is so pleasurable, so dangerous. I noticed now that Patricia was wearing eye-shadow, some foundation, subtle lipstick, adult make-up, as if someone had shown her how to do it properly. I thought back briefly to the conversation that we had had back in October, when I was the clueless newbie, she the overbearing teacher's pet, when I had had to ask her to back off in class and let me be the teacher. She had turned from confident to crushed in an instant, still a girl. She seemed different now, grown.

"So let's go for a walk," I said to Patricia, once she had paused for breath, temporarily out of second conditional questions. I realised that it was exactly the same suggestion that Marco had made to me in Envidia, a week before. Going for a walk wasn't what Marco had wanted then, I didn't stop to ask myself if that was what I really wanted now.

Patricia paused for a second, checked her watch, turned on her bright smile again and said "OK."

I drained my glass, stubbed out my eighth cigarette of the evening and stood up. I could feel Sergio's gaze on me as we passed by the counter on the way out the door. "*Adeus*," I said, just glancing in the large man's direction, wishing he would stop staring at me. *Relax*, I wanted to say, *we're just going for a walk.*

It was a relief to get out into the open air. It wasn't yet cold, the breeze coming from the city direction was light but picking up. The little noises of Graça were all around, people pulling down the shutters of bars and cafes, old geezers calling out to each other from across the road, a moped, sounding like a buzz-saw, then the creak and groan of the tram coming from the centre as it laboured its way up the hill. Patricia's chatter had slowed, she still talked on but less intensely, saying how much she liked A Lua, how her parents had taken her there after her confirmation. *Her confirmation*, I thought, *only three or four years ago.*

We drifted over towards the miradouro, the viewing point near Mario's coffee place. From there we could see half of the city below, as well as the castle, over to our left, just a little above the level we were at. The great stone structure glowered down on Lisbon like a dog protecting its master. Mario's was now closed, there were only a few people dotted around the open space, three or four perched on the wall at the edge of the miradouro, a girl and a guy sitting on the ground against the wall of the church to the right.

We sat on one of the benches facing the sheer drop to the rest of the city. No-one took any notice of us, we were just another couple out walking around Graça at midnight on a Friday. There was the kind of silence there that wasn't really silence. There were no distinct, discrete noises but Lisbon below emanated this low, constant hum, like a machine on standby, like a sleeping animal. I turned in Patricia's direction with my right arm draped over the back of the bench. She sat still, her body facing forwards, her head tilted slightly towards me.

"Do you come here with every girl you are with?" she asked, sounding like she was repeating something she had heard in a film once.

"No," I said, truthfully, "just with you."

I had never been there with Dina - she wouldn't have allowed it, it was too public - and I hadn't really been with anyone else. I had no clear plan, I didn't really know what I was doing there, though it felt temporarily right, this girl and me together, only twelve years separating us, less than half a generation. If we had both been ten years older the difference in age would have been irrelevant.

The city below continued with its low growl. I moved closer to Patricia, who seemed to shiver slightly. She had initiated this process, whatever it was, she had followed me on at least four occasions, had waited until she was sixteen to actually come and approach me on one of her stalkings, but I wondered now if she were losing her nerve with whatever it was she had had in mind.

"Cold?" I asked her.

"No, I'm fine," she said.

Patricia turned now to face me and put her left hand on my arm that was still outstretched there on the bench back, as if she had made a decision to follow through with something.

"You smell of alcohol," she said.

She smiled as she said this. We were close now, our faces maybe five or six inches apart. Time appeared to have stopped, there was nothing but the present moment. What was about to happen seemed impossible, absurd, but also inevitable. I reached out my left hand towards her face, her cheek was the softest thing I had ever felt. Patricia's dark eyes were open wide now, I thought I could see myself reflected in them. She smiled slightly at the touch of my hand, leaned her face into it. I heard a noise behind me, footsteps, distant but definite, coming closer. I paid no attention to them, wanting to prolong the touch of Patricia's skin as long as I could.

"Hey Cian!" said a voice from behind that I instantly recognised, "is you. I think, is Cian, and I'm right. You don't come for coffee today."

Mario. I turned to see his skinny frame and big grin coming towards us. My initial instinct was to tell him to fuck off.

"Hello Mario," I said, not introducing my companion. He turned to her anyway, still smiling, showing absolutely no sign that he knew what was going on.

"*Tu es Patricia Coelho, não es*?" Mario said, squinting at her now.

"*Sim, sou,*" she said, in a small voice, confirming that she was indeed who Mario thought she was.

Mario looked at me, apparently incurious still.

"Patricia is friend of my sister."

"Really?" I said.

"Yes."

He then said something else to Patricia in Portuguese, and she replied, briefly. Mario nodded, then turned to me again.

"Cian, we play football tomorrow, Nuno is.....*doente....como se diz*?" Mario looked at Patricia for help with the translation.

"Ill," she said, more sure of herself, "Nuno is ill."

"Yes," Mario went on, "Nuno is ill. You can play?"

"Sure, Mario," I said, "I can play." I didn't feel that I was in a position to refuse. "At three o'clock?"

"Yes, three."

Mario just stood there, smiling. He seemed to have run out of things to say, yet showed no sign of leaving. Time stopped. I didn't know what was going to happen, it seemed impossible that anything could. Part of me wanted Mario to go, another part wished he would stay and stop me doing whatever it was I was going to do. I could feel Patricia stirring beside me as Mario just remained there, still grinning.

Eventually she stood up.

"I have to go," she said, smiling uncertainly at me, looking like a girl again, smoothing down her clothing that wasn't in any way creased. For a few seconds both she and Mario were standing there looking down at me sitting on the bench. Then Patricia moved off, giving us both a girly wave. Mario said something to her as she went. Patricia looked at him, then at me, and said "*está bem*," - "alright".

"I go with her," Mario said, "not safe at night."

I felt paralysed, thinking I should do something, not knowing what.

"OK," I said.

"I'll see you soon, Cian," Patricia said, mature again now, somehow in control.

Mario and Patricia moved off down the hill towards the short cut to the Mouraria, where she lived. Now it was Patricia's turn to listen as Mario chatted. I could hear him from my place up above as they descended. Patricia looked back once, though I couldn't tell what she was thinking. It was getting cold, this time I shivered a little. I felt drunk, and clueless. As February turned to March Patricia and Mario disappeared from view and I stood up to look over the edge of the wall at the semi-sleeping city below.

MARCH

On the first Wednesday in March I was in our London School staffroom with Laura, Joanne and Carol. I was eating a tasteless ham sandwich, we were all lost in one activity or another when the door from the reception area opened, then closed, and Sebastian came down the narrow corridor towards us. Normally so carefully groomed, he had stains down his pale linen shirt, which was creased, and his thin, sandy hair was uncombed and sticking up, the part in it now undetectable. His eyes were red and swollen, and he was crying.

Laura looked at me as I half-heartedly chewed my sandwich. She mouthed one word - "Fernando" - to me as Seb approached. Carol was in one corner, cutting and sticking flashcards for her kids' class, Joanne was in another corner, day-dreaming, absent-mindedly picking at a salad. Neither noticed our Senior Teacher as he came sniffling into the room.

Seb and Fernando had been on and off again multiple times in the last few months, and this had been bothering Sebastian recently. He gently laid the pile of books he had been carrying on to the nearest counter-top and then slid quietly into the nearest uncomfortable armchair.

"Perry is dead," he said, neither dramatically or with much emotion. He spoke flat, as if he were imparting information that had been known for a while.

"Fuck off," said Laura, disbelieving.

Sebastian looked at her, almost blankly.

"I've been in the hospital all night. He had a heart attack at half past ten yesterday evening, was in a coma for six hours, died about five in the morning yester….no, today, this morning. I'm not even sure what day it is."

"He died?" Laura asked.

"Yes Laura, that's what I fucking said." There was no anger in his voice though, just tiredness.

"Were you with him Seb?" I asked, just to ask something.

"I was there when it happened," he replied, "it was horrible, he turned this pale colour, almost blue."

Here he broke down, put his face in his hands. Joanne had been listening too, at this stage, and now came over to him. She was small enough to be able to put her arms right around him while she stood and he sat. Her dark hair, dark skirt and blouse seemed to have been chosen for the ocasion. Sebastian shook as he wept. Laura looked on, realising that Joanne was occupying the role that she should have been playing, the comforter, the friend.

Carol had now stood up, and came over to rest her hand on Seb's trembling back.

"He was only, what, thirty,….thirty-two?" Carol asked.

"Thirty-four," Seb replied, through tears.

The scene felt unreal to me, like a play. The last time I had seen Perry was the night in Envidia when I had met Marco, and then seen him and Dina's husband sucking face against the wall of the club. Perry had been his jovial self that night, drinking a lot, disappearing every now and then, for one reason or another. He was as he always was, large, smiling, affectionate, piss-taking. The idea that he was no longer breathing was a difficult one to absorb.

Sebastian stood up. Joanne still held on to his hand. She was good at this, I could see, comforting, it came naturally to her, as it didn't at all to Laura. Seb's two best friends in the school had been Perry and Laura, though these two hadn't always seen eye to eye. Laura used to complain that Perry had no interest in women, even as company, as friends or companions. I could see her trying to force herself to be upset for Sebastian's sake.

"I have to go," Seb said, "I have to go over to his place, find his contacts book, start making calls. I don't think I can bear it."

"You want me to come with?" Laura asked, rousing herself.

"No," he said, "I need to do this. Besides, if I go we're already one teacher down, we can't lose another."

This was exactly like Seb. He seemed flighty and lax but in work he was also conscientious and responsible. To prove the point there he was, in our staffroom, hours after his best friend had died.

Laura accompanied Sebastian out to the reception area, her arm now hooked in his as they departed the staffroom. Joanne, Carol and I just looked at each other, unable to figure out what an appropriate thing was to say.

The London School grapevine was unusually quiet too, for a day or two. And then, after a decent forty-eight hours or so, the rumour and speculation began and then quickly picked up speed. The main theme was that Perry had been consuming more cocaine than was good for him and that, overweight as he had been, his heart gave out. The secondary idea bandied about, whispered in the poky bars and taverns of the traditional London School trail around the Bairro Alto, was that some kind of erotic - or auto-erotic - game had been involved, a game that had gotten out of control and gone horribly wrong. Some people even asserted that Sebastian had been involved in some way.

Jamie, my constantly drunk ex-roommate, claimed that he had an exclusive, when a few of us met up in a dark corner of the Record Bar, that Saturday night.

"I have it on good authority," he said, lowering his voice as if he were revealing state secrets, "that there was rope involved, and a swing, and a safety word that never got used."

He wasn't the only one to insist that he had the whole story. There was speculation about prescription drugs, gangsters and suicide attempts. This last one was the most unlikely to me, I had never met anyone less suicidal than Perry. What all the rumours had in common was that they painted Perry as someone involved in something deviant, perilous or semi-criminal. There was an assumption underlying all of this that being gay, he was naturally mixed up in something dodgy. To what extent the whisperings about the way Perry met his end were motivated by actual homophobia was hard to say, but there was certainly an element of resentment there against the Gay Mafia in The London School.

Whether such a thing existed or not in the school was irrelevant, the perception was there and that was enough. Laura was the first person I heard using that term - the Gay Mafia - though no doubt it was in existence before Laura or I even came to Lisbon. What was true was that there was a concentration of gay men in positions of power in the various London School centres in the city. Robert Prior, the overall Director of the school, was said to be part of this so-called Mafia. Perry, before his death, had been the Director of the Avenida school, Sebastian was Head Teacher at our school. One of the two Head Teachers at the Rossio centre, Edward Hanley, was gay, as was Seamus O'Dea, the only other Irish person on staff, who ran the Porto school in the north of the country.

It seemed unlikely that this was an actual policy. The school was owned by the woman I had met in February, Marie-Ange, who was reputed to have been a supporter of Salazar's regime, a Catholic fascist dictatorship that was clearly no friend to the gays. Yet there did seem to be a high number of gay men in school management. Laura had liked to tease Seb and Perry, speculating about the monthly meetings of the mythical London School Gay Mafia.

"I know how it goes," she said, one night in the Jazz bar in the Bairro Alto, as the two guys looked on, "you all start off plotting how to take over the whole school, scheming, planning world domination, all that. Then you get bored, someone puts Kylie on the stereo, you watch some porn, get some male strippers in, and end up banging each other until you have to get dressed and go into work the next morning."

Sebastian and Perry usually pretended to be offended, but really enjoyed the idea of this secret gay society.

"You're so wrong," Perry had replied that night in the Jazz bar, "it's Abba, we put Abba on the stereo, not Kylie."

Yet Perry wasn't even listening to Abba now, he had ceased to exist. There was a memorial service for him in the central Rossio school at midday on the Monday after he died. The only Protestant minister in Lisbon said a few words, - as if he had known Perry, as if Perry had ever darkened the door of his or any other church - muttered a few prayers and then handed the stage to Robert Prior.

Robert was very solemn, though this was his normal demeanour so it was difficult to know the difference.

"Perry," he said, looking at the gathered crowd of fifty or so teachers and other staff, some of them sniffling and dabbing at eyes with handkerchiefs, "was a wonderful person, an inspiring teacher and a great friend. We here - and I include Marie-Ange with her permission in this - are devastated by his loss."

Half the room looked around to see the shrivelled little lady sitting on a large chair at the back of the meeting room where the service was being held.

"We know that his colleagues in the school will find it hard to go on without him," Robert continued, "as we all will."

I was standing beside Sebastian as Robert said this. Our Senior Teacher covered his face with his hands. I put my hand on his arm, as I imagined Joanne would have done in the situation.

Perry's body was flown back to Brighton so his family could bury him. Talk quickly turned to his successor as Director of the school on the Avenida da Liberdade. The two favourites for the vacant position were Sebastian and Edward Hanley, both Senior Teachers, one in our school, one in Rossio.

The exact process by which the decision was to be made was a mystery, but Marie-Ange was said to be central to the outcome. Jamie opened a book on the race for the directorship, offering odds of eleven to eight on for Sebastian and eleven to ten for Edward. Sebastian, in the days leading up to when we assumed that the announcement would be made, remained calm, gave off an air of indifference, as if he really wasn't bothered whether he got the post or not. Laura, however, knew better.

"If he doesn't get Perry's job," she said, one afternoon in the staffroom, when Seb was in class, "I do not want to be around. He'll be unbearable. He sees that job as his by right, and himself as Perry's natural successor. I just hope he gets it. Or I'm emigrating."

✻ ✻ ✻ ✻ ✻ ✻ ✻

Perry's death, in the first week of March, was really only a distraction for me from my own particular situation. On Tuesday the fourth, four days after Mario had interrupted my and Patricia's little encounter, I invented a virus and rang in sick to work. I missed, among other classes, my First Certificate group which of course included Patricia Coelho. There was no problem with my taking a sick day, it was the first day I had missed for any reason since I had started. No-one was going to question the veracity of my illness, much less on a Tuesday. Monday absenteeism was high, for obvious reasons - Laura alone had missed seven in five months - while people missing midweek days was almost always assumed to be down to actual, non-alcohol related reasons.

I enjoyed my free day, went to the cinema in the afternoon, though avoided Rossio where there could have been London School management or teachers wandering around. I browsed in bookshops and went into the Cathedral, which I passed every day on the tram but which I had never actually visited. After that I mostly just sat around in the flat and luxuriated in all the space, the peace, the lack of Charlie. *I should do this more often*, I thought.

The next day I went back into work and reassured everyone that, having spent most of the previous day vomiting and negotiating bouts of diarrhoea, my stomach bug had resolved itself and I was fine, thanks. The news of Perry's demise then broke, though all continued more or less as normal, classes were prepared, students were taught, English spoken. I had dinner in A Lua that evening, though when it came to time for coffee I stayed where I was and didn't bother going to Mario's, as I normally would have. I still wasn't ready to see anyone who had been a witness to my almost seduction - or her almost-seduction of me - of my sixteen year old student the previous Friday.

I had seen Mario at the weekend, of course, at the football, though

I had turned up at the last minute, just as the game began, and left directly after, so we didn't have time to talk. He had been his normal self, had shown no sign that he thought any less of me, though I wanted to avoid being one on one with him for the foreseeable future. I couldn't, however, avoid Patricia forever. Thursday came around, and the second teenage class of the week was at four-fifteen. The kids filed in, laughing or sullen, chatting or listening to iPods. Patricia wasn't there.

"Patricia said," Sofia, her BFF in the class told me, "that she has to go to the dentist."

I figured that Patricia's dentist appointment was about as real as my stomach bug. All through the class her empty chair seemed to stare at me as I spoke. I felt it was tut-tutting as I attempted to explain the Present Perfect Continuous, giving me evils as I played the CD. *Leave me alone!* I felt like shouting, at this inanimate object of metal and wood.

Finally, on the following Tuesday, Patricia and I were in the same room again. There were only so many fake dental appointments and stomach flus you could pull. Patricia seemed to be her usual self, she sat in the same spot and chatted rapidly to Sofia beside her, though if anything she seemed to be trying too hard to give an impression that all was as it always had been. Then she began what looked to me like flirting, with Julio, the quiet, buck-toothed boy who sat on the other side of her from Sofia. Julio looked bemused at all the attention. Patricia had hardly even spoken to him before, unless it was to upbraid him for not making an effort. She didn't look my way, at least not at first.

I too was conscious of trying to appear as if nothing inappropriate had happened - or nearly happened - with any of those present, and was probably nicer and more patient with the students as a result. Sofia commented on the change.

"Cian," she said, squinting up in my direction, "why can't you be like this every class?"

Patricia, during the class, was subtly different, but only in a way that I would have noticed. She answered every question she could, was as overbearing and enthusiastic as ever, but left out the little comments, extra questions and non-sequiturs that were usually part of her classroom behaviour. Patricia was prone to going off on tangents in class, asking about song lyrics or little used phrasal verbs. Everything with her that Tuesday was uncharacteristically on point and restrained, as if she were holding herself back now, being the studious Patricia she had always been while keeping the curious girl who was constantly voracious for extra information away from the class, away from me. She was suddenly all business.

The class ended, the students snaked their way out, Patricia didn't look at me as she left. I realised that I had been sweating. It was clear that the other students, in their teenage way, were too consumed by their own petty lives and distractions to notice any tension between their teacher and his star pupil. Now that we had finally seen each other I felt better and also a little worse. It was clear that nothing could go back to the way it had been.

That Thursday we had another class, which passed off more or less the same, Patricia involved but playing it straight, me trying not to step on any toes. I wondered if I should try to say something to her, apologise or clarify, or try to seduce her again, but she blew out of there so quickly after class that there was no chance. I let her go, kept quiet.

That night I finally went back to Mario's. It had been almost two weeks, it had already become an awkward, obvious gap of time, any longer would have been a break that couldn't easily have been explained. I ate at home - Charles and Charlotte were at the cinema - and then descended our echoey steps down to street level. Largo da Graça was still busy, there was a hint of brightness left in the sky and a hum of activity remained about the place. I nodded to a few of the locals I recognised as I crossed the street and took the slight incline that led up towards the *miradouro* and Mario's coffee spot.

Mario looked up from serving another customer and smiled as I arrived. He had had his hair cut short, it was almost a skinhead now, it gave him the air of someone tougher, less boyish.

"Cian!" he said, as his previous customer, a middle-aged American lady in a baseball cap, retreated to one of the tables, "the usual?"

"Yeah Mario," I said, "the usual."

He turned to the coffee machine and in ten seconds had completed the whole sacred procedure for the preparation of a *bica*.

I performed the Portuguese sugar ceremony with my coffee and we chatted, as if nothing had happened, as if he had never come upon me trying to seduce my sixteen year old student. Mario talked, in his rapid-fire, random way, about his grandmother, and what she thought of his new crew-cut, about his boss, who was a great "*chato*" - 'a pain in the arse', I supposed - and about this girl, Margarida, who said she liked him but who would only let him kiss her, nothing more. There was no mention, from either of us, of Patricia Coelho, or of the twelve days that I had avoided his coffee place. The fifteen or so minutes I spent there failed to clear up a question I had had since that Friday night when Mario had come across Patricia and me on the bench in Graça. How aware was he of what was happening, what was about to happen that night?

I suspected that there was more to his intervention than him simply saying hello and asking me about the football, though I couldn't be sure about this. Was he, consciously or unconsciously, trying to protect Patricia - this friend of his sister - from me? Or even to protect me from her? Or was he, in fact, exactly as gormless as he seemed to be. Had he simply blundered into the middle of a situation that he didn't fully understand, or didn't think about at all? I never quite knew for sure.

Whatever the answer was, the truth is that he saved me in a way, that night. Without his role in proceedings I have no idea what would have happened. I suspect - or at least I like to think - that I would have probably kissed Patricia, maybe going a little farther, but that sense would have returned at some stage and I wouldn't have taken her the two minutes walk back to my first floor flat, wouldn't have undressed her, wouldn't have - though perhaps I wouldn't have been the first - taken her virginity. I like to think that that would have been the case, but can't in all honesty swear to it, drunk and self-pitying and horny as I was. Whatever, Mario made these questions - what would have happened? how far would I have gone? - purely hypothetical, like all of those other Second Conditional questions that Patricia had put to me in A Lua that night, about marrying her, and choosing which Corr to go on a date with, and being an animal. And for this fact I had to be grateful to him.

I did wonder too, what Mario and Patricia had talked about on their walk home. He had accompanied her back to her house that Friday night. Had he warned her about me, asked her what the hell she thought she was doing, had he played the big brother role? Or had he just talked her ear off, as he normally did to me, still apparently oblivious to what he had just prevented from happening? I couldn't ask him this, of course, this was one thing I couldn't talk to Mario - or to Patricia - about.

It also made me question myself. Had I, in fact, such a tenuous grip

on the basics of civilisation? Could drink and a pity-party reduce me
to such a level that I was prepared to sleep with my teenage stalker? I
needed to say the words to someone, to describe what had happened,
or nearly happened, to another human being who wouldn't judge me,
just to get them out of my brain. I arranged to meet Mike in his local
cafe, A Brasileira. It was the same place I had met Dina so she could
dump me.

We sat outside. I bought him a beer, and a bica for myself.

"So," Mike said, "what is it you wanted to talk about?"

Now that I was here I didn't want to say it. I went ahead anyway.

"I had an encounter, with one of my students. A female student."

"Oh yeah?" Mike was suddenly interested, "an encounter you say?"
He was smiling now.

"Yes. I'm not sure exactly what else to call it."

"Interesting. Some MILF from an Advanced class, I bet," Mike said,
smiling.

"No, from my teenage class."

"Woah!" he said, "you dark horse!" He sounded impressed.

"I don't think it's something to be proud of, Mike," I said, regretting
I had decided to confide in him now. "Anyway, nothing actually
happened. It probably would have, but we were interrupted."

"Nothing happened? Then where's the problem?"

"But I was going to....," I began, not sure exactly how to finish the
sentence.

"Wait a second, it wasn't that wee girl, your stalker? Oh fuck, man,
not the stalker!" Mike was making me feel worse by the minute.

"I'd prefer not to say who it was. And I was drunk. And had just
been dumped. In here in fact, Dina met me here to finish it," I indicated
inside, where the dumping had actually taken place. "She told me she

was going back with her husband. Anyway, that's not the point. What kind of person decides to sleep with his teenage student just because he was given the elbow?"

"Jesus, that Catholicism really did a number on you, didn't it? Let the guilt go, man. You didn't fucking do anything. Just be glad, and move on. Learn a lesson."

This actually made some sense, though didn't totally relieve the weight of that Friday night. It had helped, in the end, to at least tell someone about it, even if it was Mike, with his own dodgy past in this area. That said, I knew that I would not be free of it until the end of the year, twice a week I would have to confront what I had nearly done. It came home to me again, as I watched Patricia in class with her peers, that she was in the process of leaving adolescence, on her way out of those formative years, yet still in some senses a child. It made me uncomfortable for weeks after just to be in the same room as her, and to recognise her as an ingénue who had gotten herself into a situation with me that she had not thought through. Every Tuesday and Thursday at a quarter past four from that moment on, mixed in with all the swirling nonsense that occupied my brain at any one time, seeing Patricia Coelho in her teenage First Certificate class caused me to have one clear thought - *What the fuck was I thinking?*

✳ ✳ ✳ ✳ ✳ ✳ ✳

On the Friday after I had returned to Mario's for the first time in thirteen days, I arrived in to the school ten minutes late, hurrying in the hope that Elizabeth wouldn't notice. There was a lot of commotion going on in the staffroom as I entered, I could hear it from the corridor outside.

"But he has only been in the school five months," Sally was saying, as I walked in. No-one paid me any attention. Were they talking about me? What had I done now? I hadn't seen Sally, the long-haired, sandal-wearing vegetarian in our midst, so exercised by anything since I had met her. She was the most undemonstrative of all the staff. Laura called her 'The Ice Queen'.

"This is ludicrous," she said, loudly.

In truth, everyone was now speaking at once. As well as Sally, Laura was there, and Sebastian, Carol sat off to the side but still made comments, and even timid Joanne was looking inward and talking at a person that was sitting against the back wall, now surrounded by my colleagues.

"He is a nice boy," I could just about make out from Carol, "but how can he run a whole school?"

Carol wasn't as indignant as Sally had been, but she certainly wasn't happy either. No-one paid me any attention. I stood behind the group and peered in over Laura's shoulder. I saw that it was Mike sitting there, looking up at everyone, his shaven head beginning to show signs of regrowth, a cup of milky coffee in both hands. He saw me and half-smiled, nodded. He seemed unperturbed by the interrogation. Joanne looked around at me, the others were too intent on their questioning.

"Mike," Laura said, taking advantage of a temporary break in the stream of talk, "you are sure about this, right? You haven't got some important piece of information wrong somewhere?"

Mike took a slow sip of coffee and looked up at her.

"Look, Laura doll," - he knew it pissed her off when he called her 'doll' -, "you don't like the message, don't shoot the messenger. And don't talk to me like I'm a moron."

"Can someone please tell me what the fuck is going on," I asked, exasperated now.

Sebastian turned around, though he didn't say anything.

"They've made Adam the new director. They've given him Perry's job," Laura said to me.

"Mike is here to take Adam's classes," Joanne explained, ever helpful.

I looked at Seb. He was pale, and still hadn't said anything. He had really, really wanted that job. I wondered how long it had taken his mind, after Perry's death, to go from grief to ambition, to go from mourning his friend to coveting the job his friend's passing had just left vacant. Or whether the two impulses could co-exist comfortably.

"Oh," was all I found I could say.

For some reason I wasn't that surprised. Our tête-à-têtes with Marie-Ange now made perfect sense, and all her inane questions about who had influenced me, and if I saw myself as a leader, suddenly seemed relevant. Her meetings with first year teachers were, in effect, job interviews for positions that may open up in the future. She had been attempting, in her rigid, old-lady way, to sift through the rag-tag collection of new arrivals to find potential senior members of staff, those who could take charge if called upon. Adam had obviously scored highly on whatever warped scale she had been using. Perhaps he had betrayed a certain willingness to use torture to achieve good results in management.

"So that's all folks," Mike said, "that's all I know. I'm going outside for a smoke."

He stood up, pushed open the glass door that led to our smoking area, and stepped outside. I felt like joining him, though wanted to wait a little to see what the reaction would be to Mike's news. I found that I was personally indifferent. Adam and I had never had anything in common and his absence was nothing to me. The injustice of a guy who had worked in the school for only five months leapfrogging over a host of other candidates for the post of Director seemed entirely consistent with how the school was run.

"I take back what I said about the Gay Mafia," Laura was now saying to Seb, who still hadn't spoken. She rubbed his back awkwardly in an attempt to comfort him. "Unless Adam has changed teams."

"He definitely hasn't done that."

This came from Joanne, the last word in her clipped New Zealand accent sounding like "thet". Something in her tone made Laura turn to her.

"Why do you say that, Joanne?"

"Oh," Joanne now looked uncomfortable, her cheeks showing spots of red, "I really can't say, I shouldn't have said." All of a sudden she was a little girl, caught out.

"Joanne," Seb said, finally speaking, "what do you know?"

Joanne was Rahul's girlfriend, and had been since the second day of Basic Training back in September, three days in fact after they had met. Rahul was my and Mike's old roommate from the Pensão Imperial, and now shared a flat in Benfica with drunken Jamie and Adam - our ex-colleague and now Director of the school on the Avenida. Joanne spent half her week there at her boyfriend's apartment and so would have had a certain regular contact with Adam. Every teacher knew this, it was basic London School knowledge, like knowing who our director was, or which bar sold the cheapest Tequila.

"No, nothing, it's....," Joanne said, babbling a little now, "maybe I'm wrong."

If Joanne had been more used to dissembling she could easily have justified her comment, inventing a stream of unknown girls coming out of Adam's room each morning. She was too honest for her own good, though, and had perhaps been wanting to tell someone for weeks. She took a breath, as if before diving into the sea, and spoke.

"Adam and Elizabeth are......seeing each other."

There was a brief moment of silence, like before a thunderclap. Then the reactions came.

"Now I know you are dreaming."

"You have got to be fucking joking!"

"Adam and Elizabeth!?"

"That's not possible."

"Get the fuck out of here!"

These exclamations all came together, and at high volume. I think at least one of them came from me. Joanne looked like she was already regretting having said anything.

"Ssssssh!" she said, leaning forward and putting a tiny finger to her lips, "she might hear."

"Elizabeth's in Rossio," Sebastian told her, "some kind of summit meeting. So spill."

Joanne still looked doubtful.

"I've seen her leaving his room three times now. At about six or seven in the morning. Sometimes I can't sleep, it gets so hot in Rahul's room, so I go and sit in the lounge in the dark and listen to my iPod. Elizabeth tip-toes out of Adam's room, she only puts her shoes on in the corridor."

Everyone was staring at her now.

"I haven't even told Rahul."

This was an indication of how scared Joanne was of Elizabeth. She and Rahul told each other everything.

"Joanne," Laura said, now holding the girl's left arm, "you're not fucking with us, are you?"

"It's the truth," the Kiwi girl replied, simply.

None of us could seriously doubt her. If there was one person among us who wouldn't make something like this up it was Joanne. Mike put his head back in the door from the balcony.

"Whass goin' on?" he asked.

"Adam and Elizabeth are sleeping together," Carol told him.

"Oh that?" Mike replied, unimpressed, "I've known about that for weeks."

✳ ✳ ✳ ✳ ✳ ✳ ✳

It turned out that Adam had confided in Mike about his thing with Elizabeth, soon after it had started, back at the school's Christmas party. Somehow, Mike was someone people wanted to tell things to. I suppose it was his openness, his apparent naivety, the fact that it appeared like he might easily forget any great secret that you would entrust him with, soon after hearing it.

It was also, I suppose, because he was pretty much unshockable. This is why I had found myself telling him about my Friday night with Patricia Coelho in Graça, a week or two before. He wasn't someone you could imagine blabbing your story all over town. He would see this as beneath him. Certainly it hadn't taken Adam long to entrust Mike with the story of his fling with Elizabeth, and it seemed that Mike hadn't gossiped about that with anyone. It made me feel more secure about having given him the secret of my near miss with Patricia Coelho.

Mike fitted surprisingly well into our school, he was now seconded there indefinitely from the Rossio school and so we often met on the tram going down to the Baixa and the Metro stations there. I got on at Graça, he was usually waiting at the stop at Portas do Sol, just above our concrete football pitch. Mike had moved back into his squat again, now that the fuss about his liaison with his teenage lover had died down. Some of the original residents had moved on, according to Mike, so the remaining guys were more laid-back and welcomed his return. If Mike thought that they were laid back, that was saying something.

He and middle-aged Carol became best budds. Mike charmed and flattered her as you would imagine he might do with a prospective mother in law. He was a vegetarian, like Joanne, and they bonded over the difficulty of getting a real meat-free meal in a Lisbon restaurant. Joanne laughed at Mike's tale of how he was once offered chicken as a non-meat option by a waiter in Alfama. He had been to university in Sebastian's home city of Bath, so they had that in common, and he and Laura had a kind of love/hate thing going on, which I know they both secretly enjoyed. Sally had nothing really to say to him, though in truth she had nothing really to say to anyone. It soon became obvious that the loss of Adam had not had a detrimental effect on staff morale at all, in fact it was clear that we had gained by Mike's addition.

Fabian was the only one really put out by Adam's departure. Our French teacher had lost the only other French speaker there, which put him even more on the outside of things. He and Laura had not lasted, for whatever reason, despite their brief rekindling of things at Christmas, and so since his party and his discovery of the wager that everyone but him had known about, he had made less and less effort with his colleagues and become more and more isolated. Now with Adam gone Fabian seemed to become even more withdrawn.

Fabian was the only member of staff not invited by Sebastian down to Café Coimbra at Tuesday lunchtime on the day after St. Patrick's Day. Even Sally came down to drink a galão and listen to Seb's news. Mike and I both had beers, we had had a rare Monday night out on the seventeenth when Mike had called into play his Donegal grandfather, and claimed that it was the duty of his Irish quarter to accompany me to The Wolfhound in the Bairro Alto and to get patriotically hammered. The beer that Tuesday afternoon was cool and nutritious, it felt like it was correcting an imbalance somewhere in my system,. Mike had a baseball cap on that he pulled over his eyes as Sebastian spoke.

"I wanted to tell you all this at once so that there would be no misunderstanding," he began. "I confronted Elizabeth today about her and Adam, and his promotion."

Sebastian paused for effect. He was looking better than he had two weeks previously, after his friend's death, his tan seemed to have miraculously returned and his composure and self-possession were back too.

"Seb," Laura, sitting beside him said, "you are such a drama queen."

"You are free to leave any time you want, Laura," he said, turning to her imperiously.

She put her finger to her lips, zipped and locked them, pointedly, and then threw away the imaginary key. Sebastian carried on.

"We met in her office. I asked her straight out if she was having a relationship with someone who had been, until last week, one of her teachers." Here, he paused again to build the tension.

"She actually blushed."

Again, a pause. Sebastian looked at each of us in turn.

"I didn't even know that she could blush," said Carol, "at least, I've never seen it."

"She was speechless for about ten seconds," Seb went on, "I've never seen that either. Then she told me that that was a private matter, that she wouldn't discuss it with me. In other words, there was something to discuss." Sebastian looked even more pleased with himself than usual.

"But we know that, Seb," Mike piped up from under his baseball cap, "I told you that he told me it was happening."

Seb ignored him.

"She tried to throw me out of her office, but I wouldn't go before I heard her denying, to my face, that she had something to do with Adam getting Perry's job. I know it was her, I know that Marie-Ange loves her, but I wanted to put her on the spot before I left."

"So what did she say?" This came from Joanne, obediently setting Seb up to go on with his story.

"Nothing!" he said, triumphantly, as if this proved everything. "Well, she told me that I was crazy, though what was she going to say? Then she grabbed me by the arm and pushed me out the door, looking guilty."

For the first time since I had met her, back in October, I actually felt some sympathy for Elizabeth. Sebastian had sunk his teeth into this story now, and wasn't about to let go.

"It had to be her," he said, everyone looking at him now, he was clearly enjoying the attention, "she wanted to set her toy-boy up with his own school. How else could he have got the job?"

We dispersed eventually, Sebastian promising that the matter wouldn't rest there. I couldn't have cared less, at that stage, where the matter rested, the day went very slowly and my hangover came back about four, just when I had to teach Patricia and the teens. It probably made the class go better for me. In fact, all I could think of was getting through to the end of the day and so stopped worrying about the fact that Patricia wasn't her old self. I was back, briefly, to my old brusque, take-no-shit self, and it felt good.

By the time eight o'clock came, I was fit to crash. I found myself sharing a Metro with Carol, who was travelling back to the Baixa.

"The truth is, Cian," Carol said, turning in her seat so she was facing me, "Sebastian himself had only been in the school six months when he was made Senior Teacher. Elizabeth got the Director's job after only a year as a normal teacher like you or me, and even Perry was parachuted into the job originally from being a marketing manager with some dog-food company in the UK. That's the way this school does things, they couldn't care less about competence or seniority, they want their guys in positions of power. They want people they can control. Marie-Ange puts folks in who don't know what they're doing, so they do as they're told."

The last time I had heard ideas like these had been from Perry, who had benefited from the very policy Carol was explaining. Perry had never struck me as a yes-man, though I supposed he could have put on a good act of being so. It was, though, the first time that I had heard Carol sound so embittered and resentful about the school and her fellow teachers. Adam's promotion had done this, it had annoyed everyone in some way, except for me, Mike and Joanne, who were all indifferent to London School politics and machinations. Our indifference had varied origins. Joanne was consumed by Rahul and by her teaching, Mike was immune to the kind of collective stress and resentment that had infected the staffroom and I had never had any illusions that this school was a meritocracy, and had certainly never entertained any ambitions of promotion for myself. We three played along with the shock of the others, but it was clear that Adam's rocket-like rise made no real impact on our working lives.

It was Sebastian's birthday on the thirtieth. He was strict about keeping birthday celebrations to the actual date, but this was a Sunday and so he made all of the teachers who he wanted to attend his party promise not to get smashed on the previous Saturday so they would still be fit for the Sunday. This was an almost unheard of suggestion for the London School collective, and in truth the promise was only kept by a few. I was one, though not really by design. The changeable Lisbon March weather had landed me with a scratchy throat and streaming nose, and so I sat in on a Saturday night for literally the first time since arriving to the country, six months before. I took a sleeping tablet to knock me out, and slept for twelve hours, dreaming about being married to Patricia Coelho, about our cleaner in the school being promoted to Director, about my flatmate Charlotte getting pregnant and giving birth to lizards.

Still, I felt better after my deep deep sleep, and by nine o'clock on Sunday evening, when Sebastian's party was due to start, I was good to go. It felt wrong to be drinking on a Sunday, though this soon passed after the first few glasses of Seb's homemade sangria, which he served to all-comers in his flat near Campo Grande. Most people arrived early, for a change. Given that everyone was due in to work the next day, there were those that had planned to have a few drinks, pay their respects and – shockingly – go home before midnight.

It was easy to tell who had not kept their promise about being abstemious the night before. Fernando was sat in a corner by half eleven, nursing a coke. Joanne and Rahul came, shared a glass of sangria and left. Sylvia and Anna did the same and Carly, - who had strangely become good friends with Sebastian - was asleep on his couch by midnight.

The only ones who lasted the pace were Seb himself, Scottish Mike, Jamie, who never had enough alcohol, me, who hadn't been out the night before, Melissa, the third member of The Three As, as well as Fabian and Laura. These last two disappeared together sometime around two o'clock and were found dry-humping in the bathtub. The rest of us got shit-faced, stoned, sat on Sebastian's Iranian carpet and listened to The Doors and The Stone Roses, bitched about what pricks the London School management were and discussed our first sexual experiences. Melissa then slipped off somewhere with a smirking Mike, and I managed to gather myself together well enough to get out of there by a quarter past three. I left behind Jamie, snoring in the corner and Laura, Fabian and Sebastian dancing together with their arms linked, in the middle of the room, lit only by the weak light from an upturned lamp. A standard end to a London School party in every way except that it was happening early on a Monday morning.

I tried not to make too much noise as I stumbled in to the flat, but failed miserably in my inebriated way. I brushed my teeth, pissed inaccurately and couldn't find the light switch when I slouched my way in to my box room, and so had to turn on the lamp on my desk to the left. This was when I noticed that there was a bulge in my bed where no bulge should be.

If I had been sober I would have felt some fear, but drunk as I was I simply found it funny, as if it were a game, or a continuation of the party I had just left. My immediate thought was that Patricia Coelho had somehow gained entry, and had decided to resume her stalking activities.

I stepped closer to the bed. What poked out above the sheets was not Patricia's bush of black curls but straight, hay-coloured hair with darts of blond highlights lined within. I pulled the blanket down and poked the occupant of my bed in the shoulder.

"Dina," I said, "Dina, wake up."

She sprang awake, as if she had been waiting to be disturbed. After a second or so of a pause Dina threw back the light duvet and sat up.

Except for her boots, which were on the floor by the bed, she was fully clothed, in a dark hoody sweatshirt with MICHIGAN across the front and pair of faded jeans which always made her look good, slim and compact as she was.

"Where were you?" she asked.

She said this as if I were her husband, out without explanation or permission.

"At a party."

"On a Sunday?"

"It was Sebastian's birthday."

Sober, I might have been less willing to answer her questions, more ready with some of my own. But drunk, it still seemed like some kind of game, and I felt like playing along. I looked down at Dina, raised my eyebrows in an obvious manner, and waited for her to explain.

"I wanted to talk to someone," she began, "Charlotte let me in, she said I could wait for you. I didn't know that you would be so late." Again, it sounded like an accusation.

"Yeah, you're right," I said, "I really should stay in every night, just in case you want to call around for a chat. I'm so sorry."

I smiled, to show her that I was at least half-joking. She smiled back, but her heart wasn't in it.

"Have you got any booze?" she asked.

I laughed.

"Booze?"

I always found it funny when she used these colloquialisms.

"There's some beer in the fridge."

We sat in the small, windowless living-room with the television on for light. The main bulb had blown a week before and no-one had bothered to change it. An episode of Will and Grace was on, on the

SIC channel. It was in the original English, with Portuguese subtitles below. Will and Grace were arguing over whether their neighbour was straight or gay, and over which one of them he wanted to go out with. I thought of Sebastian, and Fabian and Laura, and how I had just left the three of them locked in an embrace together back in Seb's living-room. I turned the sound down on the TV and opened Dina's Heineken for her. She drank from the bottle, even though I had brought a glass.

"Rui and I went away this weekend," Dina began.

"Oh yeah, where did you go?"

"That's not important," Dina said, "it was Figueira da Foz, we have family there. Anyway, I told Paulo that we'd be back today,....yesterday, I mean, Sunday. We left on Friday, Rui had a day off school, Paulo didn't come, he said he had to work at the weekend. But Rui, he has asthma, you know, he needs his, you know, inhaler." Here she made a squirting gesture with her hand and brought it to her mouth.

"He lost it, forgot it on the beach in Figueira on Friday. He needs it everyday, so we had to come home early. I rang Paulo to tell him, he didn't answer. I left a message."

She took another long draught of beer, I took a sip of mine. It was actually the last thing I needed at that second. Dina stared at the screen for a moment as the scene changed to Grace's office, where Karen and Jack were talking, laughing, gesturing theatrically. Dina smiled briefly, reading the Portuguese translation at the bottom of the screen, following the dialogue.

"I used to love this show in the States," she said. "I could really have used the subtitles then though, I only understood about half, at first."

We both watched the television. I left my beer to the side, now past the stage where I could drink any more. Dina drank in silence for a while, then went on with her story.

"So I drove back to Lisbon," she said, "we got home at four, five o'clock. Rui went inside to play Madden, I go upstairs to change."

Unusually, her grammar was slipping. Her voice was flat, as if she were trying to contain herself. I felt I knew what was coming, as if it were an episode of a sit-com I had seen before.

"The door to our bedroom was half-open. I pushed it, and saw that there were two people in my bed, our bed. Paulo was there, and this.... this..."

It was like her face collapsed in on itself. It was the first time I had seen her cry.

"It was a fucking boy," she said, through tears, semi-sobs, "eighteen, nineteen, naked chest, in shorts. A fucking man!"

She fought on to tell the story.

"Paulo was totally naked. He jumped up when I walked in. He still had.....an erection. Oh, *Jesus*!"

This last word was said in Portuguese, it sounded like *Zhezoosh*. She put her head between her hands. I put my hand on to her shoulder, then slid it on to her back and rubbed gently. The Heineken bottle was tipping forward so I took it out of her hand and set it on the floor. On the screen, Jack and Will were arguing about something. In the subtitles, amid the rush of Portuguese, appeared the untranslated, untranslatable 'Gay-dar'. Dina looked up at me.

"My husband was sleeping with another man, Cian."

I pulled her closer, she hung on to me a little. I didn't think about what I said next, we were intimate, I felt relaxed, like I could say anything to her.

"It's better that you know, Dina," I told her, "I'm just glad that you found out. I've been wondering if I should tell you for the past two months or so."

This is what happens with excess alcohol, or at least what happens to me. My filter goes down, the goalkeeper that stops thought automatically becoming speech is taken away and I say things that, sober, I would know were not smart. Sober, I would have weighed up the situation, suppressed my blabbermouth self and told myself to keep certain information quiet. But I wasn't sober, I hadn't been sober for about seven hours. The alcohol and dope had dulled me and left me in no state for a conversation like this.

Dina sat up straighter and pulled away.

"Wait," she said, "hold on. What do you mean, 'tell me'? You knew about this?"

As a mark of the dull stupidity of the state I was in, it was only then I realised that I had revealed too much. It was too late to back out now and besides, I had been wanting to tell Dina this since the night I had seen Paulo with his tongue down another man's throat.

"I was in Envidia one night," I said, "I saw him there."

"Cian, what the fuck is Envidia?" she asked. Dina had stopped crying by now.

"It's a gay club in the Bairro Alto. I went there with Seb - this is the guy whose birthday it was tonight - and some other people, some gay, not all. Paulo was with another guy there, Marco, kissing him. They were against the wall when we were walking out, I recognised his forearms, they're thick, you know, like Popeye's. It was definitely him."

I was rambling now, making a mess of the story. Dina was staring at me with something close to hatred.

"I was going to tell you," I lied, improvising, "but you had just got back with him, you said that you wanted a father for Rui, I didn't want to be the one to…"

"Bullshit!" Dina shouted, "*filho da puta, foda-se, caralho da merda.*

Motherfucker. *Porquê....?"*

I had grasped a lot of what she said at first, most of the words were included in The Two Manuels' list of Portuguese curses, but then she let off a stream of language that flowed over and off me without leaving a trace.

"I don't understand you, Dina," I told her.

"No, Cian, I don't understand you. How could you not tell me? My husband is a *maricas* and you leave me in the dark!" She stood up, knocking the beer bottle as she did so. It tipped from side to side and almost fell.

"This was funny to you, right?" she went on, "entertaining! Watch Dina try to play house with her faggot husband. Well fuck you, Cian, fuck you!"

She had heavy brown boots on, with these she kicked at the green beer bottle on the floor and sent it flying towards the far wall where it smashed into various sized fragments, staining the wall and leaving a beer smell in the air. Her exit wasn't any quieter, the heavy front door was deliberately slammed, the sound of wood on wood seemed to linger on well after Dina had reached the street door below and disappeared into the Graça night.

The silence fell again, only to be broken by Charles' sinister South African voice from their room next door. His squeezed vowels and clipped consonants made even his expression of anger sound formal and controlled, though still somewhat menacing.

"Whit the feck is geng on aht theh?" it sounded like.

I ignored him. The Two Charlies had recently begun coming in late themselves, at two and three in the morning sometimes, and having loud, drunken arguments in the living-room and kitchen, with no thought for my slumber. For good measure I opened our apartment door, slammed it shut again, and did the same with my own bedroom door, partly because I could, partly because I had just realised how stupid I had been and needed a way to express this physically.

In my own tiny space I then kicked the fragile wooden child's chair that came with the desk, just as Dina had kicked her beer bottle against the wall. It briefly felt good to do this, righteous, a release, before it dawned on me that I had to clean up the remnants of Dina's anger. The green shards left over after her destruction of the Heineken bottle were still in the living room, as well as the pool of stale-smelling alcohol it had left.

I had been so close. It would have taken almost nothing to keep my mouth shut. I had become, for a brief time, someone that Dina had needed. She had come to me when she had found out about Paulo and yet in the space of two seconds I had ruined that, ruined it by speaking. I nicked my finger when picking up the glass and stained the kitchen sponge red with my blood while trying to mop up the beer.

I had forgotten to turn off the TV. Another Will and Grace episode was on, Jack and Will were in a gay club - one that looked nothing like Envidia - with an old lady in a fur coat. I switched off the set. I left the living-room not much better than it had been immediately after Dina had stormed out, now there was less sharp glass but more blood stains on the parquet floor. I didn't care. I wrapped ten squares of toilet paper around my bleeding thumb and lay down on the narrow bed that, thirty minutes before, had contained a warm Dina. It still smelled faintly of her. Fully clothed, I fell into a heavy, solid sleep, pock-marked by visions of violence, glass breaking, grown men shagging silently in a white bed.

APRIL

By late March Sebastian's standards had slipped. He had begun turning up for work unshaven, often arriving in late, beginning classes ten minutes after they should have begun, finishing early. For the majority of London School teachers this was almost par for the course, if they could get away with it. For punctual, fastidious, professional Sebastian, this was unheard of.

April arrived and things got worse. He started wearing jeans in to school, cultivated a kind of permanent stubble and stopped wearing ties or buttoning his shirts properly. Seb drank most days at lunch, half bottles of wine, glasses of brandy, beer, whiskey, and began affecting an indifference to the day-to-day running of our London School that he had been completely on top of, just three weeks before. No-one now got told off for leaving books back on the wrong shelf, for forgetting to record the contents of what they had taught in each class in our class folders, for abandoning wrappers and sandwich crusts on plates in the staffroom, all things that Seb had - in his own charming, subtle way - kept a lid on all year. It was clear that he didn't give a shit anymore.

I was in my teenage class one Tuesday afternoon, as usual trying to avoid Patricia's eye as she pretended that everything was normal. I was attempting to get the students' attention and not really succeeding, as the sun pushed its insistent way through the wide window at the back of the room. I found I couldn't concentrate, as the racket from the classroom next to mine was making it difficult to even make myself heard. There was a buzzing and a thrumming coming from the adjacent room. I went out into the corridor and knocked on the wooden classroom door, through which I could feel, with my hand pressed to its surface, the deep bass lines from the music being played inside.

Sebastian opened the door to me.

"Hey Cian," he said, "come in, join the party."

Seb's iPod was on his desk and was connected to a large set of speakers that were, at that moment, blasting out Betty Boo's one big hit from the eighties, 'Doing the Do'. His fifteen and sixteen year old students were in the middle of the floor, most of them dancing, though some of them - no doubt Seb's equivalents of Patricia Coelho - looked a little non-plussed at missing valuable English class time. Sebastian went to join them, showing off his moves, attempting to convince his students to emulate him. I walked over to his iPod, unplugged it from the speakers and took it with me back to my classroom. The sudden silence was almost as intense as the noise had been, moments before. Strangely Seb didn't put up a fight, or even really protest - although some of his students did. He knew that he had gone too far and felt that he had already made his point, whatever that was. All he said, later in the day when I returned his silver, customised iPod was, "Everyone loves Betty Boo."

The situation had to come to a head at some stage, and it was a kiss that did it. It was a Friday in the second week in April, I had just had a coffee in the Café Coimbra downstairs, and met Fernando, Sebastian's friend/boyfriend, on his way up the stairs to the school. It was unusual to see him at the school.

"Hey 'Nando," I greeted him, "what brings you here?"

"Sebastian," he said, "He's being a bitch these days. We're going for a late lunch, we have to talk."

We climbed the stairs together and reached reception. On the other side of a large glass partition we could see our two secretaries in their office. The doors of five or six classrooms opened into this reception area, and the glass wall allowed anyone in the administration office to see everything that went on there. Most of the classroom doors were ajar now, students were milling around, both adults and teens, some just finished class, others about to start. Elizabeth and Sebastian were in the office with Mafalda and Paula, they were standing around chatting, not much work was being done.

Sebastian spotted Fernando through the glass and came out of the office towards us. He had to weave around a couple of mini-knots of students who had gathered together, pre- or post-class. Sebastian walked up to Fernando, put his hand to the back of his friend's neck and kissed him, squarely on the lips. The kiss went on and on, five seconds, then ten, then twenty, with lip movements, a suggestion of tongues, until 'Nando finally managed to detach Seb, like a parent leaving down a clingy child. There were shouts from some of the people standing around, incoherent expressions of shock or hilarity, as well as a few claps and a lot of stares. Fernando, not exactly a shame-filled, retiring gay man, held Seb at arm's length and said something to him in Portuguese that included the word "*maluco*". He was, I could work out, asking him if he was fucking crazy.

Sebastian had got his audience. It was clear that this was what he had wanted. Elizabeth, skinny Mafalda and corpulent Paula - as well as fifteen or twenty students - were all watching his performance. Sebastian grabbed Fernando's hand and led him, unresisting, to the top of the stairs that Fernando and I had just climbed. They both disappeared, on their way back down to ground level. The volume of conversation in our little reception area had increased three-fold, there was laughter, a couple of still incredulous expressions, three or four people on mobile phones recounting, in word or text, what they had just seen. Elizabeth looked, through the glass partition, like she wanted to do someone harm.

It was after five by the time Seb returned. By then I had told those among the staff who mattered about the kiss. Laura came running into our shabby little teachers' room with the update.

"They're in her office," she said, "she's called him in."

As well as Laura and myself, Joanne, Carol and Mike were there. Everyone except for Mike followed Laura into the small materials room, the space - almost a cubicle - where the books, CDs and files of exercises were kept. The side wall of this little cubby hole backed on to Elizabeth's office and so we stood there, divided only by a plasterboard wall from the conversation on the other end.

At first it was only Elizabeth we could hear, and even then her voice was muffled.

"Did she say 'aubergine'?" Carol whispered, "I think she said 'aubergine'."

"Sssshhhh!" Laura told her.

We all stood there, three of us - not Joanne, she stood a little way back, and not Mike, he had remained in the staffroom proper as if he were above our eavesdropping - with our ears to the cold wall. Either Elizabeth had moved closer to us or else had begun to raise her voice. Whatever it was that had changed, her words now became much clearer.

"I've been letting your shit slide, Sebastian," she was saying, "after Perry died, but now you've stepped over the fucking limit."

".........only a kiss," we heard from Sebastian, a little farther away.

"Yes, in the middle of fucking reception," came Elizabeth's reply.

"…….same………man and a woman, Joanne and Rahul, say?" Seb was asking, "…….problem with a kiss between two men?"

Sebastian's voice was a little louder now too, and clearer.

"Don't go playing the discrimination card," Elizabeth said, forcefully, "Joanne hasn't been pissing around for the last four weeks, acting like a sulky child. And you have."

I looked over at my fellow eavesdroppers. Joanne had moved closer to the plasterboard wall, and Carol and Laura now both had their ears touching the smooth white surface. They were all concentration.

"And besides," Elizabeth added, "it is different - two guys kissing in public - and you know it is. You knew it was when you did it, that's *why* you did it, to get a reaction. You need to grow the fuck up, Sebastian."

There was a thud from inside, as if an object had been dropped or thrown.

"Sebastian!" Elizabeth roared.

"You know what you can do," he said, now clearly audible, even to Mike back in the main area of the staffroom, who raised his head as our Senior Teacher began his tirade, "you can take that over-achieving toy-boy of yours home and let him pleasure you, and then you can go and fuck yourself!"

There was more yelling after this, though it became incoherent, pure expressions of anger, blurred by the fact that both parties had moved towards the office door and were speaking - or shouting - over each other. All four of us eavesdroppers were already late for class, our students were no doubt at that moment sitting in their classrooms, waiting for their teachers and hearing the soap opera scene unfold from the direction of Elizabeth's office, as if it were an English listening comprehension exercise they would have to answer questions on. Finally the commotion subsided, we heard a concluding phrase that could have been "Fuck you too!" from Elizabeth, and then there was silence, as present and real as the argument had been seconds before.

Sebastian was suspended from his position as Senior Teacher. He gave us the full story in a typically theatrical, indignant manner when we met that weekend in what we called The Record Bar, in the Bairro Alto. We London School teachers took over the side room in the bar, as was our wont, our numbers, with the addition of partners, friends and hangers-on, tended to expand, like a gas, until we fully occupied any available space. Seb sat in the middle and held court, a paragon of offended, regal dignity.

"Robert told me," he said, waving his cigarette around as if it were a baton, "that I could come back, no problem, but only as a normal teacher, one of the plebs. After two years as a Senior Teacher! Naturally I told him to go fuck himself."

I was one hundred per cent sure that Sebastian had not told Robert Prior, our boss, to go fuck himself. They were friends, of a sort, and also had the departed Perry in common, as someone that they had been close to.

"So I'm on strike," Seb went on, "I'm protesting. I've got a labour lawyer - the guy is the best, apparently - and I'm going to take them to court. They do not scare me. I'm going to take them for all they've got."

This last word was accompanied by fist clench. Sebastian held our attention just long enough to finish his speech, and for various unenthusiastic exclamations of "Go Seb!" and "Too fucking right, Sebastian," to be heard. Our hearts weren't in it though, and we soon turned back into our various groups and cliques, we went back to our flirting, our attempts to surpass the previous weekend's level of drunkenness, our discussions as to what lucky bar would be next on the list to receive our exaggerated custom.

Sebastian, though, was true to his word. He went on strike. As the process of finding Seb's replacement as Senior Teacher was put in train, Elizabeth had to temporarily step into his shoes as liaison between management and staff. To this end she began spending more time in the staffroom, a place she usually avoided like the Queen would the servants' quarters. For us teachers Sebastian had effortlessly occupied multiple roles, organiser, confidante, authority figure, fellow-sufferer of Elizabeth's whims, ridiculer of management. It was only watching Elizabeth, now shorn of her right-hand man, trying to do the same, that we realised how good our now striking Senior Teacher had been at his job.

Sebastian began his work stoppage on the middle Monday of the month. That Wednesday there was a ten minute space before the four o'clock classes ended where I found that only I and our Director occupied the shabby staffroom. Elizabeth stood up, theatrically, poured herself a cup of coffee and took the previously empty seat beside me. Elizabeth crossed her legs and attempted to look comfortable.

"So you're Irish, Cian," she said, as if she had just discovered this fact, "didn't you all have a big celebration last week sometime? Saint Patrick, wasn't it?" I saw that her arms were freckled rather than tanned, something I hadn't noticed before.

"That was last month," I told her, "the seventeenth."

"And what do you do on that day?" Elizabeth asked me. "I imagine you all go out and get shit-faced and do that amusing dance where your arms don't move."

I wasn't sure if she was joking or whether this was her way of trying to make a connection with her underling. I couldn't stop myself glancing over at the door every thirty seconds, hoping that it would open and allow some of the others in to dilute my discomfort.

"Sure, we drink," I said, smiling to show that I was joking, even if she wasn't, "but no dancing. We have no rhythm."

"So tell me what Ireland is like," she said then, not really having listened to what I said, "is it *very* poor?"

From somewhere inside me a bubble of patriotism surfaced. In those pre-crash days I readied myself to begin my defence of the Irish economy, the million euro apartments, the conspicuous consumption, the second homes in Bulgaria, the private helicopters.

"We had a cleaning lady when I was growing up," Elizabeth continued, looking off through the open door to the balcony, as if reminiscing, "Bridget, she was called. She had some terrible stories, about pigs in the kitchen and outside toilets. It all sounded so primitive, I mean, I thought Portugal was bad."

I tried to keep my voice even.

"I've never actually seen a pig in real life, certainly not in a kitchen."

This was actually untrue, my aunt and uncle owned a pig farm in north Kerry, and I had visited often as a child. Still, I wasn't going to tell her that.

"Really?" she said, "I suspected that Bridget may have been exaggerating. Still," here she paused, looking thoughtful, "I've always wanted to spend some time there, you know, for a simpler way of life."

I had never been so happy to hear a door opening, never been so pleased to see Joanne, Carol and Laura returning from their four o'clock classes. Elizabeth took this as her cue to stand up.

"Nice talking to you, Cian," she said, staring down at me in her tall way. Then to the others she said, "Good classes, I hope?" Elizabeth began leaving the room without waiting for an answer. "Must get back to work," she said as a parting shot, before clip-clopping her way back to reception.

Laura stood in front of me and raised her eyebrows in my direction.

"I think she thought we were bonding," I said, by way of explanation. "Don't ever leave me alone in here again."

By the middle of April we all had had similar experiences. One day we were in Café Coimbra, at a table on the pavement outside, just underneath our school. The sun was undiluted by clouds, and hot enough that even sun-worshipping Laura sat under the awning as we drank our *bicas, galãos* and 7Ups.

I told the group, exaggerating for effect, about my encounter with Elizabeth. Joanne went next.

"She asked me," she said, "if New Zealand wasn't just a more provincial version of Australia, and whether it was true that there were more sheep than people."

"That is true, though, isn't it?" said Laura from behind her giant sunglasses.

"Maybe it is," said Joanne, evenly, "but it's such a cliché."

Mike had been cornered just the day before, out on the balcony, which doubled as the teachers' smoking zone. Elizabeth emerged just as he was lighting a roll-up.

"She told me," Mike began, rubbing the top of his shaved head, "that she felt sorry for my students, because even she couldn't always understand what I was staying. She said it as if she thought that I would think it was funny too, smiling at me in that gormless way she has. Since then I've been fucking paranoid in class," - here he began exaggeratedly opening his mouth wide as he spoke - "over e-nun-ci-a-ting every fuck-ing thing I say."

It was just possible that Elizabeth's cluelessness was part of an incredibly subtle plan on her part to increase morale in the staffroom. Whatever her intentions, she had succeeded in bringing her teachers together, at least temporarily. She had given us a common enemy, someone we could all feel equally patronised by. When Elizabeth showed up now in our Teachers' Room we began to take it in turns to engage her in conversation, and we fell easily into the convention that no-one could be expected to shoulder a conversation with the boss for more than five minutes at a time. We became a team, for a short time, united by the intrusive presence of Elizabeth and her blunderbuss personality.

I say "we", but this did not include Sally. She was a fourth year teacher and had never had any time for us rookies. Sally was indifferent to us all, in truth, though it didn't bother me in the slightest. She had a Portuguese boyfriend and looked down on the rest of us, except Carol, as being a bunch of feckless blow-ins, only interested in shagging and drinking. She was partly right, of course, but was so insufferable that no-one ever admitted this.

"I'm surprised she actually accepted the job," Mike said, one afternoon when every teacher except Sally was present, "it means she's going to have to actually talk to us."

Laura rubbed her thumb and forefinger together.

"Moolah," she said, "everyone has their price. But I agree, it must be killing her to know that she now has to acknowledge our existence."

"Don't be too hard on her," Carol said, "she's just shy."

"Carol," Laura replied, "you want to see the best in people, that's admirable. But Sally is not shy. She's cold, frosty, like winter."

Sally's first duty as Senior Teacher was to conduct the final observation of the year. Sebastian had observed us all back in November. He had sat in on my First Cert class, the one with Patricia in it. She had ramped up even more her efforts to make me look good, laughing at my half-hearted jokes, telling João and Eduardo beside her to pay attention, generally acting as if she had never been so entertained or fascinated by a class in her life. She was herself, squared.

I was embarrassed by this, but Sebastian, in the feedback session later, just found it funny. He spent most of our post-observation meeting warning me, correctly as it turned out of course, that Patricia had an unhealthy interest in pleasing me. Then, almost as an afterthought, he spent five minutes at the end outlining three quick activities for practicing the Present Perfect Continuous, my teaching point that day. I felt good after, as if I had been done a favour, as if I had been made better.

The same could not be said about my feedback session with Sally. She sat in on my Elementary class, where we practiced questions in the Past Tense. Sally sat beside the whiteboard - in other words directly behind me - and so, although I couldn't see her for most of the time, I was aware of her gaze burning into the back of my head for the whole hour. I felt like I was a contestant on some kind of reality gameshow - So You Think You Can Teach? - knowing I was about to be humiliated by the judges but ploughing on nevertheless.

One night on one of our pub crawls in the Bairro, Seb had told us about the technique for giving feedback, called the Praise Sandwich. You start off with something positive, then slip in any criticism you had, before finishing on another positive note, even if it was only "you have nice handwriting." Sally had obviously never heard of the Praise Sandwich.

"That wasn't great, Cian, was it?" she said as I sat down in the empty classroom directly afterwards, the mixed scents of perfume, garlic and sweat still in the air from the students in my Elementary class who had just left.

For the next twenty minutes the deficiencies in my teaching

technique were systematically and mercilessly laid before me. There was no praise, no sandwich.

"You are too concerned that your students like you, Cian," she said at the end, as I stood up to go, "you know that you can't be everyone's friend."

"*Ice Queen*," I said, under my breath, as I left the room, not looking back.

Of course I wasn't alone. We all got the Sally-treatment. Laura was literally incoherent with rage after her observation. I found her standing on the back balcony that overlooked the desolation of the internal yard, smoking rapidly and muttering.

"Board technique," she was saying, "I'll give her fucking board technique. Apparently there's now a fucking technique for writing on a fucking white board. Fucking hippie Ice Queen bitch!"

She was smoking the cigarette as if she wanted to do it damage. Laura then smiled, suddenly, as if she had just thought of something."

"On the other hand," she said, "she did make Joanne cry."

"No shit?" I said. I could have seen that coming.

"Yeah," Laura went on, still beaming, "real tears. I caught her with the red eyes and the hanky after she saw Sally, though she didn't say a word."

"I can't believe that that makes you feel better," I told her.

"Hey," she said, "we've all been Sallied. Don't tell me that you can't appreciate someone else's discomfort.

It wasn't clear whether it was deliberate, but the week after observations was when Sebastian chose to return. He hadn't even told Laura, he simply showed up one Tuesday morning, looking like his old self, trousers neatly pressed, the parting in his hair similarly impeccable, clean-shaven, in control. Given the week we had just had with his replacement, it was like the return of the messiah.

Fabian and Carol were the first to greet him. They had both had the, by now standard, treatment from Sally. Carol had been most shocked as she had been the one to defend our new Senior Teacher so much from the rest of us. Fabian had also had a lecture in his feedback session, despite Sally's patchy knowledge of French, which must have made it hard for her to understand his class.

"Sebastian," Carol said, kissing him on the cheek, "I'm so glad you're back."

Fabian shook his hand as if Seb were some kind of celebrity. Joanne then hugged him and Laura punched him on the arm, hard, for not having told her that he was returning to work that day. Mike and I both nodded at him, Sebastian acknowledged us in passing, with a brief wave of his hand.

"If only you were here last week," Laura told him, "it was observations. We all need counselling after it."

Sally was down in the admin section, we didn't have to censor what we said.

"Wouldn't have made any difference," Sebastian replied, looking around the staffroom as if he had been gone three years, not three weeks, "I'm back as a pleb, as one of you. I'm back as a teacher."

Seb didn't elaborate, he grabbed some books, took his notes off to the corner and began planning classes. He ignored our predictable requests for more information and the newly deflated mood in the room, and continued, head down, with his work. It was only two days later - two days in which Seb breezed in, taught his classes and kept his mouth shut - that we got the full story, inevitably, from Laura.

Sebastian had apparently accepted all of management's terms in coming back to the school. For all his talk, he had dropped his threat of legal action, had apologised to Elizabeth - no doubt through gritted teeth - and had returned to the school as an ordinary teacher, with the normal drop in pay. He had, in short, been defeated and yet didn't seem to care.

Sebastian had become - a word I would never, ever have associated with him before - meek. He arrived on time, dutifully taught his own classes as well as some of Sally's -which she had to give up because of her extra administration duties - and showed up without complaint for the couple of hours of compulsory materials production that we all hated. He was polite, restrained, respectful to Elizabeth, and showed not one sign of jealousy or resentment towards Sally, who had usurped his position. He did everything without drama, without flourish, with a personality so muted as to be almost extinguished. It was all totally out of character.

I didn't think much about Sebastian though, after his first two or three days back. In truth he blended in to the background so completely that he didn't intrude on many people's thoughts, beyond his entrance on the day that he returned. I had something else to ruminate on, in any event, and it came from a direction that I thought had been settled, a couple of months before.

It was April twenty-eighth, a Wednesday. I came out of my Advanced class and saw, in the middle of the open reception area, the dark curls of Patricia Coelho. Her classes were Tuesday and Thursday, so she had no reason to be in the school that day. I felt my mouth go a little dry, my stomach contract minutely. I had a sudden, rogue thought that she was about to tell me that she was pregnant, as if I could have been in any way responsible.

She saw me and approached, nervily.

"Cian, can we talk?"

It was a line that she had no doubt heard in some American rom-com or high school flick.

"What's wrong, Patricia?" I asked her, probably too sharply.

"Let's go to the café," she said.

It was the first time that we had been alone together since the night in February when I had almost seduced her. I chose a table far enough away from anyone else that we couldn't be overheard, though still not in any way intimate.

"There is a journalist," Patricia began, "a reporter for Correio de Lisboa. He stopped me the other day when I was leaving the Metro station at Martim Moniz."

She stopped and sucked on the straw she had asked for at the counter, only its pink and white top protruding from the bottle. It made her look like a child again.

"He asked me if I was having a relationship with an English teacher in the London School."

"No fucking way!"

Patricia smiled at my expletive. It was the first time that I had cursed in front of her, in front of any student.

"He was this short guy, with a beard, he gave me his card. Here."

She handed me a white business card with the legend NUNO ANTUNES, JORNALISTA, as well as a phone number and an email address. I turned it over. There was only the name of the paper, Correio de Lisboa, on the other side, in bold red letters.

"What did you say to him?" I asked her, wondering already whether this was just a scheme of Patricia's to bring us closer again. She was a good little actress, I had seen that in role-plays we had done in class. Like everything she did she threw herself into the pretend situation and - no matter how contrived it was - she was always totally convincing.

"I told him the truth, of course," Patricia said, smiling innocently at me, not elaborating on what that truth was, exactly, according to her. She looked adult again now, knowing. I suddenly remembered what had attracted me to her that Friday night in February, before Mario had - luckily or unluckily - interrupted us on that bench in Graça overlooking the city.

"He continued asking me," Patricia went on, "he was really annoying. I told him that I was going to call my uncle, who is a policeman, and he left me alone after a few minutes."

She was enjoying this, I could see. It was dramatic, it put her at the centre of the attention of two men, gave her an excuse to have a drink with me alone in a café.

"Where did he get that idea? Did you ask him? Did he say?"

I was trying to appear calm, teacherly, though I knew that I was failing.

"He said that he had a......." here she paused, unsure of the word, "*fonte, fonte, como se diz*?" Patricia muttered, flicking through a dictionary that she pulled from her bag. The backpack shaped like a teddy bear had been replaced by a very grown up leather satchel, three months before.

"He said that he had a *source*," she confirmed, after the Collins dictionary had given up the meaning she needed.

"A source," I repeated.

Suddenly I had to wonder what I was doing there. Nothing had happened between Patricia and me, there was no story there. Why were we even talking about it?

"Did you speak to anyone about...," - what was I going to call it, 'our night together', 'the time we nearly had sex'? - "....about you and me?"

"No, of course not," she said, mock-offended, "there's nothing to tell, is there?"

I wasn't sure that I believed her, about this or about anything she had said in the last ten minutes.

"OK," I said, standing, ready to get out of there now, "thanks for telling me about this Patricia. I'll see you in class. If you see that guy again, just tell him to fuck off."

I threw out the expletive on purpose, almost as a parting gift. I knew that she liked hearing authentic, English swearing.

She didn't smile at this though, she was less easy to please now. Instead she looked up at me from under her dark curls.

"Goodbye Cian," Patricia said, inscrutable now. I tried to smile, and then walked quickly away.

❋ ❋ ❋ ❋ ❋ ❋ ❋

That last Saturday in April I had a playdate with Rui. Dina had intercepted me the previous Tuesday while I was sipping a *bica* at the counter in A Lua. I was savouring the experience, letting the bitter from the coffee and the sweet from the two sachets of sugar mingle on my tongue with a pleasing smoothness that made everything briefly better.

"Hello Cian," Dina said, coming behind me. She hadn't really surprised me, I had smelled her perfume a semi-second before I heard her voice.

"Dina," I said, only glancing her way. I couldn't be sure that she didn't still have some remaining resentment she wanted to take out on me.

"Can I buy you that coffee?" she asked.

"Can you afford it?" I asked her, "I mean, it is eighty cents."

She narrowed her eyes at this and looked at me, the feline green of her irises unnerving.

"I'm trying to make peace," she said.

"Ok," I said, indicating the spot on the counter where I usually deposited my euro coin for my *bica*, "this is where you pay."

Dina gestured to Sergio to serve her a coffee of her own, and left a two euro coin in payment.

"Why didn't you tell me about Paulo?" she asked, tapping a sugar sachet in preparation for her beverage.

"It wasn't my job to tell you that your husband was gay, Dina," I said, "and anyway, would you have believed me? You had just dumped me for him, can you imagine what you would have thought if I had come out with some story about seeing Paulo in a gay bar, just weeks after you went back to him? It would have sounded fishy, wouldn't it?"

Sergio plonked the tiny round cup on the marble counter in front of his cousin. Dina just looked at me, then reached out towards the coffee cup. She had no wedding ring on her ring finger.

"I would have told you eventually anyway," I went on, not sure if I was being honest now, but liking the way it sounded, "I just needed some time to get over you."

Bingo. My appeal to my own vulnerability and my feelings for her seemed to do the trick. I still wasn't sure exactly how much I was making up.

"You know," Dina said, softer now, "I think I always kind of knew, but I couldn't admit it to myself. He's so fucking vain, and always with those body-building magazines, though he hardly ever went to the gym. And I often got the impression that he was thinking of something - or someone else - when we were in bed together. Though when I said it to him it was always a woman I accused him of thinking of. And the bastard was telling the truth, he wasn't thinking of another woman at all. *Filho da puta!*"

Dina had kicked Paulo out of the house the day after she had found him with his male lover in their bed.

"He cried like a girl," she said, "but I didn't give a shit."

She told me that Rui missed me, and was asking about me visiting again.

"And how about you, Dina," I asked, "do you want me to visit?"

"I want what is best for him," she said, "and I think that that is what you visiting him again would be."

I was non-committal, told her that I'd think about it. Inevitably I rang the next day and accepted her offer. For one thing, I kind of missed the little guy too, his bright, almost infantile positivity was a break from the compromised adult world I waded through each day. There was also the fact of the two free meals a week that Sergio promised to resume providing. I had easily gotten used to sitting down in A Lua, eating my fill and walking out without opening my wallet, like someone with an infinite line of credit that would never be paid.

So that Saturday morning I took the tram down to the square at Portas do Sol. Dina had given me directions to her house from here, this was the place that she and Paulo had recently moved into, and also the one that Paulo had even more recently moved out of. I could have walked there from my flat, but I liked the tram at the weekends, it went at the same pace as normal but the world around it seemed to have slowed down compared to a weekday. The passengers were different too. There were more Spanish visitors there for a long weekend and fewer people in suits on their commute to work, more kids and teens heading into the city centre to wander around aimlessly for a few hours and less of that mad squeeze that inevitably happened Monday to Friday where you could find yourself pressed up against a sweaty stranger for the whole journey.

The tram I caught was almost empty. It stopped at Portas do Sol, after a short, undulating journey from Graça. Down, then up, then down again and into the tiny elongated square that overlooked our five-a-side football pitch and the pink roofs of Alfama below. The five minutes inside the creaking, lumbering shack of metal and wood that was the number 28 tram was, until that point, the tranquil highlight of my week.

The square, Portas do Sol - The Gates of the Sun - was criss-crossed with tourists, as it had been every weekend since February. There were Germans in Birkenstocks and windcheaters, overdressed Italians, the Americans large and affluent, the Spanish loud and chain-smoking. A panoply of stereotypes. A few of the foreigners were observing the goings on down on the pitch where I had scored my fluky, last-minute winning goal. There was a game going on and the people above watched as if it were a show put on for their benefit, like the watered-down *fado* that went on in the bars of the Bairro Alto. Yet the game was no performance, I had a quick look myself and recognised some of the figures down there. It was the realest thing in the vicinity. The flabby and the slim, the aging and the youthful, all running around after a ball, trying to forget the rest of their mundane, city-bound lives.

I followed Dina's directions, away from the square and up towards the castle. I continued up a lane called Travessia de Santa Luzia, out of the sun - which was hot now, even at ten o'clock - and into the cooler shade thrown by the buildings around. The world there was a crossroads of the local and the international, visitors climbing towards and descending from Saint George's Castle, winding their way over two hundred year old cobbles, between the houses of families that had been there for centuries. Dina's place was number twenty-nine, it had a slanted step at the front, with a bench and two sparse trees directly opposite her green front door. It was only one hundred metres from the bustle of Portas do Sol, and yet was in as placid a setting as there was in the city, only the faint sound of the 28 in the distance shaking the calm.

I stopped before knocking, jolted by a sense of familiarity. I looked around, to my right was the building that had housed the Brazilian club that we teachers had gone to the night of our Christmas party, when we drank caipirinhas and - at least in my case - lost our memories.

I knocked, Dina answered, and gave me the two cheek kisses, as you would to a friend or acquaintance. Rui was in the living room, already playing on his X-box, I waved to him and Dina gave me a tour of their house while her son finished his game.

The place was compact, so the tour didn't take long. It was an old house that had been modernised, so the kitchen was cramped but gleaming, the living and dining rooms were joined, and there were just two bedrooms and a bathroom upstairs. Dina's bedroom was the last one she showed me, she was completely unselfconscious about this, she bounced on her bed to show me how springy her new mattress was, and got me to do the same. We synchronised our bounces for a few seconds, smiling at each other as we went up and down in unison. She then brought me over to her window to point something out.

"Spanish," she said, with something close to contempt, looking down at a group of three people passing below on their way down from the castle. They were two women and a man, all talking loudly at once. "They think they're still at home," she said.

I smiled, and stood looking at her, not sure if I should mention what I had on my mind.

"What?" she asked, eventually.

"I'm just surprised that you would stay here, in this bedroom at least. I mean, isn't this where you caught Paulo and....you know?"

Dina found this funny.

"You think I should move because of him? I like this house, it's cheap and comfortable. And I'm not going to change rooms, Rui has racing car wallpaper in his, it's a little boy's room."

I looked around at the space we were in. All evidence of a male presence had been successfully banished from the room, there were only women's clothes draped on the back of chairs, only makeup and perfume on the dressing table, a pink frilly duvet cover was under our bottoms as we sat on the bed. It had all the appearance of the room of a single woman in her thirties.

"I changed the sheets afterwards, Cian. That's enough, he's gone now."

Her hand was briefly on my arm. I felt the warmth from her skin spread before she took her hand away and returned to her persona as mother and head of family.

"Rui's downstairs," she said, "he's going to be impatient."

❊ ❊ ❊ ❊ ❊ ❊ ❊

Rui was anything but impatient, he was enthralled in his own little virtual world. We played a few games of Madden, then Dina came in to play the part of the killjoy.

"I bought you this game, Rui," she said, handing him a large black cube with a clasp on the side. Rui had his hands over his ears so she placed it on the floor in front of him.

"Não me fales em inglês!" he said, still covering his slightly protruding ears.

Dina turned to me.

"He hates it when I speak to him in English," she told me, "he doesn't mind if he's there when I'm talking to other people, but I have to speak to *him* in Portuguese. He does this every time."

"Hey Rui," I said, detaching his left hand, "how about if your mum talks to me and then I tell you what she said? Is that alright?"

He looked at his mother, unsure.

"I suppose," he said.

"Hey, it's ok, I'm only joking."

"It's not a very funny joke."

"Cian," Dina said, exaggeratedly facing me and playing along, "can you tell my son to open his present?"

Rui sat and pretended he hadn't heard.

"Rui, open your present."

He looked at me and nodded. I suddenly saw his father in him, the slight look of suspicion, the sense of contained strength, the long feminine eyelashes actually making him look more like Paulo than Dina.

He opened the dark cube. Inside were other, smaller cubes, these ones white, each with an image etched on the six sides. There were a total of twenty-seven white mini-cubes, and Rui immediately took them out and started building walls, towers and houses with them.

"*Está fixe, mama,*" he said.

"Glad you like them," Dina said to him. He gave her a dirty look from under his fringe, for having spoken to him in English again, though he quickly went back to playing with his present.

"Cian," Dina said, in her voice that she would have used to talk to her son if he would have allowed it, "can you show Rui that the cubes are for making stories. You take a few of them...," - here she picked up about seven or eight cubes - "roll them and then look at the pictures."

She did just that, coming up with a sports car, a hot air balloon, what looked like a pair of twins, an intricately detailed picture of a forest, a thick-legged elephant and the mouth of a cave.

"Now we have to tell a story including all of these elements. If we can't continue we choose another block, roll it, and get another picture to help us."

I hadn't seen Dina in this didactic role before, and it suited her. She played with us for a while, then left to do the washing. Rui quickly got the hang of it. I had to help him out with some vocabulary - 'wizard', 'stab', 'silver', 'cliff' - but his imagination was vivid and quite violent. He was strict with the rules that we had made up, only allowing me to change one cube after my throw, as we had agreed, despite the fact that chance had landed me with the pictures of five animals and a bucket to build a story.

The morning passed quickly. We could hear Rui's mother in the kitchen and at one o'clock Dina came bustling in to take her son away for lunch. She thanked me for my time, politely, but also as if I were an employee, and made no move to invite me to stay and eat with them. Within five minutes of completing my final story inspired by the solid white cubes - involving a frog who became a footballer and a princess who took to carpentry - I was back out in the late April heat, the air now heavier with warmth than it had been two hours previously.

I realised that the castle was only a five minute walk, and that I hadn't been there since my first week in Lisbon, though I saw it practically every day from one angle or another. The tourist traffic seemed to have lightened by now, most were, no doubt, sitting down in some tasca having an omelette or a *tosta mista*, so the queue for tickets was likely to be shorter. I set off up the hill, the cobbles worn smooth but still with angles and bumps that made walking slower. The sun was high now and had a real heat, a tinge of summer after the false warmth of the previous months. I felt as if I was being very slowly baked.

Without any warning a figure came up behind me, grabbed my arm and pulled me into one of the narrow lanes that branched off the main path up to the castle. There was a smell there of urine and other things, food being cooked, possibly fish, in somebody's kitchen in one of the houses nearby. I was pushed face-first against the wall and managed to turn slightly to glimpse my assailant. The square, dark, Rui-like head of Paulo stared back at me, showing his teeth like an angry dog.

"You moving in now buddy?" he said, his garlic breath in my face, the accent suddenly all American in its aggression. He still held on to my arm with his Popeye left hand. My face was to the wall. I managed to move my forehead to be the point of contact with the brick so that my nose wouldn't get squashed. Paulo had a contained strength in him, he obviously ate his spinach. My arm began to hurt, and I couldn't see how to get out of his hold.

"Hello Paulo," I said, stupidly.

"You think I didn't see you that night in Envidia?" he hissed, at the back of my head. "I saw you there with those other *maricas*. Does Dina know that you like boys? You think that she'd be interested in you if she knew?"

He had loosened his hold somewhat, so I managed to half-turn so I could see his stubbled face.

"Are you fucking kidding me?" I asked him, struck by the idiocy of what he was saying. "Now you're worried about Dina being with a gay man? Do you know what 'irony' means, Paulo?"

He pushed me hard against the wall again, though in doing so he turned me slightly to the side so I managed to twist out of his hold and face him. He was a half a head shorter than me, though still was able to reach up, put a muscled forearm against my throat and simultaneously cup my balls with his right hand. He squeezed, and I found that I couldn't, or didn't want to, breathe.

"I'm his fucking father," Paulo said now, almost ranting. I could smell garlic, cigarettes, onions from his breath. His grip tightened on my testicles.

"And I'm still her husband," he went on. "I know you told her about me, about Envidia, maybe you even set me up, huh? Paid that guy to come up to me that Saturday night, just to catch me out."

He was paranoid, possibly dangerous, I could see now. I attempted to pry his arm from my throat, while also trying to speak. I hadn't been in a fight for a while, but from growing up in Limerick city I was familiar with minor physical violence. I was a little scared but not intimidated.

"You're right, Paulo," I said, trying to mollify him, "you're Rui's father, I'm not trying to change that. I'm only teaching him English, he doesn't even like me very much."

He didn't look like he had heard me.

"He's my only son," Paulo whispered, in a voice that was plaintive, begging.

It almost made me feel bad about what I did next. I managed to manoeuvre my knee around and into his genitals, hitting the spot, finding the soft sponginess there, causing his grip on mine to loosen slightly. I twisted as he bent over, and pushed him off me, standing back as he leant for a few seconds against the wall to recover his breath. Paulo put his head down and was breathing heavily. I couldn't tell whether he was in pain, or weeping, or both. I stood about six or seven metres from him, with enough space to avoid him if he lunged at me with some concealed knife he might have. He then looked up. I felt that I had to say something.

"Look," I began, not sure where I was heading, "if you like men, enjoy it. Why be ashamed? This is a great city for being gay, there's no stigma here. I don't see why you have to have all of this self-hatred, you need to get the fuck over it. And it doesn't stop you being Rui's father, no-one is trying to change that. Dina will come around in time. Just leave me the fuck out of your issues, I'm not trying to take your place."

Paulo was eyeing me now, glaring, though he was still hunched a little. Still, I hadn't finished.

"I'm not trying to take your place," I repeated. "And anyway, if you're looking for someone to blame for her kicking you out, look at the guy who was fucking dudes while pretending to be married to Dina. That guy wasn't me."

He was significantly shorter than me, but was packed tight with muscle and looked ready to blow. There was a density to him that could surely do damage. I took a few steps back.

"Oh yeah," I said, as a parting shot, trying to sound tough, "next time we meet, stay away from my balls."

It was a weak effort, but I felt that I had to say something. I turned slowly, keeping an eye on Paulo as I did so, and hurried off back downhill towards Dina's house and Portas do Sol, my visit to the castle now forgotten. I looked over my shoulder now and then to check that I wasn't being followed and passed out a group of Italians on the way down, all in designer hiking boots, the four of them wearing Gucci sunglasses. It hurt to walk, my testicles chafed and ached as I moved. They felt bruised, squashed, like overripe fruit. There was a tram in the square when I reached it, I jumped on and stood near the back, even though there were seats free. It was less painful that way, on my feet rather than sitting. I held on to the leather strap that hung down from the ceiling for the purpose of allowing the standing passengers to steady themselves, and looked out the window, though didn't take much notice of what was happening out there. I found that my t-shirt was mostly damp from my perspiration and it also hurt a little to swallow. I could still feel the weight of Paulo's forearm on my Adam's apple. It at least served to take some of my attention away from my aching genitals.

Four days later, my genitals still ached a little. That Wednesday evening I stayed in and iced them. I had told Mike and Jamie that I might meet them later to go to the cinema, but I cried off, inventing nausea and diarrhoea, the classic London School excuse for missing anything, usually work. I lay on my bed with a bag of Charles and Charlotte's frozen peas on my balls, trying to decide whether, or how, I was going to tell Dina about my encounter with Paulo. I figured that it wasn't a good idea to keep something else from her, now that I was back in the good books, but I was afraid that she might overreact, attack her semi-psychotic soon-to-be-ex husband about it and impel him to visit me again, this time accompanied by a weapon or two other than his Popeye-like forearms.

The grating screech of the intercom buzzer interrupted my thoughts. I picked up the handset that was stuck to the wall in our hall but there was no answer, the thing had been on the blink for days now. I hung it up and went out of the door of the flat, the now only semi-frozen peas still in my hand. I descended the few steps there and went as far as the street door, where a silhouette was visible through the glass covering the top half of the partition. I heard the intercom buzzing again inside. "Alright, alright," I said, "keep your hair on." I pulled the metal frame towards me. It scraped against the floor as it moved. The figure standing there was small, solid, dark-haired, hazel-eyed, looking at me inscrutably as I completed the opening of the door.

"Maura!" I said, before I could try to be more articulate, "what the fuck are you doing here?"

MAY

I met Maura after work on the first day of May, and we went to A Brasileira, the café in Chiado where Dina had dumped me back in March. I ordered a beer, and got her a cup of tea with milk. The waitress, when I explained what I wanted, twisted her nose in disgust, as if I had asked for urine to be added to the tea.

"What's wrong with her?" Maura asked, as the bow-tied waitress disappeared.

"This isn't Ireland, they don't do tea with milk," I told her, as if the idea disgusted me too, now that I was so international and sophisticated.

We had tried to do this the night before, in Graça, when Maura had turned up at my door and left me almost speechless.

"Hi Cian," she had said, as I stood there, the now thawed bag of green vegetables still in my hand, "surprised?"

That had to be the stupidest question I had been asked in weeks, including when João Teixeira from my teenage class had asked me what the past tense of 'window' was.

"What the fuck are you doing here?" I repeated, staring now. Maura looked good, she had the beginnings of a bronzing to her skin, which always suited her, and wore a summer skirt and dark sandals. She looked like she had recently had a pedicure. It took a millisecond for the question to flash through my mind about how much effort she had put into her appearance for this little reunion.

"Listen, if this is a bad time, I can go," she said, "I'm not entirely sure why I'm here myself."

To buy time I took her to A Lua. I briefly thought about inviting her in to the flat, then decided to take her next door instead. There was something about having her in the place where I lived that seemed wrong, inappropriate somehow. We sat about half way down, at a table with a brand new white paper covering. I signalled to Sergio for a coffee and asked Maura what she wanted.

"Nothing for me," she said, "I'm not staying."

"What do you mean you're not staying?" I asked, "you just called to *my* door."

"I'm here with Ann, you remember her? She worked with Sheila in the hotel."

"Sure, yeah, Ann." I had no memory of this Ann person at all.

"We got a cheap flight, though we're going to spend most of the time in the Algarve. Ann wanted to come to Lisbon, her manager told her it was beautiful and she wanted to have something to talk to him about. She wants to impress him." Maura stopped and looked around her. "Anyway, I told her I'd meet her soon, she's in the hotel but wants to go out later."

I couldn't work out if this story about Ann wanting to come to Lisbon was real or whether Maura was leaving out something.

"And my address?" I asked her.

"I rang your mother," Maura said.

"Wow," was about all I could say to this. "Who did you say you were? She must have asked you."

"I told her that we used to share a house together in Dublin. Your parents' number is in the phone book."

"Well, I suppose that much is true, about sharing the house." It was true as far as it went, I thought, but left out a whole world of other truths.

Maura stood up.

"I've got to get back. I just wanted to call to your house for a second, to...... to say hello," Maura said.

"The last time I saw you," I said, incredulous now, "you ran away from me as fast as you could go, you took those stairs in Sheehan's two at a time. The time before that you told me that you had aborted our child. And now you travel a thousand miles to say *hello*!?"

"What can I say, I was curious," she replied. "Listen, if you want to meet me tomorrow, here's the number of our hotel. We should be there in the morning." She was still standing, looking down at me as I continued to sit, just like we had been back on New Year's Eve, when Maura had come up the stairs as I perched on the closed lid of the Sheehans' toilet. She had just handed me a piece of notepaper with Hotel Excelsior in the heading, and the number below it.

"I'm in room number thirteen, if they ask," Maura said.

Thirteen, I thought, *unlucky for some.*

Maura just stood there a few seconds longer as I saw Sergio unobtrusively observing her in the background while pretending to clean a glass. Then she said a quick, "Ok, bye", turned on her heels and was gone out the door and into Largo da Graça. It took her about thirty seconds to flag down a passing taxi, and had soon disappeared from view.

I had considered whether to phone her the next day or not, and spent a lot of a semi-sleepless night debating the issue. I could have just let her go, could have let her disappear into the city and then down to the Algarve, and I wouldn't have had to deal with whatever head-fuck she had obviously planned for me. Yet the fact of Maura, in Lisbon, the two parts of my life that I thought I had successfully separated for good, now brought together.... The temptation was just too great. And she had piqued my curiosity. I found that I needed to know what the hell she was doing there.

So I rang her hotel the next morning, and arranged to meet her after work. A Brasileira was close to her hotel, the Excelsior in Chiado, and so was easy for her to find. Maura was sitting outside when I arrived, but she wanted to have a look at the interior so we went indoors to have a drink. And that's where the waitress, in her stained apron and off-white shirt, turned up her nose at Maura's insistence on having her tea the country Irish way.

"Well if you don't have milk in it, what do you have with it?" Maura asked, amazed at the concept of milk-less tea.

"Lemon, sugar, often they put nothing in," I said, affecting boredom at her unsophisticated ways.

Our orders arrived, and I took pleasure in the Portuguese sugar ceremony, and at Maura's careful studying of me as I stirred the white granules into my dark coffee.

"You look settled, Cian," she said, "are you? Or are you just acting for my benefit?"

She had always been smart, Maura, hard to fool.

"I don't know, Maura," I said, "I don't know how to act around you. It's like we're strangers again, or else two people who used to know each other long ago, who meet when they're old. Maybe I am putting on an act for you. Or maybe this is who I am now. Who the fuck knows?"

I was rattled, obviously, unsure of how to play this. Wanting her, and wanting her to leave my city.

"I'm not sure what I'm doing here either," Maura said, sipping her light brown tea, "it was Ann who suggested we go to Portugal. She knew nothing about you and me, didn't know that that's where you were. I had been thinking about you, and trying not to, and she mentioned coming here. I suppose I took it as a kind of sign."

"A sign of what?" I asked.

"I don't know, that we had something unfinished. That the way things ended was so horrible that we needed to........oh fuck, I don't know." Maura put her head down and plunged her fingers into her thick dark hair, holding on and kneading her scalp. I reached out and touched her left forearm, stroking the skin there. It was the first physical contact we had had in more than twelve months. I took my hand away.

"What are you doing tomorrow?" I asked her.

"Sight-seeing," she said, looking up.

"Why don't I come with you two, I can show you the city." I wasn't sure that this was a good idea, but felt I had to suggest something.

"Don't you have work?"

"I feel a bout of food poisoning coming on," I told her, "dodgy fish in A Lua. It's unlikely I'll be fit for work, I'd say." Apart from that false sick-day I had taken when I had wanted to avoid Patricia Coelho in March, I hadn't missed a class since September.

"I'll talk to Ann. I'm sure she'll be delighted to have a tour guide."

❧ ❧ ❧ ❧ ❧ ❧ ❧

The number twenty-eight tram went from right outside my flat in Graça, down the hill to the Baixa and up the other side towards the Bairro Alto. On the way there was a stop that was literally twenty metres from the Excelsior Hotel where Maura and her friend Ann were staying. I took the tram first thing on Thursday morning and got off at this stop. It was already as hot now as it had been at midday the day before. It was going to be a close, boiling day. The two women were waiting for me at the door of the hotel.

Ann was short, with a mousy brown bob and a sparkling stud in her left nostril, stuck there like a diamond on a hillside. She seemed to be feeling the temperature, she was red-faced and sweating slightly, and looked uncomfortable, even in her sparkly pink Angel t-shirt and denim mini.

Maura, on the other hand, was perspiration free, as if she had grown up in thirty degree weather in rural County Limerick. I remembered how she had always, back in our house in Rathfarnham, launched herself into the back garden at the first sign of sun, how the ultra-violet rays seemed to be food and fuel to her. She was a sun-child. She tanned easily too, and already had an overlay of browner skin on her forearms, neck and face. It made her skin look like that of a local's, it gave it that caramel sheen that Portuguese girls - like Dina - carried so effortlessly.

I decided to take them to Belém. This was where Vasco da Gama had set sail from on his voyage of plunder and discovery, five hundred years before. Belém was an impressive, tourist-swamped suburb to the west of the city, full of open spaces and imposing structures that had been built to wow. In the taxi there I tried hard not to think about Maura's bronzed skin. I kept the conversation neutral and tried to pay as much attention to Ann as I did to her companion.

We went first to the monastery, where da Gama is buried, and from there to the Tower of Belém and to the monuments over by the river. Ann insisted that I take photos of her with the tower, tiny in the background, but placed so that it would look like she was holding it up, as people do with the Leaning Tower in Pisa. It didn't really work as an optical illusion, mainly because the Tower of Belém isn't tilted, yet it had become an obsession now for Ann and she wouldn't shut up until I had shown her my efforts.

Vasco da Gama was buried there in Belém, in the monastery. Ann was much more sedate when she entered the cavernous grandiosity of this building. We wandered in to escape the heat and were met with pillars the thickness of redwoods, and the ornate excesses of the crypts and the church. I realised that I was taking pride in the reactions of the girls to the immensity of the space and to its ancient beauty, as if I had had anything to do with it. It was as if it made it alright somehow that I was living here, that it made this shabby, accidental city a valid place to inhabit. I sat in a pew and watched Maura and Ann wander around, taking photos like tourists, pointing at stuff, and tried to imagine what Maura was thinking.

We took the flashy new tram back to the city.

"Hey," Ann said, as we took our seats, "we're on the Luas. Look Maura, it's the fucking Luas, in Lisbon!"

She was right, the trams from Belém were like those new ones in Dublin that were silent and airy, smooth and effortless, almost everything, in fact, that our own little number 28 from Graça was not. The word for both vehicles was 'tram' though, a fact that struck me right there as dumb, they were so different, the air-conditioned, free flowing, three-carriage rocket that went to and from Belém every day, and the rickety yellow shed on wheels that creaked and groaned its way up and down the hill to Graça. Both 'trams', both 'eléctricos' in Portuguese, one like the deformed little brother of the other.

We reached the centre in air-conditioned comfort and walked the five minutes to the tram stop beside the Cathedral. The yellow twenty eight came chugging around the corner as soon as we reached the stop.

"Now this is a tram," I told Maura and Ann, as they looked up at me. We were standing on a slope, me above them, their feminine faces turned towards me. I was suddenly aware of how stupidly proud I sounded of my scrappy little number 28, as if they had both dissed it in some way and I had to defend it. Once we got on, though, they began laughing at the noise, the jerky way the hundred year old vehicle moved, at the swaying and stuttering and whining of the thing as it struggled to get up the hill. I felt like a parent whose child was being made fun of.

Maura didn't say much on the short tram ride up the hill. Ann, who sat beside her, chatted away. I glanced back at them from my seat in front. The situation suddenly seemed impossibly wrong. I had fled Dublin to escape the mess we had made of things, and now here she was, bringing two worlds together that I had wanted kept apart. I believed that she was regretting her decision to come to Lisbon, but I couldn't be sure.

The next stop on my itinerary was the castle, so we got off at Portas do Sol, walked up past Dina's house - whose blinds were down - and by the alley to the left where Paulo had assailed me, a few days before. When we got to the castle itself and entered its manicured grounds. Ann drifted off on her own, purposely or not, and left Maura and I to wander around the different levels and the battlements, among the other tourists. We reached the edge, where we could look down at about a quarter of the city below.

"You seem happy here," Maura said.

"Do I?" I replied.

We were still wary with each other, both of us waiting for a reminder of the past, or a comment or slight from the other.

Maura just nodded.

"And you, what happened to this guy you were all hopeful about?" I asked her, remembering the email she had sent to me on the last day of February, the one that had helped to almost force me into the arms of Patricia Coelho.

"Dunno," she said, "didn't work out. Maybe I'm just toxic to men."

I paused before speaking, wondering whether I should keep my mouth shut. Then I said it anyway.

"Wait a second," I said, "is that why you're here? You're here to find out if we were a fluke, if you're actually capable of a proper relationship. Like that book, with the guy, High Fidelity, where the dude looks up all his old flames to try and find out why they all dumped him. You're here on *research.*"

"Research? Is that what you think?" she asked, "do you think I'm that cold, that calculating? Do you know me at all?"

That was a good question. It was clear that I didn't. Though I was reasonably sure that I was right about my theory. Maura was there in Lisbon to see what had gone wrong between us, to try and work out if she was really hopeless at all that or if there was some chance that she was capable of forming a healthy couple at some time in the future. She was doing research. I didn't feel like going into this.

"Let's find Ann," I said, instead. The city below went about its business, oblivious to us two above, almost fighting, not knowing where we stood well enough to know if we could row about it. I went to walk off.

"Cian, come back," Maura said. It was like a scene from a bad rom-com. I turned around, ready to be done with the whole thing.

"Come to the hotel tonight," she said, "we can have a drink, talk."

Ann appeared around the corner.

"You guys have got to see these peacocks," she said, all in a rush, "they're *gift.* Like little works of art walking around, so proud of themselves."

I turned to Maura.

"I'll see you later then," I told her, before walking off towards the exit.

* * * * * * *

It was eight o'clock when I arrived at the Hotel Excelsior in Chiado. Again, I was thankful for the tram and its route from one side of the city centre to the other. I was able to step out of my front door, walk the twenty metres to the stop in Largo da Graça, hop on to the boxy yellow tram, and be taken down to sea level, then up again towards the Bairro Alto. The stop in Chiado was thirty seconds walk from Maura's hotel. Meantime the undulating fifteen minute journey gave me a chance to have some mental space before I had to meet her, before I had to confront whatever shit she was trying to pull by following me here.

We met in the bar. I had a gin and tonic, just for something different, and because it seemed like the kind of drink you would order in a place like this. Maura ordered a glass of white wine. She had perfume on, lots of it. I looked at her, trying to form some kind of coherent thought about her that wasn't mixed up or polluted by our past. I was suspicious of her, almost afraid, I hated her a little, and wanted to be close to her, and desperately, desperately wanted to touch her, to stick my fingers into her thick dark hair, to feel the warmth of her skin, to hear her words whispered in my ear like I used to. For a period of a few months the previous year I had been consumed by this woman, totally eaten up by her, and then by her absence. Now she was here, where I had come to escape from the thought of her, and from the loss of her, and I had no idea how to react, or what I wanted.

"Have you never wondered how things could have been different?"

Maura asked, "if my mother had never gotten sick, if we had managed you moving out of Rathfarnham together?" Maura took a drink of her wine. "It was more or less a year ago, all that."

I took a mouthful too, more than I would have usually. The gin was sharp, and made me wince.

"For months I thought of almost nothing else," I told her. "I lay awake thinking about what I could have done differently. It came to me in classes sometimes last summer, I'd get distracted and start mulling it over, and forget what I was teaching. The kids would tease me about being in love. I suppose they were right, in a way, if you could call that being in love."

Maura stared again. She had been doing that a lot in the last two days.

"But in the last few months," I went on, "- really since coming here - it's been easier. I haven't thought about it, about you, much at all."

I was vaguely aware that this might hurt her in some small way, and found that I was ok with that.

"So it worked," Maura said, "coming here?"

"You think I came here because of you?"

Maura nodded.

"Well, you're probably right," I admitted, " I had no clear idea what I was doing at the time, but I suppose I was trying to escape. And maybe it did work, in a way. Bizarrely."

"So you're cured?" she asked.

"Yeah, if you want to put it like that. We were never going to work, we were an accident waiting to happen, Maura. We were forced into closeness, we shared a kitchen, a living room. We watched TV together. You cooked for me. I saw you in your slippers and dressing gown. It wasn't a normal situation. It would have collapsed anyway."

"Maybe," she said, "and maybe not. How can you be sure?"

Our roles were reversed now. She was the one trying to convince me that what we had had was worth something. I was now the one rejecting it, or at least pretending to. I wanted to believe that what she was saying was right, but couldn't bring myself to. And yet her being there, in Lisbon, where I could smell her scent, where I could reach out and touch her if I wanted, where I could hear the timbre of her voice, so familiar, the sheer physicality of her right there in front of me, made all previous progress towards indifference to this woman null and void. All previously successful attempts at forgetting were now themselves forgotten, and I couldn't think straight.

"You have no fucking idea what last summer was like for me," I told her, "I knew that I had messed things up, and you had disappeared. Why couldn't you have had this attitude then? We might have had a chance."

"We might still," Maura said. She downed her wine and stood up. "Come up to my room."

I had half been expecting this, half dreading it. I stayed sitting.

"What are you doing, Maura?" I asked.

"We need some privacy," she said.

"You don't want this," I told her.

"Don't tell me what I want, Cian."

Eventually I stood too. I couldn't not, Maura was persistent and would have outlasted me in a game of sitting/standing. We walked to the lift in silence. When it arrived it was empty, we were the only passengers to the fourth floor. I touched her on her bare arm, somehow us being alone here in the small space was much more charged than back in the bar. I could understand how people ended up having sex in elevators. Maura looked at me, though didn't move closer. The lift stopped, the doors swished open, I followed her to her room. She had managed to make it just as messy, even within two days, as her space back in Templewoods, Rathfarnham, had been.

Maura sat on the edge of her bed and slipped off her sandals. I sat on a chair that faced the bed. I felt like an alcoholic who had managed, through many months of painful deprivation, to conquer the desire for a drink, only to be faced with a free bar and an open invitation to consume anything and everything he wanted. I had shaken the habit, I had shaken Maura, and was now being drawn back in. I wanted her badly then, and wanted desperately not to want her. Her toenails were painted, I noticed, a scarlet red. My mouth was dry, I was breathing with difficulty.

"What are you thinking, Cian?" she said, looking at me through her dark lashes.

"I'm thinking that I shouldn't be here," I said, not moving.

"But you are here," she said, "we both are. Come over and lie beside me."

Still I didn't move. It felt as if I was paralysed. Maura came to me, knelt down on the carpet and took my hands briefly, released them and then put her head in my lap. It came back to me that this was a position we used to adopt, back in Rathfarnham. I'd be reading, or watching television, she would enter whatever room I was in and do exactly as she was doing just then, place her thick-haired head on my thighs. I imagined that it was something she had done with her father as a child, or even with her mother when relations had been better between them. It was the tenderest time between us, a wordless gesture that she seemed to find comforting and which never failed to both touch me and at times even turned me on. I did as I invariably had always done back in Dublin, I reached out and stroked her head, burrowed deep into her hair with my fingers, massaged her scalp a little. Her head was turned to the side, the eyes half closed. Then Maura looked up, her lids heavy, and my resistance disintegrated. She had known what would work, had played me well. I was lost.

✳ ✳ ✳ ✳ ✳ ✳ ✳

The next morning I claimed an early class and slipped out of Maura's bed at half past eight. We had ended up sleeping the same way we had done in Dublin, her on the left, me on her right. Maura sat up and watched me as I dressed. She had a t-shirt on, one that said "Material Girl" in sparkly letters, something she had borrowed from Ann. She looked wary.

"You ok?" I asked her.

"Dunno," she said, "None of this was as I had planned."

I stopped my dressing.

"Too late now, it's done," I told her. "I'll see you later."

We didn't kiss before I left. I went home to Graça and showered. My balls still ached a little from Paulo's assault a few days before, and hadn't been helped by my night with Maura. I didn't think, just acted on auto-pilot, got ready for work and caught the twenty-eight at my usual time of 11.26.

In the London School, Sally ran her first staff meeting. She made a point of asking me how I was, I assured her that I had recovered from my temporary bout of whatever it was I had lied about having. All of the teachers were there, including the newly demoted Sebastian. It took place in one of the classrooms, the very one in which I usually taught Patricia Coelho and her companions. The meeting was something to do with the Cambridge English Language exams, Sally talked about what students tend to have difficulty with, the recent changes to the exams, some useful teaching techniques. I didn't pay much attention. Joanne was taking notes and I figured that I could ask her later if I missed anything. Maura was, at that moment, somewhere in the very same city I had moved to specifically to get away from her, and that fact alone was enough to distract me from Sally's tedious lecture.

For the rest of the day in my classes I was haunted by visions and sensations of my night with Maura. I was there in my Pre-Intermediate class, lazily asking students to tell me about their last holiday as a practice of the past tense, while simultaneously smelling Maura's wine breath, feeling the heat of her skin, hearing her whispered voice. It was still with me, our night together, though it hadn't in any way gone smoothly.

It was still with me too as I sat in the staffroom and tried to take part in Mike's dissection of a film he had seen the night before. It was with me as I ate the *tosta mista* in the cafe below at three o'clock, as a kind of late lunch. It was with me as filled in my course logs with what I had covered that day in class. It was with me as I listened to Carol telling me about her macho ex-husband who didn't believe that women should work outside the home, and about how proud she was of her own daughter who had stood up to him. The sensations and emotions of the previous night followed me around like a smell, like a scent staining my clothes, sometimes pleasant, at times toxic.

The night before Maura and I had, in a kind of staccato fashion, undressed each other, both of us stopping now and then as if we weren't sure about continuing. Her skin, which I hadn't been able to stop thinking about touching for about twenty four hours, was initially a disappointment, it was just another tactile surface, another smooth plane. I had been expecting fireworks, perhaps, something profound to stir within me, but it was just warm skin. And we were out of synch, Maura was at first passionate and intense, going too fast for me, and then when she slowed down to my pace I wanted to go down on her, which she wasn't ready for, so she held me there, face to face, our bodies a mirror of each other as we tried to get a rhythm.

It was like playing a sport we had once been good at, but which we had neglected for months, years. Our technique was off. I would have thought that desire alone would have carried us along, but it was too ambivalent to be the powerful force we both needed to continue. It was Maura who called a halt first.

"Stop," she said, pushing me back, "I need to stop."

"*You're* stopping?" I said, "you started this."

I knew what she meant, but I still felt I needed to show some annoyance.

"Something's wrong, Cian," she said.

Now that we had started this, I didn't want to admit that we needed to put the brakes on.

"We'll pick it up," I said to her, "we're just out of practice."

I didn't really believe that any more than she did, but I was also inflamed now, desiring her. Not in the mood for talk.

"It's more than that, and you know it," Maura said, "this was a bad idea. I shouldn't have asked you up."

"Why the fuck did you come here?" I said, asking a question that I should have demanded the answer to a day and a half ago. "Is this some other attempt at revenge? Seduce me, get me in bed, make me think you wanted me again, and then stop in the middle?"

"Grow up, Cian, I didn't plan this," Maura said, pulling back on her t-shirt, "I haven't thought any of this through. I came here hoping to find something out, and I think that I have. It's all wrong, this, we already failed at this, I don't know why we're trying again."

I pulled myself up and leaned against the cushioned headboard. At least three things were preoccupying me at that moment, in no particular order. I wondered whether she was right, that we, for some reason, didn't work and that this little assignation of ours was a mistake, as I had suspected from the start. I also knew that my hard-on remained and that, despite the suspicion of our failure, I still wanted her. And I realised that Maura still hadn't explained herself, she still hadn't told me exactly what she was thinking in coming to my city and knocking on my door. I thought I would start there.

"Ok," I began, "explain to me exactly what the plan was in showing up here. Tell me that much at least. Because if you're confused, I'm doubly fucking so, Maura. I spent months trying not to think of you, left a city to escape you, and you follow me here."

Maura looked away, as if preparing an answer, then slid down into the bed and covered herself with the duvet. It was duck-egg blue, the duvet cover, I had noticed the colour earlier when we had had the lights on. I was now above her and looking down as she spoke.

"Time passes, I rethought things. I've been with a couple of guys since you, and they were dicks too. The same as the ones before you, feckless, immature, uncommitted, using me, or else happy to be used by me. I thought you were different, that's why what you did hurt so much."

I stayed silent though there were things I wanted to say. I had asked her to speak and she was speaking.

"That's why I came here, to try to see what we had, what was different about us, for a brief time. Because it worked, didn't it? I'm not just imagining it, am I? We were happy together, at least I was for a while, happier than I had ever been. And you did a good impersonation of being happy too. But it's gone now, we spoiled it, we killed it, whatever it was. You spoiled it when you moved out, and then slept with that French girl, I spoiled it with the way I reacted to you leaving, losing my head. The abortion."

Just then she started to cry, to weep silently but intensely. Tears fell like drops of rain, wetting the bed clothes.

"I've never seen you cry before," I told her, repressing my instinct to go over and comfort her. It was true, Maura had never cried in my presence, whether by accident or design I didn't know.

"Well congratulations," she said, between sobs, "now you have."

Maura's tears slowed, and her sobs too. She grabbed a tissue and dabbed at her eyes, soaking up the moisture without rubbing too hard.

"I can't be with you again like this," she said now, "there's too much past, too much pain. Every time we slept together I'd be thinking about how I got pregnant, about the fucking flight I took on my own to Manchester, how you weren't there."

"I would have been there if you'd told me," I said to her.

"Yes, but why didn't I want to tell you? Why didn't I want you to know?"

The weeping had almost totally subsided now, her eyes were red but dry. I felt a tenderness towards her that I couldn't remember feeling, she had never needed my comfort and protection before. I slid over to her and put my arms around her, and held her tight as she struggled to be free.

"Don't fight it, Maura," I said to her, "my Maura. Don't fight it."

She stayed quiet in my arms then, and went limp. I held her for five, maybe ten minutes, she didn't struggle, though she didn't return my embrace. We didn't talk, just remained like that, the heat of our bodies mingling, her head against my chest.

Maura then slowly detached my arms and looked into my face.

"Cian, you know that those three months that we were together in that house, they were an illusion, weren't they? Whatever we were together cannot survive in the open air. You know this, I think. I know it too, now, though I had to come here and see you, and almost sleep with you, to be sure."

I said nothing for a time, just held on, as if letting go would destroy some of the accidental intimacy we had fallen into.

"Let's just sleep," I said, eventually, "we're here now, let's just fall asleep together, like we used to do. We can do that, at least."

Maura squirmed out of my arms, and lay back on her side of the bed.

"Do what you want," she said now, "I don't care anymore."

At that she turned away from me, curled up into the foetal position as I had seen her do many times back in Rathfarnham, and left me lying there, still with a semi erection, not knowing what to do. I got up and went to the bathroom. It was past midnight and had been a long day. I stared at myself in the mirror, looked at my blue-green eyes, the long lashes that more than one woman had told me made me look feminine, and so less threatening, I suppose. I had bed hair now, it was tousled. I had managed to get some colour in my face, despite not having visited a beach since the summer had properly started. It was an ordinary face, with small teeth and too-prominent incisors, and lips that I had also been told were good to kiss, a few times by Maura in fact. I stared hard and felt that I was losing focus, that my features were melting together like in some surrealist painting. Maura had briefly, for a few months back in 2007, made me feel like I knew who I was, and now it was clear that I needed to rediscover this, remake an identity, to try and do it without her. I pissed, quickly, and returned to the bedroom.

Maura was asleep, or pretending to be. I felt that I should go, but couldn't be bothered, and also couldn't bring myself to leave her alone there in her double bed, where there was plenty of room for me. I slipped in beside Maura, and fell quickly to sleep, the scent of her in my nostrils, as I had done so often the year before.

My sleep was solid, with vivid, involved dreams that vanished as soon as I woke. I had left my phone on the locker by the bed, I checked it, it was six fifteen. Maura was in the bathroom, I could hear her moving in there, water flowing down the pipes. I lay there, facing the bathroom door, she saw me when she came back. She was in pink pyjama bottoms and the Material Girl t-shirt.

"You're still here," she said.

I just stared, as she had been doing for the last forty-eight hours. Maura got back into bed, which surprised me. I figured that she had finished with our little night together.

"Did you sleep?" I asked her.

"Not really. Tossed and turned. I watched you sleeping. Nothing bothers you, does it? None of this effects you."

I jerked, moved back exaggeratedly.

"Are you fucking serious?" I asked her. "Is that what you really believe? You think I'm immune to whatever head-fuck you're trying to pull here? Do you really think that, or are you just trying to get at me?"

We were facing each other now, both under the duvet, not in the position for an argument. Maura reached out with her left hand and punched me on the upper arm, not violently, but not playfully either. I tried not to flinch too much, but she went to do it again, and I managed to catch her fist. I couldn't tell how angry she was, or whether there was a touch of affection in her punch. I didn't let go of her fist, it was small enough that it fitted in my closed hand. She struggled a bit, but not with any great force. I think we both felt something then, a fizzing of the nervous system that seemed to wipe away all the accumulated tension and dissatisfaction of the previous twelve hours. The pressure I exerted on Maura's closed fist increased though she didn't protest. I slid further down under the duvet, and moved closer to her in the process. We didn't speak. Maura was still staring, her dark eyes blinkless in the half-light. Somehow our hands - her left and my right - were now entwined, the fingers enlaced, meshed together. I could smell her breath, it still had a hint of alcohol on it, mixed with vague human scents, straight from her insides. When we kissed, it was with fire, with teeth and lips and tongue all involved. We soon abandoned ourselves to each other, and the long empty night we had just spent was forgotten in seconds. It felt, in a strange sense, like coming home.

Afterwards, I think we both slept a little, not spooning or linked in any way, but separate. Maura had said that she hadn't slept, so now she fell into a deep sleep. I woke and dozed, looked at her lying there naked, dead to the world now, then dropped off myself for a bit. Finally, at eight, I made my attempt to get up without waking her, and had to have the parting words I had been trying to avoid before leaving.

All of this was still with me throughout the next day, in the meeting with Sally, during my classes, on the Metro home. I couldn't shift it, and couldn't get straight in my head what it meant, what we were supposed to do with it. There had been fire between Maura and I in her hotel bed, spit and teeth and nails, grasping and scraping, panting and biting. For a while that morning it was as if Maura and I had melded, like two plasticine figures squashed together into one. Our intense lovemaking had had the feeling of a goodbye about it, a signing off, maybe something of a tying up of loose ends. It had been as if we knew that it was the last time that we would do this, and wanted to make it memorable. Was that it? I wondered. Was that the end? I couldn't quite tell.

At the Cathedral stop I caught the tram up to Graça. I sat by the window and felt the breeze cool on my face while we were moving. The windows on the 28 were wooden framed, and opened vertically, creaking as they did so. This, feeling the air on your skin, was something you couldn't do on the hermetically sealed, modern version of the tram that Maura, Ann and I had travelled back from Belém on the previous day. That tram was air-conditioned and moved almost soundlessly, while its elderly cousin that took me home every day wheezed and groaned and screeched as it laboured up the hill. It may have been sentimental, but I knew which I preferred. I felt better now, being out of the darkness of the Metro and into the light. Maura was somewhere in Lisbon at that moment, but it didn't matter so much.

"Excuse me," said the man sitting next to me, who must have got on at the previous stop without my noticing, "are you a teacher in The London School?"

He was a hirsute man, with thick, dark hair up his forearms, hairier even than Paulo. His stubble too was dark, shadowed, and the hair on his head seemed to be of the same kind, black, thick, untameable. Even his nose-hair looked indestructible, intent on escaping from his nostrils to join up with his beard below. His English was neat and well-pronounced.

"Yes," I replied, "I am a teacher. Are you a student there?"

I didn't recognise him.

"Not now," he said, "I was in the past."

"Your English is good," I told him.

"Well, I can thank the London School."

"You should be on the advertisements," I told him.

We both laughed, amiably, just two people crossing each others' paths, in a city of two million.

"I always wondered," the stranger said, "if there was ever, you know, anything between the teachers and the students there. When I studied there it was obvious that there were students that would have been happy to go out with a teacher. I know two girls who did that."

I looked at him a little more closely now. His ear hair needed a trim too, I noticed.

"It hasn't happened in our school," I replied, carefully, "though maybe in some of the other centres. You know that there are four London Schools in Lisbon, I suppose."

"I know that, yes."

He said this as if it were the most obvious piece of information in existence. We were silent for a few moments as passengers got on and off at Portas do Sol. I saw Rui and two boys his size wander across the tram tracks from the direction of Alfama, punching each other on the arm and then pretending to karate kick their companions in response. One of Rui's pals slipped in mid-kick and landed on his arse, while the other two doubled over in exaggerated laughter.

"So you were ever tempted?"

This question came from my seat-mate. The strange word order was the first grammatical mistake that I had heard him make.

"Tempted to do what," I asked him, though I knew exactly what he meant.

"You know," he replied, "sleep with a student. Maybe one called Patricia."

I suddenly felt trapped. My hairy neighbour was next to the aisle, I was jammed up there against the window and the tram was now full, people stood in every available space. The moment he mentioned

Patricia's name the tram's doors folded shut, as if triggered by the sound of her name, and the vehicle lurched forward, moving in the direction of Graça. Out the window I saw Rui and his mates climb the slight incline towards his and Dina's house, and wanted more than anything at that moment to be out there with them, away from my inquisitor.

"You're the journalist," I said to him, "Nuno Antunes."

I recalled his name clearly, all the 'oo' sounds - the two in N<u>u</u>n<u>o</u>, the one in Ant<u>u</u>nes - made it memorable, resonant.

"*Exactamente*," he said, pleased with himself. He handed me his card, the same one that Patricia had been given.

"I'm just giving you a chance to tell your story, before I print something. It will be better for you to be honest." He sounded like a cop.

"Honest about what?" I asked, trying to keep my cool, "nothing happened."

Nuno raised his Frida Kahlo-like unibrow at this.

"That's not what Patricia said."

"That's bullshit man," I told him, feeling better now that I knew he was lying. "You're making stuff up. Do you know this phrasal verb 'to make something up'? It means to invent. You would have learned it in The London School. You're not telling the truth."

Nuno shrugged. Lying, I supposed, was par for the course for him as a journo. "So you don't deny that you know Patricia Coelho?" he asked me.

"She's my student."

"Just your student?"

"Absolutely."

"You see, I have a different story," the guy said, "and I'm going to print it. If you don't talk to me it makes no difference to my article."

The tram was now making the slow climb up Rua do Operário towards Graça, wheezing and straining like an old man.

"I've had enough," I said, to no-one in particular.

I stood up, ready to climb over Nuno Antunes if necessary. There was movement in the tram, possibly nervous tourists prompted by my sudden resolution into thinking that they needed to be prepared to get off, though they had eighty or a hundred seconds yet before the tram reached the stop. I just had to be out of there, I had to be as near to the door as possible when the big yellow box came to a halt. I needed air.

"Nice to talk to you," the journalist said, while he stood to let me pass. I stopped just short of punching him in the face with my left hand as I squeezed by. I didn't like his smile, or his hairy ears, or his strong cologne I got a whiff of once we were briefly centimetres apart. He slid into the place that I had just been occupying while I fought my way through the aisle-standers to get to the back door, and an anticipation of freedom.

The 28 finally reached Graça and spat me and three others out. I stepped gratefully on to the pavement and didn't look back. As a precaution, in case - as I thought likely - Nuno Antunes was watching me from his window seat, I avoided going home, or even into A Lua, and headed instead for Mario's and the calming environment of the viewing point there. No doubt the guy already knew where I lived - if he could ambush me on my tram ride home he could surely manage to find out my addresss - but I didn't want to walk into my flat in full view of the journalist, showing him the exact location of my front door.

Mario saw me coming across the small praça and had a *bica* ready for me when I got there.

"Cian," he said, as I shuffled up to the counter of the little booth, "you have a good day?"

He was smiling, in his Mario kind of way, all teeth and openness and apparent simplicity.

"Oh yeah, Mario," I said, reaching for a sugar sachet, "the best."

I'm not sure he got my sarcasm.

* * * * * * *

Nuno Antunes at least briefly took my mind off Maura. She was still there, in Lisbon somewhere, for one more day, haunting the city like a living ghost. I couldn't shake the awareness of her presence, though she was only one among two million, as she had been one among a million back in Dublin the summer before. I had given her my mobile number that morning when I left her hotel room. She rang that night, a Friday, at ten o'clock.

"Hey," she said, "it's me."

Me who? I almost asked. *Have you now won the right to introduce yourself as "me"?*

"Hello," I said, trying to appear casual.

"So we're leaving tomorrow morning," Maura said, "we get the early train to the Algarve, half past eight."

"That is early for a Saturday morning," I said.

"I thought you could come and see me before we go tomorrow?"

"Sure," I said, not certain if I meant what I said, "I can go to the hotel."

"We have to leave here at eight, Ann is paranoid about missing trains and planes, she always has to be super on time," Maura said.

"That can't be easy for you." Maura was never early for anything, she saw it as a waste to arrive even a minute before the appointed time.

"So I think we should talk before I leave."

"Talk, yeah," I said, "talk is good. Always good to have a dialogue." I had no clear idea what I was saying now. It had been a long day.

"I would suggest that we meet tonight," Maura went on, "but I don't think I can. I need to sleep on it."

"Sure," I said, "me too." This, in fact, was true. I was glad that she didn't want to talk about anything that night, my mind was clouded and heavy.

"So I'll see you here, about half seven?" she asked me.

"Half seven," I said, as if this was a normal time to be out in the world on a Saturday morning, "I'll see you then."

I knew that sleep would be fleeting and slippery that night, so I stayed up until four, eating crisps and drinking sprite like I was ten again, watching late night American re-runs on RTP. Eventually I turned off the television and sat, staring at the blank screen. I was exhausted, and yet sleepless, thinking of Nuno Antunes and his threat to write about me and Patricia Coelho, going back over my night with Maura that had stopped and started like an old car. Our lovemaking, thinking about it then, seemed out of place, a brief clear space amid all our conflicted emotions. By early Saturday morning as I sat in our windowless living room with my gaze fixed on nothing, the feel of Maura's skin had now faded and all I remembered was our misfiring attempt of earlier to get it together, my unwillingness and then hers, the wrong turnings and emptiness of the previous year. All the mistakes. It was enough, I knew then, finally. That was it, it was better to just kill it.

I fell asleep eventually there on the sofa. The alarm on my phone, which I had set the previous night, went off at five past seven. I woke as if from a coma, and for ten, fifteen seconds, wasn't sure where I was or what was happening. I saw the blank screen of the TV staring at me, and the bare walls, with the beer stain still there from when Dina had smashed her Heineken bottle against one of them months before. I slowly returned to consciousness, and remembered about Maura, waiting for me there in her hotel in Chiado. I had twenty minutes still if I wanted to go and see her. I thought about it, about leaving through our front door, walking down towards the centre and hailing a cab on the way, at that hour on a Saturday a taxi would take all of six or seven minutes to get to Chiado and Maura's hotel. I went to the kitchen, lit a cigarette by the open window, made a cup of instant coffee. I could still go and see her, we could talk, maybe find a resolution of some kind, lay a foundation for a possible future which could begin in two months, once I left Lisbon. I finished my coffee, went to the bathroom, wet my hair, brushed my teeth, and walked to the front door. On the street, on Largo da Graça, a pale cream-coloured taxi passed within about thirty seconds. I stuck out my arm and stopped it. The guy looked like he had been up all night, and the cab smelled a bit. I opened the back door, stood there, then closed it again. The driver said something to me I didn't catch, then shouted a phrase that included the words "*foda-se*", - "fuck" - though I hardly heard him. Graça was extraordinarily quiet at that time, I had never seen it so deserted in the daylight. I strolled the hundred and fifty metres over to Mario's, which of course was closed, and then looked down at the city, itself just waking up, and over to the castle on its hill to the left, the castle which had never been to sleep. I sat on the same bench that I had shared with Patricia, three months before, days after she had turned sixteen. It was peaceful.

At twenty to eight my phone vibrated in my pocked, once, twice, three times, before it stopped. It was as if Maura herself wasn't sure that she wanted to see me, she didn't even let the phone ring a sufficient amount to give me a chance to answer. Mario's boss came along at eight o'clock to open up his little cabin from which the overpriced coffee and pastries were served to tourists. I bought a bica, put the sugar in, stirred it, drank it leisurely, savouring the taste. At half past eight, at the time when Maura's train was leaving for the Algarve, I walked slowly back to our flat, which was now well and truly Charlied - Charlotte and Charles having woken up and begun to inhabit the place as they tended to do - and went to bed for the first time that day. My sleep was again deep, though more populated, with strange shapes, people that kept disappearing and reappearing, with knocks on doors and ringing of door bells, unexpected visits of friends I hadn't seen for a decade, fleeting visions of female flesh. I woke, quite refreshed, though with a feeling of loss, and a feeling of freedom, and a nagging sense that I had mislaid something important. It was lunchtime, I went to the kitchen to make a sandwich.

✳ ✳ ✳ ✳ ✳ ✳ ✳

After having kept Paulo's homosexuality from Dina, I thought I'd better tell her about his waylaying of me in the alley near the castle. Something about Paulo and Dina, and the messiness of the situation, kept me from full disclosure, however. In the dysfunctional relationship stakes Paulo and Dina left me and Maura trailing far behind. The less I got mixed up in their shit the better it would be for me.

The Saturday that Maura and Ann left for the Algarve I had a playdate with Rui. I had considered not going, but then I couldn't find a good reason to bail on our arranged Saturday afternoon, and so after I had properly woken up and eaten my toasted ham and cheese sandwich, I showered quickly and began the ten minute walk to Dina's place. It was obviously my imagination, but the city felt different, less claustrophobic. Lisbon was now Maura-less, of course, and this made all the difference. I enjoyed the walk, it was all downhill, the sun was diluted by a vague haze and the intense heat of the previous week had abated.

Dina had just been to the gym, her hair was wet and she was in a tracksuit. She smelled good. I tried not to get too close to her, in case she could somehow sense Maura off me. She had always struck me as perceptive, Dina, and at that moment it felt that I was so exposed that Dina must be able to smell her on me, to see through to the last forty-eight confusing hours. I threw myself into an hour and a half of playing and telling stories with Rui, and tried not to think about what was buzzing at the back of my mind.

When Rui and I had exhausted our store of bizarre narratives with the story blocks, I asked Dina if I could have a word. Since the resumption of our contact after her split with her husband, Dina and I had been friendly and polite, but there had been a distance there, something she had begun and I had carried on. We had again approached the status of employer/employee, a situation that neither of us was entirely comfortable with but which we didn't know how to change. Dina and I had a history, and the only way to continue our present arrangement - me as English instructor to her son, and nothing more - was to maintain a kind of formality that we had never before had.

So my asking to talk to her about something specific was a break from our status quo, and I could see that she was a little wary. I still thought about her – about her smallness, her scent, the smoothness of her lips – and wondered if she knew this, or if she thought about me too. Still, wary or not, Dina made us coffee and we sat at the kitchen table as Rui went outside with his friends.

"Last week," I began, "on Saturday afternoon after I had been here,

I met Paulo."

Dina looked at me without speaking, and then put the sugar bowl on the table so I could serve myself. I went on.

"He was upset." I paused, wondering exactly how to play this. I could tell her what had actually happened, maybe even exaggerate things a little, to ensure that her wrath would fall on Paulo without mercy. This quickly seemed like a cowardly option, and also rather pointless. Paulo was no threat now, I didn't have to put him in Dina's bad books. He had done enough to put himself there for the rest of his life.

"He seemed to think that you and I were......," I paused again, "anyway, he was upset."

If I tried, I could still feel the pressure of his hand, gripping my balls. They had been blue and black in parts for days after our little tête-à-tête in the alley, and still ached now.

"That's none of his fucking business," Dina said, "even if we were,... you know."

"Of course it's not," I replied, quickly, still trying to pick my way through the details I wanted to relate to her, the things I wanted to conceal.

"He's really concerned about Rui, and that he may not be able to spend as much time with him as he would like. I think that he's worried that he may lose touch, that he may not be able to be a father to his son."

Dina looked at me closely again. Like Maura, I suspected that she was able to see through my clumsy lying. I had never been any good at twisting the truth.

"Cian," she said, stern now, "what did he say to you? What did he do? I know him, he's not a reasonable man. He doesn't explain things to people, he tends to be more direct."

"Well, he was…," I said, and paused. I wasn't entirely sure why I was protecting the violent prick, but I still didn't want to tell her about the ball-grabbing. "…..you're right, he wasn't exactly subtle. But look, all I'm saying is that Rui needs a father, even if it is Paulo. And I know you know this, so I hope that you'll let him see his son, despite what he did to you."

I waited for Dina to start telling me that that was none of my business.

"OK," she said, instead, "you're right, I've been thinking the same thing. I still hate his guts, but we do have a child together."

Again I felt her observing me more closely.

"So why are you speaking for him?" she asked.

It was a good question, the obvious one to ask in the situation. The real answer, the one that I couldn't give her in full, involved a certain degree of self-interest. With Paulo out of the picture I was more and more being seen as the designated 'male influence' in Rui's life, and I really didn't feel ready to be some kind of surrogate father to the kid. The role of cool, trendy uncle was about as far as I could go with that, and Rui having an actual father to look up to and perhaps rebel against allowed me to play that part.

"I don't want Rui to be more effected by your split than he already is," I said to Dina, in reply to her question. "I'm not speaking for Paulo, I'm speaking for Rui."

This too was true, I realised as I said it. The kid deserved a father, even if it was a self-hating gay macho man like Paulo.

"Hmmmm," Dina said, inscrutably. "I'm surprised that you're saying this, Cian," she said, "but you do have a point. Rui has been asking about his father. He was there that day, when I caught Paulo with that…..," here Dina blinked, showing the first signs that she hadn't quite shaken off the shock of her discovery,"....that kid. I think I managed to keep him from the worst of that day. But one day Paulo was here, the next he was gone, and that's hard for Rui."

She had now dropped the veneer of formality that had existed between us for the past month. It was the first time I had seen her vulnerable since the night after she had caught Paulo, the night I had let slip that I knew all about her husband's liking for men. I stayed silent, having said all that I had prepared. The less I spoke the less chance there would be that Dina would catch me in my lie.

"I'll think about what you said," Dina told me, patting me on the hand. It was a while since we had made direct physical contact like that, skin to skin. Even for a brief moment if felt good.

"I better go," I told her. I was tired again now, I had only slept three hours that morning in my own bed after my fitful night on the sofa, and being with Rui was full-on, intense.

At the door, Dina kissed me on both cheeks, as she once had done regularly, back in November, before we had got together. I stepped out into the May heat, the air like a blanket now, thick and warm. Portas do Sol was just around the corner. I headed there, sleepy and sick and light all at once.

❖ ❖ ❖ ❖ ❖ ❖ ❖

The final weeks of May passed in a slow, sweaty haze. I had never experienced the kind of heat that now became constant in the city. I had been to Lanzarote when it was forty degrees, and on the Greek Islands when it was even hotter, but the relentless, all-encompassing summer sun that left baking traces of itself all night, even after it had safely disappeared behind the horizon, was a new experience for me.

Often even a cotton sheet was too much to sleep under. The hours of darkness were worse in their clamminess, as that was when we expected escape from the oppressiveness of the heat, an escape that never came.

The key difference between the holiday heat I had experienced before and the Lisbon summer swelter was that I had never before had to drag my pale Celtic ass to work in the morning after tossing and turning in puddles of my own sweat all night. Usually I would be in the pool, or on the beach or on a glass-bottomed boat in the middle of the Med. The temperatures made travelling on the tram even more uncomfortable than normal. Passengers were packed in in rush hour like my clothes in the tiny wardrobe in my cell in Graça. We rubbed unavoidably up against one another in the small space, sweat and perfume and garlic breath all mixed up into a pungent stink of humanity. Students too were lazier, they could feel the imminence of the summer and the end of the courses, and the orange light visible through the large windows in our London School seemed to call to them, inviting a lethargy and an unwillingness to return to the enthusiasm of their winter selves. This heat, the first non-holiday roasting that I had ever received, made me begin to see the merciless glare of the orange ball in the sky as an enemy.

The general listlessness spread to the teaching staff, and at least allowed me to cover up my post-Maura hangover by pretending to be more effected by the heat than I really was. I felt a mixture of things after Maura left, a sensation of great freedom - as if a burden had just been lifted - combined with a sharp sense of loss, an emotion close to grief. I was simultaneously lighter and emptier.

My distracted state - which was indistinguishable from the heat exhaustion that was general among the rest of the teachers - fitted in well in the staffroom. There was no air-con anywhere in our elderly building, which didn't help. Mike, in the constant thirty-five degree heat, seemed to slow down even further, if that were possible. Laura, still carrying the puppy fat that she had had when I first met her, found it difficult to stay cool and even Sally - who was in her fourth year in the country - had her fuse shortened by the high May temperatures. I heard her more than once lose her temper with Mafalda in the office, and she was even colder – if such a thing were possible – to us teachers in her day-to-day contacts.

In contrast Fabian, who was from the south of France and so used to these temperatures, and Carol, who had spent more of her life in Portugal than in Canada, were untroubled by the heat. Most unconcerned of all, though, was Sebastian. He had switched to short-sleeved shirts, but apart from that small concession to the summer it seemed that he had ice water in his veins. It was as if he didn't sweat. He certainly didn't get flustered and lose his head, or descend into ranting about trivialities, or sit there mopping his neck with a cool cloth like the rest of us. The cool he kept soon began to grate almost as much as the stifling temperatures.

"Seb," Laura said to him, one muggy Monday afternoon, near the end of May, "I think you're a reptile, like those guys in that programme V. I bet you've got gills not lungs."

"Laura, you ignoramus," Seb replied, looking up briefly from his copy of EFL Monthly, "reptiles don't have gills. That's fish, or amphibians. I can assure you that I'm all mammal."

Sebastian was also unmoved by the upcoming twenty-fifth anniversary celebrations of the London School, that were planned for June first, though in this he wasn't alone. Even Elizabeth, the ultimate company woman, made it clear that the extra work involved - putting up banners, doing press interviews, having the whole school repainted and then spring cleaned, all on orders from above - was not to her liking. And Sally showed herself to be unusually cynical - and forthcoming - about the whole thing.

"It's like North Korea," she said, "we'll be marched out there like obedient serfs and told to smile for the camera while our great leader patronises us with her presence."

It was June of 1983 that The London School had first opened, with a summer English language school in Rossio, right in the centre of the city. Marie-Ange, who had originally put the cash up for the start-up, and her hand-picked School Director Robert Prior, quickly realised that it wasn't going to work. Lisbonites didn't want language classes in stuffy classrooms in the middle of the boiling city in June, July and August, and the slow early interest from the public displayed this fact clearly. They soon decided to only open during the academic year, starting that September, and the modern London School was born. June first, however, was the date that Marie-Ange insisted on using as the birthday of the school, and that was the date on which the anniversary would be celebrated.

They had hired a banqueting hall in the Dom Fernando Hotel, right on Avenida da Liberdade, for the event. The guest-list included the fifty-odd current teachers, the thirty or so admin staff, some past teachers, right-wing political allies of Marie-Ange, a few rich ex-students and a selected pack of journalists and photographers to record the happy event of Lisbon's biggest English language school celebrating twenty-five years in the city. There would be music, speeches, dancing and a free bar, though a warning came with this last item, aimed, no doubt, at us English teachers.

Elizabeth circulated the memo that announced the festivities to us all, but also chose to come into the staffroom and read it aloud, for added emphasis. She stood there, beside the open door to the balcony, sweating a little though she only wore a short-sleeved blouse, a linen skirt and sandals. Somehow the summery attire didn't fit with her formidable personality.

"It must also be noted," Elizabeth quoted from the memo, after having sped through the practical details of the party, "that teachers will be present as representatives of The London School, and so must behave at all times with decorum and restraint. Anyone over-indulging in the free alcohol will be asked to leave."

There was general outrage at this slight on our characters, at the implication that we would abuse the free booze afforded to us. Later though, when Elizabeth had left and Sally was out of earshot, we were able to admit that the warning was probably necessary.

"A free bar!" Laura said, "and they expect 'decorum and restraint'? Have they met us?"

Still, despite the cynicism, there was a sense of expectation in the staffroom in the final week of May. Carol had bought a new dress and took it in to show us, it was a long, flowing number that was very low-cut at the front. She tried it on and we could briefly see in her some of what Carol herself had meant when she had told us how much of a knockout she used to be. Her eyes brightened as she twirled and posed, her twenty-five year old self briefly visible.

The party was planned for Sunday the first. Initially we affected indifference, but by Friday afternoon we were almost giddy. There was talk on the teachers' Facebook page that Julio César - one of the major DJs in the clubs in Alcântara, and a London School alumnus - would be playing a set at the party. There were also rumours that truffles and lobsters were on the menu for the five-course meal planned. I even went down to Rua Augusta on Saturday after my play-date with Rui, and picked up a new pair of shiny black brogues with a solid sole on for dancing.

And then Nuno Antunes' article came out.

JUNE

It was Dina who showed me Nuno Antunes' article in Correio de Lisboa. It was on the Sunday morning, the morning of the London School anniversary celebration, the first day of June. At least I wasn't hung over when I got the news, I had had a quiet Saturday night with Mike, Adam and Rahul in the Bairro, with none of the usual excess. I had hardly seen sporty Adam since his controversial promotion, and he had now become very corporate, the original company man, full of talk of the upcoming celebration, how spectacular it was going to be, how many important people were invited. I caught Mike trying not to yawn at one stage as Adam gave a little speech of admiration for Marie-Ange, our supreme leader, like an obedient party sub-boss singing the praises of Kim Jong Il. We tried not to make too much fun of him when he went to take a leak.

We all had two drinks and smoked a joint down one of the long, dark alleys that led away from the central bar district. I drifted off home at one o'clock, obscenely early for a Saturday night. Only Mike remained at that time, he headed off, saying mysteriously that he had someone to meet.

So I was well rested when Dina called out to me from the door of A Lua when I passed on the way to the bakers' to get some rolls for breakfast.

"Cian," she said, from behind me, as I neared the door of the bakery, "you should see this."

I was feeling - for the first time since Maura had left - something approaching equilibrium. I had less than a month of teaching ahead of me, a week or two in the Algarve planned to spread my tan to those places that had been covered for most of the spring, and then a space of time that was open, laden with possibilities. I had some money saved, opportunities of summer teaching in Brighton, Cork, Swansea, Barcelona, and the heavy, dark burden of the regret over Maura and me finally beginning to lift.

I had got an email from her on May 29th, saying that she was glad that I hadn't turned up, in the end, that our night together in her hotel had shown that we didn't work, and couldn't. "I'm happy that I went to Lisbon though," she had written, "if I hadn't, I would always have wondered. I would have wondered if you were some long lost love of my life, instead of a fling that had some nice moments, someone I won't forget about but not someone for me. It's time to grow up Cian, for me and for you."

Unlike her last email that had sent me towards Patricia Coelho, I read it once, then again, then closed my gmail account and went on with my day. She was exactly right, we were good together, once, for a short period, and now it was time to move on. It was time to grow up.

So in my preoccupation with Maura, and then the preparation for the anniversary celebrations of the school, by late May I had practically forgotten about Nuno Antunes, as we tend to easily forget about a promised catastrophe that never seems to come. I had even begun to wonder, when I thought of him at all, whether he really was a journalist or else just some psycho who enjoyed putting the fear of God into people. Mostly though, he had slipped from my mind, like something unpleasant but unlikely.

My illusions were dispelled that first day of June when Dina showed me her copy of Correio de Lisboa. The headline was the first thing that jumped out at me.

ESCOLA DE VICIO it screamed, in letters that were square and thick and heavy, like a hammer. 'Escola' was a word I knew well, I officially worked in A Escola London - The London School. 'Vicio' was a different matter, though I did have a suspicion about its meaning. I looked at Dina for confirmation.

"School of Vice," she said, pointing at the headline.

Underneath the fold, on the front page of the tabloid, was a photograph of the headquarters of the school, in the central square in Rossio. That was all that there was on the front page, the headline, the photo and an invitation to look inside for further details.

And the details were there on the second and third pages, laid out with obvious glee by my friend Nuno. He had a by-line on all six of the mini stories inside, and a tiny photo at the top of the page. His hirsuteness was evident even in such a small picture, though the photo had clearly been touched up to make him look less sinister.

The main story, when Dina translated it when we went inside to have a coffee, was promoted as an exposé. It was the result of a two month long investigation into what he termed *a escola de línguas mais conhecida e mais corrupta de Portugal* - the most well-known and most corrupt language school in Portugal. Nuno had, he claimed, in prose that even I could see was exaggerated and self-serving, interviewed current teachers, former teachers, admin staff, past and present students, as well as politicians and local councillors. This was all in order to reveal the sickness at the heart of The London School, which was on that day celebrating its twenty-fifth anniversary.

There were photos of Marie-Ange, Robert Prior, and another person, only displayed in silhouette, who was said to be a teacher at the school and also the main source for the revelations contained in the articles. At a table there in A Lua, as I sat beside her, Dina went on reading. She put her finger on one particular paragraph, making a face as she did so, before going on to finish the article. She came back to the part she had marked.

"'There is a....web.....of homosexuals in The London School,'" Dina quoted, "'and it is common knowledge that being gay is a big advantage to reach a senior position in the school. Heterosexuals are not promoted as easily, unless they are in a relationship with someone who is already a director.' Is this right?" Dina asked, looking up from the paper.

I didn't know how to answer her question. My instinct, strangely enough, was to defend my employers, people for whom I had been working hard for the previous nine months while being seriously underpaid.

"That's an exaggeration," I said.

"'Adam Maxwell,'" Dina went on translating, "'the now school director in Avenida da Liberdade school, only received his promotion because of his relationship with the school director of the London school beside Lisbon University.' Wait, that's your school, isn't it?"

I nodded, reading the paragraph as she explained it, getting the idea but wanting her to go on.

"'Mr. Maxwell, twenty six years of age, had only been a teacher for six months, yet was given the post of Director when the previous school head, Perry Owens, died in mysterious circumstances.'"

"What circumstances?" I asked, "does it say?" I was skimming the article now, making out words, some phrases, getting some of the gist, seeing the word 'drogas' mentioned a number of times.

"'Perry Owens,'" Dina went on, "'was only thirty-two when he died of a heart attack. It was well known that he, like many of the teachers at The London School was a......great.....no.....enthusiastic consumer of illegal drugs, especially cocaine, which is known to be a cause of heart attacks in younger people.'"

Dina looked up.

"This is kind of serious, Cian."

"I can see that."

"'Mr Owens,'" she went on, "'had had treatment in the United Kingdom for cocaine addiction, and yet was....still given the director's job because of his relationship with the general...*geral*.....not general, ...overall Director of The London School, Robert Prior.'"

"Really?" I said, genuinely surprised now, "Perry and Robert? I never heard that?"

"'Teachers in the school,'" Dina continued, "'have also sold drugs, both to other teachers and, in some cases, to their students, actually within London School buildings.'"

Dina looked across at me, her green eyes transparent in the morning light coming from the wide front window of the restaurant.

"Could this be true?" she asked.

I tried to think. In truth I found that it absolutely could be true. If the dealer wasn't one of us first year teachers - and it could have been - then it could easily have been one of the second or third years, who had better contacts and who would have felt more secure. There were a few people I knew who might have done something so reckless.

"And here," Dina said, "it talks about this woman, is she French? 'Marie-Ange Maury, who is involved with right-wing anti-immigration groups, some of which are banned in this country.' Then there is a part here," Dina pointed to the second last paragraph, "that says that 'London School teachers have been having relationships with their students, some as young as sixteen.' Wow, what kind of school do you work for, Cian?"

I couldn't reply, I could hardly speak. All I could think of was the Portuguese word there in the paragraph Dina had just read - '*dezasseis*' - sixteen. Patricia Coelho was sixteen.

"Is that all?" I managed to say, "what about this last part?"

Dina flicked through the following pages, and then returned to the original pages two and three.

"There's nothing more about it," she told me, "it just says here, in the last paragraph, 'In the following days we will be looking in more detail at the Escola de Vicio, at the drug-taking and selling, at the teacher-student relationships, and at the connection with extreme right-wing groups. It will be shocking and ..... reveal...revelating....?"

"Revealing," I said.

"Yes, revealing. I had a blank."

"Fuck," I couldn't help saying, in response to the whole thing.

"It's also true," Dina said, seeing my reaction, "that this paper is a piece of crap. Everything is a sensation, exaggerated. They just want to sell papers to the uneducated. They don't care about the truth."

"I can see that," I said, indignant on behalf of my school.

Actually though, apart from a potential false story about myself and Patricia Coelho, I didn't know for certain that anything that Antunes had written was inaccurate. He hadn't offered any real proof for his claims, but they all seemed at least possible. There was certainly more going on in the school than I knew about.

Our London School teachers' Facebook page was in uproar. Those teachers who could read Portuguese put a summary of the article up for everyone to read. I returned to my flat and sat at the kitchen table with my laptop open and read what was posted. It was basically as Dina had translated for me. There were streams of comments already, the rumour was out that Marie-Ange had exploded - as much as such a small woman could explode - and decided to shut the whole twenty-fifth anniversary down.

"They cant go on now," Sylvia St. James had typed, "think of how it would look."

"Think of how it wud look," Felicity, a third year teacher in the Cascais school had replied, "if they *did* cancel it. It'd be an admission of guilt. They're far too sure of themselves for that."

Felicity's extra two years of experience within the school had obviously taught her well. Many of us teachers met up that night for pre-party drinks in Estadio, a basic, run down bar on the edge of the Bairro Alto, and heard the confirmation from Carol - who had been told by Sally, who had been told by Elizabeth - that there were to be absolutely no changes to the organisation of the evening. Everything was to go ahead as planned.

You would have thought that the powers that be in the school hadn't even read the article. About thirty of us jammed the usually sedate Estadio bar in all our finery, had two or three shots each while standing at the counter or sitting at one of the bare tables, and then trooped down to the Hotel Dom Fernando in a convoy of taxis. We were greeted by both Robert Prior and the little walnut-like figure of Marie-Ange, both of whom insisted on shaking everyone's hand as we entered. They smiled and nodded like royalty, though with us first year teachers who arrived with the smell of alcohol already on our breath the smiles, it was obvious, were a little more forced than they were with the balding politicos and bankers that followed us into the reception area.

The school had hired the hotel's ballroom to stage the anniversary event. It was an ornate, high-ceilinged space that had a stage at the top and multiple round tables in the middle, like at an awards ceremony. Each table sat eight to ten people and every place had a printed name card demarcating where everyone was to be placed. The guests were carefully split up. The teachers were divided by school and placed mainly at a group of tables near the toilets and the exit. The admin staff - including Mafalda and Paula who I saw taking their seats in the distance - were at three tables near the front, and the VIPs were in their own area well away from the academic staff. The intention, it was clear, was that the really important guests would not be contaminated by us untrustworthy, drunken, drug-taking teachers who had to be corralled in a section far from the rest.

The atmosphere quickly became giddy and loud. We were all aware that there was work the next day - and had been warned that anyone attending the party and calling in sick on the Monday would be fired on the spot - yet this didn't stop our table calling the waiters back for a third, a fourth, a fifth bottle of wine as the meal got going. Under the influence of free booze and good food we happily managed to push that day's article out of our minds, just as the management seemed to have done. Laura and Sebastian started a mini food fight, and Carol, Mike and I began playing a drinking game once the first seafood course was despatched. The game was something involving animals and colours and the alphabet, which I ended up losing more often than not.

It was just as well that there was lots of food, to act as soakage. There was *bacalhão*, medallions of pork, *arroz de marisco* - with big chunks of crab and what appeared to be lobster - swordfish, some super sweet almond tart for dessert, followed by soft goat's cheese with freshly baked bread, coffee, liquors, cigars, all drowned in a sea of wine that kept coming in bottle after bottle, delivered by waiters that seemed to find it difficult to believe we could drink so much. It was Bacchanalian, a three hour long stream of dishes and full glasses, course after course, one sensory stimulant after another. By the time that the speeches started I was ready for a nap.

In fact, I must have dozed off a little, as I wasn't aware of anything that Robert Prior said when he got up to speak. I only really came around in the middle of Marie-Ange's speech. She was speaking in what even I could recognise as heavily accented Portuguese, but she soon switched to English to continue expressing her pride and emotion at the fact of the school reaching a quarter century. Even with the microphone her voice sounded brittle and unsteady, as she talked about the difficult early years, the sacrifices she had made, the help they had received from "good friends." Here she looked down as the assembled swells and members of the Lisbon elite that were sitting directly in front of her, and smiled a benevolent - and slightly creepy - smile in their direction. They clapped obediently, and with a certain enthusiasm, and were the first to stand up in their tuxedos and fragrant long dresses when the speech finally came to an end, giving her an ovation that lasted more than a minute. Only about half of the teachers at the back tables joined in by getting to their feet, and even then were the first to sit down. Carol, Elizabeth, Sally and Mike were the only ones who stood at our table, and Mike only did it, it was obvious, ironically, he clapped as manically as any of the others near the front, and was the last in the whole room to take his seat. I first thought that he was drunk, but it was clear, when I looked at him and he winked, that he was just taking the piss.

It was as if the article in Correio de Lisboa had never happened. There was no mention of it in the speeches, no sense that the school may be in trouble from it, no discussion of any of its contents. Though there was an undertone, in some of what Marie-Ange had said, of defiance. "We have had very many problems in the past," she had said, "and will have many more in the future, but we will overcome them all."

The only evidence of tension happened during the taking of photographs, after the speeches. The various school directors and senior teachers were dragged up, along with the "friends" that Marie-Ange had spoken of earlier, to have pictures taken with management. A largish group of men with cameras was let in at this stage, members of the press pack from local and national media, to take photos that would be even more relevant in the next day's papers after Sunday's revelations. In mid-scrum two of the large bow-tied security detail grabbed one of the photographers, an skinny, bespectacled guy, and dragged him out to the foyer as everyone looked on. The doors slammed behind them as the burly men left with the hardly struggling photographer. The two goons then reappeared a minute later, with their shoulders square and their hands empty, tugging their sleeves down over cuffs and straightening their ties.

It was Sally who clarified what had just happened when she returned to our table from posing and smiling with the top brass. She wore long dangly earrings, of the type that she tended to favour at events like this, and her skin was still pallid and tan-free, even after three months of solid sun.

"He was from Correio de Lisboa," she said, before Elizabeth came back, "he had had his permission to attend rescinded, but he came anyway. Somehow he got in, Richard told security to throw him out."

It was the first concrete reminder of the night that the article really had been published in that morning's paper. I was beginning to believe that I had imagined it, such was the level of denial in the ballroom that Sunday night. It was only then that it came back to me that there was more to come, that they had more beans to spill. Along with revelations about Marie-Ange's links to right-wing organisations and news about teachers selling drugs, Correio de Lisboa was prepared to break a story about teacher/student relationships in the London School, one involving a sixteen year old. For me, at that moment, the levity of the previous three hours disappeared in a second.

I tried to get it back by downing some peppermint schnapps that Sebastian had appropriated from the bar, but it just dulled the worry and didn't bring back the deluded joy of the beginning of the night. The music started, the DJ played a bizarre mix of fado, Portuguese rap and standard disco fare of Britney and Beyoncé. The wide dancefloor was soon full, teachers out shaking their thing beside secretaries, accountants, past students and besuited politicos dancing with their wives, as if it were still 1972. Everyone there was well-oiled on the free alcohol. Even Robert and Marie-Ange got out among the throng, getting down in their stiff way to the Beatles singing 'Twist and Shout'. Gay Robert, at least, had rhythm, his greying hair motionless even as he swung his hips, but Marie-Ange looked like what she was, a slightly drunk woman nearing her seventies, who was not used to moving like that.

I had a dance, and sat down when the sense of doom got too much to fake enjoyment. Elizabeth, I found, was sitting beside me. I had seen her with Adam only briefly, the rest of the time they had, possibly deliberately, kept a safe distance from one another. She was sitting serenely, dressed in a lime green Japanese style dress that reached her knees, looking as relaxed as I had ever seen her.

"For someone who was just written about in a national newspaper, you don't seem very worried," I said to her as she lightly tapped her right foot, a distant half-smile on her lips.

"Worried?" she replied, "I found it funny. Why should I worry about that?"

"Well, they mentioned that Adam only got his job because of you."

"Yes, that's what they said. You believe that?"

She looked straight at me now, it was the first time I had noticed that her eyes were green, like Dina's, though of a harder, more solid shade. I could almost see what Adam saw in her, with her full lips, long eyelashes, total lack of self-doubt. There was a dangerous kind of sensuality there.

"Isn't that what happened?" I asked her.

"Cian, you idiot," she said, though with something that seemed like affection, "I didn't want Adam to leave. I *liked* being his boss, it made things more exciting. He liked it too, he was fucking his superior, it turned him on. You really think that Marie-Ange listens to anything that I say?"

"Then why did they give him the job?"

"They like having people in positions of power that they can control. Do you remember that assessment you all did, your first week here? The list of multiple choice questions that you had to tick boxes beside?"

"Vaguely, I didn't spend much time on it."

"Well they use the results to target people who are efficient, conscientious and good at following orders. I think that they're looking for subjects that don't have a strong independent streak. Well organised conformists. And that's Adam exactly. He's the perfect London School director. He'll do exactly as they tell him and run the school like clockwork."

"So how did you slip through the cracks?" I asked her, "I think we both know that you're not a follower. I'd say that you have a fairly large independent streak."

She smiled, pleased with this, as if I had told her that she was beautiful.

"I'm good at faking conformity," she said.

"Why didn't you tell Sebastian this? About Adam and the job?"

"Why should I?" Elizabeth replied. "It's none of his business. He thinks that he has a right to a promotion, but Sebastian will never be a director. He won't play the game. He knows that he should, he just won't."

Elizabeth crossed her legs. Her long shins and calves were smooth, she had obviously shaved recently, though she had nicked herself near the ankle. There was a tiny scarlet scab there. I almost asked if I could run my fingers down the hairless skin.

"You know the teacher that supposedly slept with a student, a sixteen year old. From the article?" I asked her.

"Yes."

"That was me."

"Fuck off!"

She looked genuinely shocked.

"No really. Would I make this up?"

"You slept with one of our sixteen year old students? Let me guess which one. You have the Tuesday and Thursday teenage class, right? I'd say, Joanna Flores, she's fairly slutty, I imagine. Or else Carla Rodriguês, one of the two."

Did she know the names of all the students in all my classes? In everyone's? And whether they were slutty or not? I'd forgotten that behind the façade, Elizabeth was a smart cookie, razor sharp.

"Patricia Coelho," I told her.

Elizabeth was temporarily open-mouthed in wonder.

"You're shitting me. That little madame. The little goody-two-shoes. You do surprise me, Cian."

"First of all," I replied, "nothing actually happened. It might have if.....,well, it might have. But it didn't. And I didn't do any of the chasing, she stalked me for a couple of months, then...anyway, it doesn't matter. Nothing happened. I don't think we even touched."

"So what are you worried about?"

"Well, the paper isn't going to print that. They don't care about the truth, they just want a good story. And sex between a London School teacher and a student is a good story, whether it happened or not."

"So talk to Sebastian, if you're worried. He might be able to get it stopped, if anyone can."

"Sebastian?" I asked, "why would I talk to him?"

Elizabeth looked at me in that familiar way of hers, as if I were a small child, or a badly trained pet.

"He's the source. Where do you think that this guy, Nuno Antunes, got all his information from?"

"How do you know this?"

"The journalist, he's a cousin of 'Nando, Seb's friend, boyfriend, whatever the fuck he is. They probably don't remember but I met both Fernando and Nuno at a party, five years ago, when I came here first. Before Sebastian had ever heard of Lisbon. I imagine Seb went to Nando soon after Adam got the director's job Seb wanted, whinging about being passed over, discriminated against, whatever. Wanting revenge. Fernando put him in touch with his cousin, and that was it. The journalist was looking for a story, Sebastian gave him one."

Sebastian gave him one. Despite my preoccupied state, I couldn't help noticing the double-entendre, and wondering if Elizabeth had done it on purpose. I didn't know, and realised that I didn't know anything at all, really. I thought back to April, to when Sebastian had returned to the school after his suspension. From the fiery, resentful man he had been to the agreeable pussycat he became, the change was too great to be accidental. It made sense though, if he had been planning something, plotting his vendetta. Being on the inside would be useful, and pretending to be a good team player would be the perfect cover.

Before I could speak to Sebastian, I found Mike, nursing something that looked like a Coke at a table with Jamie and Rahul. I managed to get him to come with me to the bar, where we stood, half-facing each other. There were few people left now, or at least few people left drinking, besides the teachers, so we had some space.

"Mike, remember that encounter with a teenage student that I told you about?" I asked, "The one that I assumed you wouldn't say anything to anyone about?"

"Aye, I remember," he said, rubbing the top of his newly shaven head.

I waited, in case he might figure out what I was getting at without me having to actually spell it out.

"So you didn't, by any chance, mention it to anyone? Sebastian, for instance?"

Mike went quiet.

"Mike?"

"I thought that I had dreamt that," he said, looking away. "I mean, I thought, I wasn't sure....."

"What the fuck are you saying, man?"

"Me and Sebastian smoked some weed one night in his place. I went over to help him move some furniture, he said he would give me some skunk he had sourced in return for me helping him. We moved his old bed out, then set up his new one, and had a smoke. It was powerful, packed a punch. We got severely stoned, talked nonsense, I crashed on his sofa."

I ordered him a vodka, thinking it might speed things along, and poured it into his glass on top of the cola-like liquid.

"I couldn't be sure what I had told him. He started telling me stuff about his childhood, and getting bullied in his public school, and how he had lost his virginity with a sixteen year old guy in his school when he was only fourteen. Then I told him the story of Sonia, you know, the fifteen year old that I was with, and then maybe I let slip about you and your sixteen year old stalker. I'm sorry man, really, I was out of it, my judgement just goes when I smoke that skunk stuff. I can't keep my fucking mouth shut."

It was close to two o'clock before I located Sebastian. Marie-Ange and Robert Prior were long gone, and really all that were left were the teachers - most still drinking or trying to persuade the barstaff to keep serving - and some of the hardier admin staff. Mafalda, our skinny secretary, was one of these, she was dancing to the CD of Portuguese eighties rock that the DJ had left on while he chatted up Sylvia and Melissa of the Three As. Sebastian was outside in the foyer, sitting in a red cushioned armchair there, smoking with Laura and Carol.

"I need to talk to you," I whispered into his ear, with no greeting or preamble.

"What's with the drama, Cian?" he asked, looking up and sideways at me, his eyes grey and hooded in the dim light.

"Cut the crap, Seb, I'm not in the mood."

After making a show of struggling out of his chair, Sebastian came with me to the front door.

"What's on your mind, Ki-Ki?" he said.

"I need you to talk to your mate the journalist," I told him, "get him to pull his story on me."

This jolted him out of his languor a little.

"You're going to have to explain every part of that sentence," he said, tenser now, "I didn't understand any of it."

I looked at him without speaking, the force-field of alcohol making me brazen, burning off any restraint I may have had sober.

"The thing I can't believe," I said, turning towards him now, "is that you'd use your friends - me, Perry, who's dead, fuck knows who else - to get revenge on the school. That's low, Seb, lower than I thought you capable of."

I didn't stop to think that Elizabeth could be wrong, that I could be wrong. Mike had more or less confirmed what I knew now to be true. I knew I wasn't wrong, I knew from the way Sebastian was standing, his head slightly turned towards me but his body still facing out into the dark Avenida. I knew it from the rapid way that he lit a new cigarette from the butt of the old one. I knew it from what he said next.

"Get off your high horse, Cian, you don't know what you're talking about. I haven't done anything wrong."

He didn't say, "I haven't done anything", because he clearly had done something. He simply hadn't done anything "wrong". Or at least that's what he believed.

Sebastian flicked his cigarette out on to the empty pavement, and then followed it, turning right towards Rossio and Restauradores, walking at a fair clip. I started to follow him and then stopped. I was suddenly drained of all emotion, worry, anger and resentment all evaporated like water on hot stone. I watched the back of Seb's blond head as he bounced down Avenida da Liberdade, the Avenue of Liberty.

"Fuck you, Seb," I said, at normal volume, as if he were standing in front of me. Pretty soon he was out of sight. I picked up the still lit Marlboro that he had discarded on to the pavement, took a drag and inhaled some smoke into my lungs as if it were oxygen. There were taxis passing, but nothing else moved at this time on a Saturday night.

❊ ❊ ❊ ❊ ❊ ❊ ❊

Despite the warnings about being fired, Sebastian didn't show for work the next day. The staffroom was like an infirmary. Laura had had two hours sleep and sat with her head leaning against the side wall, Mike actually lay flat on the hard bench near the door and Fabian was silent and green in the corner. Only Sally and Joanne, who had both only drunk water for the second half of the previous night, were in any way compos mentis. My ailment was more spiritual than physical. My hangover was only mild and consisted of a vague sense of detachment, as if the action of reality was in fact a film or play happening around me. Though added to that was a repulsion when I thought of the prospect that I would soon be outed as a predatory sleaze by a national newspaper at some time that week.

It was a sign of my dazedness that it took me until two o'clock, in fact after my first class of the day, for me to realise that Correio de Lisboa also came out Mondays. I went cautiously down to the news-stand on the corner, looking around me guiltily all the time as if I were buying a porno mag, and handed over my euro coin for a copy of the tabloid. I opened it right there at the confluence of two streets, amid people rushing by dressed in shirts, blouses and jackets - despite the thirty-five degree heat. I went straight to the Escola London story, it was relegated to pages four and five, now that a potential scandal about a minister and a call girl had broken.

The headline ESCOLA DE VICIO was still in play, and loomed over the smaller print as the castle loomed over the city. I skim-read what

I could, seeing the words *drogas*, *estimulantes* and *traficar* appearing through the text like little signposts. There was a photo - badly focused and slightly tilted - of Perry, who had died three months before. The photo had a tag-line below it which included the word "cocaína". Perry looked large and happy in the picture, with a cigarette in one hand and a glass of beer in the other. Just to his right, and cut in half so that just his left ear was visible, was a figure with wispy fair hair, slightly taller than Perry with his arm resting on the shorter man's shoulder. It was Sebastian, I was sure.

And then I saw Mike. This photo too was of poor quality, probably taken on a mobile phone, and showed my friend and workmate in a baseball cap, half-facing the lens, his mouth open as if he were about to say something. The caption below only contained two words - "*vendia drogas*". I knew the words *A Venda* from the For Sale signs on the various buildings and houses I had seen around the city, and so could work out what they were saying. "He sold drugs," was the translation. In the text they mentioned the Glaswegian's full name, Michael Beatty, in paragraphs three, five and six, along with the words *vendia*, again, and *estudantes* - students. It was clear what they were getting at.

Mike was downstairs in the Coimbra Café, drinking a beer, when I got back to the school. I opened the page at the offending article, and looked around to see if anyone else there was reading Correio de Lisboa, and recognised my Scottish mate. No-one gave us a second glance. Mike looked at his photo briefly and smiled.

"Jeez, I look rough in that," he said.

"Mike, they say that you sold drugs, to students."

"Aye, and what if I did."

"So it's true?"

"It was hardly dealing. Two young guys in my old school, in Rossio, heard that I smoked a bit and wanted some good weed. So I gave them some for less than I had paid. I basically subsidised their stash."

"But it's in the paper now, you don't seem very surprised."

"That guy," Mike said, pointing to Nuno Antunes' photo in the top left corner, "caught up with me 'bout three weeks ago. Outside my flat. He told me that he had a story to run about me, wanted a quote or something. I was a bit out of it at the time, told him to fuck off. Probably shouldn't have done that."

I left Mike, unconcerned still, in the café, and deposited the paper in the staffroom, open on the relevant page. My classes drifted by in a haze, there were noticeably fewer students that day, whether because of the article in the tabloid or the steaming hot weather I couldn't say. In each class I had, someone brought up what Antunes had written but I feigned disinterest, saying that I couldn't read Portuguese, hadn't seen the story, that it was all lies anyway. Here my hangover helped, the whole weekend seemed unreal, so I wasn't really pretending to be detached. My students were curious, desperate for some more salacious information, and were generally disappointed when I insisted on actually teaching them some English.

Laura reported that all the boys in her teenage class had been plaguing their female classmates to admit which one of them had slept with a teacher. I was so glad that it was Monday, and that I didn't have Patricia and her gang that day, she would not have been able to stop herself giving the game away by going red, or by overreacting or storming out. I could only hope that by Tuesday some of the hype would have been dampened, and some semblance of normality could return. I got through the rest of the day, and drifted home without talking to anyone else about the new article, still in a daze.

Despite myself I managed to sleep that night. Near half past seven the next morning I fell out of bed and dragged myself to A Lua for a quick fortifying coffee, the temperature already over thirty degrees. I then went across the road to the dark, narrow shop that sold stationery and some newspapers. The old man there didn't even look at me as I handed over the money for a copy of Correio de Lisboa. I was an irrelevance in his day, a necessary evil, with my one euro coin and my air of sick anticipation.

Tuesday's theme was politics. If nothing else, this London School story was doing wonders for my Portuguese. I sat in my box room with the shutters open to the street outside, and slowly deciphered Nuno Antunes' third article, with the help of my big, square Bernard Diccionário Inglês-Português. I learned words like "*extrema-direita*" - extreme right, "*donar*" - to donate, "*a dictadura*" - the dictatorship, and "*forças perigosas*" - dangerous forces. From what I could disentangle Marie-Ange was linked to a sinister right-wing group called Defensores da Patria – Defenders of the Fatherland – who were backed by the Frente Nacional in France, and Jorg Haider's Freedom Party in Austria. Their aims were to take Portugal out of the EU, to put a strict limit on the number of immigrants allowed into the country, prioritising those from "Christian countries", and to repatriate the foreigners already inside Portugal's borders. Their youth wing, Águias da Patria - Eagles of the Fatherland - had been linked to racist attacks on black people, many of which had taken place late at night in the Bairro Alto.

Again, this was serious stuff and, if it were true, actually good journalism. I had met a victim of one of the Bairro attacks, he was a black Brazilian friend of my flatmates, a jazz musician who still had his neck in a brace a month after being kicked and beaten while on his way home one night. We had all heard rumours about Marie-Ange, about how she had been an intimate of Salazar before the dictatorship was knocked off its unstable perch back in the mid-seventies, but no-one actually believed them. She was so small, so wizened, such an unlikely fascist. If we had paid these whisperings any notice at all it was to laugh at them.

The hairy Antunes though, had done his homework. He had spoken to disaffected ex-members of the Eagles of the Fatherland, who talked of having seen Marie-Ange at meetings, and who had been told that she was a major benefactor, willing to fund training weekends for militants of the youth organisation. Some of her banker friends - who were pictured, and who I recognised from the Sunday night London School bash - were known members of the Defensores group, with dreams of re-establishing some kind of totalitarian, Catholic-inspired government that would take the country back forty years.

I didn't get all of this from Correio de Lisboa. Sergio, in A Lua, was an old-style Commie, and in his restaurant later that day filled me in on the extent of these Fatherland Defenders' reach and the breadth of their influence. He saw their hand everywhere, and I had no way of knowing if he was exaggerating or not. Like everything in Portugal, untangling fact from myth, gossip and rumour was not straightforward, and every regular in A Lua had their own theory on the shadowy group.

That was later, though. That morning I became so engrossed in the facts of Marie-Ange's political machinations that I forgot to dread my own imminent exposure. In the second last paragraph Rahul's name came up. I couldn't quite grasp what the relevance was, the sentences seemed to meander over and back without ever quite leaving a trace of their meaning. Even with the dictionary the section was opaque. I drifted out of my room and bumped into Charlotte emerging from the bathroom in shorts and one of Charles' t-shirts, two sizes too large for her.

"Charlotte," I asked, "you read Portuguese, don't you?"

"Some," she said, yawning. Their school had already finished for the summer and she and her fellow Charlie had fallen into the habit of sleeping late and lazing around the flat all day, ducking the heat.

I handed her my copy of the newspaper. She glanced at the paragraph that I indicated, the one with Rahul's name in it, and squinted at it for a few minutes.

"This is your Indian friend, right?" she asked. She had met him, of course, all of us in our insular little English-speaking community knew each other.

"Well yeah," I said, "British-Indian." This was how Rahul referred to himself.

I was on edge, I realised, and consciously attempted to at least appear more relaxed. I smiled at her, as if at a suspicious toddler.

"I'd be grateful if you could tell me what it says," I told her.

She traced the lines of script with her slender index finger, the clear nail-varnish on the tip now chipped and scratched.

"Just a second," she said, and disappeared into her and Charles' bedroom. "Darling," I could hear her say, "what does this word mean?"

There was a mumbling and gurgling of voices from inside the room, the interior of which I had only ever glimpsed in passing. Charlotte emerged, holding the newspaper, this time with her glasses on.

"Your school is a real piece of work, Cian," she said, as I stood in my bare feet on the parquet floor of the corridor. "Apparently they have a policy of never hiring non-white teachers. It's not public, obviously, but it does exist. Your friend Rahul was the first, and he only got the job because they thought his name was Raúl, like in Spanish. Apparently the owner had a canary - I'm paraphrasing here - when she found out he was actually Indian."

Charlotte handed the paper back to me.

"Tomorrow they're doing sex. The paper, I mean. Teachers and students, doing it. I think I'll buy it."

My mouth went dry. If it appeared in the paper, even one as untrustworthy as Correio de Lisboa, who was going to believe that nothing had happened between Patricia and me? I wanted to justify myself to Charlotte then and there, to assure her that she couldn't believe everything that she read, maybe to practice my denials and explanations in advance, but the words wouldn't come out. I thanked her, hoarsely, and went to get dressed for work.

Sebastian was back that day. The threat to fire anyone who took Monday off obviously hadn't been carried out, at least not yet. He was sullen, almost sulky, a very different person to the composed, obedient employee of the previous two months. He stood smoking on the balcony for most of the breaks between classes, meaning that I had to go out to the front of the building if I wanted to have a cigarette and avoid his heavy presence. Laura went out to stand with Seb near four o'clock, and came back ten minutes later and rolled her eyes, mouthing a "what's up with him?" in my direction. I shrugged, knowing the answer but not wanting to share. I had my own worries.

At least Patricia was absent that day. She too must have known what was coming, perhaps she had even told Nuno Antunes more than she had admitted to me. Maybe she had made stuff up. I couldn't think about that any more, with the story that would reveal all so close.

In desperation, I gave it one more go with Sebastian. Tuesday night we were the last two in the school, apart from the security guard, Senhor Eugenio. I waited for Seb outside his class, watching as his students filed out the door, wishing him a good night. He smiled at them, making comments as they passed, laughing as they answered him. They liked him, it was obvious, and so did I, I realised. Until that week I had even admired him. We were - or at least had been - friends, of a sort, not close but friends still. I had asked his advice on more than one occasion, he had been glad to help me, we had been drunk together ten, twenty, thirty times, he had told me about his coming out to his parents, about how his grandmother wouldn't speak to him after she found out he was gay, how she died before they had really mended fences. I had even given him an edited version of the Maura story that I had only told to Dina. I didn't like what I had to do now.

Sebastian caught sight of me as the last of his class disappeared out the exit, and his smile vanished.

"I'm surprised that you came in," I said to him.

"I have classes, students. I came in for them."

Very fucking noble, I wanted to say, but didn't. I just nodded.

"You know that Patricia and I didn't do anything," I said, walking up closer to him. "We nearly did, it could have happened but it didn't. I just stopped myself in time."

I knew that this was a lie, but it was important that I show myself in the best light possible. Sebastian said nothing.

"I'm going to lose my job if that article is printed about me. Your friend the journalist ambushed me on the tram, said that he had already spoken to Patricia, that he had information about our relationship. I assume that he got it from you. It doesn't matter if he prints lies, they will be believed, you know that. At least they will leave a stain."

"You don't care about this job, Cian," he said, putting down his briefcase and turning now to face me, "you couldn't give a shit about it. Why are you even here? You were running from something, from your little woman and all that failure in Ireland. You ended up here, it will take nothing for you to leave."

On the face of it what he said was almost true. I had just ended up there. Until Maura and the collapse of what we had together I had never even imagined living abroad, never mind in the shabby Atlantic capital of the poorest country in western Europe. Yet there I was, that was where I lived now. I didn't have a residence anywhere else and it seemed that I had found a place in the city, tenuous and fragile and short-lived as it was. It had taken me until that moment to figure that out, and my panic at the imminent destruction of all this suddenly made sense. Yet I felt that explaining my thought process to someone who had betrayed me would have meant giving Sebastian too much of myself, confiding in him as if he were a friend. I simplified it.

"Help me out Seb," I said, "I like living here, and I like this job." This too, was true, I realised. "I don't want them spoiled because of a lie."

Sebastian put his left hand to the side of my face, almost cupping my cheek there.

"This is not what I had intended, Ki-Ki," he said, more softly now. Senhor Eugenio was there in the corner waiting to close up and giving us hurry-up looks as we stood in the middle of the reception area.

"Nuno doesn't listen to me any more," Sebastian said, taking his hand away, "I never wanted him to use that stuff about Perry, and you and Patricia, I had no idea that that was true, I half made it up. I just pieced it together from....well from stuff I heard and saw, and what I saw in one of your observations. I just gave him that shit to get him interested in the story. I only wanted to hurt those pricks in management, that's all. I'm sorry Cian, it's all gone kind of wrong."

Sebastian picked up his black briefcase and moved rapidly out through the glass doors that Senhor Eugenio had pulled closed but not yet locked. I heard his hard heels clip-clop on the stairs as he descended. I returned to the empty, echoing staffroom, collected my things and followed Sebastian out the door.

I slept fine that night. I was resigned to whatever was about to happen. I could always sue Correio de Lisboa, I reasoned, get a little money for defamation, though getting Patricia to testify on my behalf could be a little tricky, I thought. Sure there may be people who believed what they read, but after all it wasn't illegal - as Mike had said sixteen was the age of consent - and I hadn't actually done anything anyway. The only newspaper I had ever had my name and photo in before was the Limerick Leader, when I was twelve and won a bronze medal for the under fourteen one hundred metres in our village Community Games. So at least it would be something new.

And the truth was - the thought hadn't left me since I had first been waylaid by Antunes on the 28 tram that Wednesday afternoon - maybe I deserved this. Sure, I hadn't done anything, I hadn't touched Patricia, I hadn't kissed her, hadn't slept with her, but how far away had I been from any of this? It was through no great display of self-control that I had avoided disaster with my sixteen year old student, it was simply a lucky break that Mario had turned up when he had. I was drunk that Friday night, and pitying myself in a particularly pathetic fashion, and may have been capable of anything. I was about to be exposed for something that I hadn't done, but which I may have been about to do, and perhaps that was justice.

It was hazy and overcast when I woke on Wednesday morning, and also muggy and humid. My sheet was stuck to me, I had to peel it off. I showered, but still felt sweaty afterward, as if the air around was part liquid. I went down the corridor in my bare feet to get some cool orange juice from the fridge. Charlotte was sitting on a stool there, leaning over a newspaper spread out on the kitchen table.

"Cian, you are so naughty."

I froze, all the repressed anxiety returning in one sheer wave. I looked at Charlotte, she was smiling at me.

"You guys in that school, gay sex rings, directors promoting their lovers, female teachers sleeping with sixteen year old boys. It's like ancient Rome. I almost want to change schools."

"Wait," I said, something not sounding right, "sixteen year old boys?"

"Yes, José Alcântara, a student in the Rossio school, told this journalist that he had spent the night with one of the teachers there, a Sylvia Saint John. Do you know her? I don't think I've met her, she sounds like a porn star."

"Sylvia?"

"In fairness, they don't have a lot on it. He may not even have been her student, he could have been lying, I suppose. Of course any sixteen year old wants to imagine that he slept with his teacher."

Sylvia? I thought. *Sylvia*? I had forgotten why I had come into the kitchen at this stage. I glanced around me at the cupboards, the fridge, the window looking out on to our bare, weed-filled concrete yard.

"Cian, are you OK?" Charlotte asked me.

"Can I see that paper?"

"Sure."

Charlotte handed me the copy of Correio de Lisboa, watching me closely. There was a photo of this boy, this José, who looked a lot more than sixteen, with stubble, a square chin, a tall, rangy figure. I found the paragraph that had Sylvia's name in it quickly. There was something about, "*passou a noite com a sua professora*" - he spent the night with his teacher - and then there were other details I couldn't follow. I looked right through the article - seeing the word 'homosexual', a number times - but couldn't locate my name anywhere, nor that of Patricia Coelho.

"Thanks Charlotte," I said, handing back the newspaper and suddenly wanting to hug her, to hug someone, "that's fantastic."

I walked back to my room, threw myself lengthways on my bed, and lit a cigarette. It tasted good, just what I had been needing. I put my left arm behind my head and stared at the ceiling. I couldn't help it, the laugh emerged all by itself, a rolling, self-sustaining phenomenon that started off quiet and then turned into an open-mouthed, belly-shaking guffaw. *Sylvia*, I thought again, *fucking Sylvia!* The original article hadn't mentioned whether the student was male or female, of course, though I hadn't noticed this at the time, in my fluster and shame. I should have at least imagined the possibility that the teacher wasn't me, I mean, it couldn't have been unusual, knowing now what was known about the London School. There must have been lots of teachers at it. I was shaking at this stage, the chuckles almost taking on a life of their own. I thought of Sylvia seducing, or being seduced by, José Alcântara, then Nuno Antunes, the journalist, tracking him down, ignoring mine and Patricia's story as unsubstantiated, vague, and anyway less interesting than a female teacher and her male teenage pupil. The joy of Antunes when young José spilled the beans.

"Sylvia," I said, out loud, in between waves of laughter, "Sylvia, you fucking star!"

✳ ✳ ✳ ✳ ✳ ✳ ✳

No-one was fired. There were only two weeks left of the school year anyway, and so much dirt had been flung around at that stage, staining so many people, including those in authority in the school, that it wasn't possible to single anyone out. Neither Mike nor Sylvia had done anything strictly illegal, as far as was known. Marijuana was more or less legal to possess for personal use in Portugal at that stage, and anyway the student who claimed that Mike had sold him weed had somehow disappeared. And, as I well knew by then, José Alcântara was not under the age of consent. According to Laura, the font of all solid gossip, Sylvia *had* actually slept with the boy, though there were a number of inconsistencies in the story.

José was actually seventeen, and was not a student of Sylvia's but was in Rahul's class and had seen the attractive female teacher around and had vowed to seduce her. According to Laura, one night in the Bairro Alto, after Sylvia had been drinking most of the day, José saw his chance and chatted her up outside Portas Largas. Sylvia didn't recognise the boy, didn't know that he was a London School student and wasn't in a state to care either way. The other two of the Three As who were there with her - Melissa and Anna - dared Sylvia to take the guy home, which she did before kicking him out immediately once the deed was done. It wasn't an untypical story of a London School Saturday night out, there was little remarkable in the account at all. Sylvia simply had the misfortune to have had the story found out by Nuno Antunes, and to have shagged a boy a couple of years younger than he said he was.

The final two weeks of the academic year petered out, there were exams, goodbye dinners, questions from students, both direct and indirect, about our sexual habits, about who among the staff was gay, about whether the school would even be there next year. The answer to this last question was the most uncertain, and was the one preoccupying a good proportion of the staffroom. Rahul and Joanne were leaving, Joanne's boyfriend was not too keen on continuing to be the only, unwelcome, non-white teacher in the school so they had decided to try and get work in Spain. Mike too, was moving on, it had been not so subtly suggested to him that remaining as an employee of The London School was not a real option for him. He had, though, the intention of staying in Lisbon, and even had a few interviews lined up for a number of other schools who either didn't read the papers or who didn't care that he had sold weed to his students.

It seemed that no-one in management had worked out that Sebastian was the source of the story. Elizabeth had, for her own reasons no doubt, not said anything to anyone about what she knew about his betrayal, and there may have been those in authority with their suspicions, but he seemed to have been left to work out his last two weeks in peace. Sebastian too was leaving, unsurprisingly, and all he would say about his plans for the future, when asked, was, "Pastures new, people, pastures new."

Sally and Carol, on the other hand, were tied to the city, and in a sense, to the school. Carol had kids in Lisbon, in fact a grandchild on the way, and Sally had just gotten engaged to her Portuguese boyfriend. For all their complaining about the London School, they both more or less needed it.

Fabian had been working on Laura to stay also for the previous month. There weren't many jobs for a French teacher, so he was happy to hold on to the one he had, and wanted Laura to remain with him. They had been spending more and more time together, Laura had almost become a stranger to those of us who were still part of the London School crocodile that continued to wind its way around the Bairro Alto on weekend nights. Laura had changed in other ways too, she was calmer, drank less, had succeeded in channelling most of her energy and quickness of mind so that it didn't push people away so much.

She had even managed to establish a civil relationship with Sally.

I overheard them one night talking about shoes – Laura admiring Sally's, Sally returning the favour – a simple, unremarkable exchange, a thousand like it every day. Yet it marked a departure for Laura that was notable. Even more notable was that at no time afterwards, once Sally had left the staffroom, did Laura seek to bitch about or denigrate our new Senior Teacher, as she would have surely done six months before. Laura, like a lot of us, seemed to be becoming an adult.

And that just left me.

AFTER

I ended up in Lisbon, in 2007, and I am still here. It's been three years now since I first arrived to this city, climbed into the back of the Ford Focus with Moustachio, my hostile, grumpy driver, and began a different life. As I said, I ended up here, as if shipwrecked, though have since found reasons to stay.

I did leave, that summer of '08, without any intention of returning to The London School. That much at least I have kept to. Back two years ago I thought that it was time to grow up, so I returned to Dublin in search of the career I believed would make me an adult. I had had my year out, doing a job that was to a large degree lacking in seriousness, so I imagined that it behoved me to try to find a professional life that was sufficiently go-ahead. I was twenty-four months from thirty, and needed to get my shit together.

Luckily, as it turned out, the Irish economy was just embarking on the greatest financial collapse in the country's history. I say 'luckily', though for the hundreds of thousands who lost jobs, savings, homes, businesses, it would be difficult to find the silver lining. Yet there was a deal of fortune, for me, in the depression that hit Ireland like a wrecking ball. If the boom had continued, and jobs could have been found as easily as before, I would have fallen back into an old routine that had made me - unbeknownst to myself - miserable. The summer of 2008 was a barren time for web designers looking for work. There was a glut on the market, a nerd-surplus. For someone who wasn't super motivated, or mega committed to his profession - like me - finding a job was not a runner.

To buy time I went back to the English Institute. This was the place in Dame Street where I had taught the previous summer, though 'taught' is, of course, a relative term. The year before I had improvised, basically winged it. That next year, however, I had the strange sensation of feeling like I actually knew what I was doing.

I was able to combine a lot of the games and pissing around that I had done in my first year with some actual teaching activities, and was amazed to see that this job was actually doable. There were two rookie teachers there that second summer, two callow country girls called Shauna and Miriam, fresh out of their TEFL course and about as clueless as I had been twelve months before. It took me about three weeks to realise that I was in a position to help them, to alleviate their looks of shock and bewilderment. I taught them Alibi, my favourite game from my first summer, which I had refined and developed slightly in Lisbon, and felt something close to pride when they both reported back that the game had gone down a storm with their French, Belgian, Croatian and Danish teens. *Wow*, I thought, *look at me, a real teacher!*

The institute gave me some part time work in September and October, while I looked for what I considered a real job. I did have a few interviews - with Google, with a company called Adventure - but it was clear that my prospective employers could tell that I didn't really want the jobs I had applied for. I got PFA after PFA, and I was, in truth, glad of each rejection letter. I knew that I should want these IT jobs, and also knew, somewhere, that they were absolutely the last thing I really desired. There was too much competition out there now for companies to be hiring well-qualified but unmotivated guys like me. In the past, on the strength of my CV alone, I could have walked into a job in any of these places, but the crash had changed the game and, luckily for me, it stopped me doing something I had really no interest in.

I bumped into Sheila, Maura's cousin, one day in Brown Thomas. I was half-heartedly looking for a pair of runners, with a vague idea to get fit and become a physical specimen like my old colleague Adam. Sheila had a pair of pink Nikes in her hand, was looking at them dubiously. I saw who it was, and could have turned and scampered before she noticed me, but I had had enough of running away.

"Hello Sheila," I said, coming up beside her. She was even smaller than I remembered, though I could still see some of that genetic residue that she shared with Maura in her face, the dark eyes, the long lashes. Sheila looked at me, recognition failing to dawn for five, ten seconds.

"Jesus, Cian," she said, eventually, "what are you doing here?"

I told her, gave her the abbreviated version. She was still in the Rathfarnham house, she had stayed even after Maura had left. Her boyfriend, Philip, had moved into Maura's old room, so they were now cohabiting, just as Maura and I had done a year and a half before. Inevitably, the topic of Sheila's cousin came up.

"Maura's in Limerick City," Sheila told me, "in Limerick General there. Bernadette, her mother, died three months ago. The cancer came back. It was awful quick." Sheila's voice broke a little.

I gave her my condolences, meaning it. I reached out and put my hand on her shoulder for three seconds, then took it away.

"Maura wanted to be nearer her dad, now that he's on his own. They are close, you know."

I realised that I hadn't known that.

"It's been hard on her," Sheila went on, "Maura and her mother didn't really get on, and now she feels guilty."

"Yeah," I said, "it must be difficult." All I had access to were platitudes.

We said goodbye, imagining we would bump into each other again somewhere, not swapping numbers. Sheila's attitude to me was much more benign than the last time I had seen her, at the door to the Rathfarnham house after I had just discovered that Maura had moved out. That day in Brown Thomas we talked just as if we were two people who had once shared a house, which was exactly what we were. Her rancour had gone too, like Maura's.

I had thought about Maura, of course, since being back in Dublin, though less than I had expected to. We still had each other's email addresses, each other's mobile numbers, but there had been no contact since the day in May when I didn't turn up to see her off at the train to the Algarve. The cord had been cut then, and though in some of the darker times in my aimless months since leaving Lisbon I had thought of phoning her number, the temptation had never really grown. And now I knew that it was over. Sheila had told me that Maura's mother was dead, and I had no intention of sending my regards, concerns, thoughts or prayers. She had lost a parent, had not told me about it, and there was no question that it was my place to phone and commiserate. I was sad for her, that much I did know, and wished her the best, but those wishes would not be communicated to Maura by me. It seemed that we were finally done.

✳ ✳ ✳ ✳ ✳ ✳ ✳

It was an email from Charlotte in November that drew me back to Lisbon. She and Charles were still there, still in Graça, with another sucker now living in the shoebox they called their spare room. Not much had changed for the Two Charlies, they also continued working in the grandly titled Communicate Institute where they had both been for three years. Their school, according to her email, was going through something of a crisis. Three of their teachers had just upped and left to start their own school, leaving their institute short-handed. Charlotte asked me if I knew of anyone in Dublin who might be able to fly in at short notice and cover some classes while they found someone more permanent. It took me all of five minutes, three hundred seconds spent staring out of the window at a rainy, dark, November afternoon to begin looking up the Aer Lingus website for the next flight to Lisbon International.

My intention - or at least what I told myself that my intention was - was to go back just until Christmas and fill in for the few weeks that it would take The Two Charlies' school to hire more permanent staff. I would swoop in, earn the eternal gratitude and respect of an institute under pressure and go back to Dublin at the end of December, ready to resume my real, adult life.

Needless to say, nothing of the sort happened. I arrived on November ninth, booked into a *pensão* in the Baixa, a bare functional place only half a step up from the Pensão Imperial that I had stayed in fourteen months before, and showed up at the Communicate Institute the next morning. It was a Monday, and I expected to be welcomed as some type of hero. It turned out that the brewing crisis there had been averted. The school had amalgamated some classes, drafted in a couple of retired teachers to help out, and really only gave me work at all because I had come half way across Europe to help out. In the end I had two measly teaching hours, twice a week. I had gone from underemployed in Dublin, to even less employed back in Lisbon.

At least it meant that I had plenty of time to reconnect with the old gang. Amazingly, Laura was the only one of the teachers that had started with me in the University school that was still there. She didn't say as much, but it was obvious that it was Fabian who held her in The London School. She was even living in his swish apartment in Lumiar now. I could imagine them both at weekends, like Charles and Charlotte, lazing around Fabian's place half-dressed, happy in their coupledom, two sides of the same coin.

Laura and Fabian met me one Thursday night in the Record Bar in the Bairro Alto. Fabian's English had gotten a lot better, he was now coming out with phrases like, "we were really 'ammered last night", and "Laura, she likes winding me up." I had shared a staffroom with the guy for nine months and had thought him haughty and standoffish, though the truth was that he just couldn't communicate. Now that he could it seemed that he was warm, funny and deeply devoted to his live-in lover.

Fabian went to the bathroom at one stage. I took a sip of my sangria and turned to Laura.

"I think I saw him literally kissing the ground you walked on when you came in here tonight," I told her, as the tall figure departed on his way towards the manky toilets.

"Yeah, I know," she said, "he worships me. I think I could get used to being worshipped."

"I'm fascinated to know how you are going to explain to your kids how you first hooked up," I said then, smiling.

"I'll tell them the truth, Cian, you asshole," she said, "our eyes met across a crowded staffroom."

"Ok, and you'll leave out the part where you won him in a contest."

Laura punched me, hard, on the upper arm. I didn't mind, it was her signature move, one of the ways that she expressed affection. The stinging in my deltoid felt familiar, comforting almost.

As always, Laura was a good source of information about the rest of my ex-workmates. She seemed to have reached a kind of equilibrium as far as Sally was concerned. "Oh she's still snooty," Laura said, when I asked her about her new Senior Teacher, "though not quite as snooty." I was kind of disappointed with this, I had expected her to have reached boiling point by now with the woman that she used to call Ice Queen Hippie Bitch.

She then began talking about the first year teachers that had just begun with them, two months earlier.

"They're such fucking children," she said, "they don't plan any classes, show up late on Mondays so I have to cover, and all they talk about is who is shagging who. I can't believe that we were ever that bad."

I looked at her incredulously.

"Laura, that sounds *exactly* like us."

"Nah," she said, "we had more class than that. Or at least we were more subtle."

There were only three new teachers in the University school that year. Laura described them as "two bitchy teenagers and a nerd." That's all that she would say about them. Her disgust wouldn't allow her to elaborate. It was clear now why her antipathy to Sally had abated. She finally saw things from Sally's point of view. It's hard to continue despising someone when you find yourself cast in their role.

"And I don't even have Carol to lean on any more," Laura added, taking a long drink of her G and T.

"Carol's gone?" I had thought that Carol was a lifer there, like Mafalda or Senhor Eugenio.

"Yeah, she's in primary schools, teaching the little ones English.

She has like three or four schools that she goes to. She's using them as guinea pigs for her children's book, like a captive focus group."

"Her children's book?"

"She's writing another one. She had one published during the summer," Laura explained.

"Yes," Fabian offered, "it's called Mr. Squirrel and the Square Squid." I could tell that he enjoyed saying the title of the book. "It's very clever, I bought one for my *nee-ess*."

"It's pronounced 'niece', honey," Laura said to him, quietly.

"Yes, for my *neese*." He held her hand as he said this. I suddenly wanted to hug them both, they were so cute there together.

"And Sebastian is in Japan, in Tokyo," Laura continued.

"Oh yeah?" I tried not to let my indifference show. I wasn't sure how much Laura knew. It was common knowledge that Seb had been the main source for the series of articles back in June. Laura definitely knew that much, though I couldn't be sure whether he had told her about Patricia Coelho and my almost seduction of my sixteen year old student.

"He says that the gay scene there is really weird, they're all into this kinky stuff."

"Right up his ally then," I said, dryly.

I could feel Laura looking at me closely.

"He might come to visit at Christmas," she went on, "the school will pay for one flight back to Europe and he doesn't want to go back to London."

I nodded. By now I had heard enough about our former Senior Teacher, my former friend.

"So Joanne and Rahul are in India," I told them, glad to have some info that Laura was unlikely to have.

"Oh yeah, isn't it very hot out there to be wearing so much black?" Laura replied.

"Rahul's getting in touch with his roots, and trying to get his parents off his back in the process." I said "He told them that he's learning about Hinduism, though they are really just slumming it and taking lots of drugs in Goa."

We drank some more, and got slowly, contentedly drunk. Like happy couples everywhere Laura and Fabian - or Laurian as I began calling them, which they initially pretended to dislike and then started using themselves - decided that I needed a partner and promised to set me up with one of Fabian's female French friends. They had a short argument about who would be more suitable for me, Matilde or Ninon, though even the way that they argued was full of playful tickles and slaps and squeezes. Laura, in becoming one half of Laurian, had turned into someone more malleable, less cynical, right with the world. It was an impressive transformation.

Two nights later I met Mike and Jamie in A Lua for dinner. Mike was still in his commune in Alfama, but was now the longest serving resident there, the Aussies who had set it up having moved on. He was sharing with a bunch of people from the local circus school, according to Mike they were a bunch of loose-moralled hippies who smoked too much weed. They must have been really something for Mike, of all people, to describe them like this.

Mike was now teaching part time in a school in Benfica, to subsidise his new business venture, which involved giving alternative tours of the city to tourists who had more specialised tastes. He was very vague about it, and about how it was going, how he was publicising it, but he did give some details.

"The circus school is the first stop," Mike said, rubbing his still shaved head as he tended to do when thinking, or explaining things, "and then we 'come across' this capoeira group that I know, while walking the streets of Alfama. They do their stuff for half an hour, the tourists are impressed - these guys are the real deal, pure martial arts Brazilian spectacular - and then we head to Simão's place."

I had met Simão once in Mike's company. Mike tended to collect these eccentrics - and lunatics - though it was never clear where he picked them up. Simão lived in a small flat behind the Feira da Ladra, from where he ran the world's smallest Fado bar. Patrons would come in, occupy the six available seats in his tiny living room, receive a glass of cheap red and be entertained for half an hour by an assortment of amateur fado singers from the neighbourhood. It was total kitsch, a series of novelty performers, authentic and not at the same time. Perfect for Mike's alternative Lisbon tour.

Jamie, too, had moved on. I had heard on the London School grapevine - which I was still connected to in a minor way - that he had changed. The stories ranged from rehab to a religious conversion, from a new woman to liver collapse, but whatever the reason the word was that he had quit drinking. On first sight that much seemed to be true, with his steak and chips he had ordered a pineapple juice, and was now on to his second while Mike and I had another bottle of wine between us.

Jamie, like Laura, had also stayed in the London School. He was still in Rossio, in the HQ, near where Marie-Ange and Robert Prior had their offices. Rossio was the centre of power, and so the rumours and soft information that filtered through from there were likely to be near to the mark. Jamie had always had a way of finding things out anyway, his air of harmless dopiness tended to seduce people into trusting him. For this reason he had almost the whole story on the fallout from Nuno

Antunes' series of articles back in June.

"They all pretended that there was no problem," Jamie told us, his Brummie accent noticeably less sharp than it had been a year before. "They're really good at pretending though there was a sense of desperation from Robert, he walked everywhere really fast that week and forced a smile for everyone he met. It was creepy, he never smiled before. The directors were called over for meetings four times in ten days. There were dudes in suits in and out of the building every ten minutes. Lawyers, I suppose, and PR consultants. Typical London School shit, everything fine on the surface, a teeming mass of maggots underneath."

"So glad I'm out of there," Mike said, as if it had been his choice.

Jamie looked over at him, they were sitting side by side. Jamie had mostly been speaking to me up until then, I guess Mike had heard this already.

"Nah man," Jamie said, "things are better now. They're all so concerned with their image, with not being seen as racist, or as a den of homosexuality, they've given us more leeway, though you would expect the opposite. There's been no observations yet, less paperwork, all of this fatuous bullshit that they haven't got time for anymore. They're just so happy with you if you simply manage to avoid sleeping with any of your students, or selling them drugs."

Ouch. Mike didn't seem to even notice that he had just been implicated, and Jamie didn't care if Mike was offended. Mike looked at me instead, briefly. I didn't return his gaze. It was already ten months since my night with Patricia Coelho, a night in which absolutely nothing happened, and yet I still hadn't totally shaken it off. Maybe that was right, maybe I didn't deserve to be rid of it so easily. I was still getting looks from the only other person - besides Patricia herself, Mario and

Sebastian - who knew about it.

"Anyway," Jamie went on, "they're on the offensive now. Student numbers are definitely down this year, naturally, but there's obviously some serious PR muscle behind the school. Marie-Ange has been seen at this Sport Against Racism event - the school sponsored it. That's got to kill the old dear. Salazar would be spinning in his grave seeing her there surrounded by all these little black and brown kids. She was smiling in the photos like someone had just told her that her dog had died."

"So they're still going?" I asked. "I thought that those articles might close the school down."

"Nah," Jamie said, "ten years before we arrived they had this big fraud scandal. There were only two schools then, Rossio and Cascais. Apparently there was some creative accounting going on and they ended up owing tonnes of tax. Millions. But they weathered it, and two years later they opened your school by the university, a year after that the Avenida school. The London School is a cockroach, man, indestructible. Give them two years, they'll be bigger than they ever were."

Mike and I drank on, wine, then beer, then back to wine again. Jamie stayed on the wagon, happily sipping a series of pineapple juices. He had started smoking though, and bummed cigarette after cigarette off me, something he had never done when he was drinking. We talked on, reminiscing about the old times as if we were at a reunion twenty years after the events, though a lot of what we remembered had only taken place in March or April. We talked about Fabian's party, and about The London School anniversary celebration, just four months before, and even back to our communal room in the Pensão Imperial, which had ended up housing four of us though it was cramped enough for two. We got by turns morose and hysterical, laughing like old men at the antics of our youthful selves.

Most of the nights that we recalled had ended up with Jamie asleep in some corner or other, passed out happily after consuming his weight in booze. I had passed the stage of wanting to respect his feelings, and just wanted to know.

"So what happened, man?" I asked, after a millisecond lull in the conversation, "really? Pineapple juice?"

"You mean, why aren't I drinking?" Jamie asked, in return, his accent suddenly stronger.

"That's exactly what I was getting at, yes."

Jamie bit his lip for a few seconds, looking around him, suddenly seeming like a little boy.

"Have either of you two ever pissed yourselves?" he asked, looking at Mike and me in turn.

"Well, obviously, when I was a kid..." Mike said.

"As an adult," Jamie clarified.

Both Mike and I shook our heads, tentatively, as if we weren't sure.

"It happened to me at the end of the last school year," Jamie began, looking uncomfortable now, but determined. "A couple of us went to the Algarve on holiday, once the teaching was over, rented an apartment. You know, Melissa and Anna, Rahul and Joanne, Adam and Felicity and Jackson from Adam's school. Carly was there too."

I had almost forgotten about Carly. Our obsessive note-taker from Basic Training. She had had the straightest hair of any girl I had ever met, as if she ironed it.

"Shit, Carly!" I said, "what's she doing now?"

"Well she's not doing me, I know that much," Jamie said, sadly. He shrugged. "We got it together one night in the Algarve. I'd liked her for a long time, but it had never happened. Then in Lagos, you know, booze, sun, no teaching, we hooked up. Ended up in bed together."

Jamie took a gulp of the thick yellow juice in front of him that suddenly reminded me of urine. I could almost see what was coming.

"So I couldn't really get it up. I was too pissed. We fooled around a bit, then went to sleep. When I woke up, Carly was shouting, "Jesus Christ, Jesus Christ! I'm all wet!" We were in her bed in the apartment. I realised that I was soaking too, and the quilt we were sleeping under. You can guess what had happened. I had pissed on her in my sleep."

"Fuck" I said. Jamie looked like he needed a hug.

"I never saw her again after that. She left the Algarve early, went back to Kent. I really liked her," Jamie said. "So I made a change. I haven't had a drink since."

"Jesus man," Mike said, "from one extreme to the other."

"No, it's good," Jamie replied, "no more hangovers, I can remember nights out. I've even got a girlfriend."

Jamie was seeing an Irish girl called Mary who had started in the Rossio school that September. I admired the enormous break he had made with his past. Everyone, it seemed, was moving forward, making changes, growing up. I was stuck, worse than stuck, I had gone backwards. Mike had a new business, Jamie had gone off the booze, Laura had managed to form a healthy relationship, Carol had written a book. I was an underemployed reluctant English teacher who couldn't face going back to Dublin as I would have to look for a real job there.

Then I bumped in to Dina. I had thought about her, of course, had thought about calling to her house, but it had been awkward when I left, back in June. Rui hadn't felt any of the awkwardness, at the end of our last playdate he hugged me, hard, his little head now up to my chest, and I felt genuine sadness at the thought that I may very well never see him again. Dina, though, looked unsure for once, she hung back, as if she didn't know if she too should embrace me or kiss me or just shake hands. Eventually she combined two of the options, clasped my left hand and kissed me on both cheeks, then stood back again. There was this distance between us still, this invisible barrier, a gap that neither of us had managed - or perhaps wanted - to bridge in the last three months. I left my email address and then headed off towards Portas do Sol for the last time, promising to visit, knowing I wouldn't.

Inevitably, it was in A Lua that I bumped into her again. I still went up to my old local restaurant in Graça once a week, just to be in a place where people knew who I was. The city, since I had come back, had felt less mine, I was less part of it now than I had been even when I had just arrived, yet the alternative, returning to Dublin, was even worse. In A Lua, at least, Sergio was always there, predictably large and accommodating. The Two Manuels popped in and out, insistent still on teaching me rude words, though they had pretty much exhausted the Portuguese language's large store of curses at this stage and were simply recycling. A Lua was familiar and unchanging, there was no-one moving on in their lives here, no-one writing books or starting businesses or giving up the drink. It was an eternal present there with the same décor, the same stodgy menu, the same reassuring stability.

I was drinking a *bica* at the counter one quiet Tuesday afternoon in early December when I had nothing better to do. Dina came in, stood beside me for at least three minutes without noticing me, ordered a *galão* and an almond pastry - usually comfort food for her - and ate and drank silently while exchanging a few words with her cousin. I was literally standing a metre from her all this time. Sergio, who of course knew that we knew each other, made no comment, and made no attempt to point out that I was standing there right beside her. I sipped on my bica, and turned towards Dina as she talked and drank and ate, oblivious to my presence.

In a break in her conversation with her cousin I spoke.

"Hi Dina," I said.

She turned towards me, and looked at me as if I were a stranger.

"Cian, shit, sorry. I'm miles away, under pressure. Wait, wait a second.. what..what are you doing here?"

We sat at one of the bare tables and talked. I was surprised at the sheer pleasure I felt at being in her company again. She looked similar to the very first time that I had seen her, a year before, harried, hair mussed, but still managing her stress. Unbreakable, in a way. Dina's skin was as sallow and smooth as ever, and I had the immediate and familiar sensation of wanting to reach out and touch it. She had coloured her hair since I had last seen her, it was now lighter, streaked with blond. It suited her, and highlighted the green of her eyes. She still wore the same perfume.

I gave her an edited version of my stay in Dublin and how I had ended up in Lisbon again. I could see she was distracted and trying to be polite.

"So you're stressed, Dina," I said, cutting short my narrative. I was tired of it anyway.

"I'm trying to set up this import business," she said, "or at least, import/export. It's for Portuguese emigrants, and *retornados*, those who have returned. I got the idea from Rui, he was always asking for those American candies that you can't get here, Reece's Pieces, and Twinkies, stuff like that." Her accent was suddenly really American, saying the brand names of the products, like a real New Englander.

"So I got some of my friends in Rhode Island to send me some, and I gave them to friends here, who had also come back. And there's a market for them, not just for the returnees, lots of people like them. I have a whole range available from a cheap supplier in Connecticut. And then there's the opposite, the Portuguese in the States who want Portuguese food sent over to them, you know, a taste of home. So I'm working both sides of the Atlantic, it's a growing business. But I need a website for it, of course, and my fucking web-designer has let me down. Well, he went out of business, and won't finish my site. So I've been trying to find someone to do it who won't charge lots of money."

"You want me to take a look?" I asked.

"Shit, of course," Dina said, "you used to do something like that, didn't you? I forgot."

The guy who Dina had doing her website was a bit of a chancer. He had left a lot of things half-done, links that went nowhere, badly written code, poor design. It didn't take me long to tidy things up, to get at least a basic version of her site up and running, where she could display some of the products available and accept orders by email and payments by Paypal. Within an afternoon the address productosparaportugueses. com was current and live, a fully functioning part of the World Wide Web.

"Cian," Dina said, with something close to wonder, "how did you do this?" She was genuinely surprised at my competence.

"This?" I said, aware I was laying it on a bit thick, "this was easy."

In the coming days I expanded her site, set up a proper 'Store' section where people could buy online after registering, and generally made the thing look more professional. I enjoyed the work, enjoyed the craft of sculpting out a virtual space accessible to the whole world for the first time in a couple of years. I worked in Dina's kitchen, when she was there she came and stared over my shoulder at the screen in silence for a few minutes before walking away, as if I were involved in some kind of sacred ritual. I enjoyed the power of it, the power that the possession of a certain skill that others don't have gives you. I liked when she looked over my shoulder, it was good to feel her silent presence there behind me, concerned, curious, maybe a little impressed.

And that's where it started. It was obvious, though something that had, in my obtuse state, never occurred to me. Why don't I just design websites in Lisbon? I began small, setting up basic sites for Mike and his alternative tours of the city, and then for Fabian, who wanted to market online French lessons to English speakers. I had forgotten about the cachet of the English language, most of the web designers in Lisbon spoke good English, but none of them were native speakers, and I was soon in demand, among the companies in the city with business in the English speaking world, and then with those who wanted to break into this world. I was freelance, cheaper than outsourcing to a big web-design company and yet just as good, if not better. I stayed in Lisbon that Christmas, to work on some projects and build up my client base and generally devote myself to my little startup venture.

In Dublin, before Maura, before my flight to Portugal, I had slowly begun to lose the initial enthusiasm that I had had when starting off my career straight out of college. I was stuck in the mythical rut and what I did no longer seemed in any way creative. In Lisbon I discovered that I wasn't in fact bad at my profession, that I had an expertise that people appreciated, and when it was my own little company that was at stake suddenly it seemed that the quality of my work went up. I cared again. What I was doing wasn't any more challenging than my work with Avatar in Dublin, but the context had changed. Now it mattered. Now it mattered a lot.

My parents were surprisingly sanguine about my no-show for the Christmas holidays. They realised that I was almost thirty and was making my own way, finally. In truth they were probably glad of the freedom from my frustrated presence there in my native village, a village that seemed smaller every time I returned there. Christmas in Lisbon was a novelty, mild weather combined with the typical iconography of a Northern Yuletide, snowmen and Santa Claus and reindeer in fifteen degree daytime temperatures.

I went to Dina's for Christmas dinner. We had fish. There wasn't a turkey in sight, something I was glad of as I had never really been fond of the dry, white meat of the Christmas bird. Maria, Dina's mother, was also invited, and I could see Dina attempting to restrain her annoyance at Maria's insistence on meddling in the preparation of the meal. Maria eventually got the message and came and kept me company in the living room as her daughter finished cooking. She was still flirty with me, I thought, though that could have just been my ego playing tricks.

Rui was there too. He had grown now, was not quite at puberty yet but was getting there, there was a squareness coming into his jaw, some of the little-boyishness was being slowly washed out of him. Still, he wasn't too grown up to play and beat me in Madden, his American football game that I still hadn't mastered. We played a quick game before he went to his dad's for dessert, Dina and Paulo having come to an agreement about Rui splitting time between them. The kid's parents seemed to have reached an accommodation.

"I suppose I feel sorry for him now," Dina told me, as we sat at the kitchen table, drinking port. Maria was now asleep on the sofa in the living room, or at least pretending to be so as to give us some time alone. I was never sure exactly how much Dina's mother knew about her daughter and me. I just nodded as Dina went on.

"He's a very confused man. He was brought up in this macho culture, you can imagine how many gay builders there are in Alfama.

Not many. So he felt he had to continue this myth with me and Rui, and meet these men on the side to satisfy himself. It started while we were here and went on in the States. It's kind of sad."

"You're very forgiving," I said, aware that this was dangerous territory for me. I couldn't tell if she had really forgiven me for not telling her about Paulo in the first place.

"Not really," Dina said, taking a drink and lifting a cigarette out of my packet, "it's just easier. Rui still loves him, and we have to deal with that situation. Being angry all the time is tiring."

I had heard this before, but not from Dina. Maura had said it, or something like it, almost a year before, on New Year's Eve, in Manus Sheehan's house in Ballyhayes. Though that time she had been talking about me.

Eventually Maria woke up, came in to join us for a final glass of port, and left for the two minute walk back to her own house. I picked at some chocolate cake that was left over and then got up to leave too. As I stood there in Dina's kitchen, just around the corner from Portas do Sol, she took my hand and came around to face me.

"Stay," she said.

I thought for a millisecond about declining, and then couldn't find a good reason to do so. She had taken off her heels and so was now her usual six inches shorter than me. I looked down at her, unnoticed by me she had lit candles and turned off the main light. Her green eyes were startling in the half-light. I reached down and put my arm around her warm waist, and our lips locked for the first time in twelve months.

❈ ❈ ❈ ❈ ❈ ❈ ❈

I got my own place in Alfama, just at the back of an open area called Campo Santa Clara, round the corner from the amateur fado bar that Mike took his alternative tourists to on his improvised tour. Twice weekly the Feira da Ladra appeared in the open space in front of my front door. This translates as 'The Thief's Fair', a market that happens on Tuesdays and Saturdays, bustling and hectic while the selling is going on, sedate and tranquil the rest of the time. It was a small flat, with a tiny sleeping space, more of a chamber than a room, walled off from the rest of the flat by a curtain. There was a basic kitchen, and a petite windowless living room between front door and kitchen. It did possess a small room off the kitchen that was big enough for a desk, a desktop computer I got second hand and a small electric heater in the corner that I turned on when it got cold. My first office. I noticed that when I turned on the shower the lights in the other rooms dipped or went off totally, and there was no central heating, yet it was cheap, central, and it was mine.

It was also only five minutes walk from Graça and A Lua in one direction, and five minutes from Dina's in the other, right on the edge the ancient, winding streets of Alfama. I took to walking around at night, getting blissfully lost in the allies and lanes, going up stone steps and down cobbled mini-streets, then eventually trying to orientate myself by heading upwards and upwards again until I emerged at a landmark that I knew. Often this was Portas do Sol, the triangular square overlooking our five-a-side pitch and just around the corner from Dina and Rui's terraced house. From there I could find my way home to my narrow apartment.

Dina and I began something that Christmas and now, two years later, we have kept it going. I say 'something', as exactly what it is is not entirely well defined. We still live in our own separate residences, she suggested a year ago that I move in with her but I declined, citing the failure of my previous experience of living with a woman. And it is true that this is on my mind - how could it not be? My three intense months with Maura in Rathfarnham is in the past but still exists, in some amorphous way. It is still with me, like a guardian angel, or a curse. It is diluted and faded now, but lives on in the decisions I make and the turns I take. What I had with Dina was worth preserving, I thought, and moving in together was tempting fate, just daring things to all fall apart again.

Yet at some stage I am just going to have to get over it. I am an adult now, have recently entered my fourth decade and have a small business that initially prospered before being hit by the crisis that has swallowed Portugal up two years after having washed over Ireland. It's still going, my little enterprise. I have clients and am still designing websites, but have found that I have only enough work for about half a week, and so have gone back to teaching again, though this time I am an instructor in web-design in a small local private institute. My year and a half as an English teacher stands to me, I think back to what the now deceased Perry told me after my first observation in October. *You're the sheriff*, he had said, *you're the boss*. It's valuable advice, and all I have left of him really, besides a few random memories, and I try to follow it. Teaching is about playing a role, sometimes pretending that you know more than you do, adopting a mask that gives this air of control and wisdom, even if you don't feel it. That's one thing that my year in The London School has given me, at least.

The other thing is that I am teaching through Portuguese. In bad Portuguese, admittedly, but Portuguese nonetheless. I have done a few courses - bizarrely in The London School in Rossio - and Dina and Rui have helped me prepare the expressions and vocabulary that

I need to impart the basics of web-design to my mainly teenage and twenty-something students. In truth I am supposed to be managing in Portuguese, but it is in reality far more of a mixture, most of the people in the classes have Intermediate level English or above and I usually succeed in getting my point across in one language or another. Still, I find that all those evenings spent hanging around A Lua with Sergio and the Two Manuels have finally begun to pay off, the students laugh at me and what they call my *calão*, my slang. Without realising it the Portuguese that I have picked up is the language of the street, *estou-me nas tintas, tanto faz, de caraças*, all of these expressions - non-offensive but authentic - that I have soaked up from my tormentors in the restaurant in Graça are now standing to me and giving me some much needed cred. And I am finally teaching something that I know something about. I may be instructing my future competition, but for now it is giving me a strange sense of satisfaction and is paying the bills.

Mike is still here, though Jamie and Laura have moved on. Jamie is in Saudi Arabia. He fell off the wagon while in Lisbon, around the time that Mary from Cobh dumped him, just after Christmas 2009, and struggled with on-again-off-again attempts at sobriety. His solution was to take a well paying job in the country in the world where it is hardest to get an alcoholic drink. For his send-off we had a small party in A Lua, with discreet bottles of wine and a cake with a camel on it. The night ended with everyone but Jamie well inebriated, though this didn't stop Jamie himself leading a chorus of "*Allahu Akbar*", as if he were some kind of Salafi Mullah. I miss his dozy face around the place, his fundamental good nature. His struggle with the drink will probably never be over, I suppose, but I hope to see him again.

Laura and Fabian are in Marseille. They lasted two more years in total in Lisbon, and then wanted to move on. The choice was Manchester or the South of France. Unsurprisingly, Fabian won. He's teaching French lit at a local secondary school, and Laura is now assistant director of a language school in the city centre. I laughed out loud when I read her email giving me this news, I texted her three words, with a smiley face after - "Poacher turned gamekeeper". Laura was now management. Anything is possible, I thought.

More extraordinarily, she rang me last week to say that she is pregnant. Twenty-eight and pregnant. I told her that I was proud of her, and this is absolutely true. She has become a real person, and is carrying new life, has grown from the funny, sharp, but slightly bitter young woman I first met in September 2007. I almost cried a little when I spoke to her, I managed to cover it with a cough but there was definitely a catch in my throat. I admire what Laura has done, in her small way the distance she has travelled is more than any of us.

I still see Mike every week. He of all people hasn't really changed. He still smokes more dope than is good for him, and his alternative tours venture is going strong, though hasn't really changed since 2009 when he got a mention in The Rough Guide to Lisbon. He's been living off the glow ever since. I'm not entirely sure how he survives financially, I think he gives some private lessons in English, and has some other mysterious sources of income that may be related to the sale of semi-illegal substances. He has become a kind of Buddhist - I told him that it was a logical progression, after all he already had the bald head - though he doesn't really follow all the dietary requirements, and is certainly not as chaste as the religion strictly requires. But he calms me when we meet, and is a link to my past in this city, a reminder of where I have come from, of where we all started.

And in some indefinable way it is partly the city itself that holds me. I'm not entirely sure what that means exactly, but I know it is true. I have been here almost four years now, on and off, not a long stretch of time in the context of the history of Lisbon - or even within my own thirty-one short years on the planet - but enough for us to grow together, and to intertwine in a tiny way. We have effected each other, though of course my impact on Lisbon is miniscule and probably unquantifiable. Neverthelesss, whoever I am now is partly down to the narrow, cosy streets of Alfama, to the sleepy deep age of the buildings and monuments, to the smell of sardines being grilled that is everywhere in May and June, to the yellow and red trams that screech and groan their way up and down the many hills of the city, to the whining, sibilant, ssshhhing sound of spoken Portuguese, and to *Lisboetas* themselves, the people of this place. It is a city no better and no worse than others but it has become mine, and it is mine in a way that Dublin never was.

And Dina holds me here too. We fit, and have probably grown together, like the city and me. After Maura I was cautious, and with a twelve year old son, caution in relationships is something of a given for Dina. I am light relief for her, though not always on purpose, and she grounds me, and has helped me to be at least a semblance of an adult. And what we have is not heavy, though it should be. It should be because she has a violent, gay ex-husband and a child, and I have my own baggage and a tendency towards immaturity. But we stay light together, we make each other's lives richer, we have somehow worked it out. The next step is in sharing a living space, something that will happen in time. I can't let Maura - or my failure with Maura - haunt the rest of my life. And Dina is not Maura, is not even close. I'm just going to have to man up about it.

I can't believe how callow the guy who got off that Aer Lingus plane back in September 2007 was. How clueless. Of course I am still a little clueless, just less so. I was running, four years ago, though my flight was headless, without a real destination. My arrival in Lisbon was all down to push factors, there was no pull. I left Dublin like a scalded cat, and Lisbon was where I ended up. And somehow it has worked for me, me and the city have melded, I feel safe here, as you are supposed to feel in a place that is a haven, a harbour. I still only have an imperfect knowledge of the language, the politics of Portugal are a mystery to me and the country outside of the city is largely unknown, but then this last is true of most *Lisboetas*. Just last week I found myself giving directions from the Baixa to Graça to a group of visitors from Porto in the north. The two men and a woman thanked me - "*Obrigadinho*" - when I had finished directing them up the hill and towards the tram stop at the Cathedral, all of us aware of the irony of this foreigner with a hit-or-miss pronunciation telling these Portuguese people where to go in their own country. I am a *Lisboeta* now, or at least I claim that title, I know the names of the Metro lines, the numbers of buses and trams, I know where to get the best *arroz de marisco* in the city, what time the various bars in the Bairro Alto stop serving, where to get good dope if I have to.

And I know more of the history of the city than most people who were born here. I know about the Phoenicians, who established a colony here three thousand years ago, naming it *Allis Ubbo*, "safe harbour", before the Romans moved in and changed the title to Olissipo. I have read about the Muslim conquest of Portugal, when they took over the city and established the first traces of Alfama, the place where I now live. I have studied the Christian reconquest, the forced conversion of Muslims and Jews, the pogroms that took place in the old city and which ended with bonfires of the burning corpses of Jewish *Lisboetas* in the centre of Rossio square. The voyages of discovery left from here, da Gama and Henriquês sailed off to find India and China and came back with riches and spice. An earthquake demolished the place in 1755, much of the destruction sparked by a tsunami from the Atlantic. The Marquês de Pombal rebuilt the city, Napoleon invaded it, Salazar controlled it and let his secret police loose on anyone who stood up to him. Democracy arrived in 1975, when, as Dina proudly told me on our trip to O Covil in November '07, the people put carnations in the rifles of the soldiers and the fascists slunk off with their tails between their legs. I have made it my business to know this stuff, and to know more about it than the natives, to orientate myself within the history of this place, to know where I stand. It is important to understand my context, where I fit into this living, breathing, urban animal. I am here now, and don't believe I'll be leaving any time soon.

About the Author

Lorcan McNamee is a language teacher, writer and translator. He has lived in Northern Ireland, London, Reykjavik and Lisbon, and currently lives in the West of Ireland. *A Year in Lisbon* is his first novel.

Contact the author: **mcnameelorcan@gmail.com**